D1495456

TAKE
OR
DESTROY!

Also by John Harris

Army of Shadows
Cotton's War
Covenant with Death
The Fox from His Lair
The Mercenaries
The Mustering of the Hawks
Ride Out the Storm
The Sea Shall Not Have Them

TAKE
OR
DESTROY!

John Harris

EAST CLEVELAND PUBLIC LIBRARY

Walker and Company
New York

Oz Editions

Copyright © 1984 by John Harris

All rights reserved. No part of this book may be
reproduced or transmitted in any form or by any
means, electric or mechanical, including photocopying,
recording, or by any information storage and retrieval
system, without permission in writing from the Publisher.

All the characters and events portrayed in this story
are fictitious.

First published in the United States of America
in 1984 by the Walker Publishing Company, Inc.

Library of Congress Cataloging in Publication Data

Harris, John, 1916–
    Take or destroy!

    Reprint. Originally published: U.K. : Arrow Books,
1978.
    1. al'Alamayn, Battle of, 1942—Fiction. I. Title.
PR6058.A6886T3 1984   823'.914   83-40577
ISBN 0-8027-0786-6

Printed in the United States of America

10 9 8 7 6 5 4 3 2 1

The qualities of a successful poacher, cat burglar and gunman would content me.

Field Marshal Lord Wavell, describing his idea of a good infantryman, in a lecture to the Royal United Service Institution, 15 February 1933

You will usually find that the enemy has three courses open to him, and of these he will usually adopt the fourth.

Helmuth von Moltke

Your prime and main duty will be to take or destroy at the earliest opportunity the German–Italian Army commanded by Field Marshal Rommel together with all its supplies and establishments in Egypt and Libya.

Winston Churchill, in his directive to
General Alexander, Commander in Chief
in the Middle East, 10 August, 1942

The quotations at the head of each chapter are taken from the official report on Operation Cut-Price, 29 October to 1 November, 1942

Part 1

THE PLAN

1

Information reaching Eighth Army Intelligence indicated that unexpected quantities of petrol and ammunition for Field Marshal Rommel had arrived at the port of Qaba.

The white Egyptian town, hanging between the blazing sky and its reflection in the mirage which swept and rolled over the harbour, began to take on tinges of bronze and salmon pink as the blazing orb of the North African sun sank. The throat-parching heat, dusty from the desert and dry enough to strike everyone speechless by day, lifted as the earth cooled. The torment of the flies ceased and the figures moving sluggishly between the houses began to raise their heads and walk with a new energy, as though a weight had been lifted from their shoulders.

The signs on the walls, orange in the gaudy rays of fading light, were German over the old British and Arabic. They were peremptory, efficient and showed firmly who was in control. Young men, blond but burned black by the sun and wearing the stiff-peaked caps of the Deutsche Afrika Korps, moved about in the quickening twilight. Their uniforms were faded and sometimes consisted only of the briefest of shorts that left their brown legs bare to the groin. Among them were a few Italians, shabby in ill-fitting coats and baggy trousers like unbuckled plus fours.

Few of the houses in the narrow streets had escaped the scars of war. The struggle in North Africa had been going on for three years now and during the British occupation Mussolini's Regia Aeronautica and later the German Luftwaffe had taken their toll. Since the Germans had arrived after the battle of Gazala and the retreat to El Alamein earlier in the year, it had been the RAF which had added to the destruction. Everything was pocked by bomb splinters, and on the whitewashed wall of one mauled wreck there was still the hand-written boast, 'Score – 50 – not out.' Over it the word, 'Vinceremo', had been daubed by some optimistic Italian.

Qaba had once been a pleasant watering place for wealthy Egyptians from Cairo, two hundred miles away. The Shariah Jedid, its steep central street, with its open-fronted garage-like shops, cut it in half like a sword stroke as it dropped down from the desert to the sea. To the west, dominated by the Ibn al As Mosque, lay the old Arab quarter below the rising ground known as Mas el Bub. It was a sprawling area of narrow alleys, called Wogtown by the departed British and the Borgo Nero by the newly arrived Italians. To the east, in the direction of the air-field and Ibrahimiya, a scruffy Arab village in a dip in the cliffs, lay the more modern residential area, with white bunga-lows stretching away along the edge of the sea. Most of these were occupied now by the garrison, the staff of the prisoner of war compound, and a few other fortunate Italians.

The old and the new came together on the waterfront at the Bab al Gawla, at the bottom of the Shariah Jedid, held apart, it seemed, by the remains of a Roman arch built by the Emperor Hadrian in the year A.D. 130. On the eastern side of the arch were a few larger buildings such as the Boujaffar Hotel, which had been taken over by the German town major for his head-quarters, while on a small headland alongside the harbour stood the Mantazeh Palace, once the residence of a wealthy pasha, but now partly ruined, its mosaic floors smashed, its filigree work splintered and dusty.

Behind the town, at the top of the hill where the Shariah Jedid became the road to the desert, there was a stretch of orchard and vineyard which in turn gave way to patchy grass and saltbush. In front, where scrubby date palms shaded the water's edge near the Ibn al As Mosque, there were two brilliantly white beaches, now occupied by the hulks of three bombed ships. Between these beaches lay a rocky promontory on which had been built the mole that circled the harbour.

The mole was a long one and ran in a rough arc over a base

of concrete blocks lowered into position by the Egyptians in the Thirties and improved on by the British in 1940. It was high enough to keep away the wind, but it was uneven and broken here and there where it had been hit by British, Italian or German bombs. Inside, the rusting masts, funnels and wheelhouses of dead freighters protruded from the water, every one of them pitted and twisted by high explosive until they were almost unrecognizable as vessels.

What living shipping there was in the harbour was all concentrated towards a stone warehouse at the end of the mole – three large coastal vessels lying on a trot one outside the other, with a fourth on its own nearer the entrance. It was an awkward arrangement but it had been forced on the harbour authorities by the absence of a tug and the demolitions the British had set in motion on their June retreat from Cyrenaica which had scuttled ships, desolated scrawny streets with holes, and brought down roofs and splintered trees.

The four coasters had arrived in the early hours of that morning. They had not been unexpected because signals had preceded them from Taranto, Corfu, Crete and finally Tobruk and Bardia, as they had made their hazardous voyage across the Mediterranean and along the North African Coast. Originally, there had been seven of them but one had been sunk by the watchful RAF off Corfu; a second had had to turn back to Tobruk with boiler trouble; a third, *Umberto Uno,* had had problems with her rudder and, three hours behind the others during the night crossing from Crete, had been picked up at dawn by a British destroyer.

Since there had been nothing much happening in Qaba for a fortnight, the whole of the town major's staff had turned out to see the ships arrive – Colonel Hochstätter, the town major himself; Major Nietzsche, the military commander; Captain Wutka, the engineer; Fregattenkapitän von Steen, the harbourmaster; Captain Hrabak, the supply officer; even Captain Veledetti, the Italian in charge of the prisoner of war compound which had been set up near the harbour to keep the bombs away.

'Petrol,' Hochstätter said. 'Petrol for the panzers!'

As the ships began with difficulty to edge alongside, they were eyed sullenly by Private Gaspare Bontempelli, of the 97th Mixed Engineer Company attached to the Pistoia Division of the Army Reserve. Plump and – because he was always hungry – known to his friends as Double Ration, Bontempelli, like so many Italians, couldn't have cared less who won the war in North Africa, so long as he didn't have to die in it. It wasn't so much that he didn't possess the *dono di coraggio* – the gift of courage – but that, as an extremely realistic young man, he preferred not to risk his neck in something for which he didn't have much sympathy.

He regarded the desert with a loathing he found impossible to put into words, and for the life of him he couldn't understand why three great nations should involve themselves in such a titanic struggle for its possession. Because he didn't understand it, to Bontempelli the desert seemed bewitched. Like everyone else from the teeming cities of Italy, he hated the disembodied silences and the terrifying ghibli that clothed him in a cloud of fire, certain he'd be found days afterwards when it stopped blowing, with his own bullet in his temple and his eyes and mouth full of sand.

Bontempelli lived by the black inert shape of a 47 mm. gun on the Mas el Bub side of the town, tormented by a desperate longing for Naples where his home was. In Taranto, where he'd last been stationed, there had at least been a young widow by the name of Maddalena Corri whose loneliness had made up for his homesickness. This place had nothing. *Nothing.* No beauty. No comfort. No music beyond the wailing half-notes of Arab wind instruments. Not even women. Apart, that was, he admitted, from Zulfica Ifzi, a plump seventeen-year-old Levantine he had discovered two months before in one of the two brothels the town sported, who had given up work to devote herself entirely to Bontempelli.

Not even Zulfica Ifzi's attentions could make up for the discomforts of Qaba, however, and Bontempelli therefore detested his NCO, Sergente Barbella; his officer, Sottotenente Baldissera; the Prussian who ran the harbour gangs, Unteroffizier Upholz; and the German supply officer, Captain Hrabak – all of whom he considered pushed him around far too much. He also generously detested Marshal Ettore Bastico, his commander-in-chief; Field Marshal Erwin Rommel, the absent German commander; General Stumme, his very present deputy; Hitler; Mussolini; Churchill; Stalin; and everybody else he considered had contributed, however indirectly, to his presence in Qaba.

As a result, as the ships arrived – when he'd half-hoped the campaign in North Africa would come to a stop through lack of supplies and they could all go home – he raised a cynical cheer. To his surprise a man on his right echoed it and someone else took it up, until it swelled and spread, so that in no time at all every man of the 97th Mixed Engineer Company and Captain Hrabak's few Germans was yelling hysterically, and the sullen look on Bontempelli's dark handsome face changed to a smile of delight as he marvelled at the influence he could bring to bear when he felt like it.

Colonel Hochstätter didn't share his happiness. 'For God's sake, Hrabak,' he snapped. 'Do you want the whole of North Africa to know these ships have arrived? Shut those men up!'

As the cheers died and the winches began to clatter, lorry-loads of camouflage netting began to roll towards the mole. Von Steen had spent three whole days scouring the back areas of the line for every scrap he could find, and as the ships' engines stopped, his sailors began to swarm aboard and swing the nets into place so that the vessels began to merge in with the land. Smoke generators were also set up to create an artificial fog if necessary and Hochstätter watched with quiet pleasure.

'A good job well done, Herr Hafenmeister,' he said.

Von Steen eyed him indifferently. Hochstätter had been a good officer once, but the effects of wounds had slowed down not only his movements but also his processes of thought; and his mind, as they all knew, was all too often occupied with worry for his wife and two daughters in Düsseldorf, because Düsseldorf was a regular target for the RAF and he hadn't heard from them for months now. Hrabak was quite certain they were dead, and it was felt that Hrabak had good reason to know because his own wife and daughter had disappeared in one of the holocausts that had struck Essen.

Almost before their engines were shut down the ships' captains were collected by car and taken to Hochstätter's quarters in the Boujaffar Hotel.

'Four ships out of seven,' the elderly German commodore of the convoy observed bitterly as he accepted a drink. 'It's not many. Have you heard what happened to *Umberto Uno*?'

'She's in Alexandria harbour now,' Captain Tarnow, the signals officer said. 'Our agents report her anchored close inshore with British soldiers on board and a guard ship alongside.'

Hochstätter gestured. 'We could have used the weapons she was carrying,' he said. 'But thank God we have –' he glanced at the list von Steen had handed him ' – *Giuseppe Bianchi, Andolfo, Guglielmotti* and *Cassandra*.'

As the sun died, like a gigantic gun-flash in the western sky, the usual evening breeze started, stirring the palms and rolling little puffs of dust along the streets, and the Bedou traders who had spent the day huddled in their galabiyas in the shade of the trees near the mosque, their heads down, indifferent to the war that had spread along the whole north coast of Africa, began to rise. One after the other, gangling rope-haltered camels kneeling under the palms lurched to their feet and stood patiently, gurgling wetly as they disgorged. Then slowly they began to move off past the harbour.

Beyond the town, on the black ribbon of road that ran east and west along the coast, a group of bored Italians were cooking an evening meal of soup, pasta and beans among the broken walls. As the camels approached, one of them stood up stiffly, holding a rifle. The camels came to a shuffling halt, the dust they had stirred up drifting past the little encampment on the breeze. There was a brief exchange in a mixture of tongues, and then the Italian waved them on.

'Aiee!' The leading driver jabbed with a pointed stick at his animal's testicles and the little caravan, stinking of uncured hides and dates, headed out of town towards Akka Dub, the next village along the coast in the direction of Fuka and the fig plantations of Daba. The Italians didn't bother to look up. The evening movement of camels between Qaba and Akka Dub was normal enough. The Bedouin had been spectators of the North African struggle ever since the first forward pushes in 1940, looking on disinterestedly as fortunes swayed back and forth between El Agheila and El Alamein, even sharing the waterholes with lorry-borne young men of the long-range groups of both sides. Sometimes they lost a village hit by bombs or a camel killed by a mine. Sometimes they murdered a lost soldier or profited by a rifle stolen from a corpse, a can of petrol from a wrecked car, or a few tins of food from an abandoned lorry. But, profit or loss, it was always wise to be wary of the Messerschmitts and Hurricanes that prowled the sky during daylight hours, and they took care to remain within easy reach of shelter when the sun rose, and only moved their caravans during the first hours after dusk. It had been going on so long now that neither side took much notice of them; the Italians, who had ages since grown sick of the war, least of all.

The caravan moved slowly eastwards, the camels like ungainly ships on a rough sea, their riders muffled to the eyes against the grit stirred up by the breeze. Occasionally a single rider turned north to where his family huddled with his few animals among the hills in a flat black tent smelling of sheep dung. Slowly the convoy became strung out, the leader a good half-mile from the last straggling beast, a dark brown animal with a hide covered with sores. Its rider crouched on its back, his head down, the grimiest of the whole string of grimy riders, the only portion of his face that could be seen the grey eyes glinting under his head-dress and a large hooked nose poking through the wrapping of rags that surrounded his face.

Gradually the distance between the main group and the last rider increased until he had dropped far behind. Then, as night fell and the sky overhead became thronged with glowing stars, he sat up straighter on his limping animal and turned, not north but south, into the desert. Down there rolled the Great Sand Sea, known to the Arabs as 'the Devil's country', almost impassable to anything but a camel, but interspersed with great areas of rocky outcrop, stony wastes and loose sand where vehicles could move.

After an hour's riding, the camel halted and the rider stared about him. In front, the land rose a little, and on the horizon against the lighter hue of the night sky, he saw a square angular shape which didn't fit into the landscape. The camel snorted and, as it moved forward again, a stone rattled under its great flat feet. From the direction of the square silhouette came the click of a rifle bolt being shoved home.

A light flashed briefly and figures appeared against the skyline. A few muffled words were exchanged and the rider of the camel slipped from the beast's back. At the other side of the ridge, white blurs of faces turned, figures moved in the shadows and engines were started. The muffled shape in the grimy galabiya climbed into a lorry and someone offered him a cigarette. As he drew in a deep grateful puff and the smoke floated away on the night air, he gestured towards the east.

'Let's go,' he said. 'And pile the coal on, please. I've got news that'll make their hair stand on end at HQ.'

2

The decision was therefore made to mount a special operation to disrupt these important supplies, together with large amounts of spare parts for the Luftwaffe and the Afrika Korps panzer divisions which were also known to be in Qaba.

Brigadier Loftus, of Eighth Army Intelligence, was a big man with far too much flesh on his bones, and he was sweating profusely because his tent was stuffy in the morning sunshine. He was a dedicated man, and it never occurred to him to take an hour off for a breather, because he had already given his complete allegiance to the new commander of the Eighth Army and was prepared to work every hour that God sent to make him successful.

The new man hadn't been long in North Africa – barely long enough to get his knees brown, in fact – and to the sunburnt desert veterans, he hadn't any particularly remarkable physical attributes with his fair hair, sharp enquiring nose and pale blue eyes. Pale though they were, however, those piercing eyes seemed to Loftus to miss nothing and there was a steely quality behind them that indicated an unexpected depth of character. It was said the general was lacking in warmth, but he was incisive, firm of purpose and, as quite a number of indifferent officers had already found out, not over-willing to make allowances for the fallibility of others. He mightn't look very much like the sort of man who would win the hearts of his soldiers, but he did seem to be the very man who might do something about the Afrika Korps and especially about Rommel.

Rommel had caught the imagination of every man in North Africa, and his soldiers – Erwin's Army, they were called – with their palm tree insignia, sun-bleached hair and bright blue eyes, had built up a legend of invincibility that was hard to break down. Because their general was good and an honourable man, too, his Afrika Korps was good also and its soldiers were clean fighters. Well equipped with excellent weapons, they envied the British nothing except their cigarettes, and it was little wonder the Eighth Army admired them.

They still stood, however, for German *Schrecklichkeit* – that toxic frightfulness of the Nazis – and since they had to be beaten, it was Loftus's opinion that another legend was needed to combat the one Rommel had built up. And oddly enough, the long-nosed general, who'd come out from England only as a second choice, had already started one of his own, different but strangely similar in its austerity and ruthlessness. His attitude was quite clearly not to dance to the German tune, but to play one of his own – only better – and first. In the desert, the wolves of Europe were suddenly facing bigger and craftier wolves.

Brigadier Loftus had a whole series of situation reports to prepare, and despite the heat he still went on with them because every minute was important if the Germans were to be defeated. The three arms of their *Drang nach Osten* had all by the grace of God come to a stop at last – the Russian one at Stalingrad and Moscow, the Balkan one at Crete, and the North African one at Alamein, only a few short miles from Alexandria – but it was still necessary to guarantee the Mediterranean and somehow re-establish a footing in Europe, and the only way to do that was by the conquest of Libya and the driving out of North Africa of every last vestige of the German–Italian occupation.

Since the new commander of the Eighth Army seemed to have some pretty solid ideas on the subject, and vast new supplies of tanks and 25-pounder guns, to Brigadier Loftus it seemed that the extra effort might well be worth while, so when the starched and laundered young staff captain appeared in his doorway, he looked up with a frown at the interruption.

'Chap called Hockold to see you, sir,' the captain said.

The man in the scruffy galabiya appeared, his skin still dark with the stain on it. His face was lean and, without the ragged headdress, his straight fair hair fell over his eyes like the broken wing of a yellow bird.

'Hello, George,' Loftus said. 'Made it, I see. Brought some good news?'

'Depends which way you look at it, sir.' Hockold moved to Loftus's table, and a mug of tea appeared. 'I've just come from Qaba.'

Loftus studied him carefully over his spectacles. 'What's special about Qaba?' he asked.

'That's where Rommel's got his petrol.'

Loftus gestured. 'Rommel hasn't got any petrol. He's supposed to need thirty thousand tons and, before he can move again, another thirty-five. He's supposed to be in Berlin, in fact, begging on his bended knees for it.'

'I think it's different now. There are three petrol ships in Qaba. They came in forty-eight hours ago.'

Loftus's eyebrows rose. 'The RAF reported nothing,' he said.

'They rigged up camouflage. They had it up within a matter of hours.'

'How much petrol is there?'

'I worked it out at thirty thousand tons – at least.'

Loftus whistled. 'That would make a hell of a difference to how he fights.'

'Are we expecting an attack?'

'We're not. *He* is. The new commander's all set to go. Chap called Montgomery. Know him?'

'Instructor at Camberley when I was there.'

'Well, I hope he puts the wind up 'em. For my money he's all right. He says he's going to knock Rommel for six clean out of Africa.'

Hockold gave a little smile. 'It might be harder than he thinks now,' he pointed out. 'There's also a ship loaded with ammunition, a refuelling post in the town where there are two sheds of spare parts, and a dump a mile inland from the harbour. Fortunately for us, their administrative services are unstable and they have no lighters, tugs or lorries.'

Loftus sighed. 'We'd better let 'em know at AHQ,' he said. 'They'll get an RAF bang laid on, I suppose.'

'Not this time. There's a prisoner of war cage right alongside the harbour.'

Loftus stared at Hockold for a long moment. 'Got any ideas?'

'I was thinking of a raid.'

'Not a hope. Monty's dead against sideshows. The navy set one up against Benghazi and Tobruk in September. It was a dead loss.'

'There's no minefield,' Hockold persisted. 'And I've got a chart.' He placed an envelope on the desk. 'A few other things too : Numbers. Positions of the ships. Gun emplacements. Three old French 47s and heavy machine guns, but not much else. Flak guns are all inland.'

Loftus paused; then he smiled and pushed his papers away. 'You make out a good case,' he admitted. 'Perhaps we should let the bigwigs decide.'

As it happened, even as Hockold prepared to head for Eighth Army headquarters to lay his ideas before the new general in command, the signals that Colonel Hochstätter had made about the arrival of the four supply ships to General Stumme, holding the fort for Rommel at Afrika Korps headquarters, were just starting to bear fruit. Qaba, which was normally used only when Mersa Matruh and Bardia were full, had increased enormously in importance since the British retreat in June. Now the lines of communication went all the way back to Tripoli, and as it suddenly occurred to someone that they were incredibly vulnerable, a message was directed to Hochstätter that the four ships were to be unloaded at once.

Captain Hrabak, the supply officer, permitted himself a cynical smile. 'What with?' he asked. 'We're short of lorries.'

'Lighters then,' Hochstätter suggested. 'Across to the concrete below the POW compound.' He turned to the signals officer. 'Ask for lighters, Tarnow.'

'Where from?' Tarnow demanded. He was popularly supposed

to be a member of the *Feldsicherheitspolizei* or the *Liebstandarte Adolf Hitler Waffen S.S.* and was surly, arrogant and indifferent in manner, which gave the stories a substance of truth and made them all wary of him.

Hochstätter drew a deep breath. 'Try the navy at Mersa Matruh,' he said. 'And we can hire all the Arabs we want.'

'They work too slowly. It's not their war.' Hrabak gestured angrily. 'We need *transport*. The panzers took all ours at the end of August. It never came back. If they want what we've got, we've got to have lorries.'

Hochstätter frowned. What Hrabak said was only too true. A few lorries had been commandeered, together with everything the wretched Italians possessed, but it was obviously not going to be enough by a long way. Unknown to Hochstätter, however, his signals to army headquarters had been duly noted, and General Stumme was well aware there was a considerable amount of worry in the forward areas caused by a shortage of petrol. He also knew that a British Commando brigade had been sent to the Middle East the previous year and, though it was known to have been badly cut up in Crete, he had no knowledge of whether its losses had been made good and he was very concerned in case it attempted something against his supplies.

'Tell Colonel Hochstätter that the defences of Qaba must be strengthened,' he directed. 'At once. And keep me informed about what's being done because we don't really know yet what the Eighth Army's up to.'

The Eighth Army was up to a lot of things, chief of which were the new general's preparations to knock the Afrika Korps out of Africa, for which the plans, code-named Lightfoot, had been pushed ahead at tremendous speed.

Army headquarters was a group of caravans at Burg el Arab, twenty miles from Alexandria, set on the coast where the staff could walk straight from their work into the sea. Despite the rumours that he allowed no smoking and no drinking, the new commander was not a killjoy.

'He'll laugh if it's funny,' Loftus said as his jeep jolted along. 'And he doesn't give a damn about saluting. They say that Freyberg suggested that, since the New Zealanders didn't go in for it much, he should try waving at them. To everybody's surprise he did, and they waved back.'

His belly jerked as he laughed. 'The chaps who've flogged up and down the same bit of desert till they're sick of it love him,' he went on. 'Though he's a bit difficult with generals. He says they know a lot about fighting but not much about war, and the machine's running properly now for the first time since Wavell left.'

As the dusty jeep drew to a stop, the new general was standing at a table under a strip of camouflage netting which threw a speckled shadow over the map he was studying. As the brakes squealed, several of the officers round him turned to look at it and, though the army commander didn't even bother to lift his head, what he said was sharp enough to bring their attention hurriedly back to the map again.

As he finished speaking, Loftus stepped forward and saluted. 'Colonel Hockold, sir,' he said.

The narrow head seemed to duck and lift, and the pale blue eyes stared piercingly upwards. 'Still up to your tricks, I see, Hockold,' the general said. 'I seem to remember a nasty little night exercise when I was instructing at Camberley in 1930. You won, if I remember rightly, with rather a dirty trick.' The thin severe face cracked into a frosty smile. 'Just the type we need, because we're fighting some pretty tough customers out here.' He patted a folder on the table alongside the map. 'I've read your report.'

He paused and Hockold waited. The general's head ducked again and the pale eyes came up once more to his face.

'Not keen on sideshows,' he went on. 'Waste of time. Waste of time. Didn't think much of the one on Benghazi and Tobruk in September. A frontal assault on a heavily defended base seems unnecessarily hazardous. Are you sure about that swept minefield?'

'Certain, sir,' Hockold said. 'The harbour clearance units are still busy at Bardia and Mersa Matruh for the next sweep forward.'

The general frowned. 'There'll be no sweep anywhere if I have anything to do with it,' he observed acidly. 'The only sweeping that's going to be done will be done by me.' He stood for a moment with his hands behind his back, his sharp nose thrust forward, then he looked up again. 'So perhaps we'd better set something up, if only to make them think we're coming in by the back door. And you'd better handle it yourself since you know where everything is. It'll take about a week to organize, I imagine, and that'll work out just about right, because I'll be ready around the night of 23 October.'

He stared thoughtfully at his feet. 'You must accept that we're a bit stretched at the moment,' he went on. 'And there are one or two other things to take into consideration, too, because in early November I gather we're going into Morocco, Tunis and Algeria.' He turned to one of the officers behind him, a thin good-looking man in shorts. 'Freddie, see that he gets full authority for this thing and have the navy and the RAF warned that he's coming.' He swung back to Hockold, lean, tense, and excited by his own imaginings. 'We've got to pull it off this time, Hockold, but I think we shall do it all right. I think we shall. We're going to knock him clean out of Africa this time, so that there can be no coming back for more. Get him down to Gorton, Freddie. He'll fix him up.'

As it happened, however, when Hockold arrived in Cairo General Gorton was in no position to fix anybody up. He had been whipped off half an hour before to hospital with an agonizing ear infection he'd been fighting for days, and in his place was an entirely different officer who was still a little lost in his new job. He didn't seem very willing to make decisions and Hockold had a suspicion he wouldn't last long under the new régime.

'Go and see General Pierson,' he said. 'I'll tell him you're coming.'

General Pierson, however, was busy near Ismailia, and

Hockold was shunted through several officers with Baden-Powell
shorts and chests like the contents of a paint box to see a Major-
General Murray, a heavy-featured man with a bulldog jaw and
a hostile frown who stared at him discouragingly as he entered.
'Qaba,' he said at once. 'They tell me you're going to put on a bit
of a show there. Do a bit of damage and all that.'

Hockold swallowed. There was always an enervating lassitude
over Cairo; the tropical rain from the highlands of Ethiopia and
the swamps of Uganda swept down to distribute the muddy
water in a thousand and one canals across the Delta, so that out
of the steamy soil the foetid heat intensified in a pall of dust and
filth that lay over the streets of the city. The dirt was persistent
and Cairo – corrupt, lackadaisical, easy-going and flashily
romantic at night, despite the war only a hundred miles away –
showed no sign of a spartan warrior existence. Too many battles
had already been lost there, too many plans ruined, and Hockold,
still only a lieutenant-colonel, felt he had to come to the point
quickly.

'Sir,' he said, 'please don't pass me on again. This operation's
been authorized by the army commander himself and I've only
just over a week to set it up.'

Murray scowled back at him under his heavy eyebrows; then
a sudden unexpected smile changed his whole face.

'Better sit down and tell me what you want,' he said.

Hockold drew a deep breath. 'I want transport –' he began.

'Lorries?'

'No, sir. We're going by sea.'

'Can't be done!' Murray sat up briskly. 'The navy's got
nothing to spare.'

'It's the only way it *can* be done, sir.'

Murray's smile came again. 'Well, we'll leave that for the
moment,' he said. 'What else?'

'Men, sir.'

'How many?'

'Five hundred, sir. Trained men. Not people who've just
arrived.'

The frown returned to Murray's face. 'General Montgomery

got rid of all specialist sub-units,' he pointed out. 'And we're already scraping the gutters for his battle. Every decent outfit we could find's already moved up into the blue.' He paused, his face thoughtful. 'You'll have to rehearse. Where are you going to do it?'

'Gott el Scouab. There are ravines there, one of them steep like the Shariah Jedid at Qaba.'

'Could you do it in a week?'

'If they're the right chaps, sir.'

'I'll see what I can do. Go on.'

'What about naval support fire, sir?'

'Not a chance.'

'The general said there had to be no mistake, sir.'

Murray's heavy body sagged. 'Unfortunately, Monty's not an admiral.'

'Sir, there are three 47s guarding the harbour.'

Murray wrote something on a pad. 'Well, we won't start shouting "Abandon ship" till the bloody thing goes down,' he said. 'Anything else?'

'Signallers. Medical people. Demolition experts.'

Murray thought for a moment then he gave an unexpected grin and tapped Hockold's plan. 'Sounds all rather worth while,' he said. 'I'm told you've been behind Jerry's lines for three months.'

'Four, sir.'

'Well, you can't sit around with your thumb in your bum till I've talked to everybody. How'd you like to nip out for a drink with my planning officer? I'd laid it on to go myself but I suspect now I'm going to be busy for an hour or two.'

Hockold smiled, grateful that out of all Cairo's armchair warriors he'd found one who was prepared to forsake his evening gin to do some work. 'I've a little drinking to catch up with, sir,' he admitted.

Murray nodded. 'Good. My planning officer's got transport. Sound operator. B.A., Aberdeen. But see you're back by seven o'clock because I suspect we shall be whipping you off to see the Navy or somebody.'

He pressed a bell and an ATS officer appeared. She had a splendid figure and Hockold was quietly admiring it when Murray gestured. 'Kirstie,' he said. 'This is Colonel Hockold. Hockold, this is my niece and my planning officer – Kirstie McRuer.'

3

It was decided the attack should involve all three services and take the form of a Combined Operations raid.

Kirstie McRuer was twenty-five, tall and straight-backed, with green eyes and thick chestnut hair. She had been in the Middle East for eighteen months and was wary of predatory officers.

'Because I'm with the army,' she explained, 'most of them seem to think I'm a sort of camp-follower. In fact, quite a lot of us are in Planning now and doing very well at it, too.'

They were sitting on the terrace of the officers' club, and in the odd moments of silence they could hear the grumble of the guns to the west. It seemed a strange sound in the light-hearted atmosphere about them, which was like that of an expensive Thames-side pub on a Sunday morning in peacetime. There was even a Cairo tennis professional in white flannels watching a group round the pool where a few Egyptian girls smiled, beautifully dressed and poised. Kirstie wondered how much they detested the British.

She was unobtrusively studying Hockold as they chatted over their drinks. He had sat in silence as they had driven from Murray's office through endless lines of ammunition trucks – even a column of German prisoners, singing the song that every army in North Africa sang.

> *'Deine Schritte kennt sie, deinen zieren Gang,*
> *Alle Abend brennt sie, doch mich vergass sie lang . . .'*

At the club Hockold had helped her from the jeep with an

29

old-fashioned solemnity which was strange in Cairo where everybody accepted women officers as equals. It told her he'd been a long time away from female company and was faintly embarrassed by it.

Nearby, two cavalrymen in faded drill were playing table tennis as if the result of the war were at stake. They were both burned black and looked as though they'd just come in from the desert. There was something of the same worn look about Hockold. He was tall and slender, thin-hipped in a pair of old doeskin trousers bleached almost white, but under the mixture of nonchalance and professionalism which made up the side of him that was a soldier, there was also an uncertain discomfort that told her he was shy.

A young officer in neat khaki was eyeing her hungrily from a nearby table, and she decided he'd probably been on a troopship coming round the Cape for two months and was desperate for female company. Trying to draw Hockold out, she indicated him with her eyes.

'You'd be surprised how often one of them tells me I'm beautiful,' she pointed out. 'If I were, I might be flattered. But I'm not.'

'You look all right to me,' Hockold said with a brisk enthusiasm that was overstressed enough to tell her that he wasn't in the habit of paying compliments to women.

'You've been in the desert a long time,' she smiled. 'It's what you'd call a good Scots face. Scotswomen have a tendency to look better as they grow older.'

'At least that's something for Scots husbands to look forward to.' Hockold's comment was brusque. 'Often in England it's the other way round. Leads to quite a lot of ill-will after about twenty years.'

He sipped at his drink, staring into it as though he were searching for something else to say. He still looked grim and ill at ease, and she guessed that some of his awkwardness had come from being lanky and ungainly in his youth.

'Are you engaged or married or anything?' he asked.

'I'm a widow.'

'Oh!' He looked uncomfortable and she saw to her surprise that he was actually blushing. 'Rude of me to ask.'

It was a long time since she'd seen a mature man blush in front of her and it oddly endeared him to her. 'It's a normal enough question,' she said quickly, encouragingly. 'I don't mind.'

He tried to make up for his gaffe. 'Was your husband army?'

'Yes.'

'Dunkirk?'

'No. Bomb. He was with Bomb Disposal. One of them killed him.'

'I'm sorry.'

She shrugged. 'It's history now. We didn't know each other long and we were only married two months. What about you?'

'Much the same as usual.' Hockold gestured with his glass. 'Regular cavalry. Got a little tired of swanning up and down in the blue in a tin box on wheels so I did a bit of long range stuff for a change and finally found myself attached to Loftus's lot. They left me behind in June to see what I could find out.'

'When did you come out here?'

It was the question everybody asked sooner or later and he smiled because he'd arrived in the Middle East even before Dunkirk, one of Wavell's small and rather amateur force which had deluded Graziani into believing it was twice as strong as it was and in 1940 had even smashed him back beyond Benghazi.

'I was one of the first,' he said slowly, and she knew he wasn't shooting a line. 'But they've decided now that I've had enough, and there's talk of bringing me back after this next little business.'

'Do you want to come back?'

He sat for a moment thinking of the wastes of shaly soil and trying to exist on a meagre quarter of a gallon of water a day.

'Yes,' he said in the clipped way he had of speaking to her, so different from the way he spoke to Murray. 'Been spitting sand out for three years now almost without a break. Should be pleasant to be able to take a bath regularly.'

'At least you're honest.'

He shrugged. 'No. Just frightened. Can't go on for ever. Been nicked twice. Nothing much, but it's a sign. We all catch it in the end if we go on too long. This time Loftus insists.' He smiled again. 'If I survive.'

She didn't know what to say, sensing an honesty that had become unexpected in Cairo where everyone still contrived to live as if it were peacetime, dining and drinking and apparently not connected at all with the war in the desert.

'Is it going to be difficult?' she asked.

'Well, it's not going to be easy and I have a suspicion it's already become bigger than I originally intended.' Hockold paused and finished his drink. 'Suppose we ought really to be getting back now,' he said. 'Time's up.' He hesitated, then went on in a breathless, stumbling rush. 'Any chance of buying you another drink sometime?'

She looked up at him. His skin seemed to be burned to the eyebrows so that it looked beaten and raw, and his eyes were tired. He was a severe individual, meditative and brooding, a pensive, lonely, quiet man, but she suspected that he was also uncompromising, unflinching and honourable.

She deliberately put on her best smile to encourage him. 'I'd like that,' she said.

When they got back to Murray's office, he was on the telephone. He waved at Hockold and went on talking.

'No,' he was saying loudly. 'The bloody man can't take compassionate leave! Every other poor bugger's having to work his guts out and a few of 'em are going to end up dead, so why should *he* get away with it?' He slammed the telephone down and closed the file in front of him; as he smiled at Hockold his whole face changed. 'Take a pew,' he said. 'I've laid on a meeting with the navy and the RAF. We'll go straight along. I've also got a few facts for you. None of 'em very encouraging, I'm afraid.'

'Better tell me the worst, sir.'

'Right. Bad news first: there'll be no warships. That's a dead cert. According to a staff appreciation made only a week ago there's nothing anywhere until Monty's battle's over. The navy's had a rough time in the last two years and everything they've still got at this end of the Med's earmarked for the advance. That

means there'll be no naval support fire. One other thing:
Freddie de Guingand says Monty can contribute nothing either.
He says he needs everybody he's got and I expect he does because
he's determined that when he punches his hole in Rommel's line
he'll have enough men for the follow-through.' He glanced at
Hockold's taut face and his cheerful smile appeared again. 'But
don't worry, my boy. We'll find your men even if we have to turn
out storekeepers, clerks, cooks, elderly staff officers like me, and
the man who fought the monkey in the dustbin.'

Murray's meeting took place at RAF, Bir Farouk. It was the
usual flat expanse of nothing alongside the road, with a few
tents, huts and screens where aeroplanes were serviced. The
station commander had laid on a large empty marquee with a
table and chairs and maps of the desert and the coast.

Murray took his place with Hockold. 'Who's coming for the
RAF?' he demanded.

An RAF officer by the maps looked up. 'Air Vice-Marshal
de Berry, sir.'

'And the naval adviser?'

The airman coughed. 'Rear-Admiral Bryant, sir.'

Murray pulled a face. 'Damn,' he said as he spread his papers.
'Those two detest each other and they can foul anything up if
they're in the mood.'

The two men – the airman tall, slim and elegant and wearing
a string of decorations dating from the days when he'd been a
fighter ace over the Western Front, and the admiral, short,
square, stocky, every inch of him a saltwater sailor – began to
eye each other warily the minute they arrived. Hockold pushed
forward the plan he'd made of Qaba and began to outline his
idea, aware of a deep distrust from the other side of the table at
once. He described Qaba with its long mole and beaches and the
positions of the petrol depot, the ships and the warehouses full
of spare parts.

'How did you arrive at these distances?' Bryant demanded
sharply.

'I walked them.'

'Under the eyes of the Germans?' Bryant sounded as though he didn't believe it.

'I worked for seven days with a labouring gang shovelling concrete. I walked along the mole fourteen times – seven there, seven back. I measured it every time.'

'How many paces?'

De Berry leaned forward. He had a fly-whisk hanging from his wrist and was smoking a cigarette in a long amber holder. 'Couldn't we assume that Colonel Hockold knows what he's talking about?' he said.

Bryant turned to stare at de Berry but when he drew on his pipe and said nothing, Murray touched Hockold's arm. 'Go on,' he urged quickly.

Hockold drew a deep breath. 'We want a ship which can place my troops on the outside of the mole – '

Bryant was immediately hostile. 'That's a matter for the navy, I think,' he growled. 'Why not go in alongside this single ship here – *Giuseppe Bianchi* – and blow her up with a time fuse. She'll probably take the others with her. You could then make for the depot, blow that up en route, and finally head out into the desert.'

'Without vehicles, petrol or water?' de Berry asked.

'They'll have to expect casualties.'

Hockold drew a deep breath. 'There's just one snag with that plan, sir,' he said, and Bryant's head jerked round. 'The Germans have dragged the hull of an old lighter across the entrance. There may even be two now. It's blocked. And the prisoners of war have to be released first or they'll go up with the ships. Two thousand of them. Do we have to accept *that* many casualties?'

Bryant was silent and Hockold went on. 'There's only one way to do it: We have to put a ship against the outside of the mole and go across it.'

Bryant frowned. 'It's not possible. It's shallow water.'

'There's one place – here –' Hockold pointed at the chart ' – where the water's about nine feet deep. I gather the Germans dredged it and, until the harbour was cleared, moored a lighter there and unloaded across her.'

Bryant frowned. 'Why can't we go in close and shell the ships through the harbour entrance?'

'Because there's a big sand-bank with a wrecked freighter in the way. There are also three Italian 47s – here, here and here – which could effectively stop anything smaller than a destroyer. The only way it can be done is by getting aboard the ships and placing charges.'

Bryant frowned. 'What's the opposition?'

Hockold pushed forward a sheet of paper containing numbers and names of units. 'There are also the 47s. They've been well sited and, in addition to firing to seaward, every one of them could be worked round at a pinch to fire towards the Roman arch. And it's round the Roman arch that we have to have a strongpoint, or no one will get into the town to destroy anything.'

Murray took up the story, feeling that Hockold was battling against too much rank. 'We're proposing that a lighter or something goes alongside the mole at the point Colonel Hockold suggests and that the following vessels lay alongside her.'

'What following vessels?' Bryant tossed a file across. 'Take a look at that, and tell me where they're coming from.'

Murray didn't bother to pick up the file and Bryant went on coldly. 'When the army make demands of the navy they should make sure of getting a soldier who knows something about the sea.'

'Or an admiral who knows something about the land,' de Berry murmured.

Murray leaned his head on his hand, saying nothing, and Hockold stared in amazement as the two men glared at each other.

'Support fire's out of the question,' Bryant growled, staring aggressively round the table as if challenging them to dispute his words. 'Force K lost a cruiser and a destroyer and two cruisers damaged. *Valiant* and *Queen Elizabeth* were damaged by Italian charioteers. *Jackal, Kipling* and *Lively* went in May and *Sikh* in that damn' silly raid on Tobruk. We've also given up everything we can spare for the other end of Africa, yet we still have to keep the men and supplies flowing without

35

interruption through the Red Sea and make sure the Levantine convoys come through with fuel. On top of all that, Montgomery still insists on full back-up and a feint raid near Fuka as the barrage starts. Every damn' thing we've got's earmarked and you can't produce ships like rabbits out of a hat.'

Nobody said anything and he seemed to feel he had overdone his indignation. 'Anyway,' he went on gruffly, 'why *another* raid, for God's sake? Didn't the one on Tobruk prove this sort of thing can't be done?' He glared at de Berry. 'How about the RAF? Can't they help?'

De Berry sucked at his cigarette for a moment. 'African air space doesn't belong to the Germans,' he pointed out. 'But, for the same reasons the navy gives, we can't offer much.'

'An air raid's out of the question,' Hockold said, aware of a sinking feeling of despair. 'Because of the prisoner of war compound.'

Bryant sucked at his pipe for a moment. 'Does this raid *have* to go in?' he asked bluntly.

'It does,' Murray said.

Bryant stared at his files. De Berry's offer of help seemed to stir him. 'We have one or two launches,' he said.

'Launches aren't very big,' de Berry observed.

'Are you talking as an airman or a sailor?'

'I'm talking as a man who was a lieutenant in the Rifles and, before he transferred to the RFC in 1916, went over the top more times than he likes to remember. The RAF knows the job of both the army *and* the navy because that's where most of us served before we became airmen.'

Bryant glared, and Hockold listened with a sad feeling that they were getting nowhere. When the meeting broke up all he had was a promise to see what could be done.

'For God's sake, sir,' he said to Murray when they climbed into the car, 'who are we fighting – the Germans or each other?'

Murray smiled. 'Military plans demanding navy support always did give rise to a lot of tooth-sucking,' he said. 'And so far, the RAF's always considered one bit of air like any other bit of

36

air, and supporting a landing no different from dropping a few bombs.'

'Combined Operations isn't a black art, sir.'

Murray smiled again. 'No. But there's also a saying that Combined Ops HQ's the only lunatic asylum in the world run by its own inmates. Leave it to me. I'm sure it won't end here. They're both intelligent men, despite what you might think. They'll come up with something. They've got to. Everything's got to go into winning this damn battle of Montgomery's and they know it.'

The problem of men and equipment which was worrying Colonel Hockold was also beginning to worry his opposite number, Colonel Hochstätter, in Qaba. He was occupied with unloading *Andolfo* when Stumme's signal arrived and, calling a conference of all the officers concerned with the port, he put to them what he'd been instructed to do.

'Strengthen the defences?' Major Nietzsche looked up with a frown from the lists he held. 'What with? Where do we get the men?' He stared at Hochstätter and, watching the cautious way he lowered himself into his chair because of his wounds, remembered his own stiff leg and Hrabak's half-blind eye. With the Reich suddenly in trouble in Russia and now awaiting the biggest attack yet in Africa, there were no able-bodied men to spare for the lines of communication. 'It's all very well telling us to set the defences in order,' he continued. 'Every damned soldier who appears in this town gets snatched up and sent to the front.'

Hochstätter sighed. 'Get in touch with Major Zöhler, Tarnow,' he suggested. 'Tell him we need help.'

The signals officer nodded but he didn't expect much success. Major Zöhler, the *Panzerarmee* representative, who lived at the airfield at Ibrahimiya, was a man who'd twice been wounded in the desert and for six months had served on Rommel's staff before being hit yet again by a bomb splinter in the gallop from Gazala after the British. He was by no means the man to allow a worn-out old cripple like Hochstätter to push him around.

He looked up, prepared to argue, but in his vague other-worldly way Hochstätter seemed to have slipped away from them. He was looking through the window at a group of sailors with a launch trying to tow a second lighter into place beyond the hulk that had been anchored across the harbour entrance.

'The boom?' he asked. 'How is it coming along?'

'We need chain cable,' von Steen said. 'And for chain cable we need power – and welders – and time. We have to buoy them to take the weight and then get tractors on the landward side to haul them across. I'll need some of Wutka's men.'

'Not likely,' Wutka said. 'I need every one of them myself.'

'What about guns?' Nietzsche, the military commander, demanded. 'We can't hold off a seaborne attack with rifles.'

'We have three 47s as general purpose guns,' Major Schoeler, the garrison gunnery officer, said. 'It's not much.'

'What about tanks?' This time it was Captain Schlabren-dorff, of 2 *Brigade Flakartillerie,* who commanded the anti-aircraft defences outside the town. 'Damaged ones. We can dig them in to cover the harbour. Surely Zöhler has one or two without engines which can be towed into position.'

Hochstätter turned to Tarnow. 'Ask headquarters for more guns,' he said. 'And gunners. *Any* gunners.'

'*And* pioneers,' Hrabak put in. 'We still have to get these ships unloaded.'

'A few engineers wouldn't come amiss either,' Wutka added. 'We still haven't filled in that last gap in the mole. It's still only a wooden bridge.'

'It must be hurried.' Hochstätter said.

'We *are* hurrying,' Wutka said. 'But we haven't the men. They were all taken away to build gun positions and strongpoints for this damned attack that's coming in the desert. And if Schoeler's thinking of building fresh gun positions here and digging tanks in, there'll be still less.'

Hochstätter stared at his hands spread on the desk in front of him. His face was impassive and for a moment there was silence. Then through the open window they heard some nostalgic Rhinelander playing '*Warum Ist Es Am Rhein So*

Schön?' and Wutka, who came from Remagen, felt old and lonely and sick of the war. Had he only known it, it was making Hochstätter think of Düsseldorf and the wife and daughters he hadn't heard from in months.

The older man took a deep breath that seemed almost painful. 'I think we shall have to re-examine our resources,' he said slowly. 'I'd like suggestions as soon as possible. Shall we say tomorrow?'

4

*Troops not worked into the plan for the major
battle then pending were to be used.*

Murray seemed more enthusiastic about things when he appeared just before lunch the following day.

'Your men.' He gestured at Hockold with a cigarette. 'General
Pierson tells me that No. 1 IBD at Akkaba close to the canal
has a lot of chaps who haven't been worked into Monty's plan.
They belong to every unit known to God except the Boy Scouts
and the Salvation Army and they've all put their names down
for Combined Operations. There are four hundred and sixty-
seven of them. Will *they* do?'

'Sound just what I'm looking for, sir.'

Murray pulled a wry face. '*Some* of 'em,' he corrected. 'You
know the types who volunteer. The usual dedicated chaps, of
course, who've spent too long sitting on their bums or are sick
of running away from Jerry and want to hit back, but they also
include the hotheads, the lunatics, the bored, the frustrated, the
ones who've spent too much time in the desert and are a bit
sand-happy, and the bad lots who've been given the alternative
of volunteering for something that'll take them away from their
units or being court-martialled for some mayhem they've committed. You'll get as many bad soldiers as good ones.'

'Beggars can't be choosers, sir.'

'Well –' Murray smiled ' – at least they're all supposed to
be trained, though, of course, they're not trained for anything
in particular. They just know which end of a gun the bullet comes
out. There's a fairly high percentage of regulars among them,

though – chaps who were out here when the war started – but, on the other hand, some of 'em haven't ever been in a fight before.'

Hockold opened his mouth to ask a question but Murray held up his hand. 'Just one more thing,' he said. 'There's a small nucleus of commandos among them.'

Hockold's heart leapt. He felt he was getting somewhere at last.

'Don't hoist the flag yet,' Murray warned. 'There aren't many. You know they sent out 7, 8 and 11 Commandos last year and then didn't know what to do with them. They laid on a few small raids – one on Bardia and that one on Beda Littoria when Geoffrey Keyes was killed – then they were used in Crete and Syria, and by the time that lot was finished there weren't many of them left. A few of them went into Special Air Service and the Long Range Desert Group, but there were also a few who applied to go back to Europe where they thought there might be more happening, and ended up in No. 1 IBD. You could promote a few to show the others what to do.'

'What about morale, sir?'

'They seem to have plenty of spirit – '

'That's a help.'

' – Unfortunately, as usual, they use most of it up on each other. As far as I can make out, they spend all their time fighting among themselves. Jocks against English. Irish against Welsh. Australians against everybody. The British army in the field always did spend more time attacking each other than they did their enemies. Think they'll be any good to you?'

Hockold drew a deep breath. 'I'd better go and have a look at 'em first, sir.'

Murray nodded. 'I think you better had,' he said. 'I gave orders last night for 'em to be rounded up. There's also a couple of rather good chaps who were lying about loose who I've arranged to come and see you. They might be of some use too.'

Hockold was still pondering the quality of the troops he'd so unexpectedly acquired when the first of his recruits arrived.

He still wasn't sure that he'd been wise to accept the direction of the operation because he was well aware that his personality had never made him good at handling men. He was best in the blue, he'd discovered, working independently with a few loyal followers in an area where his temperament didn't matter, and he'd been rather hurried into the command when he'd expected that someone with more experience of raiding would have been given the job.

There was another thing, too. After hours of thinking about the problem the night before, he had at last dropped off into a fitful sleep only to awaken sweating with fear, dreaming he was dead. He had seen himself quite clearly, sprawled under the sun among the debris of wrecked houses, the dust of the desert on his dry lips and congealed in his eyes; his blood blackening the sand, his hands still clawing at his body where he'd felt the pain. He had started to consciousness in an extremity of terror, sickened with a presentiment of death. His face had been covered with wounds as though he had been hit again and again about the head. The image had been too clear to push away, and he was wondering uneasily if it were an omen.

He was still frowning at his own troubled thoughts when the door was opened by a youthful captain recently out of hospital after an attack of jaundice brought on by a too-extensive sojourn in the desert.

'John Watson,' he said. 'Yeomanry. They said I might be of help.'

'You a commando?' Hockold asked.

Watson smiled. Becoming a commando was one of the few ways he'd worked out as a means of getting home. On his overseas leave he'd married a girl whose parents had considered their daughter too young to be swept into marriage to a man they didn't know, and he knew they'd only given their consent because he was going away and they suspected he might not be coming back. He'd been fully aware of their hostility. *And* of the dangers of parting, because he'd spent only two nights with his wife and the Eighth Army was full of stories of wives who'd gone astray.

42

He tried briefly to tell Hockold how much he needed to see the war won, and Hockold listened with sympathy. With a broken home, bullying at school because he was over-tall and awkward, and a chronic lack of money which had always obliged him to eschew social occasions, parties and girls, he had never considered that he had had a life filled with much warmth either.

They were still talking when the door opened again and a burly figure with a shaggy ginger moustache and spectacles appeared.

'Alexander Mackay Murdoch,' he said in a marked Inverness-shire accent. 'Major, Black Watch. I haird there was a wee bit o' fun being planned.'

Hockold studied Murdoch across the desk. He was an ex-NCO, tall and strong. Yet though he wore a kilt, bonnet and brogues, he still managed somehow to look like a professor from a university.

'Doubt if I'd call it fun,' Hockold explained. 'It's a raid along the coast behind Jerry's lines.'

The Scot's face didn't change, and there was something quiet – and curiously deadly – about him, so that a sudden flash of understanding came to Hockold.

'You done this sort of thing before?' he asked.

'A few times.'

'Where?'

Murdoch smiled. 'Spanish Civil War. Before that, Abyssinia.'

He was intelligent, cold, and sure of himself, a throw-back to the efficient, single-minded Scottish soldiers of fortune who had fought in every war from the sixteenth to the eighteenth centuries, and Hockold found himself setting out his ideas for him with enthusiasm.

'We have a few experienced men,' he explained. 'Belonging originally to 7, 8 and 11 Commandos. They're at No. 1 IBD.'

'Aye, I know.' The circular army spectacles gleamed. 'I took 'em into Crete last year. We came oot with our blankets lashed together with bootlaces to make sails. We also did yon raid on

Bardia. It was no' very successful but we blew up a few guns. I've been in hospital a wee while since.'

His matter-of-fact tones intrigued Hockold and he smiled. Murdoch's self-sufficient cool-headedness reminded him of the army commander.

'Our job's to destroy ships,' he said. 'The general also wants us to create as much hell as we can in the hope that it'll distract the Germans just when they're getting worked up about his battle. Can you prepare troops for the job?'

'Are they trained men?'

'They're not commandos.'

Murdoch gave a thin smile. 'They will be when I've finished with 'em,' he said.

According to its occupants, No. 2 Transit Camp at Akkaba was a bastard at the best of times, and when it was windy, it was the nearest thing you could get to hell.

It was really part of another vast grouping of huts and tents known as No. 1 Infantry Base Depot, from which it was separated by a wire fence. The scenery around was as stark as if it were on the moon, with sand stretching to the horizon on every side and making the eye and the mind alike ache with its arid uncompromising harshness. Beneath the strident sun, it was imposed on a landscape of bleak desolation, which, every time the wind blew, lifted up and rolled past them in clouds of dust. *'Dear Mum,'* they wrote, *'we are now sixty miles inside Egypt. Fifty miles of it just blew into our tent.'*

Though almost empty now, until recently No. 1 IBD had had every British infantry regiment in Egypt represented in its lines, each company with its own area of tents, parade spaces and huts to house company offices, stores and mess kitchens. It was the most God-forsaken hole in Egypt and No. 2 Transit, on its southern fringe, was the most God-forgotten part of it. Since most of those inside No. 2 Transit were volunteers for Combined Operations training, it had become known to the rest of No. 1 IBD as Death Valley.

The inhabitants of Death Valley were a pretty mixed lot, speaking with every accent of the British Isles, and mostly they were private soldiers who considered themselves entirely forgotten and far from home. With the bored, the frustrated and the rebellious, they were a pretty fair mixture of good and bad, ardent and indifferent, intelligent and stupid – in fact, the warp and weft of a reasonably normal unit.

There were seventeen officers, all of them subalterns. One of them, Lieutenant Collier, was a keen yachtsman who had been turned down by the navy, and felt that since the commandos went to war in boats instead of lorries, they were the next best thing. Another, Lieutenant Swann, had gone into the army straight from school. His ambition was simply to get among the action. He wasn't very clever, but he was brave enough and so far he hadn't managed to hear a single shot fired in anger.

The rest were much the same in terms of aggressiveness and ambition, types like Lieutenant Brandison who had played rugby for his county and considered himself ideally suited in build and temperament for a commando. But there was one, Second-Lieutenant Sotheby, who was nervous and stuttered and, considered a little slow in his own regiment, had been encouraged by his colonel to volunteer as a means of getting rid of him. His father had been killed at Dunkirk and he hoped he might be able to avenge him.

Among the NCOs, Sergeant Jacka was there quite simply because he was a commando and wanted to get on with his job. Sergeant Freelove was there because he considered he ought to be a sergeant-major and had been passed over for some creeper who didn't know his arse from his elbow. Sergeant Berringer had an undoubted gift of command. Sergeant Bunch was an NCO of the old school and a man of limited vocabulary – 'Get fell in,' 'Get spread out,' 'Get sat down' – who was reputed to salute the telephone when speaking to an officer. A little old for action, he was there because he thought the modern army nothing but bumph and wanted to join something that had been invented for fighting.

Then there was Corporal Sidebottom who had served in

Egypt and India for more years than most people had lived. He spoke a language of his own composed of Arabic, Urdu and Hindi, and had crazy light-blue eyes. He was widely believed to be a little mad, and was known to everyone as Sidi-Bot-Om or Mo-for-Mohammed. Corporal Curtiss of Signals had tired of punching keys and filling in message forms, and Corporal Snow, who had lost his whole family in the blitz on Coventry, simply wanted to slit a few German throats.

The private soldiers similarly reflected the diversity of the army. Some came from the far corners of the earth where a meeting with another human being was an event of some importance, some came from cities as crowded as anthills, their chief adventure a Saturday afternoon football match. There was a South African who'd joined because he didn't approve of the Afrikaaner opposition to Smuts' support of the United Kingdom, and there were New Zealanders who'd volunteered for fighting and after Crete had grown bored with not having any. Private Willow had once beamed on holidaymakers as he'd peddled ice cream along the crowded beaches of East Sussex, but Private Comrie had acquired his bitter ill-humour fighting the sea as a fisherman beyond the lonely stretches of the northern isles.

Private Belcher was an ex-barrow-boy – independent, self-reliant and quick-witted – who had heard, quite rightly, that at the sharp end of an army neither the officers nor the sergeants stood on their dignity too much, and that a private soldier was as good as any man if he could do his job. He had already worked out a neat little scheme for cornering all the camp's spare fags and selling them back at a profit during shortages.

Private Auchmuty never said two words if one would do, and not even one if a grunt would suffice. He had spent most of his life alone as a shepherd in his native Banffshire and liked it that way. He had volunteered because he'd been doing guard duties near the canal where, as in all units away from the firing line, there was a strange belief that an idle soldier was an inefficient soldier. Baragwanath Eva, dark as a gipsy, had carried a gun ever since he could walk. In his native Cornwall, he had man-

aged to live from poaching other people's game, farmers'
handouts when he'd cleared their farms of rabbits, and the money
he got from the sale of the skins. He could thread a needle with
a rifle.

Owen John Jones – Taffy to most people – was a handsome
bull of a man, a big talker and a great lover. Coming from a
village on the border, he barely scraped in as a Welshman and,
anyway, had spent most of his adult life patting water into
butter in a Shrewsbury grocer's. A man constantly at odds with
the fortitude that obsessed him, he had taken the Charles Atlas
Mr World course and looked like a Greek god. He was fond of
saying what he was going to do to the Nazis and was at Akkaba
because of the jeerings of his comrades in the East Yorks who
had said he should put up or shut up.

David Evan Bradshaw came from the heart of the Brecknock
hills but, though he was twice as Welsh as Taffy Jones, he never
sounded Welsh and was *never* called Taffy. Yet his name was
unaccountably the source of constant confusion. Officers and
the NCOs variously addressed him as Braddock, Bradwell,
Bradley, Bradbury, Bradford and Bradway. His fellow privates
further complicated matters with Bulstrode, Oxshott and anything else that came into their heads – even, sometimes, when
they'd had a few soapy Egyptian beers, 'De Vere Anstruther,
darling'. To Bradshaw, a quiet, self-contained, curiously confident man who could usually be identified by the book in his
hand, it was a matter of supreme indifference how he was
addressed. An American airman had moved into Bradshaw's
bed not long after he'd moved out en route for Egypt and he'd
volunteered in the hope of being posted home again – not, as
one might have supposed, to black his wife's eye but to rescue
his books which she'd consigned to the garage. Between him and
Taffy Jones there was a curious lack of accord.

Scrapper Keely of the Argylls was more Irish than Scots and
had finally compounded a whole string of villainies – most of
which consisted of pounding military policemen senseless – by
being caught out of bounds in Cairo wearing nothing but his
boots. His excuse – 'I got lost in the black-out, sorr' – hadn't

convinced his colonel, who had offered him a choice of volunteering or going before a court-martial.

Private Gardner, from Barnsley in Yorkshire, had inevitably found himself in the Royal Welch, just as Taffy Jones had arrived in the East Yorks. Private Docwra from Cumberland didn't see eye to eye with the desert because it was about as different from his native fells as chalk was from cheese. Private Kirkpatrick's face was scarred from burns received when the motor-boat in which he'd been chased out of Greece had been set on fire. Private Fidge had volunteered in the hope of being posted home, so he could then report sick with some none-too-well-defined disease until he could look around his native Birmingham and find himself a cushy posting or even go over the wall and disappear among a few friends who lived off the black market and managed to avoid the army.

Mitchell, Smith and Chamberlain – each of them over six feet tall – had grown up together, enlisted together, whored together and raised hell together, and were known as the Three Stooges. Private Sugarwhite, an even-tempered young man with guileless eyes, was there chiefly because he didn't like his own name and was sick of people addressing him as 'Sweetie' or 'Sugarpie' and thought he might find a different breed of men in the commandos. Ed By had the shape and demeanour of a Suffolk Punch – large, slow, plodding, not very clever, but willing, hard-working and proud, six-feet-five of human being built like a brewery dray and all encompassed in four small letters.

Rounding them off – literally, since his name began with a W and he was always down at the end of every list – was Herbert Kitchener Waterhouse, a vulgar, light-hearted irrepressible young man with concave cheeks and a thatch of ginger hair like a copper pan-scrubber, who spoke – even at close quarters – in shouts and yelps that were thick with a catarrhal cold-in-the-nose sound which came from too many years of breathing coaldust. Private Waterhouse had no idea why he'd volunteered, unless it was for a change, and didn't care much anyway.

They were all ordinary soldiers, with ordinary faces and ordinary feelings, and nobody knew what to do with them except drill them and march them and nag them – chiefly Sergeant Bunch, who was a master of every army joke that had ever been made. 'Straighten your back,' he roared. 'You're not Quasimodo! Chests out! Not that nasty thing, Bradway! You look pregnant! Fists nicely closed! Heads up! Bags of swank!'

Once there had been a corporal who'd nagged them like Bunch, and when Bradshaw had told him to go and get stuffed he'd merely slunk off. Bunch was different. The last time Bunch had laughed was firmly believed to be for his mother when she'd shaken his rattle at his pram, but he commanded a certain amount of grudging respect because he'd fought on the Somme in 'Sixteen, aged just that; at Cambrai in 'Seventeen; in Belgium in 'Eighteen; in Russia in 'Nineteen; and in India and Palestine in the 'Twenties and 'Thirties; to say nothing of Dunkirk in 1940, Tobruk in 1941 and Gazala earlier in the year. With that awesome record, they accepted as normal his strange method of command – 'Left turn! By the Christ – quick march!' – their only consolation that he was always there with them, keeping up the step, carrying as much equipment as they did and not even saving his breath for marching but wasting it on shouting.

To keep everybody happy, No. 2 Transit contained a cinema run by an Egyptian called Sharif and known as Sharif's Shambles because of the number of times it broke down. There were also the usual church parades on Sunday when padres with nothing better to do set up their stalls in the Naafi while nearly everybody else searched out their books and packs of cards and pocket chess-sets and fought to get seats at the back. The sermons invariably started off with a swear-word and a risqué joke, which pleased the padre and raised a smile among the faithful in the front rows but didn't for a moment disturb the more distant murmurs of 'I'll go a bundle', 'Two no trumps' or 'Knight takes bishop and that, cock, is bloody checkmate'.

Life was a round of PT, collecting rubbish, route marches and lectures on venereal disease. Because they were bored, it never required more than an abrasive jest – usually about a regiment – for belts to be brandished. Captain Francis Amos,

once of the Light Ack-Ack and now in charge of No. 2 Transit
while he recovered from a bout of dysentery caught in the desert,
had long since given them up as a bad job and put in for a
posting himself.

'If the buggers fight the Germans half as hard as they fight
each other,' he said bitterly, 'they'll be unstoppable.'

Since it didn't seem as though they were to be involved in the
coming battle in the desert, every night at No. 2 Transit had come
to be regarded as a Saturday night. When Murray's order to fetch
them all in had arrived, almost everybody not on duty was in the
clubs, canteens and gin mills in the in-bounds area of Akkaba;
and the Paradise Dance Hall, a misnomer if ever there were one,
was full to the door jambs, the noise so violent the walls seemed
to billow like a marquee in a high wind. Despite the fact that the
bar looked like the Charge of the Light Brigade they'd gone
quietly enough, forming up by the lorries to be transported back
to camp. From behind her desk, Madame had shouted in an
excess of emotion, 'God bless you, boys, I love you all' – 'She'll
have her work cut out,' Sergeant Bunch observed – and they were
taken away, bouncing about in the backs of the lorries like corks
on a rough sea. Except for the difficult few like Private Fidge,
who at that precise moment in time was rolling in a bed that
stank like a dog's basket with a half-caste Arab girl wearing only
a white blouse. When the patrols arrived he managed to dive
through the window while the girl swore blind she'd been alone.

With the bored and the penniless in camp there should have
been no problem. But there was, of course. There always was.

The Naafi was full of men trying to forget they were a long
way from wives, girl friends, children and good English bitter
by trying to suck down the frothy swill that in Egypt went by the
name of beer. The Scots were sitting in suspicious little groups
muttering about clans despite the fact that most of them came
from Lowland cities. The cavalry were calling the infantry mud-
crushers and the infantry were calling the cavalry horse-shit
collectors. The Hostilities Onlys were jeering at the Regulars
who, they claimed, had only joined the army because they were
too dim to earn a living as civilians, while the Regulars were

calling the Hostilities Onlys rotten skiving bastards who'd sat smugly on their fat backsides and let the Germans chuck the BEF out of France. They were as friendly as a lot of cats in a sack. The British Army off duty.

It should have tailed off into the usual sullen fed-up sort of evening, everybody going quietly to bed and only the diehards determined to show they were drunk when they weren't by bawling a few dreary songs, but instead Herbert Kitchener Waterhouse, a lunatic if ever there were one, discovered Sugarwhite's first names and started doing what Sugarwhite found all ill-mannered bastards always did in those circumstances.

Because Sugarwhite carried a burden which would have made the Garden of Eden turn sour. Not only was he called Sugarwhite, which was bad enough in anybody's language, but he also bore the Christian names of Lancelot Harold. He'd often wondered what his mother and father had been at when they'd chosen them. 'Lancelot Harold' he might just have got away with, but 'Lancelot Harold Sugarwhite' was enough to make a man worry rats. Still a virgin despite his ambitions to the contrary, Sugarwhite blamed even that on his name. For God's sake, any girl looking bright-eyed across the pillow, all rumpled, flushed and pleased with herself, to ask 'Well, it's about time I got to know your name, isn't it?' and getting 'Lancelot Harold Sugarwhite' as a reply, would more than likely fall out of bed laughing.

So when Waterhouse gave his great adenoidal yell of glee and slapped his thighs – 'Lancelot Harold Sugarwhite, for Christ's sake! Oh, sweetheart, where have you beed all by life?' – Sugarwhite didn't hesitate. He simply threw his beer at him.

Unfortunately, Waterhouse ducked and the beer went over a Royal Sussex who promptly lashed out and in a moment the canteen was a mass of brawling figures, with the elderly Egyptian who ran it down on his knees behind the counter praying to Allah to take the infidels out of his beloved country and sink them in the slime of the Nile delta.

Not far from where the main struggle was going on, Private By was sitting at a table which looked more like a tea-tray under his vast fist. It took a lot to rouse Ed By but when he *was* roused, he was capable of taking on a whole army corps, and when someone landed a backhander on his nose that made his eyes water, he swung a haymaker that caught Waterhouse on the jaw and lifted him clean off the floor. The top of Waterhouse's head struck the taller Sugarwhite under the chin, and *his* head cannoned into a third man's with a click like a billiard ball.

'Mon,' an awed Seaforth had said as the Military Police arrived to pick up the bodies. 'Three o' the buggers wi' one crack!'

When Hockold arrived next morning the prisoners were all waiting in the corridor outside Captain Amos's office. The sergeant-major, six foot of lean hard Regular by the name of Rabbitt – a dangerous label in the electric atmosphere of No. 2 Transit – stood chatting with the corporal of the escort, and as Amos swept past him he turned and followed.

'What was it this time, Mr Rabbitt? Bannockburn or the Peterloo massacre?'

'Boredom chiefly, sir.'

'Well, we're all bored, but we can't tear the British army apart because of that, can we? What shall we do with 'em? Crucify 'em or just give 'em twenty years in the glasshouse to slow 'em down?'

The waiting men heard every word and were just visualizing a life of endless stamping about the detention barracks when the door at the end of the corridor opened and an officer appeared. He was tall, beak-nosed, and wearing desert boots. As he stalked past them into Amos's office they saw he was a lieutenant-colonel.

The door swung shut behind him so that they could hear only muffled voices, though once they caught Amos's voice raised in a single startled exclamation. 'Let 'em *off*, sir?'

There was another long wait and a great deal more muttering beyond the door, then Sergeant-Major Rabbitt appeared. 'All right, you lot,' he said briskly. 'Something's come up. March 'em off, Corporal. Find 'em something to do for an hour.'

As the startled men about-turned and marched out of the

building, Amos watched them through the window. He was delighted to learn he was losing the bored unwilling soldiers who had made his life a misery but he was also having sudden visions of some spiteful army authority promptly filling the empty camp up again with another ration of similar types.

'Not wanting an extra officer or two, are you, sir?' he asked.

Hockold turned. 'Want to come along?'

'Can you fix it, sir?'

Hockold smiled. 'Anybody else?'

Amos grinned. 'Mr Rabbitt's beginning to look as though he's got mange,' he said.

Shortly afterwards a lorry stopped outside the guard-room where Rabbitt's four criminals were now scrubbing the verandah. Fidge jumped out, unshaven, frowsty and ashamed.

The military policeman who had accompanied him gave him a push. 'Go on,' he said. 'Shove off.'

'Ain't Oi gowing in the knocker?' Fidge asked.

'Not as far as I know. Better find some blankets and get your head down. You'll be needing all the sleep you can get before long.'

The buzz went round the camp like wildfire. They were being posted. It stuck out a mile. They were being sent home for training at last. Scotland was where they trained commandos, wasn't it? And the beer up there was good. For the first time in weeks, there was an air of excitement in the camp.

'We're moving on Friday,' the next buzz said. 'And it's Cape Town, not Scotland. They've set up a commando camp in the middle of the Karroo and the instructors have all been drawn from the Special Service Battalion because they've got a reputation for not liking the British.'

Kits were packed in readiness. And not a moment too soon, because almost immediately they were paraded and told to be ready in an hour. Sergeant Bunch got them into a column. 'Heads up,' he roared. 'Backs straight! Chests out!' A glittering eye like the muzzle of a Spandau swept over them. 'You look like a lot of nasty old age pensioners,' he complained. 'You're

not lumps of pudden, you're human beans. Right! Company –
le-eft turn! By the Christ – qui-ick march . . . !'

They were crammed into the lorries waiting outside the gate
until they looked like sardines. The engines started and the convoy
began to move. Someone started a song that inevitably lapsed
into the usual filthy ballad.

> 'Stanna shwaya. Oh desire!
> Stanna shwaya, pull your wire!'

Private Docwra, staring around with a dropped jaw, stopped
it dead. 'Wheyhey,' he said. 'Where are they takkin' us? This
isnae the way to Cape Town.'

No more it was. They were heading west, which was nearer
the fighting.

They finally stopped, alongside a stretch of drab tents, for-
lornly flapping in the dusty breeze as though they'd been
standing there on the edge of the desert since Napoleon had
fought the Battle of the Pyramids. There was no village – just
an escarpment with a succession of wadis, a puddle of water
round a few rocks and a couple of palms. To the Arabs it was
known as Gott el Scouab. In addition to the tents, it contained
a few huts and two or three marquees, a lorry park, a cookhouse,
a petrol store, an arms store, a Naafi, a bored staff and a church.
Since it had once been used as a prisoner of war camp for
Catholic Italians, one of the wire-mesh windows of the church
had been taken out and reverently replaced with one made from
the bottoms of brown, green and white beer bottles. It now served
every denomination in the army, and was known as St Martin's-
in-the-Sands.

A fat dough-faced cook-corporal called Rogers and a dozen
greasy minions served them a meal. Then Sergeant-Major
Rabbitt, who had arrived by car half an hour ahead of them,
began to get them organized. 'All right, all right, all right,' he
roared. 'Get yourselves into a half-circle! The colonel wants a
word with you!'

Aware that whatever it was they'd landed this time it was
obviously going to be infinitely worse than Death Valley, they

reluctantly shuffled into place. When Hockold appeared, Sugar-white and Waterhouse recognized him at once as the man who'd got them off when they'd looked like spending the rest of their natural lives pounding the dusty square at Akkaba. They began to cheer up. If he could work one miracle of that sort, he could perhaps work a few more.

'Right – ' someone had placed an ammunition box on the sand and Hockold climbed on to it ' – just gather round, so you can hear.'

'Thingks 'e's the gederal.' Waterhouse's nasal whisper sounded above the muttering as they moved nearer. ''*E* goes id for this, they say.'

Hockold lifted his cane to indicate that the muttering should stop. 'As of this moment,' he said, 'you are no longer Jocks, Welsh or British. You're not East Yorks, Argylls, Seaforths, Susseckers, Buffs or whatever else you were before.'

There was a buzz of comment. No British soldier liked to have his regiment snatched from under his feet. To lose your regiment was one degree worse than losing your trousers. If you joined as a light infantryman, you were a light infantryman for the rest of your life, while a Guardsman remained a Guardsman for ever and ever, amen, right to the Last Trump. A Buff was a Buff. A Diehard was a Diehard. And nothing on God's earth could make a Gordon into a Black Watch. Except authority. And authority seemed to be throwing its weight around at that moment.

Hockold drew a deep breath. 'As of now, you are Number 97 Commando,' he said, and waited with bated breath for a bolt of thunder and lightning from Combined Operations HQ to strike him down because he had no authority whatsoever as yet to give them such a title and it had only been agreed on as a temporary means of giving them an identity.

There was a moment's silence then Bradshaw grinned. 'De-tribalized, by God,' he said, and there was another buzz of muttered conversation. They weren't sure whether to be pleased or not, but in most of them there was a feeling of relief. A few were even happy, because it meant they were on their way. In a few breasts like Lieutenant Swann's, glory even lit a small lamp.

To one or two others – like Private Fidge – the announcement brought a quiver of alarm. This was something he hadn't expected. When the buzz had gone round that they were going to South Africa, his day had been made. There was no conscription in South Africa and all you had to do was get on a train to Johannesburg and call yourself Cronje.

Hockold was speaking again.

'I've looked at your records,' he was saying, 'and I notice some of you have been out here since the war started. That's a long time, but if it's any consolation, so have I.'

Well, that's something, they thought grudgingly. At least he wasn't some toffee-nosed puff from Cairo who hadn't yet got his knees brown.

'We're here to train,' Hockold went on. 'For a special operation that could have a great deal of influence on the battle which we all know is brewing up out here. We don't have long so it's going to be tough and you're going to have to work hard.' He jerked a hand at the silent figure standing just to his right, and everybody's eyes switched direction. 'This is Major Murdoch, and it'll pay you to give attention to what he says. It might save your lives.'

They all took a good look at Alexander Mackay Murdoch who stared back at them with his cold yellow eyes. He had dressed for the occasion and he looked like a walking armoury. He wore his kilt and, in addition to a Highland dirk honed to razor sharpness, he carried a .45, a .38, and a sniper's rifle with a telescopic sight with which he'd shot more than one man in Spain. They didn't like the look of Murdoch, and Murdoch didn't like the look of them. The advantages were all on Murdoch's side, of course, because he knew he could do something about them, while they knew they couldn't do a damn thing about him.

Hockold was speaking again, searching his mind for something funny to say that would jerk them out of their apathy. 'I expect you to do as you're told,' he went on. 'And do it well because we want to pull this thing off and win ourselves VCs.

He was pleased to hear a distinct laugh this time. You didn't go out and get a VC because they looked nice on your coat.

VCs were usually handed over at Buckingham Palace to your widow or your bereaved mum.

He paused. 'I can't tell you yet when it'll be,' he said. 'Or where it'll be, or what it's for. But I *will* see that you do all know before we leave, because no one can do anything well unless he knows *what* he's supposed to do. There's just one snag – '

' 'Ere it comes,' Waterhouse said.

Hockold sensed the waiting hostility and went on quickly. 'From now on, just to prove you're no longer what you were, we're going to separate you all.'

Sugarwhite's eyes flicked to Waterhouse's. Waterhouse looked at By. In similar fashion, the Argylls looked at the Gordons, and the Gordons looked at the West Yorkshires, and the West Yorkshires at the Royal Sussex. The look went right round the whole crowded half circle.

Hockold continued mercilessly, accepting that Murdoch, who had suggested the move, had the experience to know what was best. 'Regimental loyalties are no longer important,' he said. '*The only thing you think of now is this unit.*' He gestured at the small group of commandos under Sergeant Jacka. 'Ask these chaps. They know what I mean. There will be two of them in each tent to encourage and advise. Otherwise, no tent will be made up exclusively from any particular regiment. That's all. Training will start tomorrow.'

While they were still gaping, startled, shocked and disgusted, Hockold stepped from the box, thankful it was done. He turned to the sergeant-major with a forced smile. 'It's all yours now, Mr Rabbitt,' he said, trying to drum up another joke to break the silence that hung over the gathering like the kiss of death. 'Let t'battle commence.'

5

*A training programme was organized and naval
vessels were earmarked for the task.*

As Colonel Hockold was dismissing his men from his mind,
Colonel Hochstätter was busy examining his. His conclusion was
much the same as Hockold's.

'They're a pretty mixed lot,' he said. 'And there aren't many
of them.'

Major Nietzsche, who had called the parade, shrugged.
'Qaba's not very big,' he pointed out. 'And after all the Luftwaffe's
responsible for the airfield.'

He glanced at Captain Schlabrendorff, for an outline of the
anti-aircraft position. Schlabrendorff was none too confident.
'The town's ringed by guns,' he said. The whole area's covered by
heavy and light flak. Unfortunately, if they get into trouble in
the desert, they'll take them all away.'

Hochstätter looked at his lists. 'A few guns,' he said. 'A few
engineers, a few gunners, and a few transport men, together with
eighty-seven experienced grenadiers. Two hundred and fifty-
three altogether. Tarnow –' he swung round in his chair to the
signals officer ' – did you inform army headquarters of our
needs?'

Tarnow's cold face was impassive. 'As strongly as I could.'

Hochstätter stared again at his lists, and finally at the map of
Qaba and its defences. 'Wutka,' he said, looking up. 'We must
have your engineers.'

Wutka's head rose. Like Hochstätter, Nietzsche and Hrabak,
he was there to recover from injuries received in battle, and he

limped badly and was always glad to sit down. He was also
overworked, sick of the war, sick of Qaba, even sick of Adolf
Hitler. 'Not a hope,' he commented flatly.

'There must be.' Hochstätter pushed across the signal that had
come in from army headquarters. 'We must have more strongpoints, road blocks, wire barriers, mines and booby traps.'

'My men can't do guard duties *and* build strongpoints,'
Nietzsche said.

'And my men can't repair damaged harbour walls and
transport supplies *and* stand in for *your* men,' Wutka snapped
back.

Hochstätter sighed. He liked to consider himself a civilized
soldier and a believer in *Krieg ohne Hass* – war without hate.
But while, on the whole, the units of the German army in North
Africa managed to leave acrimony out of their dealings with the
British, they found it hard to leave it out of their dealings with
the Italians and each other.

'You must try,' he said patiently.

'We've tried,' Nietzsche growled.

'Then you must try harder. We must have your men. If only
for a few days.'

Wutka frowned. 'Very well,' he agreed. 'You can have thirty.
But I'd like it in writing.'

'I'll see that you get it. Veledetti, how many can *you* spare?'

Captain Veledetti's brown eyes moved unhappily. He already
considered he had barely enough to patrol the perimeter of the
prison compound and he was afraid that if he had less the
prisoners would break out and murder him as he slept.

'Ten,' he suggested warily.

'Come, Veledetti.'

'Twenty, then.'

'That's better. Hrabak?'

'I can let you have thirty,' Hrabak said. 'But I must have them
back the minute we get transport.'

Hochstätter nodded. 'Von Steen?'

'Twenty,' von Steen said. 'Not one more, or the whole operation of the port will come to a stop.'

'Twenty then,' Hochstätter said. 'That makes three hundred and fifty-three engaged purely on defence. Tarnow, ask army headquarters if we can't borrow from Tobruk. What about guns?'

Schoeler, the artilleryman, looked up. 'Zöhler got a smashed-up Mark III from 15th Panzers. We're digging it in now. It can't be repaired and won't move and he had to tow it into position, but the turret can be cranked. He's also got two old British tanks armed with two-pounders.'

'Is that all?'

'The panzers are sitting on everything they have,' Schoeler said. 'In case they have to be cannibalized for spares. They're expecting to need them before long.'

Hochstätter frowned. 'Aren't they all getting a little worked up about this big attack?' he asked.

Nietzche shrugged. 'This time they seem to think they need to.'

'What about tank men?'

'Zöhler sent down fifteen and an officer. All convalescents!'

'*Himmelherrgott!*' Hochstätter gestured wearily. 'Have we nothing but the halt, the blind and the lame? I just hope that the British are having the same difficulties we are.'

As it so happened, they were – as the explosive mixture crammed into the tented camp at Gott el Scouab indicated.

At that precise moment in time, the camp was chiefly notable for the sullen atmosphere that hung over it. Most of its inhabitants were moving about with frowning faces and saying very little. Hockold watched them from the doorway of his headquarters, a drab wooden hut which, following a raid by the Luftwaffe in July, didn't even stand erect but leaned at an angle. Amos and Watson were behind him, Amos sitting at the desk working at a training programme Murdoch had written out, Watson staring at the tent lists and wondering if the idea of separating everyone from his friends had been a good one.

When he'd first arrived in Egypt, like everybody else who'd left England in the dark days of 1940, he'd never expected to go home again because he'd thought the war would go on for ever.

It had made the pain of being separated from his wife all the worse and for a long time he'd just accepted that he must be grateful simply for having known her. Now, however, with the old piratical days of 1940 and 1941 gone, the desert filling up with armed men, and the certainty growing that this time they really *were* going to knock the enemy out of Africa, the longing to go home had become an agony and he was impatient to finish the job.

'Think it'll work?' he asked.

Amos lifted his head. 'It'll work,' he said confidently. 'By tonight they'll be swopping fags.'

At that moment they were swopping nothing but uncomplimentary remarks about their new commanding officer.

'Fuddy bugger, isd't 'e?' Private Waterhouse was yelling, a gormless, untroubled grin on his face. 'Proper cobedian. Let t' battle commence, eh? What a lot o' drippingg. It makes me fair roll od the bloody groud.'

On the whole they were in complete agreement. Gott el Scouab was clearly a bigger hell-hole than No. 2 Transit and the vastness around was oppressive, limitless and awful. Sand seeped into everything, a fair proportion filling their socks, while the brooding sun stuck their shirts to their backs with a board-like consistency and made their necks raw with the gritty dust.

'If this is the commandos,' Sugarwhite observed, 'we should have joined the chain gang.'

They were all set for a good grumble, but Murdoch didn't give them that long and sent the sergeants and corporals round the tents to chase them out. They came unwillingly because they were still feeling they'd been cheated, and Murdoch stared contemptuously at them as they turned up in dribs and drabs.

'When I say I want y'on parade,' he said in his quiet low voice, 'I mean I want y'on parade – now!' His voice remained quiet but there was something deadly in it now that made them uneasy. 'I'm a commando. You *want* to be commandos. Well, the fairst thing you'd better learn is discipline – without question. Contrary to what Errol Flynn would have you believe, toughness isnae bashing another chap's head in. Toughness is keeping on going when everybody else has stopped. And *that* depends on stamina, temperament, will – and discipline. Well, we cannae change your characters or make you stronger than you were born. But we *can* give you discipline.'

He paused and the yellow gaze flickered across their faces as what he'd said sank in. 'I was in Abyssinia and Spain,' he went on. 'So I ken what I'm talking about. Yon Abyssinians and yon Spanish were brave enough but they didnae savvy much aboot discipline and it was that that did for 'em. With a bit o' discipline – a couple of commandos or the Fairst Black Watch, for instance – we could have seen off both Mussolini *and* Franco, and then Hitler might no' have bothered to go to war.'

As he stopped to draw breath, there were no funny comments because they all knew that what he said was the truth. 'So!' he ended. 'I shall be doing everything you're doing, as will all the other officers and sergeants, so you've no need to think you've got it tough.'

A few glances were exchanged and Murdoch went on. 'You're fully trained soldiers,' he said, his foxy eyes gleaming behind his glasses. 'When I've finished with you, you'll be *fit* fully trained soldiers – with courage, physical endurance, initiative, resource, activity, self reliance and an aggressive spirit towards the war.'

'Jesus!' Waterhouse let his breath out in a bleat of horror.

'In the words o' Garibaldi –'

'Wha the hell's Garibaldi?' Keely muttered.

'Some bloody Eyetie ice-cream merchant,' Belcher pointed out. 'Shut up.'

' – you'll know "*fame, sete, marcie forzate, battaglia e morte.*" Churchill puts it a different way. "Blood, sweat an' tears," he called it. There'll no' be much red tape, but there *will* be bull, because a clean soldier's a good soldier and it's all only normal infantry training. A wee bit quicker and a wee bit harder, to make you persevere, when the time comes, right to the end. Any man can cover seven miles an hour if he wishes – even out here. It's our job to see that you *do* wish.'

There were a few shocked looks but Murdoch seemed impervious.

'Most o' what you do, therefore,' he continued, 'will be done at the double, carrying heavy weights. When you've finished you'll be better men, and when you leave here every one of you will walk on the earth as if he owns it. To the Germans he will have to face, he will be as a wolf is to a lamb. Now, who are the engineers?'

A group of men shuffled forward, none too willingly, because it was the oldest dodge in the army to ask who were bird-watchers or Baptists or who could ride a bicycle, and then give you the job of cleaning out latrines.

This time, it was different.

Murdoch turned to Jacka, the commando sergeant. 'I want an assault course constructed. So that they can learn to do the things they might have to do. I want it finished by tonight.'

As the others tramped away, the engineers stared at Jacka.

'What the hell's an assault course?' they demanded.

Jacka grinned. 'A few ups and a few downs,' he said. 'A few unders and a few overs. That sort of thing.'

'Where do we get the gear? There's nothing here.'

'No, there isn't, is there?' Jacka looked at the speaker contemptuously. '*Then find the bloody stuff!*' he roared.

It was their first lesson in independence and in no time they'd begged, borrowed or stolen from neighbouring camps or the intervening desert, nets, poles, rope, boxes, boards, spades, rolls of barbed wire, even wrecked cars, old lorries and one rusty tank.

The rest of the men had grouped round Murdoch who was balancing a rifle and bayonet in his hand. He looked murderous despite his glasses.

'Weapon training,' he said quietly. 'You all know about weapons and how to handle 'em. Some o' you might even have had a pot-shot at a Jerry. In the commandos, the aim o' weapon training is no' to take pot-shots, but to *kill*.' His voice rose slightly so that he seemed to be the embodiment of a diabolical will, and anyone who'd thought up to then that there was any other aim to weapon training realized he'd been kidding himself.

They were all a little sober as they headed back to camp at the end of the morning and all a great deal dustier after four hours of solid marching to see what they could do.

'Gawd chase me up and down Wapping Steps,' Belcher said, brushing the sweat from his eyes. 'I feel like ten men – nine dead and one paralysed all down one side. Who's that feller think 'e is, anyway? Bew Guest?'

By this time a lot of Jacka's assault course had been put up and there was a contrivance of derricks and wires stretching across the sand from one of the huts. 'What's yon for?' Keely asked.

'You'll soon find out!'

The words had an ominous ring and there were no further questions. They'd already learned that the commandos weren't in the habit of enlarging on things too much, and asking them for explanations was about as rewarding as trying to nail jelly to a wall. It seemed safer to wait and see.

Training was no part of Hockold's business at this stage because he had too many other things to attend to in Cairo.

Kirstie gave him the best smile she could manage as he appeared. In Murray's office he was brisk, keen and to the point. With her he was grimly silent and she felt it her duty – even more than her duty – to give him a degree of encouragement. It had clearly worked so far because, instead of crashing past, taking half the furniture with him as he had the first time he'd appeared, he stopped by her desk.

'How about a drink when we've finished?' he barked.

She beamed at him, and he blushed and vanished into Murray's room. Murray was on the telephone. He seemed to spend half his life on the telephone. He waved Hockold to a chair and went on with his conversation. When he'd finished, he seemed to surface slowly, lit a cigarette, and smiled.

'Things are looking up,' he said. 'There's another meeting and Bryant telephoned to say he's got you half a dozen launches and something to go alongside the pier.'

Hockold didn't reply and Murray looked quickly at him.

'It's a beginning,' he said.

'Yes, sir. But I'm a bit worried about those guns.'

'So am I. But we'll come up with something.'

Hockold drew a deep breath. 'I was thinking of tanks, sir,' he said.

Murray's eyebrows shot up. 'Tanks?' he said. 'Tanks can't operate in the dark.'

'They might, sir. After all, we always used the dark to get into position, so why not use it to fight? We did at Beda Farafra last year. Jerry was all round us, so we took off the black-out shields and switched on the lights. They were so surprised, it worked.'

'You'll need more than headlights,' Murray grunted.

'We could arrange for the RAF to drop flares and fit extra lights on the turrets. We don't need anything big. Or anything very new. Honeys, for instance. They're fast. There's a wide slip alongside the mole and if we could get them on to the beach they could go up there. If they're quick, all those 47s could well be facing the wrong way.

Murray pressed a bell and Kirstie appeared. She didn't look at Hockold.

'Get me Alec Gatehouse,' Murray said. 'If anyone knows whether it can be done, he will.'

Bryant and de Berry were more forthcoming this time but not much more friendly towards each other. 'So far I've got you half a dozen launches,' Bryant said. 'Three naval Fairmile Type Bs, and three RAF high-speed rescue jobs which are under naval command. There's also an Egyptian water-boat, *Horambeb*, to go alongside the pier for your troops to land across. She draws only four feet unladen. We can mount guns.'

'How about the launches?'

'MLs – three-pounders and machine guns. HSLs – stern-mounted Oerlikons and waist-mounted point-threes in turrets.'

It didn't seem much and Bryant seemed to recognize the fact. 'At the moment that's as far as I can commit myself,' he said.

'*They* won't get us ashore,' de Berry pointed out. 'And we have to bridge the water gap.' He smiled. 'Like Jonah and the whale which vomited him on to dry land. He formed a neat parabola through the air, I believe.'

'Something that's impractical with tanks,' Murray interjected sharply.

Bryant's head jerked round. 'When did we start talking about tanks?'

'Just now.' Murray made himself sound casual. 'We're proposing to use them.'

'At night?'

Murray smiled. 'That's what everybody says. I said it myself at first. But why not? 1st and 10th Armoured are moving up in the dark when Monty starts his battle. I think it'd shake 'em rotten in Qaba if they saw British tanks waddling up the main street.'

Bryant grunted. 'For tanks you need landing craft.'

Murray grinned. 'I happen to know you have one or two in this neck of the woods.'

'They're obsolete.' Bryant made a wash-out gesture with his hand. 'They're Mark 1s and they've never been used as landing craft because they were no sooner built than they were proved out-of-date.'

Murray's bulldog jaw stuck out and he looked as obdurate as Bryant. 'We're not asking for a Spithead review,' he growled. 'Just a landing craft. And I know there's one in Alex.'

Bryant's eyebrows shot up and Murray continued. 'She carries three forty-ton tanks one behind the other,' he said. 'Steams at a nominal ten knots; and discharges her cargo through her bows. She draws three foot six inches forward, and she was sent out here with others in sections as deck cargo. She was ferrying supplies and, until she moved to Alex, she was at Kabrit in the Great Bitter Lake.'

Bryant seemed amused. 'You've done your homework,' he admitted. 'Very well, you can have her. We can even mount machine guns.' For the first time he seemed to be giving his full co-operation. 'I'm trying also to get you a frigate but it's unlikely. All our spare units are earmarked for the feint on the day Montgomery's battle starts.'

'Six launches, a water-boat, an LCT and the hope of a frigate,' Murray said. 'You'll have to do better than that.'

They seemed to have reached an impasse once more. Hockold looked at de Berry. 'What about a raid on the airfield?' he asked. 'We need to make them switch on their searchlights so we can see. Flares would help too – as near the town as possible.'

'We could do that.' De Berry nodded. 'We might even be able to make the raid seem bigger than it is. They've been experimenting with some new metallic strip. I can get hold of some.'

Bryant was frowning heavily at Murray. 'What losses do you estimate?' he asked.

'Thirty per cent.'

'I'd put it higher than that. Can't you work out some way of withdrawing into the desert to be picked up by the army as they come through. You'll be holding the centre of the town and the road to the airfield. You might be able to get out that way.'

Hockold stared at the map. 'I'm still worried about getting *in*,' he said.

It was a thought that worried Hockold a great deal because, with the arrival of the Afrika Korps, the war had become very professional in the last year. In 1940 and 1941 when there'd been only the Italians to attend to, it had even been enjoyable, with the sun rising in a red ball in the mornings and the world clean and good, and a whisky and water at night out of an enamelled mug near a flapping tent. It had been German efficiency that had shaken them out of their self-satisfaction.

The memory was a bitter one and all the worse for coming back to him as he ate a hurried meal in the officers' club with Kirstie McRuer. Around them the usual desk-drivers from all three services were sipping their pink gins and discussing the latest 'buzzes' from the desert. Cairo was a place where everybody seemed to be busy yet nothing seemed to get done, and the thought reminded Hockold how little progress he'd made.

'We still haven't picked up any signallers,' he pointed out.

Kirstie made a note in a pocket book. 'I'll see what we can do,' she said. 'But it won't be easy. Everybody's busy with the coming

67

battle and the general's a stickler for getting what he wants. That's why you're stuck with me instead of a man.'

The words took the edge from Hockold's worry, and his smile was encouraging. 'You're doing fine, really,' he said. 'But I've got to have everything in hand by tomorrow. I must have a model of Qaba, too, and some demolition experts who won't make mistakes when the bullets are flying.'

She looked up over her plate. 'How bad will it be, George?'

The question was unexpected and Hockold was silent for a while.

'Not bad,' he said eventually.

Her eyes shone with her anger. 'I don't believe it. The Germans know the Eighth Army's going to attack soon. They won't be unready.'

Hockold said nothing because he knew she was right. The Germans *would* be ready. When they'd chased the Italians back in 1940, he'd come out of the desert with torn trousers, matted hair and a lorry full of Zeiss binoculars. But when they'd gone the other way it had been different, and he could still remember the big fire in Derna and the explosions and the smoke, and drunken soldiers staggering from the Naafi store with crates of whisky. He'd often thought since that he ought to have made more effort than he had to stop the rout, but it had been so colossal it had been more than one man – or many men, for that matter – could handle, and in the end he'd gone along with the rest.

He badly wanted to get his own back for it, but he'd also learned from experience that you didn't just lash out at the Afrika Korps in a fit of pique and hope for the best. You had to think of every tiny detail, because if you found yourself short of something you desperately needed in the desert it could make all the difference between life and death.

He realized Kirstie was watching his face, and tried to be nonchalant. 'It'll be a bit messy perhaps,' he agreed. 'Nothing we can't cope with, though.'

'But at what cost?'

Hockold shrugged again. 'Always a cost,' he admitted. 'Oldest military cliché in the world is that you can't make an omelette without breaking eggs. Somebody's bound to get hurt.'

'Take care, George!'

He looked up quickly. Her eyes were clear and bright and steady.

'Does it matter?'

'The one thing I've never liked about my job here,' she said, 'is meeting people and then learning that they've been killed. It's something I can't ever get used to.'

'I'll try to bring back the news of our success personally.'

He seemed suddenly to ease with her and she smiled. 'Do that, George. Try to do that.'

He jerked a hand at a military driver waiting with a staff car near the entrance to the club. 'As somebody much cleverer than me once said,' he pointed out, 'it all depends on that article.' He paused. 'Don't think they'll let me down though,' he ended. 'I wonder how they're settling in.'

At that particular moment, they weren't.

In Tent 7, his eyes anxious, Private Sugarwhite sat on his blankets and sucked at a cigarette. It was one of the Victory Vs to which everybody was reduced from time to time. They were said to be made in India but everybody was convinced they were manufactured locally from bat shit and camel dung scraped up round the Pyramids. In his pack he had a tin of fifty Players but he had no intention of producing them in the company he was having to keep at that moment. It was much easier to make a martyr of himself. The misery even seemed a comfort in the prevailing gloom.

He'd never been in such a rotten tent, he decided.

Opposite him was the big ugly brute who'd flattened him the night before and next door to him the lunatic who'd started it all, still caterwauling his blocked-nose catch-phrases as though he were defying the army to get him down, so that the man next to him gave him a weary look. He was a Royal Welch from Barnsley and beyond him there was an East Yorks from Wales. On his other side was an Argyll and a gloomy-looking Durham, while opposite there was a Rifleman who looked like a gipsy, and a Middlesex who'd never stopped reading from the minute he'd arrived. The tent's senior commando was a silent ex-Grenadier lance-corporal called Cobbe who knew all there was to know about war because he'd walked all the way from Brussels to Dunkirk in 1940 and been among the last to leave.

To Private Sugarwhite they looked the most unprepossessing crew he'd ever seen, and at any moment now, he suspected, the ginger-haired madman who appeared to be called Waterhouse was going to start his song and dance about his name and they'd all start rolling about in heaps again.

He was just mentally flexing his fists at the thought when the Royal Welch on his left, who was digging into his kitbag for note-paper and pencil for a letter home, looked round and sniffed.

'Those are lousy fags.' The flat North Country voice took Sugarwhite by surprise. 'Better have a Woodbine.'

In his soured mood Sugarwhite automatically assumed a sneer but, as he turned, he saw a tin being held out to him. He stared at it, a little startled, then he pulled himself together.

'Thanks,' he said.

The other man offered him a light. 'What's your name?' he asked.

Here we go, Sugarwhite thought. He frowned and gulped.

'Sugarwhite,' he said, waiting for the peals of laughter.

To his surprise, none came. 'What do your pals call you? Darkie?'

'Darkie?'

'Sugarwhite – Darkie. A feller's short, they call him Lofty. He's six-foot-five, they call him Tiny. My pal's name was Slowe, so we called him Blitz.'

Sugarwhite's mouth clicked shut. He couldn't imagine why he'd never thought of this simple solution before. 'That's it,' he said. 'Darkie. Sometimes other things.'

'My name's Gardner,' the Yorkshireman said. 'So they call me Spade. Sometimes even Shovel. I was just going to write a letter to my girl to tell her we've gone into the blue again.' He pushed a photograph across. 'That's her. The one and only.'

Sugarwhite stared down at a nondescript-looking young woman in a dress that looked like a flower-stall at a bazaar and
wondered what made her so special.

'We've never – you know. She's different. Not like the others.
You got a girl?'

Sugarwhite had not got a girl, and it made him feel as in-
adequate as a spayed tom-cat. He fished in his wallet. He'd
picked up a few photographs during his career and, in the desperation of youth, had clung on to them. He sorted them out
like a hand of whist and pushed the one he thought was best-
looking at Gardner. He couldn't even remember her name.

Gardner passed the photograph to the Durham who had come
far enough out of his gloom to look interested. 'Wheyhey!' he
said. 'She's all right, man!'

Sugarwhite made a moue of modesty and the others in the tent
began to make shy forward movements to join in. Had Sugarwhite only known it, they'd all been feeling much the same as
himself and were only waiting for someone to break the ice. They
passed the photographs round, making suitable comments.

'You'm lucky, me dear,' the swarthy-looking Rifleman said,
holding one of them at arm's length. 'She's all right. Does she?'

'Does she what?'

'*Does she what.* You'm a dark one, edden you? What's your
name? Abdul the Bul-Bul Emir?'

While they were talking, the East Yorks took a watch from
his pocket. 'My girl gave me this when I left,' he said in a high
Welsh voice full of bombast. 'Thinks a lot of me, see, she does.
Likes a man with a bit of virility and a good body.'

They all politely but without much interest studied the
Welshman's bulging biceps and narrow hips, and he went on
without a trace of self-consciousness. 'I did a Charles Atlas
course, see. I can take any three on, one hand behind my back.
Girls like fellers like that, you know. I have been with a few in
my time. She gave it to me so I can work out just what she is
doing at any given moment. I look at it a lot at bedtime.' He
clicked the back open. 'Bought in Cardiff it was. I'm Welsh, see.
Cwmru am Byth. Wales for ever.'

They admired the watch, even the Guardsman who was growing bored with his own company by this time. He was actually a gregarious young man and it was only because he'd always been taught that a Guardsman was equal to any six other soldiers and a commando to any further six that he'd got a lofty built-in superiority complex.

As they talked they swopped identities. 'I'm from Barnsley,' Gardner said. 'My proper name's Phil.'

'I'm Jim,' the Durham said.

'I'm Taffy.'

Waterhouse's face split in a mad grin under the pan-scrubber hair. 'I'b buggered,' he said.

They all looked at the little Rifleman. His jetty eyes stared back at them expressionlessly.

'Sometimes they call me Cornish Jack,' he said. 'Sometimes Tinner. Me name's Baragwanath. Baragwanath Eva.'

The Welshman laughed. 'What sort of name's that?' he said contemptuously. 'A bloody girl's, look you! What did you do when you were at home?'

'I earned me livin' catchin' rabbits.'

The Welshman laughed. 'Well, it is not rabbits you are fighting out here, is it now?'

There was a moment's silence because the Cornishman, small and shadowy as he was, seemed to be a law to himself and clearly didn't welcome personal comments about his name. There was a sudden awareness in the tent that enemies had been made, but Welsh Taffy said nothing further. A Royal Sussex, who'd been shaving outside, came into the tent to break the unexpected silence.

'My name's Willow,' he said. 'Tom Willow. They call me Tit.'

They were glad to change the subject. 'Why dot Tits?' Waterhouse yelled. 'You odly got one?'

'I think it's some song.' Willow began to sing. ' "On a tree by a river a little tom-tit, Sang Willow, Tit-Willow, Tit-Willow." '

'Know any more?' Gardner asked.

'No.'

'Pity. We could have had a concert.'

'All Welshmen can sing –' Taffy Jones started, but the Cornishman interrupted him, fishing in his side pack.

'I got some whisky,' he said. 'Leastways, they mucky toads in Akkaba who sold it me said it was whisky.' He jabbed a blunt finger at the gaudy label. ' "Fine Olde English King Anne Whisky." That's a laugh, edden it? 'Tes distilled gnats' piss, I think.'

There was a guffaw and fags were handed round.

'Bit of a rum do we're on,' Gardner said. 'A week to get ready. Good job we're all trained men.'

They were pleased to acknowledge that they were trained men, experts, wise in the ways of war, old soldiers, cunning in their worn uniforms, never at a loss, knowing their way about, hard-bitten, aloof, unresponsive, conscious of the psychological barrier between themselves and newcomers, and above all capable of mayhem if a German got in the way. If they'd only known it, it was the beginning of a pride in their new unit.

They passed the bottle of distilled gnats' piss round. It was enough to peel the enamel from the mug but, to a group of men who a few seconds before were as far down in the dumps as they could be it wasn't bad. Cigarettes were handed round – not Victory Vs but decent fags from old carefully hoarded stores – even Sugarwhite's Players. The Welshman dragged out a brown packet of Capstan Strong. 'I like these best,' he said, not bothering to offer them. 'Strong, see. Mild smokes are for kids.'

Then Lance-Corporal Cobbe began a long-winded yarn about the retreat from Dunkirk and a sergeant of the Coldstream who'd insisted on stopping after every battle for his section to polish their brass and clean their boots. 'They say he had a button stick in his hand when Jerry put him in the bag,' he said.

They all nodded appreciatively, acknowledging that bastards with button sticks were a menace in anybody's army, but nobody said anything out loud because it was accepted that Guards bull was what helped them to do the Homeric things they did.

'Nil illegitibi carborunddum,' Private Waterhouse yelped, looking half-drunk already. 'Don't let the bastards gride you dowd. I reckon they picked us for this job because we'd beed at

73

Death Valley so log they knew we'd all got spiteful enough to do a lot of damage.'

'And because we are all fit and strong, look you –'

'They got us cheap,' the Royal Welch said.

'Cut-price.' The Middlesex with the book spoke for the first time.

'The cut-price commandos,' Sugarwhite added, and to his surprise they all seemed to think it clever.

'Cut-Price Commandos,' Gardner said. 'That's a good name, Abdul. That's clever.'

Sugarwhite's youthful heart filled and he beamed with pleasure. He'd got a new name and a new reputation already. His smile grew wider. Abdul Sugarwhite, the Cut-Price Commando card. He decided he was going to enjoy being in this mob after all.

6

A plan was formulated to enable the raiding force to make a landing.

'Heard what they're calling us, sir?' Amos asked Hockold the next morning. 'The Cut-Price Commandos. Somebody coined it last evening and it's spread like wildfire. I think they like it. A bit like the Eighth Army calling itself the Desert Rats.'

Hockold wasn't so sure that self-disparagement was a good idea, because it seemed important that their approach should be one of utter self-confidence. Not that he felt utterly self-confident himself; most of the night he'd tossed and turned on his blankets after starting awake again with his dream about dying. There was no reason for it. He didn't feel ill – nothing more than an enormous tiredness that had been growing on him for some time – but he was becoming quite certain that he was going to be killed at Qaba and his chief worry was that, with all the difficulties they were facing, too many of his command would be killed with him.

By this time, the enterprise was gaining momentum. Amos was a man of incredible industry who revelled in the detailed minutiae of administration, while it had been obvious from the start that there was nothing to worry about in Murdoch's training. He had laid out sections of the desert and the ravines round Gott el Scouab with white tape, one square representing a block of houses, another a ship, another the prisoner of war compound, a fourth the warehouse, a fifth the fuel dump.

'It's got to be fast, y'see,' he said. 'We've got to have yon bridge across the gap in the mole. If we're slow about that, we might just

as well wrap up and go home. The most difficult job will be the
lorry park and the petrol compound.'

'I thought of you for that,' Hockold said. 'But it's nearly a
mile from the docks, and getting back again will be the big
problem. If things go wrong, you're the one who's going to be
put in the bag.'

Murdoch gave a low laugh. 'They'll no' put me in the bag,'
he said.

Hockold's first call of the day was to see the army commander.

The desert road was full of vehicles but they all seemed to be
turning south and he guessed it was part of the great deception
for the coming battle, and that they'd all be heading north again
after dark. Among them were dummy tanks constructed from
canvas-covered frames on three-ton trucks; new guns obscured
from the German spotter planes under netting on dummy lorries;
water carts, ammunition trucks, and scout cars, all being dispersed away from prying eyes. Brand new refuelling posts were also
being set up, along with petrol and ammunition dumps, field
hospitals and first aid posts, to say nothing of repair shops, spare
part depots, bakeries, and stores where the air smelled pungently
of petrol and oil and melting asphalt.

Over all there was an atmosphere such as Hockold had never
before experienced in all the time he'd been in North Africa, a
sense of impending victory, a feeling of confidence that he could
put down only to the presence of Montgomery and the new faces
he'd introduced to replace the bewildered leaders of the past. It
was something everybody else obviously felt too. They all seemed
invigorated and exhilarated, and it made him believe that when
they went into Qaba the army wouldn't be far behind.

The army commander was away on one of his tours of inspection and it was de Guingand who saw him. He seemed about to
take off himself and was cramming papers into a canvas bag as
he talked.

'Monty's been thinking about this little diversion of yours,
Hockold,' he said. 'And he's getting very enthusiastic. We've
arranged a feint landing on the night we start and a convoy's

sailing west in the afternoon from Alex. All but a few fast craft will put back after dark, of course, but there'll be shelling and mortar and machine-gun fire and light signals, all timed to take place three hours after the guns open up in the hope of tying down their reserves.'

He began to buckle the canvas bag, and reached for a folder of maps. 'Strategic surprise's out of the question, naturally,' he went on, 'because they know we're coming. So we can only delude them as to weight, date, time and direction. We're doing what we can, of course, but anything anyone can contribute will help.'

An officer appeared in the doorway and de Guingand reached for his cap. 'Brigadier Torrance is waiting to put you in the picture,' he concluded. 'We're relying a lot on you, Hockold, because the one thing that mustn't happen is that the panzers get that petrol. Once the battle starts, we'll be ready for counter-attacks, and they'll only end with the destruction of their tanks. But if they run out of petrol as well, it'll put the lid on the Afrika Korps for good and we can grab the lot.'

Brigadier Torrance had a face that had been burnt brick-red by the sun, and he appeared to be trying to model himself on Montgomery.

'The plan's got to be elastic,' he said sharply. 'Your men have to be quick.'

'They won't be slow,' Hockold interrupted brusquely, irritated by the apparent assumption that he didn't know his job.

'Good. Good.' Torrance peered at him. 'This feint we're making on the day we go in. The loading'll be done where enemy agents can see. Tanks'll be shipped and troops marched aboard. They'll all be disembarked later, of course, because they're ear-marked for support roles after the breakthrough, and when nothing happens Jerry'll assume it's a feint. But then your people will hit Qaba, and he'll think they've finally arrived after all.'

And react all the more violently, Hockold thought.

Torrance continued. 'We feel,' he said, 'that your operation should therefore be timed for the third night of the attack, when they're preoccupied with watching their rear. After that first dummy raid, a genuine one could have them running about like hens in hysterics. The longer you can stay there the better.'

Hockold frowned. The operation, which he'd envisaged as a quick in-and-out, seemed to be growing into something else entirely.

Torrance seemed unaware of his increasing anger and was talking rapidly so that Hockold wondered how much his opinions were his own and how much the general's. 'We mustn't have another woolly operation like that one against Benghazi and Tobruk,' he was saying. 'They were trying to win the war on the cheap in those days. Typical Delta staff work. Too complicated. Dismal failure. All the seaborne people landing in the wrong places. What are the chances of releasing the prisoners at Qaba?'

'We *have* to release them,' Hockold snapped. 'Before we can do the rest of the job.'

Torrance looked up, startled. 'Oh! Do you?'

'But we can't look after them. We'll be too busy.'

'We were expecting –'.

Hockold shook his head. 'My responsibility's to destroy the ships and the petrol dump, sir. They'll have to take their chance.'

Torrance stared at him, frowning, and Hockold continued.

'If I'm successful and the army's successful, sir, any who don't make it will be released within a matter of days anyway, so it isn't worth making too much of them. Their only importance is that they must be allowed to disperse before the ships go up. We can't afford to be hampered and the ships come first. *They must be destroyed.*'

How though?

It was still a question that troubled Hockold a great deal.

Kirstie was also looking worried as he passed her desk. 'I've got your signallers, George,' she said. 'But demolition experts are harder to come by. They've formed an Administrative Assault Force to open up the ports after their capture, and they've roped in everybody who knows anything about it. However, the RAF's got a few they use for airfields. Would they be any good?'

'Do they know how to blow up ships?'

'I shouldn't think so.'

Hockold sighed. He wasn't sure that it would matter in the end, anyway, because he couldn't imagine anyone back home losing any sleep over a raid on Qaba, whether it were successful or not, and he wouldn't be there, in any case, to answer the arguments.

The blank spots that had been occurring in his mind ever since daylight had continued all morning so that it was as if his brain had melted and the earth had stood still, and he'd seen himself quite clearly, dusty with death as he'd seen so many other men in the last three years. The khamseen sifted through the bones they'd scattered like ivory splinters across the desert, and for the first time since arriving in the Middle East he felt certain that his own were going to join them.

He realized he hadn't spoken and that Kirstie was staring up at him. She looked tired and seemed to think he wasn't satisfied with her efforts.

'George,' she said, 'believe me, I'm doing everything I can. I really am. I've got a stake in this operation, too, you know. And not just that –' she looked down at the desk ' – I told you yesterday. I want *you* to come back.'

He wondered if his thoughts showed in his face, and made an effort to indicate his gratitude for what she'd done. 'Of course.' he said. 'I know that really. It's just that everybody wants me to do so many things but can't give me the means.'

When he went into Murray's office, however, Murray seemed surprisingly cheerful.

'Qaba,' he said at once. 'Bryant's come up with rather a bright idea. Or at least one of his chaps has. You might find it interesting.'

They climbed into Murray's car and headed for Alex, moving through suburbs where native children, their stick-like legs twinkling, ran alongside crying for biscuits and bully and baksheesh. Murray was in good spirits.

'Things are looking up,' he said. 'I've got you a couple of old Honeys. They're not so hot and 9th Armoured, where I found 'em, apologize profusely because they're not so new either. But they've got the modified armour – fifty millimetres on the nose – and 37 mm guns with plenty of traverse and elevation. You'll know more about them than I do. 3rd Hussars who own them, say they'd be very happy if you'd simply abandon 'em when you've finished with 'em so they can put 'em down as "Lost due to enemy action", and get two new ones.'

Hockold said nothing. The sun was hot and the streets contained the usual hordes of cringing dogs, blind beggars, shoe-shine boys, fly-whisk vendors, acrobats and snake charmers. It all seemed a little unreal in his odd mood of foreboding, so that it was a pleasure as they turned out of Ras el Tin Street to see a smartly dressed, well-ironed Marine guard drinking tea in a hut by the dock gate and the painted initials indicating the offices of high-ranking naval men.

Smudges of barrage balloons marked the sky. Between the buildings they could see dazzle-painted merchantmen cross-hatched by the spars and masts of native vessels, and not far away a ship on its side, its upperworks ripped and twisted, a great deal of rust showing underneath.

'Business before pleasure,' Murray said. 'We'll inspect the LCT before we go to receive the glad hand about the plan. Then we'll know what we're talking about.'

Landing Craft (Tank) 11 was old and badly in need of a lick of paint, and her captain seemed as battered as his ship. He was a middle-aged ex-Merchant Navy officer called Carter and he led them about the ship, scruffy, draggle-tailed and ugly, singing to himself as he went – 'I'd like to sleep with Nazimova. . . .' It was only as he pushed past that Hockold caught the words, with a mouthful of bad breath.

With his ravaged face and a tatty beard that made him look like a rat peering through a hedge, Hockold wondered what he'd picked up. Even his ship looked as though it were something the navy was trying to get rid of, a cross between a barge and a Noah's Ark with its dredger-like bows and patches of rust. Lying nearby were three big Fairmiles and three elderly teak-built RAF rescue launches. Like the landing craft they all looked very much as though they were considered expendable.

Murray pulled a face. 'Not what you'd call exactly prepossessing,' he said. 'Let's hope the plan's got more weight to it than they have.'

The plan proved to be the brainchild of a commander on Bryant's planning staff called Babington. He was small and grey-haired and looked vaguely like a bus conductor, but he was clearly a man with drive.

'You sure about this swept channel outside Qaba?' he asked immediately.

'Absolutely sure,' Hockold said.

'Well, we'll have to do a bit of checking on our own, of course, but if you're right, I think I can help you.'

'Do we have a ship yet?' Hockold asked.

'Yes.' Babington smiled and went on cheerfully. 'She's even got a gun.'

'What is she?'

'*Umberto Uno*. Italian coaster we picked up a fortnight ago full of arms and ammunition for the Afrika Korps.'

'For God's sake!' Hockold glanced at Murray. 'You're not offering me a coaster, are you?'

Murray's face didn't change its expression. Neither did Babington's. 'Yes, I am,' he smiled. 'And if you'll listen, you'll see I'm offering you not only a coaster – and a pretty fast one at that which'll be more than big enough to remove your two thousand prisoners – but I'm also offering you a plan. Courtesy of the Royal Navy Christmas Parcels and Free Gift Scheme.'

He leaned forward. 'I've been over your suggestions,' he went on, 'and I visualize what you're going to do to be this: our ship – whatever she happens to be and at the moment she happens to be *Umberto Uno* – goes down the outside of the mole, with the water-boat *Horambeb* hard alongside. *Horambeb* goes up against the wall where the Germans moored their lighter, and you get your ladders against the mole from her. Is that roughly how you saw it?'

'Roughly.'

'Right. Shore parties! How many had you visualized?'

Hockold was frowning. 'Five,' he said. 'One to hold the centre of the town, the others to blow the ships and dumps and release the prisoners.'

Babington smiled again. 'I take it that the party by the Roman arch is the key to the whole operation.'

'Without them in position, the others won't be able to move.' Hockold was sitting up straight now, his eyes angry, his lips tight. 'And we haven't got them *off* yet,' he reminded. 'That sea wall's a long run and it's covered every bit of the way by machine guns. We need something to keep the Germans busy until we get the tanks ashore.'

Babington held up his hands in protest. 'Give me a chance,' he said. 'I've thought of that. While *Umberto* and *Horambeb* are getting alongside, the LCT's disembarking her tanks on to the beach at the landward end of the mole to deal with the guns. They go up the slip and hit the guns one after the other – bedoink – bedoink – bedoink.' He was smiling and to the worried Hockold he seemed to regard the affair as a joke. 'With them are the party to deal with the fuel depot and they nip up the Shariah Jedid while the Germans are busy with the tanks. The warehouse party travel in the naval launches and disembark across *Horambeb*. The POW party are in the RAF launches which break off outside the harbour and head for a point behind the Mantazeh Palace. The ships demolition party and the town centre party disembark from *Umberto Uno*.' He sat back, pulled forward a chart of Alexandria Harbour and jabbed a finger at it. 'At this moment,' he said. '*Umberto*'s anchored just there. I can arrange for her to be fixed up with a few extra guns. Not much, and mostly light, but they'll work. I can even hide 'em in wooden boxes that look like deck cargo. I can also give you a good gunnery officer, and put grapnels and gangways aboard her, too, so that the men inside her can be off her in a matter of minutes.'

Hockold glanced again at Murray but Murray's face was still a mask. 'Providing we can get her alongside,' he said doggedly. 'How do you propose to do that?'

Babington smiled. 'Force and fraud are cardinal virtues in war,' he said. 'Suppose she escapes?'

'Escapes?'

'It would have to look real, of course, because the Germans would be as suspicious as hell. But if it seemed genuine they'd allow her to approach Qaba near enough for her to run in, wouldn't they?'

Hockold's interest was caught. 'Go on,' he said.

Babington grinned. 'At the moment, she's got an old motor launch alongside as a guardship and her crew's still aboard, together with a few pongoes with rifles. Suppose during the night "the harsh and boisterous tongue of war" is heard – not only in the ships nearby but all over the bloody shore, too – and the launch sinks and *Umberto* up-anchors and disappears. What would one think?'

'That she'd fought her way out.'

Babington's spectacles seemed to gleam with pleasure. 'Exactly. And the beautiful thing is that nobody'll be surprised. They'll just assume we've been bloody careless again.'

'Go on.'

'German agents – and, believe me, we know there are plenty of them in Alex – hear of the incident. Bodies in British uniform are even picked up next day by bumboatmen who assume quite rightly that they're from the guardship.'

'You can't fake a body,' Murray interrupted. 'Where do they come from?'

'Two of them are Italians from *Umberto*. Four of 'em were wounded when we picked her up, and these two – one of them the captain – obligingly died last night. We also have two prisoners of war who equally obligingly stabbed each other to death in a fight, and the crew of a spotter plane which was shot down near the harbour yesterday.' Babington smiled. 'I've arranged to have them all put on ice.'

'And *Umberto*?'

'By this time she'll have been secretly unloaded and will have an additional conning position built near the hand steering in case there's a hit on the bridge. She'll also be fitted with steel plates at crucial points and have concrete round the engines. She'll also have splinter mats and she'll have been filled with your chaps and their weapons. She heads for Qaba, which is a sensible place to go, of course, because Mersa's full and it's on her manifest, anyway.'

Hockold was interested despite his doubts. 'What about challenges?' he asked. 'They're bound to throw signals at us.'

'Then you'll need an Italian-speaking signaller. I know where I can lay my hands on one. Leading hand called Fusco. We've used him before. He'll fend 'em off with broken signals in plain.'

'Won't they be suspicious of plain language?'

'Not if they think *Umberto*'s taken a hit on the bridge as she escapes, which killed her master and mate and damaged the code books. We can arrange that they will. Given that, our Italian ought to be able to fox 'em long enough for you to get alongside.'

Hockold drew a deep breath and Babington smiled, accepting his silence as agreement. 'They'll soon know in Qaba that you're on your way,' he said, 'and they'll be waiting to welcome you home. Since it's just about two hundred miles as the crow flies, that makes the time-table just about right. Given a diversion by the RAF big enough to keep them busy, they ought to let you in. How does it sound?'

Hockold swallowed. It seemed that an awful lot was having to be taken for granted, but with the time and equipment at their disposal he could see no alternative.

'I don't think we'll come up with anything better,' he admitted.

7

*Training was started at once, and demolition
and other experts enlisted.*

Every military movement, every feint, every attack, has to have a
name. And since the one destined for Qaba could hardly be
called 'Operation to blow up four ships, a warehouse, and a fuel
dump', a title which could soon reach the wrong ears, it had to
be coded.

'Why not call it "Cut-Price"?' Amos suggested, and after a
lot of argument 'Cut-Price' it was.

The signallers had arrived at Gott el Scouab at last, and ex-
Corporal Curtiss, now a sergeant, was out to show he was the
best trainer of signallers in the British army. He blindfolded his
men and had them establishing communication without in-
forming them of frequencies; when he was satisfied they could
work in the dark, he took them out into the wadis with a
breeze lashing the grit against their skins like barbed wire, and,
surrounded by escarpments, he made them work like slaves to
maintain touch with each other.

Sidebottom had also been promoted sergeant, so that to
Bunch's stream of 'By the Christs – !' was added Mo-for-
Mohammed's crazy 'Iggery! Jildy! Jiloh! Yallah, yallah!'
Several lance-corporals had also been upped and Cobbe's extra
stripe had given great pleasure to Tent 7. 'Gi'e us a kiss, Corp!'
Waterhouse said warmly.

Cobbe treated the suggestion with the contempt it deserved,
strutting up and down in front of them, six-foot-two of bone and

stringy muscle, offering the patter on how to scale a wall that he'd learned as a commando.

'Eight feet high,' he said, facing a bank of smooth escarpment and talking in a high, strained instructor's voice, as though someone was clutching him by the throat. 'You can't jump it. You can't fly. You're not monkeys. So how do you go about it? Easy. You have a little teet-a-teet, which is Frog lingo for getting your 'eads together, and two of you 'old your rifles as a mounting block for your pals. A light spring with one foot on it carries you up and over.'

'With bloody great packs on, Corp?' Waterhouse asked disbelievingly.

Cobbe gave a tight-lipped smile and turned to the biggest of the Stooges. 'Cop hold of this rifle, Chamberlain. And see he gets a really good bunk-up so he won't forget.'

Waterhouse sailed over the escarpment to land on his face, the breath knocked from his body by his pack. 'You rotten bugger, Corp,' he gasped. 'And there I was, thinkig we was mates.'

Further on, Sergeant Jacka was facing another group whom he was instructing in street fighting. 'I'm now about to put you through the wringer a little bit,' he warned. 'But it's all in a good cause and at the moment you're about as much use as a grasshopper's fart in a gale. We will consider first how to take cover.'

'A good idea by my reckoning,' Bradshaw observed quietly.

Jacka agreed. 'And so it should be,' he said. 'All that about dying for your country's just a load of cock. Much better to make the other bugger die for *his*. So – if they start shooting at you, what do you do? You find somewhere to get behind, don't you? A cigarette box'll do. You'd be surprised how small you can make yourself when some fella's trying to hit you. Anyone ever done any ju-jitsu?'

Jones the Body, Mr World himself, was pushed forward and, being what he was, he couldn't resist boasting. 'Why, aye, I know a bit, all right, Sergeant. It is fit I am, see.'

'Right,' Jacka said. 'Let's see what you can do to me then. And don't hold back. I'm not a cream puff.'

Two minutes later, Taffy was being carried away, grey-faced

and groaning that he wasn't ready, and Jacka was staring after him, puzzled. 'I thought he knew something about it,' he said.

At the butts they'd set up in one of the wadis, Baragwanath Eva was showing Sergeant Sidebottom what he could do. 'Five bulls out of five,' Sidebottom observed. 'You're good with a bundook. There'll be a few black camels turning up if you use that thing right.'

'Black camels, Sarge?'

'Islamic belief, lad. When you're going to die a black camel arrives at your door.'

'How d'you know that, Sarge?'

'Thinking of turning Moslem, son. That's how.'

And, of course, there was always By-the-Christ Bunch – 97 Commando's Ancient Pistol – as rigidly at attention as if he'd set like plaster of Paris. Bunch's methods consisted of sarcasm. 'You couldn't fight your way through the skin off a old rice pudding,' he complained. 'You'd make my old mum weep to look at you, so I'm going to see you turn out nice because I can't stand the sight of a woman's tears.'

The specialist parties worked at their own particular tasks, Ed By using his huge coal-grab hands to hurl Mills bombs vast distances, to explode so far away they were almost out of sight. The rest of them Murdoch had sweating in the sunshine for hour after hour, with the sergeants yapping at their heels like terriers as they scrambled round and over and under the collection of boxes, drums, nets, poles and old vehicles they'd collected, cornering in their panic like puppies coming up the cellar steps.

'Pick up yon magazine, Mr Sotheby,' Murdoch rapped as they came to a stop, panting and streaming with sweat. 'And try not to drop it again. It gets sand in it and that'll jam your gun. It'll also make a clatter and that'll get you shot. Mr Swann, for the love of God, stop nagging your men. And Corporal Snow, when someone tells you to move your section, make gey sure it's a proper order and no' just somebody in a panic. The rest of you: there's too much grumbling, too much talking, too much puffing and panting. Remember, only he who gives himself up for lost *is* lost.'

As they marched off, Murdoch kept Bradshaw back. 'You ever thought of applying for a commission, Bradwell?' he asked.

Bradshaw was an easy-going unambitious man, who'd never expected to be a soldier at all yet somehow managed to be a good one.

'No, sir,' he said. 'I'd rather be one of the boys.'

Murdoch stared at him with contempt. 'Has it no' occurred to you,' he snapped, 'that intelligent boys grow up into men? As of now, you're a lance-corporal.'

De Berry was poring over maps in his office when Hockold arrived to see him.

'They tell me you want our help,' he said. 'Rubber dinghies and so on to get ashore.'

'More than that, sir,' Hockold explained. 'Things have changed. We'd like your diversion to draw off as many people as possible.'

De Berry's eyebrows rose. 'What do you want? Paratroops?'

It was meant in jest but Hockold nodded. 'Yes, sir,' he said. 'That's *exactly* what we want. Dummies. While your chaps are dropping their bombs, could they also toss out dummies on parachutes?'

De Berry smiled. 'Bombers are bombers,' he said. 'You can't shovel dummies out of 'em just like that. You'd need the right aircraft.'

'Have you got any, sir?'

De Berry stared at Hockold for a moment. '202 Group have a few Bombays. What do you want?'

'Anything you can arrange, sir. Shop dummies. Tailors' dummies. Even overalls stuffed with straw.'

'How long have we got?'

'Eight days now.'

'How many do you want? Fifty?'

'Couldn't make it a hundred, sir, could you?'

The Plan

A mock-up of their destination arrived in the bottom of a truck as Hockold returned to Scouab, and that evening he stood at the far side of it with an old billiard cue Amos had produced for use as a pointer while all the officers and senior NCOs crowded round.

'That's Qaba, by God!' Brandison's spontaneous exclamation could be heard all over the hut and Murdoch turned slowly, his eyes icy.

'I think we'll just forget you said that, Brandison,' he commented and Hockold wished he'd been quicker and said it himself because, somehow, it added to Murdoch's growing reputation for crisp leadership.

He jabbed with the pointer. 'That's the harbour area,' he said. 'There are four ships in there and it's our job to destroy them. Since three of them contain petrol and one ammunition, it shouldn't be too difficult.'

Sotheby tried a nervous question. Because he was aware of everybody looking at him, his stammer was worse than usual. 'Sus-sus-sir! Who does it?'

'Not you, Sotheby,' Hockold said. 'There will be five parties. Number One will hold the road and the harbour by the Roman arch – here. Number Two will concentrate on the ships. Number Three's job will be to open the prisoner of war cage and deal with any Germans on the east side of the town.'

'What do we do with 'em, sir?' Swann asked.

'For Christ's sake, mon,' Murdoch said, his accent suddenly more marked. 'What d'ye think? Play kiss in the ring?'

'Not the Germans, sir.' Swann looked embarrassed. 'The prisoners.'

Hockold tucked the billiard cue under his arm and lit a cigarette to avoid too sharp a retort. 'We leave 'em to their own devices, Swann,' he said.

'Thank you, sir, I just wondered –'

'That's all right, Swann, but don't interrupt again until you've got your orders.'

'I just thought –'

'Shut up,' Murdoch snapped. This time Swann shut up.

Hockold drew a deep breath. Murdoch seemed to be managing the affair better than he was. 'There'll be two more parties,' he went on. 'Number Four will head for this warehouse – here. Get it clearly in your heads. There are alleys into Wogtown from the Shariah Jedid and it's not an alley you're looking for, it's a road. The last party, Number Five, will destroy the fuel depot. Any questions?'

'It'll bub-be dark, sir,' Sotheby said. 'How do we know where the Germans are?'

'Eat carrots,' Collier grinned. 'Like the night-fighter boys.'

'Take a cat with us,' Brandison added. 'And aim where it's looking.'

Murdoch silenced them with his bark. 'There'll be a moon and sairchlights at the airfield,' he said. 'And there'll be flames. How about dress, sir?'

'Drill trousers, battledress blouses; berets, bonnets, steel helmets or whatever you prefer; gym shoes or rubber-soled boots. We want no noise and with all that petrol splashing about we want no sparks from hobnails. As little webbing as you can manage with. As much ammunition as you can carry.'

Hockold paused and the pointer jabbed again. 'A last word. The Ibn al As Mosque. See that it's respected. We'll have enough with the Germans, so we don't want the Arabs sniping at us, too.'

At RAF, Sheikh Kafesh, Flying Officer Devenish was bored.

It had been his idea when he'd first joined the RAF to become an air-gunner but, unfortunately, just when he was seeing himself heading for Canada or Rhodesia for training, with the proud white flash of an air-crew cadet in his cap, he had discovered something about himself that he'd never before been aware of. He was colour blind.

In desperation, he had looked round for something in which he could prove himself and had discovered that a small and very select branch was being formed expressly for Demolition. As his subjects were physics and chemistry, he had volunteered at once and, encouraged by an unorthodox commanding officer, had developed into an expert. Posted to the Middle East he had gathered round him a small group of men, which included a Palestinian Arab called Uri Rouat who had turned up from God alone knew where and insisted he was part of Devenish's outfit, and their work consisted chiefly of blowing up damaged enemy planes on captured aerodromes. Devenish considered it dull and unexciting, however, and was still itching to gain a little glory, so that when Hockold, on Kirstie McRuer's advice, descended on Sheikh Kafesh, he was more than willing to offer his services.

'Ships,' Hockold reminded him quietly. 'You've had no experience of ships.'

Devenish's scholarly face twisted in a slight smile. 'All you have to know is where to put your firework,' he pointed out.

'Would you be prepared to volunteer?'

Devenish didn't hesitate. He still felt he had a long way to go. 'Yes, I would,' he said. 'I can't speak for the rest of my people, of course, though I think they'd come along.'

'How long would it take you to find out?'

'About five minutes.'

Meanwhile, Commander Babington hadn't been idle. During the night he had moved his empty ammunition lighters up alongside *Umberto Uno* and had started to remove her crew and cargo. Because of prying eyes ashore, the work had stopped before daybreak, and the lighters were now lying nearby, apparently completely unconnected with the coaster. During the coming night, more would take their places and these would be replaced nightly by others containing carpenters and armourers to replace the deck cargo with guns and dummy crates. The gangways and ladders to be used at Qaba were being prepared ashore; because they'd be spotted the minute they were put in place, they were to be carried aboard at the very last minute. For the same reason the splinter mats and steel plates which were to cover the bridge and upperworks of *Horambeb* were stowed out of sight in the holds and would not be fitted until the ship was at sea.

Extra petrol tanks were being fitted to the Fairmiles and high-speed launches, which were also being stripped to make room for the soldiers they were to carry. Stores were being amassed and routes marked on charts and the commander of ML 112, which was lying alongside *Umberto* as guard-ship, was at that moment arranging several pounds of explosive in the stern bilges of his command. Their detonation at the moment of departure would suggest she had been hit by gunfire from *Umberto*, but only seven already dead men would be likely to be harmed. They were to be brought aboard the night before, and the bodies, in lifejackets and attached to spars, would float into the water as the launch sank.

It all seemed easy enough and the commander of ML 112, a breezy young volunteer reserve lieutenant called Dysart, seemed quite capable of doing his part effectively.

'What about your crew?' Babington asked.

'Mostly awkward bastards, sir,' Dysart said cheerfully. 'Chaps who misbehave themselves ashore get sent out here to work off their bad temper.'

'How about you?'

'I can handle 'em,' Dysart said cheerfully.

'I didn't mean that. I meant, are *you* here because you've misbehaved yourself, too?'

'Oh!' Dysart grinned. 'In a way, sir. I called my superior officer a stupid bugger without looking round first to see if he were within earshot.'

Babington said nothing but he thought it might be a good idea to find out who Dysart's commanding officer was, because Dysart impressed him with his self-confidence.

'These chaps of yours,' he asked. 'Have they ever been put on charges?'

Dysart grinned again. 'More than once, sir. Either by the Regulating Branch or the civilian police.'

'Let's have a look at them.'

The twenty-three sullen members of the crew were lined up on the foredeck and Babington studied a list in his hand that contained the vital statistics of the seven dead men at present lying in the mortuary. He jerked a hand at a beefy leading seaman running to fat.

'He'll do,' he said. 'What's his name?'

'Gaukrodger, sir.'

'It fits, I think. What about the little chap in the middle?'

'Smith.'

'That goes with him, too. I'll have the chap next to him, too, and the three on the end.'

Dysart looked at Babington admiringly. 'The six most awkward bastards I've got, sir. You couldn't have done better with a divining rod.'

Babington smiled. 'All the better. Have they got records?'

'Not half, sir. Tiny Gaukrodger's cleared the Fleet Club more than once and smashed up the Tipperary more times than I can remember. The owner starts calling up reinforcements the minute he arrives.'

'And the others?'

'Smith starts the fight Gaukrodger finishes. And the others aren't exactly backward.'

'Good. Get them all in your cabin, will you?'

Puzzled, Dysart told the six men to report below and from the little desk alongside Dysart's bunk Babington looked up at them. 'You're going to take part in a small deception we've planned for Jerry,' he said. 'I want you one at a time to turn out your pockets and wallets on the table there. You first, Gaukrodger.'

Unwillingly, the big man laid his belongings on the table.

'This everything?'

'Yes, sir.'

'Anything of particular value to you?'

Gaukrodger squinted at the articles on the table. 'Just the photo, sir,' he said. 'It's me ma.'

'Take it. And your money.'

As Gaukrodger picked up the photograph and the money, Babington swept the other articles to the other end of the table. 'Label 'em, Dysart, and give him a receipt. You next, Smith.'

Smith's pockets contained much the same – fags, matches, a

93

bundle of obscene photographs, and a dozen contraceptives in paper packets.

Babington stared at them. 'You must go at it like a ferret,' he said mildly.

Smith grinned. 'Them Egyptian bints, sir.'

'No wonder you're not very big. You don't give yourself a chance.'

Babington went through the personal belongings of all six, taking everything except treasured photographs and letters. When he'd finished, he had a pile of packets of cigarettes, matches contraceptives, even a few letters and unwanted photographs of girls. He looked at his list, then up at Dysart who was grinning at his men. 'Now you,' he said.

Dysart's cheerful expression faded. 'Me, sir?'

'Why not?'

Dysart began to fish in his pockets. There was a contraceptive among his belongings, too. 'I see you go in for it as well,' Babington said dryly. 'Letters?'

Dysart stared at the dog-eared papers. 'There's a mess bill I haven't paid.'

Babington grunted and looked up at the six men. 'Right, shove off. And keep it quiet. And I mean quiet.'

As the door closed, Dysart gestured at the table. 'What's all this for, anyway, sir?'

Babington smiled. 'You're going to be picked up dead in the harbour,' he said.

It had taken Devenish half an hour to round up his men and equipment and get them into a couple of lorries. Two hours later, watched by Hockold, they were getting to know what made a ship tick and, clambering round the bowels of a freighter with his men, Devenish suddenly discovered a new excitement in his job. This was better by a long way than being aircrew and dropping bombs.

'One bang in the hold of a petrol carrier,' the naval lieutenant who was leading the conducted tour pointed out, 'and the bloody lot'll go sky-high. If the hatch is closed, you'll need one of these.' He swung what looked like a four-foot iron spanner. 'That'll unclamp the dogs.'

By this time, two Honeys were parked on the quayside alongside Landing Craft (Tank) 11, and Hockold found Lieutenant Carter pottering round the cabin of the vessel, singing to himself. There was a gin bottle on the table and he seemed to be sorting out papers; judging by the way he was tossing them to the floor, he didn't have much use for most of them

> 'Eternal Father, strong to save,' he sang,
> 'Whose arm doth bind the restless wave....'

'Bumph,' he announced cheerfully in his cracked, boozy voice as Hockold appeared. 'Don't believe in filling in forms.'

Hockold looked round. The place smelled like a bar. 'You going to be able to do this job, Carter?' he asked sharply.

Carter lifted an eyebrow. 'You been hearing the stories?' he asked.

'What stories?'

'About me being slung out of the Merchant Navy and only getting in this lot because of the emergency.' He gestured at the bottle. 'That was the cause of it. That and the bitch I married.'

'I'm not interested in your private life,' Hockold said. 'Only if you can do the job or not.'

Carter grinned. 'I can do the job,' he said. 'With one hand tied behind my back.'

The tank men were young and, as usual, covered with oil. A lieutenant called Meinertz was in command of one Honey and a sergeant called Gleeson the other. Hockold studied the high-sterned, square shape of the tanks and turned to Meinertz. 'You know what you've got to do?' he asked.

Despite his youth, Meinertz had eighteen months' experience in the desert behind him and was only in Alexandria because he was supposed to be resting. He nodded and smiled.

'Think you can do it?'

'Sure we can, sir. My gunner couldn't hit a bull in a barn door at the moment – he's new out here – but I'll get him out in the desert and see that he gets some practice.'

'Anything you want?'

Meinertz glanced at the Honeys. Nothing except a Panzer Mark IV, he thought.

Leaving Meinertz, Hockold called on Babington. He was sitting at his desk, staring at seven brown paper bags.

'Seven dead men there,' he said. He turned one of the bags upside down and spilled out letters, keys, money, cigarettes, lighter, photographs and a contraceptive. 'Belongings of Lieutenant Jeremy Edward Dysart, RNVR,' he said. 'They'll be placed in the pockets of Captain Matteotti, of *Umberto Uno*, who will be found floating in the harbour the morning after you leave. Captain Matteotti doesn't know it, of course, because he's already dead.'

'How about the ship?'

'Going ahead all right. Steel plates and concrete ready with the extra conning positions. You've already got two collapsible crates on the fore deck full of Oerlikon and we'll have two more aboard tonight. How are you doing for demolition experts, by the way, because I think I can lend you one or two.'

'It so happens,' Hockold said, 'that the RAF got in first.'

'The RAF won't know how to blow ships.'

'This chap will. He's got quite a reputation and he's already aboard a ship in the harbour finding out all about it.'

Babington looked disappointed. 'I was going to supply you with a sub-lieutenant and a party of jolly jack tars.'

Hockold smiled. 'I'll be glad to have them,' he said. 'But your sub-lieutenant can't blow four ships at once. The RAF stays in charge.'

'This is a naval operation.'

'It's a combined operation.'

'Oh, well – '

'Don't back away, Babington,' Hockold said sharply. 'I want your party. I want anybody I can get.'

'Funny you should say that,' Babington mused. 'Because I've got this American as well: Captain Cornelius H. Cadish. Nice chap. Been sent here to learn. He has twenty men he could bring along too.'

'No special terms of reference,' Hockold said shortly. 'They do what everybody else does.'

'I'll put it to him.' Babington looked up. 'About the minefield at Qaba: you were right. There isn't one. The gap's wide open. I shall have the chart in front of me when we go in.'

Hockold stared. 'Are *you* going?'

'As you said – ' Babington's face cracked into a grin ' – this is a combined operation and, if we're going to have a nice little nocturnal jolly ashore, I might as well look after the seaborne end.'

8

*The men were hardened in the desert by rigorous
training under expert instructors.*

The defences of Qaba had taken a turn for the better and
Colonel Hochstätter was feeling much happier.

Headquarters had suddenly gone mad. Balloon equipment,
searchlights and light and heavy flak had been ordered up and,
in addition to Zöhler's damaged Mark III, two captured British
Honeys and a damaged Grant had been sent to the town. Since
the Honeys were too light for the Western Desert and the Grant
had its gun mounted in a side sponson, it was thought they might
be of more use to Hochstätter than they would to the panzers.
Finally, two 75 PAK 97/38 guns arrived.

Schoeler eyed them without much enthusiasm. 'They might
have sent us something better,' he complained. 'They're only
French 75s on German carriages. They're hard to handle and
they're unstable when they're firing.'

Nevertheless, they were better than nothing, and he found
sites for them behind the POW compound on the Ibrahimiya
side of the town and alongside the searchlight at Mas el Bub.
And when two further 47s and two captured two-pounders
arrived, he began to change his tune as he realized he was beginning to build up quite a formidable battery.

'If we're not careful,' he said, 'they'll be pressing *Panzer-
jägers* on us.'

This wasn't all either, because there had been a signal to the
effect that eight hundred men from a *Pionier-Lehrbataillon* on
their way from Tobruk were due to pass through the town with

all their transport and were to be held for harbour defence until further notice. It was quite clear army headquarters was growing concerned about the coming British attack, and the whole of the rear area was being showered with demands to clear the line and get things moving before it started. Hochstätter had heard, in fact, that all was not as well with the Afrika Korps as appeared on the surface. Thanks to the RAF and the Royal Navy, which regularly intercepted stores and reinforcements from Europe, units were under strength, and it was well known that water supplies in the forward areas were now considered to be critical. There were even alarming rumours that the fighting troops were undernourished and that the sickness rate was rising, while the British, always well supported, were growing stronger every day.

It was a disturbing situation, and Hochstätter knew that General Stumme had made a depressing report to Berlin on his position and the bitterness that existed between the panzers and the Luftwaffe. It was obviously essential that Hochstätter's supplies should be set in motion as quickly as possible but all Hrabak could do was seize the lorries which dragged in the guns, and organize parties of men to push drums on handcarts, and Arabs with camels to haul them on sledge-like constructions of poles. His conscripted engineers, sailors, convalescents, artillerymen, pioneers and Italians began to wish they'd never seen North Africa. It was hot and dusty and some of them were even beginning to loathe their beloved leaders who had brought them there.

None more than that homesick skiver, Private Gaspare Bontempelli. He was sick of the war, sicker still of Qaba, and sickest of all of the Germans for giving all the dirty jobs to the Italians. People like himself from Naples were used to going hungry, but gracefully and to the accompaniment of music and beauty; not, as in Qaba, to the Germanic shouts of Sottotenente Baldissera, a dedicated Fascist who tried hard to model himself on the brisk young men of the Afrika Korps, and Unteroffizier Upholz who, despite his lower rank, had the power to tell even Baldissera what to do.

Bontempelli sighed. There had been a time earlier in the year when he'd thought it was all coming to an end as the British had bolted back from Gazala, and they had moved up through deserted British camps towards Cairo. The windscreens had flashed in the sun as they'd dropped down from Sollum, already visualizing waving palms and water and green meadows, and the unlimited lust to which they were entitled as conquerors at the expense of terrified Egyptian women. They had joked of having harems and being appointed governor of Heliopolis, but when they'd stopped the only thing that had interested them was to fling off their clothes and rush stark naked into the indigo Mediterranean. Cairo could wait a day or two longer.

Unfortunately, Cairo was still waiting. Rommel had tried to outflank the British, but his favourite trick hadn't come off for once and they had come to a stop. Now the Eighth Army was supposed to be receiving reinforcements, and instead of the luxury and lust, they'd got only the burning sand of Qaba, itching skins, sores, dysentery and jaundice.

Bontempelli stared with reddened eyes at the four ships in the glittering little harbour. Then a butterfly landed on the drum he'd been pushing, and as it palpitated there it reminded him somehow of the white body of Maddalena Corri in Taranto and how he'd seen her shuddering with suppressed excitement as she'd waited for him to make love to her. He drew a deep painful breath, stifled by his own erotic thoughts, and forced her out of his mind. It was time he went to see Zulfica Ifzi again.

Zulfica Ifzi lived in the Borgo Nero among the close-huddled houses of whitewashed mud-brick, and even if she weren't as beautiful or as fragile as the lost Maddalena, at least she was hot-blooded and moved well in bed. Because Qaba had been occupied by the British for so long, her sole conversation at first had been 'Hello, Angleesh swaddy! No spikka other bints,' but she was young enough to learn and had the Eastern habit of oiling her body with perfumed unguents which made contact with her all the more exciting.

Bontempelli shuddered and shook his head as he tried to force

the picture from his mind. '*Maria, Madre di Gesu*,' he murmured agonizedly. 'Preserve us all.'

Then he became aware of Unteroffizier Upholz staring at him
from the door of the hut where he had his office, and as he
returned to the ship, Sottotenente Baldissera appeared in front
of him, small, strutting, his hands on his hips, his arms akimbo,
his jaw with its neatly combed Balbo beard thrust forward in the
style of Mussolini.

'Daydreaming again, Double Ration?' he asked.

'*Si*, Signor Sottotenente,' Bontempelli admitted. '*Un poco*.'

'What about?'

'Women, Signor Sottotenente.'

Baldissera's adam's apple worked because it was something he
often dreamed about himself. 'Then don't, *ragazzo mio*,' he said.
'The Germans are watching.'

The position was surprisingly similar at Gott el Scouab where
quite a few of the Cut-Price Commandos were beginning to
regret their hasty decision to volunteer.

Their life was still dominated by the fierce influence of the sun.
Every day they saw it rise from under the eastern rim of the
desert and, growing rapidly in heat and light, climb its course
across the glaring sky. Cut off from the rest of the army, they
knew only hard work, the emptiness of the desert – and the flies.
Because the Italian prisoners had never been careful with the
disposal of their rubbish, there were millions of them at Gott el
Scouab, enjoying the moisture in human sweat and swarming
round the ears, nose and mouth. Desert sores drew them like
magnets, and whenever food was put down they arrived in their
squadrons and brigades and divisions for first bite.

'They've got no bloody discretion,' Belcher complained bitterly. 'Gettin' in a man's tinned fruit like that. I thought the bastard
was a raisin and there it was – ett!'

A few fights enlivened the proceedings. On one memorable
occasion even the Three Stooges set about each other, bringing
down four tents in their titanic struggles until someone thought

of By who incredibly managed to hold three large and very angry young men at arm's length in his great fists at once.

'Once round By,' Belcher said, 'twice round the gasworks.'

One pleasure was football which Murdoch encouraged as a means of keeping them fit. The sergeants played the corporals and the corporals played the privates who, being more numerous, had four teams. The camp cooks had a team, too, picked by Cook-Corporal Rogers, but like all cooks they were too fat and couldn't run. They lost by forty-three to nil to Privates 4, which was captained by Jones the Body who claimed to have had a trial for Cardiff City before the war. Triumphantly, he threw out a challenge to the officers, so that everybody could laugh when they made fools of themselves; but Murdoch played as if he'd been capped for Scotland and they beat Privates 4 easily, chiefly due to the efforts of Second-Lieutenant Sotheby who, despite his stammer and nervous appearance, turned out to be a born footballer and ran rings round Taffy Jones to score seven goals.

As they lay in their tents, docile, cantankerous, suspicious, swapping grievances and jokes, they tried to remember what it was like to be cold and miserable instead of hot and miserable.

'When we was on Salisbury Plain,' Belcher said, 'we used to share a hut wiv about eight hundred rats. How the poor fings survived the cold and damp, I dunno. It was lovely.'

'I wish I was 'obe,' Waterhouse wailed in mock woe. 'Stuck out 'ere, I feel like a bloke who's bird's dropped 'im. Slung away like the paper after she's fidished 'er fish ad chips.'

'Actually —' Bradshaw lifted his head ' — you're better off out here with Monty than you realize.'

'Well —' Waterhouse spoke grudgingly ' — I suppose Monty's a good gederal.'

'Wavell was a good general, too,' Sugarwhite said gravely, and Waterhouse burst into song at once: " *'But dow 'e contemplates his navel —' "*

Bradshaw let them sort out who was the best general, then he mildly brought them back to the point. 'Actually, I wasn't talking about the army.' It stopped them dead.

Waterhouse turned. 'Well, what was you talkig about?'

'This place.'

'It's the bloody sand that gets me dowd.'

'Actually,' Bradshaw said, 'the sand's mostly dust.'

'I suppose you know a lot about it, don't you?' Taffy said aggressively.

'Yes,' Bradshaw agreed. 'I was in the gallop up to Gazala and back.'

That stopped the argument dead again because Bradshaw had allowed them to think he was a newcomer like the rest of them. Taffy was the first to recover.

'I was nearly in that, look you.'

Baragwanath Eva turned. 'You was never, you gert liar.'

'I was. Mad I was when I missed it. What was it like being up in the blue?'

'Marvellous. No one else but us and the Germans.'

'And the bloody flies,' Waterhouse yelped. 'The flies, the sand, the 'eat and the 'ard tack!'

'What's wrong with that?' Bradshaw asked. 'I've never found the desert a scene of fretful discontent and disillusion, have you? And if you have to make war, where better? Any man who's been part of this army will sit back in his old age and say, "I was one of God's chosen few." '

The thought gave them a measure of consolation as Murdoch drove them. It was exhausting work in the extremes of temperature but he never let up, drumming advice into them until their brains hung limp between their ears. The sergeants also never let up. The training went on all day, humping weapons and ammunition, running under the blazing sun, their shirts dark with sweat, dropping flat in the dust, getting up and running again. They shed weight by the pound.

'I think the idea's to dehydrate us,' Bradshaw observed solemnly. 'So they can shovel us into the sea from aeroplanes – whereupon we swell up and become soldiers again. A whole regiment landed behind the German lines in a brown paper bag.'

Once a 'shufti-wallah' came over, droning stridently from the

west to look for the Eighth Army. But it was a long time since
the Luftwaffe had dominated desert airspace and five Hurricanes dropped on to its tail immediately. For a while, the
machines moved about against the blue sky like a lot of flies, and
they could hear the bursts of firing as the German streaked for
safety. Then one of the Hurricanes slipped into position and the
'shufti-wallah' faltered, lost altitude, and with a deepening howl,
nose-dived into the ground beyond the ridges a mile from camp.
They all heard the crash and saw the pink and yellow mush-
room of smoke, flame and sand blossom upwards.

'Better send a section over,' Captain Watson said flatly to
Bunch in the silence that followed. 'Somebody might have
escaped.'

He didn't sound very hopeful and all they found were a few
charred hands and feet.

Of necessity, their amusements were simple and it was Auchmuty – inevitably Auchmuty, the solitary, silent ex-shepherd –
who discovered that among the camelthorn that surrounded
them there was a surprising amount of animal life. Jerboas
warrened the ground in the gravelly patches. Insects abounded :
white-shelled snails, large long-legged ants, and revolting black
dung beetles which lived on animal droppings and could always
be heard scrambling around in the area of the latrines. There
was also a picturesque but sinister selection of sand spiders,
tarantulas and scorpions, and scorpion-baiting became a minor
sport.

In addition to these pastimes, they could always smoke, drink
tea or sing; for a treat they could even take their boots off and
think about women. Not much, though, because the desert made
them as sterile as itself, and sexual appetites disappeared – something that worried Captain Watson, whose marriage was so far
bounded entirely by two days and two nights.

Only Kiss of Death Jones, the Hearts and Flowers Kid,
bothered to dwell on the subject. 'A kiss, look you,' he pointed
out, 'is only an application at the top of the building for a job
in the basement.'

Sugarwhite's ears flapped. Though Taffy didn't know it, in

Sugarwhite he had the best listener in the tent, because inside the 'Cut-Price Commando card' there was still an uncertain boy determined that if he ever got back to civilization again he'd go for the first sizeable skirt he saw. To the experienced, Taffy's claims always had a hollow ring and his talk meant only that for some reason of his own he needed to put himself across to them, but the fact that in less enlightened days he would have had his ears cropped for his lies made no difference to Sugarwhite. To him, Taffy was the Minstrel Boy himself, the Man of Harlech, Owen Glendower and the red dragon of Welsh Wales all rolled into one for his skill with women. Sugarwhite had been brooding for months on the disaster of his overseas leave when, feeling he might die in battle without ever having experienced physical love, he'd tramped unsuccessfully for hours round London looking for a willing girl.

'The left one,' Taffy was continuing with the sureness of an expert. 'And there's a state she will be in, boy, because that is where her heart is, see.'

Bradshaw, who had been trying against odds to read, lifted his head from his book and interrupted the diatribe in a bored voice. 'I always thought your heart was in the centre,' he said. 'And since a woman's ticker's made of untreated granite, anyway, massaging her mammary glands isn't likely to stir a virgin's passions to the point when she gives away what she prizes above rubies.'

Taffy's open mouth shut with a click. Bradshaw always seemed to interrupt him with a disputatious comment just when he was at full throttle, and usually in words he couldn't understand. Since he was only too well aware of his own failings, he was certain Bradshaw did it deliberately, and he'd often considered taking refuge in the last extremity of offering to go outside with him to settle their disagreements with fists like the Stooges. Despite his bulging muscles, however, Taffy was unsure of his courage and there was a strange quiet self-confidence about Bradshaw.

'There is ignorant for you,' he said indignantly, smoothing his hair and turning to less imaginative listeners. 'I am not Tyrone

Power but I do not have to wear a sack over my head to warn the girls I am coming.'

'I rackon they gurls disappear like rabbits down a 'ole when 'ee appears, me dear,' Eva growled. 'I would, was I a gurl. 'Tes nothin' but wind and piss you are. I 'ad a ferret once just like you, but I never did breed from the mucky toad. 'Twas useless 'e was.'

Taffy jeered. 'Maybe it is jealous you are because *you* do not have any success.' He turned hurriedly to the undemanding Sugarwhite. 'What I always do, look you, is get them with their left arm behind their back and hold their right under my left –'

'But that's rape,' Sugarwhite protested.

'Or else a thumping great fib,' Bradshaw said. 'I bet all he's ever done is tried not very successfully to roger some poor bloody barmaid against the railings one night when she'd had a few gins over the Plimsoll Line after the local eisteddfod.'

'I know what I am talking about,' Taffy said furiously.

'I doubt it,' Bradshaw said. 'Most of the time you talk the most blistering balls. You know what the Good Book says : *Pe llefarwn â thafodau dynion ac angylion a heb gennyf gariad yr wyf fel efydd yn seinio neu symbal yn tincian.*'

Taffy's jaw dropped. 'That's Welsh,' he said.

Bradshaw smiled. 'Yes. And you'll perhaps know what it means? It means, "Though I speak with the tongues of men and of angels, and have not charity, I am become as sounding brass or a tinkling cymbal." First Corinthians, Thirteen, verse one.'

Taffy's eyes were popping. 'You speak Welsh, man?'

'Welsh is the language of Paradise, Taffy bach.' Bradshaw's voice was suddenly thick with Celtic intonation.

'It's Welsh you are yourself?'

Bradshaw's smile became a broad grin. 'But not such a bloody welsher as you are, Taff.'

9

The troops were praised by the general, specialized equipment was drawn, and ways and means of getting ashore were worked out.

To tell his men what they were going to do and where they were going to do it, Hockold used the general's method and had them sit down round him in a little amphitheatre of sand in one of the wadis. Captain Amos had produced a blackboard with a rough plan of Qaba drawn on it.

'Qaba,' Hockold said, jabbing with a billiard cue. 'Two hundred miles away, fifty east of Mersa and twenty west of Fuka. There's a prisoner of war cage there that contains two thousand of your chums whom we hope to set free.'

The information put an immediate expression of interest on their faces. They all knew someone who'd been slipped into the bag and the thought that they might release a few friends was good for their morale.

'Our object : to destroy a fuel dump, a spare parts depot, and these four ships here. I know they're there because I was in Qaba a week ago.'

It was news to them that Hockold had been behind the German lines and they regarded him with new interest. Previously he'd been just an ordinary sort of half-colonel, brusque in manner and difficult to approach, who'd been appointed to push them around.

'We shall be split up into several parties,' he went on. 'And every officer and sergeant will be given a map of the town. I want you all to look at them and familiarize yourself with the details so that if anything happens to your officer or sergeant, someone else can take up where he left off. We shall go in by ship, so that when you've done your job, you will make your way to the beaches or the mole and return aboard as fast as possible. Any way you can. Swim –'

'I cad't swib,' Waterhouse yelled from the back.

'Then you'll have to take a running jump,' Murdoch said and there was a yell of laughter.

Hockold was glad to see the growing cheerfulness, and he was just beginning to feel that he had them in the palm of his hand when they became aware of a cloud of dust approaching. Almost immediately, without warning, they found themselves facing the new general. The briefing was hurriedly postponed and the general climbed to the seat of his car, squinting into the sun like an actor under a spotlight. 'Come closer,' he said, gesturing. 'As close as you can. So you can hear me.' Then he told them everything, his plan for the coming battle and what he expected of his men.

'When I assumed command of this army,' he said, 'my orders were simply to go down into the desert and destroy Rommel. And that's exactly what I intend to do. So give your minds and your hearts to your jobs and do them with all your might, so that with God's help we can throw the Germans out of Africa and set about cleaning up the mess they've made in Europe.'

And that was it, and he was tossing out packets of fags handed to him by an aide. 'Have a smoke,' he said. 'Enjoy them. With luck before long you'll be smoking German cigars.'

While they were still scrambling for the cigarettes the car drew away. Rabbitt hurriedly called them to attention and Hockold stood at the salute with Murdoch and Sergeant Bunch – set in concrete as usual – and someone raised a scattered cheer. To one or two of the cleverer ones like Bradshaw it was obvious that the chat – not quite so spontaneous as it seemed – was a calculated attempt to get their tails up; but to most of them it was just the Old Man, coming down among his pals, the swaddies, the chaps he knew had to do the dirty work. And any general who came and talked without spit and polish and without you having to stand in the hot sun for an hour while he had a pink gin with the

colonel, any general who told you what he was going to do and
chucked fags about, was all right.

The next day the equipment lorries arrived, containing everything they wanted. Working on the principle that the army never
gave you half what you needed, Hockold had indented for twice
as much as he thought he'd get, and when it came it was twice
what he'd expected, twice as many Brens, twice as many radios,
twice as many Tommy-guns, binoculars, compasses, pistols and
Stens.

Feeling like new men, they were divided into squads. Amos
was with Hockold because he knew what was going on, all the
distances, all the times and numbers. Number Five Party, which
had a job that isolated them, could safely be left to the experienced
Murdoch who would think well ahead and handle emergencies
with his usual ruthless efficiency. Watson, who had proved
experienced, able and cool-headed, had been given the ships.
Second-Lieutenant Sotheby was with Collier's POW party
because that seemed the place where someone who was nervous
and not very bright could get into the least trouble. Blood-and-
Guts Swann was considered more than capable of handling the
refuelling post and warehouse; especially since Brandison, whose
job was to capture the bridge on the mole, would be around to
back him up.

At this point, Tent 7 was split up yet again. Bradshaw was
with Devenish and Sergeant Bunch in the ships party; Belcher
was with the dour, sour Comrie in the warehouse party under
Swann and Brandison, while Keely was stuck with Fidge in
Collier's group. Because he could shoot the eye out of a rat at
half a mile, Baragwanath Eva was with Docwra in a group of
snipers whose job was to stop anybody picking off the leader of
the operation. This party also included Willow, Gardner, Sugarwhite and Waterhouse; while, due to his size and the fact that
he could run at full speed with a load like a drayhorse without
even noticing it, Ed By was with the Three Stooges in Murdoch's
party, travelling in the landing craft, with Auchmuty and Cobbe
and the rest of those built on the heroic scale. Jones the Body was

with this party, too, but only after loud complaints that he was as strong as anybody, look you, and had joined up to get into a bit of action.

Waterhouse was loud in his derision. 'I'll tell you why *I'b* 'ere!' He raised his voice in a riotous yell. 'I'b 'ere because I got called up and got no choice. That's why I'b 'ere.'

Belcher grinned. '*I* joined to get the judies,' he said. 'Uniform does something for a feller.'

'Oh, agreed!' Bradshaw looked up from his book. 'Nobody was interested in me in civvies, but when I put on a uniform, vast lustful village girls with breasts like clock-weights and bums like garden rollers ran after me down the street to drag me off my bike.'

'Did they catch you?' Waterhouse asked.

'Sometimes. But I gritted my teeth and endured it like a man.'

That afternoon the officers drove to Cairo where Rear-Admiral Bryant had set up a briefing conference. There was a large blackboard with a map of Qaba drawn on it with the gun positions marked, and Bryant stood up to tell them what to expect.

'German headquarters,' he said, using a pointer. 'POW compound. Naval barracks. Mosque. Batteries – each of which consists of one 47 and light weapons. There are also machine guns on the roof of the naval barracks and the German headquarters, and in these houses here. Colonel Hockold will tell you more about them.'

He went on to explain what preparations had been made and what weather, currents, and conditions they might expect. Then General Murray gave them a rundown on Montgomery's battle plan and how they were to fit into it. Next, Commander Babington rose and began on the real details.

'Start signal will be *Umberto*'s gun and the explosion aboard ML 112 at 0100 hours. You understand that, Dysart?'

Lieutenant Dysart nodded indifferently. His job was already done. All he had to do now was touch two wires together.

Babington's gaze took in the ships' captains – Lieutenant-Commander Hardness, who was to have *Umberto*; Lieutenant

Stretton, an ex-Merchant sailor like Carter, who was to command *Horambeb*; Carter himself, lined-faced and so casual he seemed drunk; and the skippers of the launches, all of them young enough to look like boys. 'As the convoy arrives off Qaba,' he went on, 'the RAF launches will break off and go in fast to their beach. *Horambeb* will go into this stretch of dredged water – here – on the outside of the mole, and will get her ropes ashore. *Umberto*'s troops will disembark across her. Landing Craft 11 –' he looked at Carter who seemed to be asleep ' – Landing Craft 11,' he repeated.

Carter looked up. 'I'm listening,' he said.

'It's your job to put your ship as close to the harbour as possible and get the tanks ashore quickly, so they can deal with the 47 just above the slip.'

'Provided that the 47 just above the slip doesn't deal with me first,' Carter observed.

'It'll be your job to see it doesn't,' Bryant snapped.

As Babington sat down, Hockold reached for the pointer. 'Four parties will go into the town,' he said. 'Major Murdoch's will go as fast as possible for the fuel dump. The main party will set up a medical aid station and headquarters near the Roman arch and keep open the Bab al Gawla and the Shariah Jedid for their return. The first party ashore will be the ladder party, which will capture the wooden bridge on the mole before it can be destroyed, with the main party close behind ready to pass through them. The refuelling station and warehouse party will pass through the main party when they're established by the arch. The explosives parties will remain below until they're certain the mole's in our hands. Any questions? Meinertz, how about you?'

Lieutenant Meinertz looked at the plan of Qaba and decided that what seemed easy to the navy was going to look a lot different to a man shut up in a little tin chamber pot; especially as he still wasn't happy about his gunner, who seemed to have been born with a congenital defect in his eyesight and couldn't have hit a bull in a passage after dark. Since, however there was little chance at this stage of getting a new gunner, there didn't therefore seem to be any relevant question, and he shook his head.

As Hockold sat down, Air Vice-Marshal de Berry straightened his long legs.

Towering above the table, puffing at a cigarette in the amber holder, he outlined the RAF's share in the operation. 'We've planned a course to bring the aircraft in from the sea so that their engines will drown the noise of the launches. Blenheims will go in first in groups of three, dropping metallic strip and flares, but they will then circle to the south and come in again to drop their bombs. They'll be followed by Bostons, who will also arrive in threes, interspersed at four-minute intervals with Bombays, so that the bombs and the flares and the dummy parachutists are dropping over a long period to keep the Germans guessing. The Bostons and Blenheims will be loaded with high explosive, anti-personnel bombs and incendiaries to cause as many incidents at the airfield as possible.'

As he sat down Hardness, the captain of *Umberto,* asked a question. 'I notice we have no fire support,' he pointed out.

'You won't need it,' Babington said. 'In addition to the RAF's effort, you've got the biggest diversion it's possible for anyone to have and it'll have been going on for several days when you arrive. You've got the whole of the Eighth Army making it.'

After the conference was over, Hockold drove Kirstie to the club for a drink. She wasn't in a talkative mood because the battle was near now and the thought saddened her. Her eyes gentle, she watched Hockold as he jerked out his case to offer her a cigarette. At the conference he'd seemed sure of himself but now he was brusque and clumsy again as he always was with her.

'How do you feel about it now, George?' she asked.

Hockold frowned. 'Think we'll pull it off, given normal luck,' he said.

'Does it mean a lot to you?'

'There'll be a lot of lives lost if we don't.'

'I didn't mean that. I meant, from the point of view of your career.'

He was silent for a while then he lifted his head. 'It would be nice to make brigadier,' he said. 'And pulling this off would help. I've not moved fast in the army – others my age have done better – but I've never expected to hit the headlines. Not even in wartime. I was never at the top of the ladder, Kirstie. Just one of the ordinary people in the middle. That's what I am, I'm afraid.'

It was the first time he'd really talked to her about himself and her heart went out to him for his modesty, his self-deprecation and his honesty.

'So I think brigadier would satisfy me,' he went on. 'And this is my chance. If it doesn't come off, I never shall do it, because to get to the top any other way you have to trample on people and I'm afraid I'm not made that way.'

It was the longest speech he'd ever made to her and certainly the most he'd ever said about himself. She looked at him, seeing a sensitive, kind, painstaking man who took refuge behind his frowns and silences, and she felt curiously close to tears.

Later he drove her home. She shared a flat with several other ATS officers in a shabby block near a restaurant that dispensed over-spiced oily food. Nightshirted pimps stood on the next corner selling their sisters or blue Egyptian sex books. Not far away they could hear packed trams pounding by on rusty rails and the cry of the muezzin coming like a mourning wail across the close-packed flat-roofed houses. Somehow, the place went with her, modest, unsophisticated, but worldly. Some of the English-women in Cairo had acquired house-boats on the Nile opposite the Gezira Club and still discussed the Wine Society's lists and regarded *Lili Marlene* only as a tune that grew boring with too much repetition; somehow it pleased Hockold that Kirstie hadn't opted for that.

They sat for a while in the old Humber, talking, ignoring the scruffy urchins who passed with the hawkers wearing galabiyahs like empty laundry bags.

'When it's finished, George,' Kirstie asked. 'What then? What happens after that?'

He sat in silence for a moment, because he wasn't sure there was going to be any 'then', or any 'after' either. The image he'd seen of himself, lying among the wreckage of Qaba, still troubled him by coming at the most unexpected moments. He had almost mastered it now, but not quite, and he had never managed to discuss it with Amos or Watson, and certainly not Murdoch, because he'd always felt that people who told others about their presentiments were being unnecessarily maudlin.

'George?'

He realized she was looking at him, wondering at his silence, and he pulled himself together.

'I suppose,' he said slowly, 'that we shall join up with the rest of the army and move west.'

She frowned. 'So that when you leave, it'll probably be the last we shall see of each other.'

Hockold's head turned quickly and she smiled. 'I hope not, George,' she said. 'But I think we ought to have a last drink in case, don't you? To celebrate. Or to wish you well. Or until we meet again or something.'

He handed her the brief-case she'd carried. The setting sun was in his eyes as he glanced at the white buildings and at the telegraph poles and the odd gharry laden with noisy soldiers of the Cairo garrison. For a moment they had a strange sort of clarity, illuminated by a bright light as if he were seeing them for the last time. He was quiet for a moment and she spoke quickly to break the silence. 'Have you ever been to Peebles, George?' she asked.

'Once. I come from Cumberland. It's not far.'

'My father farms there. We have a few acres.'

He opened his door, climbed out and appeared by the passenger seat. She looked up. 'I think we ought to try to keep in touch, don't you?' She was trying hard not to make demands of him or frighten him off, but she felt somehow that he needed to know that there was someone on his side somewhere, waving flags for him and shouting encouragement. 'After the war even. Perhaps I could persuade you to visit us.'

He looked down at her. For a moment she seemed to be miles away so that she was small and dimly outlined. 'Yes,' he said, thinking that after the war, even after Qaba, there would be no visiting anybody for him, none of the quiet things he enjoyed in life, nothing but silence and an aloof darkness. It was a strange feeling which – because it seemed so inevitable – didn't depress him in the slightest. 'You must visit Cumberland, too,' he added.

'I'd like that, George.'

'Truly?' He was really only making conversation because under the circumstances none of it had much meaning.

'I mean it. Honestly I do.'

He didn't answer and there was another long silence as he wondered how she'd feel when she learned what had happened to him. He went on explosively. 'Why didn't you marry again, Kirstie?'

'Nobody asked me.' She smiled. 'At least, nobody I wanted. I had plenty of proposals, of course, but not many of them for marriage.' There was another silence. 'Why didn't *you* marry, George? I've never asked you.'

Hockold shrugged. 'Just never thought about it,' he said. 'Even thought I ought not to with the war.'

He managed to help her from the car without wrenching her arm, but for a long time neither of them moved, both of them busy with their thoughts. Then she turned and headed for the door. With her hand on the knob she turned. Her face was curiously sad as she stared at Hockold.

'War's a time when people *should* marry and have families, George,' she said. 'If only to make up for everybody who gets killed.'

10

RAF and naval experts and American troops joined the force. Morale was remarkably high.

With the plan settled, the training grew more particular.

Quite unnoticed, as the days had passed, a metamorphosis had occurred and, although they could hardly even now be called commandos, they were still a lot better than most. Brandison's party could run the length of the mole in a matter of seconds, while Murdoch's party, despite packs weighing up to ninety pounds and spare magazines for the Brens, could run the mile they would have to run in a matter of eight and a half minutes. They even began to get ideas; and Eva and Docwra, both experienced at trussing other people's sheep, devised what they considered a good method of securing prisoners so they couldn't escape, only to be quietly corrected by Murdoch who showed them a much better one with the prisoner's thumbs fastened behind his back and a loop round his neck. 'If he tries to free his hands, he'll strangle himself,' he pointed out.

A few began to show off a bit. Jones the Body had acquired a throwing knife, swearing after his noisy fashion that he was going to do a German or two. It never seemed to hit the target, however, and didn't even stick in much.

'Try it this way, son.' Jacka flicked his wrist so that the knife stuck quivering within half an inch of the bull, and Taffy stared after him, his jaw dropped, as he sauntered away.

There had never been much time, however, and the cost was measured in broken bones. Nagged by Murdoch's shouts, they continued to push a little harder and, because Bunch was nearly twice as old as most of them and could still keep up despite his age, a few who were young pushed still harder to prove themselves; one man sprained an ankle and was ruled out of the operation, while another twisted his back and a third broke three fingers.

Some of the accidents were serious. Murdoch's engineers had bridged a shallow twelve-foot-wide wadi for Brandison's gangway party to practise on but as they rushed towards it in the heat of the day, one over-eager youngster tripped and fell in. It was a trivial accident and he ought to have walked away from it, but his Sten, in the manner of Stens, went off unexpectedly; and instead of a man with a sprained ankle, they found they had a man with the best part of his stomach blown away and only a faint chance of survival.

Inevitably the careful instructions of experience were ignored. 'Don't pull the pin out with your teeth,' Corporal Cobbe had warned as he drilled them in the use of the Mills bomb, but others knew better and one man was carried away dead and another dying.

Even Babington seemed to have been caught up in the general atmosphere of over-confidence, and when Hockold arrived for a last discussion about the plans he was staring at an assorted selection of weapons on his desk.

'I've been torpedoed twice,' he said, 'had my home bombed, lost my brother at Dunkirk, and haven't seen my kids for over two years. I feel I have a little spite to work off. It'll be a piece of cake.'

Hockold had an uneasy feeling that Babington was simplifying things too much. Nothing in which men put their lives at risk was a piece of cake. But they were committed now, and there was no question of changing the plans at this stage.

When he returned to camp, Captain Cadish and his squad of Americans had arrived. Cadish was a tall good-looking young man who reminded Hockold of a few Hollywood heroes he'd seen at the cinema. He was festooned with weapons and had what seemed to be an inordinate amount of transport for twenty-one men.

Stiff and correct, Hockold laid his cards on the table. 'From now on your people will walk,' he announced. 'They will also be split up among my people –'

Cadish made an uncertain protest. 'They won't like that, Colonel.'

'Neither did my people. But they've got used to it. They might even discover to their surprise that Americans aren't overpaid, overfed and oversexed, as a lot of them believe. And, doubtless, your people will teach *them* a thing or two – even if it's only how to play poker.'

The arrival of the Americans brought out the members of 97 Commando to watch, and Tent 7 waited suspiciously as a tall thin youth with acne proceeded to toss down his equipment.

'Hank Broecker,' he introduced himself. 'From Paris, Illinois.'

'Paris is in France,' Encyclopaedia Jones pointed out firmly, determined not to be pushed around by any smart-Alick Yank.

'Yeah?' Broecker seemed surprised. 'Well, the one I'm talking about is in Illinois in the good old USA. There's another in Arkansas, and one in Idaho, and one in Tennessee, and one in Texas. We got two Londons I know about, a Moscow, a coupla Berlins, two Dublins, six Manchesters and about eleven Chesters. Anybody want a smoke?'

Waterhouse thought he could do with one, and Broecker started tossing around not single cigarettes as they'd expected but whole packs, twenty to each man. 'We kinda get a lot,' he explained.

The Americans had no sooner sorted themselves out when Devenish and twenty airmen arrived. With them were thirty naval men under a sub-lieutenant who were greeted at once by Waterhouse's mad screech as they climbed from their lorries.

> 'Never trust a sailor
> An inch above the knee.
> I did, and look what he left me –
> A bastard on my knee!'

The sailors were merely supposed to be guides but they'd noticeably taken the precaution of arming themselves with automatic weapons, while Devenish had brought with him three hundred pounds of plastic explosive, one thousand pounds of gun cotton, a hundred and fifty pounds of ammonal, a hundred and fifty incendiary devices, sixty gun cotton primers and fourteen hundred feet of fuse.

'Thought we'd better bring plenty,' he explained.

They settled in quickly and, despite his cherubic expression and mild eyes, Devenish acquired a quick reputation as the only man ever to disconcert Murdoch.

They were being instructed in the Thomson sub-machine gun, and Murdoch was showing them how to dismantle and reassemble it blindfold when he noticed Devenish playing with a lump of plastic explosive.

'I hope you know how to use that,' he said sharply.

Devenish raised his eyes. 'Oh, yes,' he said. 'Of course. Catch!'

He tossed the plastic pudding at Murdoch who snatched it instinctively out of the air to turn on him with a red and furious face. 'Don't ever do that again, you mad bugger!'

Devenish smiled. 'I always get the chaps tossing it about like that,' he said. 'To get them used to it.'

On the same day that Hockold's additional forces arrived, so did Hochstätter's in Qaba, and he began to feel that things were turning out well after all. Although the balloons and extra searchlights he'd expected had been diverted at the final moment to the desert forces, his pioneers had turned up at last.

He had almost fallen on the officer in command and dragged him to the Boujaffar to ply him with grateful drinks. The officer, who knew nothing of the anxiety existing in Qaba, was only anxious to be shot of him so he could find a billet and get his head down for a decent night's sleep.

'For God's sake, Colonel,' he protested, 'my people must have some rest!'

'Major,' Hochstätter said, 'my men are falling asleep as they work.'

The officer glared at him, his face taut under its mask of dust. Then he recognized the strain in Hochstätter's face, too, and nodded.

Hochstätter turned to Nietzsche as he left. 'Tomorrow you shall have everybody back for defence, Nietzsche! I think we've won!'

Everybody was thinking that they'd got the whole thing buttoned up.

Though the administrative situation was unchanged, General Stumme was warily optimistic. Ritter von Thoma, in command of the panzers, went further. He was certain they had nothing to fear.

On the other side of the line, however, the Eighth Army were bursting out of their skins with the certainty of success. General Montgomery, as full of bounce as ever, had not – and never had had – the slightest doubts about his plan. His Chief of Staff, Freddie de Guingand, even felt sure enough of their administrative organization to take a couple of days off in Alexandria.

As the *Pionier-Lehrbataillon* got down to work with Wutka's men and Hrabak's men and Baldissera's Italians, the old hands at Gott el Scoub began chasing across the desert again with their new arrivals to see if they could beat their best time now that they were hampered by Yanks, sailors and RAF men with explosives. They were all aware that time was going to count.

Hockold knew exactly where he was going to establish Number One Party's strongpoint and which buildings he intended to fortify, while the men who had to destroy the ships or race for the fuel depot felt they knew enough about Qaba now not to make mistakes. Swann's job wasn't difficult either, so long as he didn't get excited and lose his head, while Collier's was a simple two-hundred-yard dash with the wirecutters to where the prisoners were held. Once there, they'd all be knee-deep in escaped men, every one of them itching to bash some German's head in. It just had to be done fast and without hesitation, that was all, and crowded little conferences were held in Hockold's office to iron things out.

'These 47s,' Meinertz the Hussar said. 'I can probably knock the first one out without being seen, but the next one could easily pick me off while I'm doing it. How long have we got?'

Hockold turned to Devenish. 'How long do you need?'

Devenish looked at the naval sub-lieutenant Babington had supplied. 'We think twenty minutes to half an hour.'

Hockold swung back to Meinertz. 'Let's say half an hour and five minutes after we hit.'

'Prisoners?' Amos asked.

'We're not taking any.'

'Wounded?'

'Captain Cadish has organized an American medical party to join us, but anybody who can't be moved easily will have to stay behind.'

Final adjustments were made because it was found that the tallest men weren't always the fastest, and the most perfectly developed weren't always the strongest. Finally, the Three Stooges were switched to Hockold's group because it seemed to consist of all the smallest men in the camp and might well need a little strength. With them went Mr World, complaining loudly about being badly treated, look you. Murdoch ignored his bleats. His party had a long way to go and was the only one which had to be entirely self-supporting, so that it needed plenty of determination, speed and strength. The fastest and the strongest of them all, in fact, was Honorary Airman Second Class Uri Rouat and Murdoch watched in disgust as, loaded with equipment, he ran like a stag.

'It's no' a bloody race,' he said furiously to the RAF sergeant in command of his demolition party.

'You told him to move fast, sir,' the airman said patiently. 'So he moved fast. His English isn't all that good.'

Speed was also in Sergeant Jacka's mind but in a different context. 'You will be watching me for the signal to go,' he told his party. 'Like a moggie with its eye on a bit of herring. And when it comes you will get up them ladders and down that mole like a load of mad dogs was after you. You will give it big licks. You will play it loud and use both hands. If you don't, you won't half catch a cold from me. If you do, you'll find it as easy as eating your dinner. Well, perhaps not as easy as that, but a bloody sight easier than if you hang about like you were trying to decide what to buy mummy for Christmas.'

They became men apart, different even from the men waiting in the desert for the battle to begin. The rehearsals were different, too, because the blanks that had been exploding around them as they ran and climbed and cursed suddenly became alive.

'Duw, man,' Taffy Jones yelped, hopping about like a cat on hot bricks in alarm. 'It is trying to knock us off before we start they are!'

No one was hurt but it was only because they'd learned their lesson quickly and they even began to take a pride in the bangs so that a few dummy graves were dug near the cookhouse.

'Blokes who failed the course,' Cook-Corporal Rogers explained gravely to visitors.

At last even Murdoch seemed pleased with them. 'I'm no' worried about the fighting,' he said. 'I reckon you're bloody-minded enough now to cope with that. The man I'll be watching for is the runner who's away with a message, and feels tired enough to have a smoke before he sets off back; and the feller who grabs the first man to be hit and hurries him to the rear without orders. Remember the words of the song – It's not what you do, it's the way that you do it. Any common or garden mob can do our job if they try; only *you* can do it in the time allotted.'

It was heady stuff and it made them feel supermen; in the warm feeling that even Bunch was a part of things – especially with that awesome war record of his – Tent 7 encouraged him to describe what a real battle was like. They soon wished they hadn't.

'July· 1st, 1916,' he said. 'Opposite Serre, wasn't we, and going in with the pipes squawking round the corner like strangled moggies, and me brisk as a kipper and innocent as half a pint of water. Well, it was going to be a piece of cake, wasn't it? The general said so. Easy as oiling a bike. By three o'clock that afternoon I looked like I'd been dragged out of a knacker's yard, buried and dug up again. You know how many was knocked over that morning? Sixty thousand. All lovely fellers. And two weeks later I was one of 'em meself, with a lump out of me bum as big as your fist and feeling as lost as a bone in the stew. They said the brigadier was that fed up he put his head in the oven and gev himself a gas supper.'

Bunch was no orator, but he so managed to convey that, despite the most careful preparations, things sometimes went wrong, they all suddenly started wondering whether they'd paid sufficient attention to everything they'd been told, whether they'd put their backs into things sufficiently, even whether they had the courage they'd always thought they had.

Sugarwhite, the youngest in the tent, found himself studying the men with whom he was shortly to go to war with a new interest, as though he saw them clearly for the very first time.

Taffy Jones – and it would have troubled Taffy Jones to discover it – had never counted for much with him as a warrior, and as he listened to him going on about his body and his muscles, Sugarwhite wrote him off quickly. Taffy was all empty threats and bombast, and Bradshaw could always quell him with a sentence so that he had to retire, defeated by nothing more than a superior morale.

As he looked at Bradshaw, Sugarwhite smiled. He enjoyed hearing Bradshaw taking the mickey out of Taffy because he sounded so urbane and civilized. Bradshaw was sound, he knew. Come what may, he would do what he was expected to do, perhaps even more.

Ed By was safe, too. He was writing a letter home with a small frown of concentration between his brows. He could hurl heavy objects vast distances without effort and separate whole platoons of fighting men with nothing but his bare hands, but holding a pencil in his great fist and writing a letter was hard work to By. He looked like the Rock of Gibraltar as he sat on his blankets, but he was always gentle and hard to stir to anger. By was sound.

So was Tinner Eva. Taffy contemptuously called him a gipsy
and Belcher, the Cockney, a Five-to-Two – a Jew – but it wasn't
from the Phoenicians or the Romanies that Eva inherited his
dark good looks but from the survivors of the Spaniards who had
fought their great Armada all the way along the Channel from
Lisbon, up the North Sea and round Scotland down to the West
Country. Somewhere inside that dark shadowy character there
was a proud independence that, like Bradshaw's urbane intellect,
had always baffled Taffy Jones. Eva was safe.

So too, was Auchmuty, with his long silences and his love of
loneliness. He had always been one of the few men who had
never minded the emptiness of the desert. Gardner was another
good soldier, a product of industrial South Yorkshire who had
learned through the dark days of the Depression the one thing
that above all was needed of Hockold's group when they got to
Qaba – how to hang on. And Docwra, his eyes as distant as his
native fells, and the aloof, withdrawn Cobbe, bolstered by the
tradition of a regiment that went back to the time of Charles II;
even little Tit Willow, with his willingness and ready smile.

As he reached Waterhouse, an old deep distrust came up in
Sugarwhite that stemmed from that first deadly adenoidal insult
back at No 2 Transit on the night before they'd come to Scouab.
But then he realized that there was also more to Waterhouse
than met the eye. From his first week in uniform, Waterhouse had
spent half his career confined to barracks for one thing or an
other; but, noisy, vulgar and brash, nothing in the world had
ever got him down. Came the Germans, even the four corners of
the world in arms, against him, he wouldn't be dismayed. The
copper-wire hair would only stand up straighter, and the lantern
jaw below the hollow miner's cheeks would merely twist in the
half-witted grin they all knew before some equally half-witted
jingle put the matter in its proper perspective.

Waterhouse was lazy, and far from being the best of soldiers,
but there was something about him that every unit needed.
Waterhouse kept them laughing. He was like the soldier Sugarwhite had heard of in the waste of Dunkirk who, surrounded by
the wreckage of a whole defeated army and threatened by the

German dive bombers, had still raised his voice with a yell of light-hearted defiance: 'You rotten bugger, 'Itler! Just you bloody wait!'

Waterhouse was sound, too, he realized, and suddenly Sugar-white was glad to be a part of them all.

11

Due to the exigencies of the battle which had begun in the Western Desert, the operation had to be put off.

They were ready. All they needed now was the start of the greater battle of which they were a part.

As their training ran to a halt, they became aware of movement across the face of the desert. It had been building up for some time, hardly noticeable at first and largely manifested by the low growl of the RAF high in the sky, heading west against the German artillery and lines of communication. Now, however, lorries began to roll forward past the camp, first in small groups, then bigger ones, then in whole columns, grinding by in the last light of the day so that the dust had settled before dawn when the 'shufti wallahs' might be overhead. Among them were tanks — new Shermans, Matildas and Crusaders; self-propelled artillery made out of Valentines, and the new American Priests; and hundreds and hundreds of 6-pounder anti-tank guns to kill Rommel's armour when it poked its nose out.

The battle was to be different from any previous desert operation and more like the battles of the First World War. It was to be on a grand scale, plain old-fashioned attrition, and the old untidy idea of outflanking movements had been drilled out of the army to be replaced by a faith in a strong frontal breakthrough, a head-on night assault against fixed defences.

For two years the British army had been facing the enemy across this same dusty wasteland, where, mummified by the sun or suffocated by sand, men had died not only of wounds but of loneliness, thirst, starvation and sheer weariness. Now, those who had been at Dunkirk or Norway or Greece or Crete, those war-weary men who'd been chased out of every country almost from the North Pole to the Equator, sensed that this time the Germans were going to do the running for a change.

The evening of 23 October came in quietly and they were all restless as they waited about the camp at Gott el Scouab. That morning they'd been paraded to hear Montgomery's message read out to them by Hockold in his slow, unemotional voice. It was the usual exhortation to do and die, which they'd all heard before, but somehow this time it seemed different.

As the light began to fade and the desert turned silvery, there was a cold wind blowing from the sea to chafe the gritty dust against the skin. A few of the older hands were quiet and thoughtful, thinking of friends who already lay in the desert, beneath crooked crosses jammed into old petrol tins full of sand or sticking out of piles of snake-infested rocks.

Bradshaw was watching Sugarwhite as he clutched a pencil and pad. He was fulfilling an urgent need to write home to the girl next door. She meant nothing to him, never had and never would, but he couldn't go into battle, he felt, without putting his thoughts down for someone.

'How do you feel?' Bradshaw asked him.

'Frightened. It's a big thing, a battle, isn't it?'

'It is a bit.'

'What's it like?'

'As far as I can remember, hot, dusty and uncomfortable.'

'Were *you* frightened?'

'Mostly I was just so tired I only wanted to be allowed to go to sleep.'

It didn't sound too bad and Sugarwhite felt satisfied he'd be able to cope. 'After all, we've been trained for it,' he said. He was trying to convince himself that the likelihood of survival was good when deep down he wasn't so sure. 'We've got a good chance, haven't we? I don't like to think of being killed.'

Bradshaw considered. 'So long as they don't put up memorials to us like they did after the last war, and half-baked intellectual poets don't write all that bilge about "Friend Death" and

"Sweet Death". I'd much rather read poems to sweet life. I've rather enjoyed mine.'

'But your marriage –' Sugarwhite was young enough to imagine that love was eternal, a deep romantic attachment consisting of sitting warm and comfortable at opposite sides of the fireplace, interspersed with frequently recurring periods of tremendous sexual passion where you were lifted to unimaginable heights of ecstasy. 'Will you take her back?'

'Shouldn't think so.' Bradshaw sounded terribly casual. 'I think next time I'll just look round for some warm-hearted child and live with her till I'm sure.'

For Sugarwhite, to whom love, even if not sex, was always legal and honest, it was hard to accept.

As zero hour drew nearer and the sky darkened, they noticed that the desert was growing quieter. Despite the vastness, there were always small sounds somewhere – an unseen lorry's gears grinding in the distance, the faint growl of a tank, the stutter of a machine gun or the thud of a far-off anti-tank weapon – but now even these small familiar noises were disappearing.

It left them with an uneasy feeling of half-formed anxiety that things might go wrong, that the battle might be lost, that it all might turn out like the last one, so they'd have to run back way beyond their own start line or even to India, that the bloody war might go on for ever and ever till they were all old men.

'It winnae be that easy,' Keely said, his dark Scots-Irish face worried. 'There innae ony flies on Jerry.'

'He is lying doggo just, to let us know he knows,' Taffy Jones agreed uneasily.

With the rising of the moon Tenth Corps, which was to support Thirtieth Corps in punching the hole in the German line, began to move up to its start line, and an endless stream of vehicles began to rumble by. The coating of dust on the faces of the men inside and the impassive expressions they wore made them look as if they were wearing masks. Then, as the moon climbed higher into the sky – bloated and florid – all movement stopped and they experienced the strange sensation of the whole desert holding its breath. In the distance they could hear the drone of aircraft over the enemy's forward positions, but over many hundreds of miles there was unbroken silence as though they hung in space. It was an illusion. The desert contained thousands of men, all within a short distance of each other, all armed to the teeth. They had been there all day, lying in holes in the ground, roasted by the sun and tormented by the flies, forbidden to move for any purpose whatsoever. Only as the sun had disappeared in its crimson fury behind the German lines had they climbed out, and now, with the stars like a million lamps in the sky, they were forming up with creaking equipment in sections and platoons and companies, and beginning to look at their watches.

The moon was high now, serene, illuminating the desert with a blue light. In the artillery gun pits, the order 'Take Post' had been given. The weapons were loaded and the layers had set their drift scales and range readers to the charge settings. The shells had been rammed home. Only an occasional Very light or a burst of fire from a light weapon broke the stillness. Outside Tent 7 they began to look at their watches.

'Nothing can stop it now,' Bradshaw said in a flat voice. 'The guns are placed, the tanks ready, even the empty beds in the hospitals back in the Delta.'

Taffy looked at him. 'You have got the wind up, Oxshott, man?' For a moment he was hoping in his misery that he had found someone with whom he could share his fears.

Bradshaw shook his head. 'Oh, God, no,' he said, unaware of Taffy's torment. 'I'm as bloodthirsty as the next man. It's just the thought that any moment now several thousand lives are going to be cut off – just like that.' He snapped his fingers. 'Quite deliberately. Ours and theirs.'

There was another silence. Sergeant Bunch, who could remember the big attacks of the First War, recalled how quiet it had been at Cambrai before zero hour. To Hockold, waiting in a forward gun position in the white moonlight, the silence came almost as a shock. Not a gun nor a rifle fired. The seconds ticked on. He had never heard such a silence before.

'It's too bloody still,' an officer nearby said uneasily. 'It'll give the game away.'

A battery commander further back had obviously had the same thought and there was a series of sharp staccato cracks and the rush and whirr of shells going over.

'Six-pounders,' someone said. 'That'll make 'em think. Solid shot bouncing around in their trenches.'

At Gott el Scouab the minutes continued to tick by. They looked at their watches again.

'Now,' Docwra said.

'No.' Taffy shook his head. 'A bit longer, look you.'

He had just worked out the time and raised his head to inform them when the whole sky turned pink. For a moment the silence held, then the noise of the guns hit them in a solid wall of sound that shook the desert and split the sky in two.

It hadn't the volcanic horror of the First War barrages, but there was a clamorous quality about it that they knew they would never forget, a strange assurance, a certainty that was irresistible, and they stood with their mouths open, entranced by the spectacle, their ears assailed by the violence, their minds awed by the racket and by the incredible confidence that seemed inherent in the din. To north and south the flickering lightning flashes played, fluttering round them, it seemed, like huge moths.

'Over a thousand guns, man,' Taffy said exultantly. 'All calibres. One every twelve yards.'

As nearby batteries he hadn't even suspected crashed out, Hockold flinched, watching the whole front sparkling with light. The night was seared with flame, convulsing the horizon with a ceaseless glare. Then he heard the clear-cut nonchalant bark of a German 88 in the maelstrom of sound, and saw the metallic spitting of machine-gun fire. There seemed to be little reaction from the Germans, just an occasional explosion as though an odd gun had got off a single round before it had been obliterated, and by now whole squadrons of aeroplanes were going over so that the sky was resonant with throbbing. The din was heartening and Hockold listened with a thumping heart.

A deep glow on the horizon marked the end of an Axis gun

position, then there was a pause as the artillery switched targets
and he knew that the infantry had begun to move forward. In
the distance he could see the periodic bursts of a Bofors marking
the line of advance with tracer shell, and the beams of searchlights directed towards the sky as beacons, then somewhere in the
darkness a voice called out. 'Charge Two! Zero-three degrees
two-oh minutes! Four-eight-oh-oh! Fire by order, five rounds
gunfire! B troop, fire!'

As the battery crashed out, he saw waiting officers and orderlies
trying to shelter from the concussion, then he heard the thin wail
of bagpipes and saw line upon line of steel-helmeted figures in
shorts and shirts moving up, their rifles at the high port, the moon
glinting on their bayonets, and heard the chafing clink of tanks
lurching warily forward.

As the bitter pre-dawn wind faded and the sun came up the
next morning, the blue of the western horizon was blurred by
smoke and dust and there was a strange reek of cordite in the
air. When Hockold appeared by car in a cloud of dust, Murdoch
was standing in the doorway of the signals tent, and he could
hear the radio bleeping. 'They reckon the Jocks have gained all
their objectives and there's no sign of a counter-attack,' he said.

As he spoke, the guns, which had slackened during the night,
started up again with sharp salvoes. Groups of British bombers
escorted by fighters were sailing overhead and a few dog-fights
started away in the distance beyond the German lines, with
occasional rattles of firing and the long deepening drones of
diving aircraft. The desert, which had been empty for so much
of their stay at Gott el Scouab, was filled with vehicles now. There
were more batches moving up behind them so that the route past
the camp, normally gritty gravel, was powdered by the moving
wheels to a substance as soft and fine as dry cement which lifted
about the streams of vehicles in great man-made clouds.

Everywhere you looked the desert was crammed with human-
ity. Convoy after convoy rumbling past with whining tyres, sand-
coloured and drab. Lumbering armour, making a tremendous
din with their engines and tracks, their guns jerking and lifting,

their antennae whipping as they lurched over the jolts. And battery upon battery of guns, light and heavy, rolling past on portees or towed by lorries; all served by men in the areas behind, who pulled out piles of shining shells from beneath their draping of camouflage netting.

That night Hockold held his last conferences with Babington and the RAF. Then, back at Gott el Scouab, he called the officers together and went over the whole thing once more.

'Warehouse party,' he warned. 'Avoid the alleys. There are dozens leading into Wogtown and all you'll do is get lost. And if anybody's in doubt who's opposite, shout for the password. It's "War Weapons Week, Weymouth". The Italians don't have a W in their alphabet and Germans pronounce it as a V, so neither of them should be able to imitate it.'

The last day was tense. As the sun rose a few men appeared and shaved; then, as the morning advanced, the tent walls were rolled up and the interiors cleared of the rubbish turned out of pockets the night before. Kits were stacked and the piles marked. There was a spate of letter-writing, and a few torn sheets of paper and discarded photographs fluttered about. Automatically they arranged bedding but there was no inspection. A few chores were performed and after breakfast they lay in the shade of the tents, reading, smoking, sipping water from the chattees and gazing towards the west where the rumble of battle continued.

'I wouldn't mind a swim,' Sugarwhite said.

'You'll p'r'aps get all the swibbig you wadt toborrow night,' Waterhouse bawled.

The day was a Sunday and, to everybody's disgust, Bunch came down on the tents like an avenging angel to drive them out to a church parade.

' 'Oo wadts to go to church?' Waterhouse yelled. 'Kneelig down there grousig to some bloke you cand't see.'

But Bunch, as usual, was way ahead of them when it came to tactics. 'God'll like you better for it,' he announced. 'And where you're going it might be a good idea to 'ave 'Im on your side.'

At midday, Murdoch got them round him for his last pep talk. 'No bunching,' he urged. 'No rushing. Just keep y'r heads and don't do anything blindly. Don't shoot unless you have to. It'll only draw attention to where you are.'

They were only small points but it was good to hear them, and made them realize that Murdoch had thought of everything and left nothing to chance.

He glanced at his notebook, not because he didn't know what followed, but to give them time to absorb the things he'd already told them. Then he went on again in his quiet, steady, unemotional voice, as if he were announcing plans to take a troop of Boy Scouts on a camping holiday. 'If you have to send a message, use a proper form, no' a scruffy bit of paper. And just make sure you're no' in need of a pee when you land. We cannae have everybody stopping for that just when he's needed.'

Hockold stood behind him, listening, envious that somehow in his own murderous way Murdoch had done what he himself could never do, and had captured the imagination of the men around him. With his own limitations of personality, and with time short so that the preparations and the demands he had had to make had kept him away from contact with them, it had always been Murdoch's personality which had impressed them most. Perhaps, he thought calmly, it was as well; and right that his own share in Cut-Price was to be no more than taking the brunt of the German counter-attacks so that the other parties were free to do their jobs. Only the night before he had experienced another of the unnerving blank spots when he could see nothing but the sprawled body among the wreckage, clawing at its wounded head.

Beyond the camp there was still the grind and rattle of tanks moving, and the low sustained roar of lorry engines as they headed westwards. There was little information on the general situation, but someone brought the news that the Germans were resisting strongly and that the Greeks had caught a nasty packet in a feint down by Hemeimet.

'Wops, see.' Taffy, of course, knew the reason why. 'They cannot fight.'

'Modern war being what it is, however,' Bradshaw pointed

out cheerfully, 'those who aren't naturally heroic are sometimes obliged to become so, while those who are likely to thrill to the sound of the charge are all too often left guarding the bogs. You can't always pick your spot.'

A little later the word was that the Free French had caught a packet too. Nobody knew how such news got around the desert but it always did and no one doubted that it was true.

Sugarwhite looked anxious. 'I hope this one doesn't end up like all the others,' he said.

'It wod't,' Waterhouse reassured him. 'Not this time.'

'Suppose we win it, boy?' Taffy was doing a big planning job for the future. 'What will you do with the peace? What will be the first thing you will do when it is all over and we can all go home.'

Waterhouse looked at him with contempt. 'You know the adswer to that as well as I do: Go upstairs with the girl friend. And then take me pack off.'

Somebody noticed that Sidi-Bot-Om, old Mo-for-Mohammed, was reading an Everyman edition of the Koran.

'What's that, Sarge?' Belcher asked.

'It's a bit like Kipling, son,' Sidebottom said gravely. 'Only more holy.'

Even Bunch found himself suddenly popular with nervous youngsters who hoped that from his vast store of knowledge he could produce something reassuring. 'J'ever see a cavalry charge?' he said. 'I did. Last there was. On the Somme. Ten minutes later they was all lying dead.'

'The men, Sarge?'

Bunch's dim honest face stirred. 'Oh, yes,' he said. 'They was killed too.'

They brewed tea, making it in cans in the old desert way, independent of Cook-Corporal Rogers. A few names came in of men of their old units who were said to have been wounded or killed. Once more, nobody knew where they came from but nobody doubted. As the sun began to sink they saw a Boston in the distance hit by anti-aircraft fire and explode, to fall in a thousand fragments away from the rest of the formation as it forged steadily on. A few lorries came back, some of them damaged, some of them containing damaged equipment for repair, some of them damaged men. The sight made them realize that the noise and smoke ahead were not mere histrionics, but the sound and fury of battle.

The day dragged. The lorries continued to pass them going east, and it suddenly occurred to Fidge that he ought to get aboard one, because then he could be in the back areas before anyone missed him.

The sun grew hotter. They tried not to talk about the battle. Belcher got a game of crown and anchor going and everyone seemed willing to lose everything he possessed, as though hoarding money were a temptation to Fate. Sugarwhite tried to finish his letter to the girl next door. Baragwanath Eva cleaned his rifle for the thousandth time, his face placid as though he were looking forward to what lay ahead. Jones the Great Warrior, trying to hide the unease that was filling his mind to bursting point, told them yet again how he was going to win the war. Bradshaw read.

Then, just when they were all beginning to think about preparing themselves for the evening move, a staff car came tearing into the camp, bursting like a bullet out of the streams of traffic grinding past. A moment later, Sotheby was seen running to Hockold's tent.

A few curious men managed to see the officers arguing inside the headquarters hut. Then the staff officer came out, and as his car swung out of camp, Hockold called for the old Humber brake he used. He climbed into it and drove away, his face angry, heading after the staff car.

Almost immediately the news flashed round the camp like wildfire.

It was off!

Operation Cut-Price had been cancelled!

Part 2

THE RAID

1

With the operations west of El Alamein changing direction, a new date was set so as to support Operation Supercharge.

There was considerable activity round Montgomery's tactical headquarters when Hockold arrived. Up ahead he could see the horizon clouded with smoke and dust and the moon yellowed by the millions of gritty particles hanging in the air.

A young major met him. 'We're keeping the gnats out of the flan,' he said, 'though we're behind schedule here and there. Thirteenth Corps seems to be held up in the south, but the Old Man's as cool as cucumber. Went to bed at his usual time last night and slept like a baby, I'm told.'

De Guingand was busy but far from flustered. 'Hello, Hockold,' he said. 'Sorry we had to hold you. You'd better come along and see the general.'

Montgomery was sitting on a stool, examining a map fastened to the side of a lorry. He seemed quite unmoved by the thump of ack-ack guns, and the occasional vicious whistle and crump of a nearby bomb. 'Ah, Hockold,' he said. 'Sorry about your show. We're just making a few adjustments, that's all.'

'Then we're still going, sir?'

Montgomery rose. 'Are you ready?'

'We can go any time, sir.'

'Excellent. Excellent. Then you shall.' Montgomery gestured at the map. 'Everything's going very well. Excellent progress. The situation round the Miteirya Ridge's a bit congested but we're breaking clear. 10th Armoured's two thousand yards west of the minefield area and in touch with 1st Armoured, and the

New Zealanders and 8th Armoured are through too. All very encouraging. Most encouraging. But the enemy's waking up now.' He jabbed a finger at the map. 'There's some heavy fighting just here and it's becoming a little expensive, so we're going to switch directions. I'm going to use wet hen tactics and get the German reserves rushing backwards and forwards trying to find out where we are. They'll start hitting back properly tomorrow. I'd like you to put your men in some time after that. Don't change your arrangements. You'll be warned when to go.'

'Very good, sir. What do I tell my people?'

Montgomery, who had turned away, stopped, paused, then looked round. 'You don't,' he said. 'As far as they're concerned, it's *off*.'

'Off?' Fidge whined. 'For Chroist's sake! After Oi slogged oop and down that bloody desert till Oi bloody near dropped?'

It had taken some doing to screw themselves to the pitch of battle readiness, and in their highly charged emotional state the let-down left them bewildered and slightly sick. Morale drooped at once, and to show their disapproval someone wrote 'Balls to Montgomery' on the walls of the latrines alongside 'Joe for King', the bawdy verses, and 'A merry Christmas to all our readers'.

With the sky the colour of dirty pewter, Gott el Scouab was in a sullen mood and there was a great deal of angry muttering. There were a few, however, who sent up a silent prayer of gratitude and relief. Some, uncertain all along of their courage, managed a thankful quip as though they didn't care – 'Those Jerries don't know how lucky they are!' Others like Fidge made no bones about their attitude. 'Oi'm no 'ero,' he said. 'Oi just do what Oi'm towld. That's moi mottow.'

And one or two, their hearts still thumping in their chests and thankful above everything for their deliverance, were unwise enough to raise their voices in feigned fury.

'I am fed up, I am,' Taffy Jones announced loudly. 'I think I will transfer to the Tank Corps, look you, and have done.'

'Gerroff, you'd die of fright,' Waterhouse said.

'No, man! You can go for the Jerries in the Tank Corps. Like the charge of the Light Brigade. I'd have liked to have been in that.' The heady relief that had swept over Taffy was making him over-ebullient. 'Or else, perhaps, I will change to the sappers. Lifting mines. Or to the air force and become a rear gunner.'

Waterhouse glared, but nobody made any further comment because they were all used to Taffy shooting off his mouth. But then, unexpectedly, Baragwanath Eva spoke, his dark face twisted with contempt.

'You'm a bloody liar,' he said slowly and deliberately.

Taffy turned, startled, and for a long moment the tent was absolutely silent. Bradshaw glanced at Sugarwhite and laid down his book, placing it carefully on the blanket alongside him.

Eva gestured. 'You'm the biggest bloody liar I ever yurr,' he said, spacing his words to add point. 'You'm always talking like that but there's a yeller streak a mile wide runnin' straight through the middle of 'ee.'

Taffy had stopped dead, shocked, then, because he knew – as they all knew – that Eva was right, he returned to the fray explosively and without much thought.

'And you,' he said in his high indignant voice, 'you are a bloody dirty, scruffy, thieving gipsy, look you!'

Sitting with their mouths agape at the sudden hot hatred that was in the tent, they were all taken by surprise as Eva dived for his bayonet. All except Bradshaw, who leapt after him so that the two of them sprawled on the ground, fighting for possession of the weapon, while Taffy, his jaw dropped, his face suddenly white, stood petrified, his back against the tent pole.

'Lemme go!' Eva grated.

'No, you bloody fool!' Holding him to the ground with his superior weight, Bradshaw flung an order over his shoulder. 'For Christ's sake,' he said. 'Wake up and get that bloody gas-bag outside!'

The words brought them to life. Gardner, Willow and Auchmuty dragged Taffy into the sunshine while Sugarwhite and Waterhouse went to Bradshaw's help and wrenched away the bayonet.

There was a long silence. They'd all been aware of the dislike that existed between Eva and Taffy Jones. It had been building up from the first day they'd been brought together, like two explosive ingredients in close contact with each other, but the violence had still been unexpected. It left them all shocked and Sugarwhite suddenly realized why it was that they all listened to Bradshaw, why Murdoch thought he should be an officer.

He was climbing to his feet now, allowing the Cornishman to sit up. He thrust the bayonet which Sugarwhite handed to him back into the scabbard, and Eva pushed the hair from his eyes and lit a cigarette without saying anything.

After a while Taffy reappeared. He looked uncertain and uneasy as he stuck out his hand.

'Shake, Tinner,' he said.

Eva looked at him contemptuously. ' 'Tes daft you be,' he said.

The matter was dropped, and even forgotten as news came in that there was a hell of a battle working up round a place called Kidney Ridge. Nobody seemed to know where Kidney Ridge was, though, and a story was going round that the staff had had to send out a survey party to find out.

Unable to pass on the truth, Hockold was miserable for his men. Having steeled himself for the battle, he also felt let down, annoyed at having to make the psychological adjustment, yet aware also of a sneaking sense of relief and joy that for a few more days he was to be allowed to live and breathe, and see the sun and the stars.

A film show was hurriedly summoned from base but it turned out to be Gloria Swanson and was so old it broke down nine times and everything appeared to be taking place in a downpour. The next morning there was another, bigger 'Balls to Montgomery' in the latrines and from the tents came the sound of Waterhouse's voice raised in raucous defiance – not just of Montgomery or the Eighth Army, but of Hockold, too, and Murdoch and all the officers and sergeants, King's Regulations, and everybody in authority right down to the man who fought the monkey in the dustbin.

The Raid

'Let cowards scoff ad traitors sneer,
We'll keep the bloody red flag flyig 'ere!'

Only Fidge was satisfied. If they weren't to be flung into battle, he decided, there was no point in bolting towards the rear and he settled back to enjoy the rest.

A few prisoners appeared, marching east, slovenly files of weary men with their arms in splints and field dressings on their faces, covered with dust and blood and wearing their greatcoats like cloaks. Most of them were Italians, disillusioned, undersized men clutching cardboard suitcases and bottles of chianti; the white towels they'd waved in surrender still round their necks. A few were Germans, however, and it made a change to see the master race being put in the bag, arrogant bastards every one of them, singing 'Wir fahren gegen England' at the tops of their voices to show they didn't give a monkey's for the whole of the Eighth Army and certainly not for 97 Commando.

Vehicles and tanks were still moving forward and the whole of the western horizon was a mounting cloud of smoke and dust. The guns were still rattling and muttering, but further away now because the army was moving northwards; news came that when the panzers had switched the direction of their counter-attacks up there they had lost fifty tanks at once. According to the griff, everybody at army headquarters was delighted with the way things were going. But if the generals were happy, 97 Commando wasn't, and being held back at the last moment left them deflated and angry.

In the office, the question that occupied everybody's mind was, should they start training again? Should they risk making the men stale and bored with the whole thing by going over it once more, or should they simply let them rest?

By that evening, Hockold could wait no longer and, climbing into the Humber brake, he went to find out for himself what was expected of them.

Headquarters was throbbing with activity and Montgomery was in conference with his divisional commanders, so that it was

Brigadier Torrance he saw in the flapping gaslit gloom of a marquee.

'When are we going in, sir?' he demanded.

'No idea.' Torrance shrugged.

'Are things going wrong?'

Torrance's eyebrows shot up. 'Good God, no!' he said. 'Anything but. We're a touch behind schedule, that's all. There's a hell of a barney still going on round Kidney Ridge and we've switched 9th Australian Div. up there. We knew it would take a few days, and it is. We've got Jerry in a salient near the coast and we're going to trap him there. Plans are being made for the break-out – code name Supercharge. That's when we'll need you.'

'I can't keep my chaps up to battle pitch for days, sir,' Hockold protested.

'Can't you?' Torrance's reply reminded him how distant headquarters remained, even with the best will in the world, from the men who did the fighting and the dying. 'In that case we'll have to find someone who can.'

When no word came the following day, Hockold was forced to decide that training should start again and they went at it sullenly, not trying very hard because they felt nobody cared and it was just army bull to keep them busy. To be despised was intolerable and a bitter sense of resentment developed. If the Eighth Army wanted to do the whole bloody thing on their own, well, let 'em! The great victory everybody was talking about didn't seem to concern them and they even started to wonder if there would be a victory at all.

Determined not to put his back into things, one man timed a jump badly and broke his ankle. Two more went down with dysentery – 'Can't 'ave 'em stopping to ask the way to the bogs,' Bunch observed – while a huge sand sore on Tit Willow's knee made it obvious that he, too, should be out of the running.

'That thing's not healing,' Hickey, the American doctor Cadish had produced, pointed out. 'I think you'd better go to hospital.'

Nothing changed except that Lieutenant Dysart's corpses had been placed on blocks of ice in the hold of *Umberto*. The crew, being sailors and superstitious, didn't like it much. The sun shone. The flies persisted.

'I found one in me tea yesterday,' Waterhouse said. 'It was as big as a bloody midget. I expected it to adswer me back when I took it out.'

The desert looked as arid, brown and boring as it always had. Headquarters, concerned with the rings and arrows chalked with chinagraph on their situation maps, seemed to have forgotten them entirely; they felt orphaned, despised, unwanted. The whole bloody army was involved, it seemed, except 97 Commando.

With the exception of Fidge, Taffy Jones and one or two more, they were almost suicidal by the evening of the 28th when, with the battle five days old, word came that Cut-Price was on after all, that this time they really were on their way. The news arrived by staff car.

'Supercharge starts in the early hours of November 2nd,' Hockold was told. 'You embark tomorrow. We want you to create as much confusion as possible.'

Hockold drew a deep breath. The words seemed a death sentence. A law of averages existed in the desert and he had occasionally felt that with two slight wounds he had drawn his share of hurt. This time, though, it was different. This time, it was as if warnings had been transmitted to him, loud and clear, to prepare himself for oblivion. He stood stock-still for a moment, seeing once more with a terrifying clarity that tormented image of himself with its bloodied head. Then he drew a deep painful breath and turned slowly to Amos. 'Better let the chaps know,' he said quietly.

There were worried men in Qaba as well by now. With the battle shifting across their front, there was even an element of fear, because they knew better than anyone how important the fuel they were struggling to unload was to Field Marshal Rommel.

They had known fuel was important long before he'd disappeared to Germany for treatment for his liver complaint, but as the four supply ships had crept in, hearts had lifted because, with what was already in the dumps, there was now enough for the panzers to fall on any attack the Eighth Army chose to mount.

But then, for God's sake, after dark on the evening of the 23rd, there'd been one great, white, Godalmighty flash and a roar along the front, and the shells had come down along the whole line. Instead of the Afrika Korps falling on the Eighth Army, the Eighth Army had fallen on the Afrika Korps!

Almost immediately the telephone had rung in Hochstätter's headquarters. Hochstätter answered it and Nietzsche, his head down over the plan of Qaba, heard his irritation.

'Of course we're ready! Do you think we're blind and deaf and stupid?'

The following day, the 24th, the first wounded had started to find their way back from the front. The guns hadn't stopped for a minute and it was said now that whole squadrons of British tanks were getting through, charging like horsemen with pennants flying and guns going, and that the line had been overrun, with the British infantry bursting through the minefields, indifferent to their casualties.

The explanation came in the evening: General Stumme had been dead since early morning when his car had run into British fire while out on reconnaissance. When he had jumped out to scuttle for safety, he had fallen dead of heart failure. His place had been taken by von Thoma, a lean, scarred, experienced old warrior who, thank God, claimed to be satisfied with the situation.

Then, on the 25th, to everybody's joy Rommel himself came back and that evening he actually appeared in Qaba in person. Private Bontempelli, sweating by the water's edge, saw him step from the small dusty car that was taking him to his forward headquarters; a wiry, energetic man holding his arms straight down at his sides and standing with his stomach thrust out as he stared at the supply ships and bellowed his rage at Colonel Hochstätter.

'I've been pleading for this for months,' he yelled. 'All the time I've been in Berlin I've been begging for a drop in the ocean that's been going to Russia.'

He wore his motor cyclist's goggles over the high-peaked cap

with the eagle on it, a simple tunic, shorts and yellow boots like
Bontempelli's. When he took off his cap, Bontempelli could see
the white mark against his sunburned face and a vein bulging in
his neck as he shouted.

As he drove from the harbour, Rommel's pug-nosed face was
a great deal more cheerful. 'With these supplies,' he said, 'I think
we can trade the British punch for punch.'

Almost immediately a notice went up signed 'Erwin Rommel,'
cancelling all leave, all days off, all breaks for meals, all sleeping,
even all breathing, and then the panic started. For ten days
Hochstätter had been waiting for instructions, begging again and
again for pioneer companies, for more men to replace the slow-
witted Italians and half-hearted Arabs, for transport, tarpaulins
and drivers – even for his missing balloons and searchlights. No
one had taken the slightest notice but now, at last, clear orders
had been given – by Rommel himself.

To Hochstätter's delight a signal arrived at once to warn him
that a convoy of lorries would appear the following morning to
start moving the petrol, and he called Hrabak and Nietzsche into
his office and offered them a drink before they got down to
organizing their working parties. But as dawn came up over the
desert on the 26th, and they stared towards Mersa Matruh and
Bardia for the first sign of the cloud of dust that would herald
the arrival of the convoy, Tarnow brought in a message to the
effect that the previous day's signal had been cancelled.

A coffee cup went over and crumbs burst from Hrabak's
mouth as he exploded into rage. But while they were still trying
to contact headquarters, he discovered that the lorries had been
diverted by some desperate panzer general to carrying supplies
from the forward dumps to his hard-pressed tanks, and for two
hours Hochstätter and von Steen shouted into telephones demanding help.

'For God's sake,' one officer shouted back, 'we need the
damned lorries here! I can actually see the Tommies from where
I'm standing! Any minute now they'll be driving down the telephone!'

By midday, to everybody's surprise, because they'd been

expecting it for days to fade out as usual, the British attack had been stepped up again, and a nagging worry started. With the faith they'd had in Rommel, they'd expected his mere presence to stem the tide, but there were even rumours now that he'd been killed and that they were burning papers in Fuka and even as far back as Mersa Matruh.

They were still wondering if the lorries would come when Zöhler arrived to snatch away the Grant tank he'd given them, the two Honeys, the tankmen, even the shattered Mark III.

'Is it bad?' Nietzsche asked.

Zöhler pulled a face. 'Erwin's anxious,' he said. 'But he's not contemplating a defeat.'

They were still worried by the news when another signal arrived, snatching away most of the pioneers and every one of their lorries.

'For God's sake,' Hrabak stormed. 'We need them! Is the army being run by zombies?'

2

*The troops, brought to a high degree of skill,
were transported to Alexandria.*

When they learned at Gott el Scouab that they were going after
all, they nearly lifted the roof off the desert.

As Hockold's car was seen leaving the camp, little groups of
men began to drift towards headquarters, all trying to look as
though they were doing a job but every one of them waiting to
catch the first whiff of griff. They were all aware that Erwin's
Boys were having difficulty hanging on and that a final hard
blow now would knock them clean off-balance. His communi-
cations ravaged, the sand drifting over the bodies of his dead,
Erwin was ripe for a big new attack if one could only be mounted
in time. From being brittle and precarious at the beginning, the
situation had strengthened and there was a certainty now that
victory was in the air. The Mark IVs, feared ever since Gazala,
had been smashed to pieces by gunners who, red-eyed with
peering and croaking from the heat and the dust, had not given
an inch.

The air was full of speculation. Huge traffic congestions were
building up to the north as units swung to newly allotted routes
and the armour flowed forward, choking on its own exhaust
fumes.

The dead were laid in their dusty graves, split sandbags
replaced, fresh piles of shining shells built behind the guns, and
as the scrap iron was towed away to give a clear field of fire,
the army prepared itself for the next trial of strength.

As Murdoch appeared with a sheaf of papers in his hand,

Rabbitt began to signal with his arms. 'Fetch 'em out!' he shouted. 'Fetch 'em out!'

Sergeants went down the lines of tents, slapping the slack canvas so that men came running. A few came from the cookhouse and a few from the Naafi, two or three from the latrines, one even from St Martin's-in-the-Sands where he'd been having a quick grumble to God about the way he was being mucked about. They gathered round Murdoch, eager, curious, their sullenness gone, Rabbitt pushing them into a half-circle.

Murdoch stepped forward. 'Listen carefully,' he said. 'We're on our way. There's a big new attack going in any moment now and we're to arrive on Jerry's back doorstep just in time to throw him off-balance. We leave tomorrow at the original time.'

Taffy Jones heard him in an agony of apprehension, his frantic mind trying to cope with the question of whether he'd be alive or dead when it was all over, whether he'd be whole or maimed for the rest of his days, blind, mad, or fated to spend the rest of his life on his back.

That evening, because they found they had time on their hands, there was an impromptu concert. It started with someone dragging out his mouth organ and playing all the songs that Vera Lynn and Anne Shelton sang to make homesick swaddies even more homesick and from these, it was only one step to 'When This Blooming War Is Over', the old complaint that was as timeless as Corporal Nym and Ancient Pistol – probably even By-the-Christ Bunch. Then Caruso Jones, who had made a bob or two in the past singing in pubs and clubs, announced that he was going to give them 'Ave Maria'. His thoughts were rushing about in his mind like demented mice and he had to do something to stop them; being a Welshman, singing was the first thing that occurred to him.

'In its original Italian,' he explained.

'I thought the original was Latin,' Bradshaw said.

'Oh, is it, bach?' Jones stared at him, for once unwilling to take up the cudgels. 'Well, it makes no difference, see. I was going to make it up as I went along.'

Waterhouse, who possessed a tenor that was high enough to crack glasses, tried to get in with a few musical comedy favourites, but when he started on 'The Desert Song', he got no further than '. . . sad kissig a boodlit sky . . .' when a great howl of derision stopped him dead and he had to change to the infamous ballad everybody knew about King Farouk and his queen.

> 'Quais ketir, King Farouk,
> Let the swaddies have a look . . .'

The Welsh sang 'Sospan Bach', as they always did, as if they were all professionals and had been rehearsing it for months. And as a grand finale, Auchmuty produced a set of pipes from somewhere and gave them a selection that set their blood stirring, whether they came from Inverness or Cardiff or even Bognor Regis.

As they went to their tents, the air seemed to be charged with emotion, a sense of loneliness but of grim determination too. Beyond the horizon men were dying to bring the war in Africa to an end, and in most of them there was a clear willingness to be part of it. They were all sick of the war. The whole world was sick of the war and anything that would bring its end nearer was worth chancing your arm for.

The next day they rose at leisure, sluggishly, like drugged bees. Nobody was talking much; they'd done all their talking long since. They put their kits and equipment together quietly, while worried officers checked their lists, and harassed sergeants made sure everybody had what he ought to have. The guns were still rumbling in the distance and they were all a little subdued and preoccupied.

At midday Hockold went over the whole thing with them again, hoping to God he wasn't boring them. But their faces were tense and earnest and they appeared to be taking it all in. By this time they were all dead serious. Leg-pulling had stopped, comments were sober, and he tried to match their mood.

Unable to hold back his enthusiasm, Cook-Corporal Rogers had given them bacon and eggs for breakfast, though the bacon was tinned and the eggs were Egyptian and no bigger than marbles. At lunchtime he went mad with stew and ginger pud with gyppo, so that they were all in a good mood, laughing and eating at the tops of their voices. During the afternoon they lay and smoked and talked, listening to the rumble in the west. Then, because of the possibility of infection, they changed into clean shirts, socks and underwear; and, to make the dressing of face wounds easier, shaved carefully.

'Anybody got a spare blade?' Bradshaw asked.

Sugarwhite fished in his pack. A strange affinity had grown up between them, because Sugarwhite considered Bradshaw the most experienced and educated man he'd ever met and because Bradshaw needed Sugarwhite's innocence to combat his own cynicism.

' 'E's going to castrate Taffy,' Waterhouse said. 'So 'e can't go out stoating no more.' He grinned up at the Welshman, aware like all of them that his bluff had been called at last. 'There must be birds all the way from Lad's Edd to Johd o' Groats, weeping and wailing and gnashing their teeth because you've sent 'em 'urtling down the slippery slope.'

Fidge was still anxiously watching the horizon for lorries heading east, but there were no lorries in sight at all now and he began to admit to himself that he'd left it too late. 'Do yow think the battle's owver?' he asked.

'No,' Belcher said. 'They're keeping it goin' till you get there.'

Fidge glared. 'Oi down't think that's foony,' he growled.

Then someone noticed that Sidi-Bot-Om was busier than usual over his Koran and, with a feeling that even if he were put on a charge it couldn't hurt much more than where he was going, Waterhouse dared to pull his leg.

'Must be a bit of all right being a Bohammedad, Sarge,' he said. 'All them wives.'

'Polygamy's largely a myth, son,' Sidebottom answered quietly, his crazy eyes not blinking. 'Not pukka. Designed to discredit the Faith.'

'Wouldn't mind that part all the same. All them birds. You 'eard that one about the 'arem?'

And Waterhouse began to recite at the top of his voice, as he did everything else, even eating and sleeping.

'It was Christbas day in the 'arem,
The euduchs were stood by the walls,
When in strode the bold bad sultan
And gazed at 'is marble 'alls.
"What would you like for Christbas, boys," 'e yelled,
Ad the euduchs answered "Balls".'

When the whistles went and the lorries began to arrive, they collected in groups, dressed with as much care as debutantes at their first parties, Waterhouse as outrageous, uproarious and cheerfully indifferent as ever to the solemnity of the occasion.

'I feel as done up as a bowl of rabbit stew,' he said.

'All dressed up, look you –' Taffy bared his teeth in a grimace ' – and nowhere to go.'

They gathered under their officers and NCOs. Khaki drill trousers and battledress blouses, Hockold had told them, with headgear of their own choice, but Murdoch had ignored orders and dressed himself in his kilt.

'In full fig,' Bradshaw said as he hitched his webbing on to his shoulders. 'The men of Waterloo and Inkerman. When the last strap is in place and the last buckle tightened, eyeballs will not protrude more than one and a half inches from the head.'

He watched Taffy fastening his buckles with unsteady fingers, aware with his shrewd intellect how he felt. His voice became gentle. 'And the Man of Harlech himself,' he said. 'Contriving as usual to appear the *dernier cri* even in this witches' sabbath we're going to. Cwmru am Byth, Taffy bach. Cwmru am Byth.'

Taffy turned. Bradshaw had always puzzled him but this time he was glad of the friendly tone of his voice. 'Yes,' he said, managing an agonized smile. 'A clean soldier is a good soldier. Cwmru am Byth to you, too, Oxshott.'

When the whistles went Bradshaw saw him sigh as he picked up his Sten gun and he laid a hand on his shoulder. Taffy's head turned and for a moment in his eyes there was no boasting, no sign of self-justification, merely a mute gratitude that Bradshaw

153

had shown this brief sign of comradeship. This was the moment when they had to face themselves and discover whether they were as stout-hearted as other men, and he had a miserable feeling that he wasn't.

As they gathered by the lorries Fidge stared at the vehicles in sour disgust. The transport towards the east he'd been awaiting for so long had arrived at last. But they were the wrong lorries and he wouldn't need to scrounge a lift in them; he was being offered one with the compliments of the Eighth Army.

The breeze coming off the sea was cool as they clambered aboard, the heavily-laden pushed up by their friends. There was a lot of fidgeting with equipment and a lot of nervous coughing. Nobody was saying much and a lot of people seemed to be brooding; even the occasional catcall seemed unfunny and forced.

They were all aboard at last, carefully segregated into their groups, with Devenish's men tucked into the middle with their explosives. The men who'd been running the cookhouse and the canteen and the petrol store and the transport section turned out to see them off, standing silently alongside as the last tailgates were·jammed into place with a clang. Then Murdoch moved to the leading lorry and waved his arm as he climbed aboard, and the convoy rolled out of camp and began to move east.

Bang on time.

3

Embarkation took place after dark, the ships leaving in the early hours of 30 October.

In Cairo the evening was warm, so that Hockold's neck ran and he felt stupidly – unendurably – hot. There was a radio playing somewhere, full of the sentiment that the people at home loved – 'Here's one for Private Dogsbody from his ever-loving wife' – and he wondered if Private Dogsbody out in the desert was asking himself bitterly if it were just to keep him happy while his ever-loving wife slipped into bed with a gunner from the 8th Air Force. The tragedy in North Africa, he felt, was growing stale.

He tried to push his thoughts away. There was no time for the luxury of introspection. He knew he was going to see men die and finally die himself; and since 1940 he'd seen it so often he'd learned to keep his dismay private, a detached thing which could easily be hidden under his normal brusque exterior.

As his thoughts ran on, he realized his glass was empty and he put it down, reluctantly because in his heart of hearts he had no wish to go. Despite his care, it clattered against the table.

'I must be frightened, Kirstie,' he said, trying to make a joke of it.

She followed the pretence and laughed with him, but she had the feeling that he was near the end of his tether, that he'd been living on his nerves too long.

Hockold's smile died. He was certain he was looking at her for the last time and was wondering if he could face death with a measure of dignity as he'd seen so many other men face it.

He looked up to find her eyes on his face. 'Well,' he said briskly. 'This is it. I've got to get moving.'

She nodded. She had said goodbye to so many men in the past eighteen months, there was nothing unusual in the parting. She was showing no excitement or anxiety but inside she was a tumult of unhappiness. Quite by chance in a book she'd been reading in bed the previous night she'd come across a disturbing quotation. 'A tree with a straight trunk is the first to be chopped down,' it had said. 'A well with sweet water is the first to be drawn dry,' and she knew it meant men like Hockold. Not necessarily the most personable or the most handsome, but always the most honest, truthful and steadfast, who had a sense of rightness and, despite their dread, selflessly believed in living by it.

She found difficulty in replying to him. 'Be careful, George,' she managed.

'I'll be back, Kirstie.'

Oh, God, please yes, she prayed. She'd waved off so many men she'd never seen again, it was like having part of herself cut away. Most of them hadn't meant a thing to her; a few had meant a little; one or two like Hockold, for one reason or another, had meant a lot; but it was always the same.

Hockold was hitching at his belt now. She handed him his cap, studying him unhappily. This is an odd pair of boots, she'd decided the first time they'd met, but she'd learned since that behind this lean, dour-faced North Countryman with the beak nose, who didn't always seem to be listening to what she said, whose eyes seemed always to be seeking out infinite distances because he'd lived with them so long, was a much finer man than anyone gave him credit for. She'd heard what people had said of him – 'Poor as a church-mouse,' 'Stiff as a yard-broom,' 'A good lead-horse, no more' – but there was more to him than that; more, very often, than there was to the men who criticized him. Behind that strong resolute face there was a curious Puritan concept of duty which was the key to his character. Standing up in front of men, leading them, telling them what to do, was as unnatural to a man of his modesty as flying. Yet he conceived it to be what he had to do and did it, if without brilliance, at least well.

He was fumbling with his cap. 'So long, Kirstie,' he said.

'So long, George. I'll have a long cold drink waiting for you when you come back.'

He hesitated, frowning and wondering what to say. Then, on an impulse, she kissed him full on the mouth. He smiled and, to her surprise, grabbed her shoulders and kissed her back.

Then he was gone, and she was standing alone, her hands at her sides, staring at the blank door, wondering if she'd meant it or whether it was just another of the unstable excesses of emotion people who stayed behind felt when decent, kind, honourable men went off to the war probably never to return.

Babington was waiting near the dock gates when Hockold arrived.

'Bit of trouble,' he said immediately. 'The skipper of the leading Fairmile's been whipped off to hospital with galloping appendicitis. Seems he's been hanging on for three days in the hope that we'd go but it was just too much today and he had to report sick. They've already operated.'

Hockold's mind was still full of Kirstie and he had to force himself to concentrate. 'Will that cause problems?' he asked.

'Not really. We've just moved 'em round. The skipper of 146 has been briefed what to do. He'll be able to handle it.'

Hockold nodded and Babington went on enthusiastically. 'I have a man with a car to guide your vehicles to the debussing point. Hot soup's laid on in a godown there with bully beef, pickles and a few things like that. They'll be glad of a bite before they go on board.'

The moon was out and by its faint grey light Hockold watched the men falling into groups, every one of them laden like a Christmas tree. There was no talking. They did it quickly and without orders. Then, faintly, Hockold heard Bunch's voice.

'97 Commando, atte-en-shun! Le-eft – turn! By the Christ – !'

Then Hockold knew that this was something Murdoch, Amos, Rabbitt and the sergeants had cooked up between them – a tribute to him or a tribute to the men, it didn't matter which – and as the leading files swung past him, heading towards the water, and he came to attention, every head clicked round.

They were actually enjoying it, Hockold thought, marching with a precision that would have made a chorus line look silly, moving as one man, swinging their free arms to shoulder level, fingers clenched, thumbs flat, hands down at the wrist to make a straight line, really feeling they were someone. The army was a funny institution. Composed chiefly of tough, hard-boiled soldiers not given to emotion, it still had a gift of moving a man and he found himself very close to tears.

There were no lights on in the warehouse where the navy had set up tables with dixies of tea and great iron pots of soup; just one or two hurricane lamps to give a ghostly look to the line of men filing past.

'Keep your voices down, lads,' Rabbitt was saying quietly as he moved among the muttering groups. 'And take your time.'

There was surprisingly little talk. Most of them just ate and drank, and when they'd finished Rabbitt got them into lines. They shuffled to silence and Hockold moved into the centre of the hollow square they'd formed.

'A few last tips,' he said. 'When you arrive, spread out quickly. And keep it quiet. Above all, try to imagine what it's going to be like for the other side. They're not going to realize what's happening until they hear the first bangs. They're going to be scared stiff.'

They stared back at him soberly. He was just like the rest of them, hung about with binoculars, map case and ammunition, with a Sten gun under his arm. He'd said more than once that he expected the officers to do as much of the dirty work as the men.

They were just about to start moving the tanks on board the landing craft when Murdoch appeared, driving Hockold's ancient Humber brake on first.

'Room for one more?' he asked, relaxed and grinning as they'd never seen him before.

The tanks lurched over the ramp, Sergeant Gleeson knocking

a great dent in the brake as he edged his vehicle into place. Then
the men began to file quietly after them and take up their positions alongside – a small sea of packs, weapons, steel helmets and
webbing straps.

Hockold drew Meinertz aside as they pushed past. 'You quite
happy, Meinertz?' he asked.

Meinertz wasn't sure whether to be happy or not. A lot seemed
to depend on him and his crew; and although he'd had him
practising day and night, his gunner still hadn't managed to
hit much. Since, however, the range was likely to be point blank,
he felt they ought to manage. And now was no time, anyway, to
say, No, he wasn't happy – quite the contrary – he didn't want
to die and he was bloody unhappy.

'Yes, sir,' he said, surprised at the calmness of his voice. 'I think
we shall cope.'

One of the American medical orderlies was by the ramp
handing out tablets from a large brown clinical bottle, and Cobbe
bent his head and squinted at the label. 'Avomine,' he said. 'For
seasickness. It's also given to expectant mothers for early morning
sickness.'

Stinking of cigarettes but stone-cold sober, Lieutenant Carter
leaned over the bridge where his crew were beginning to secure
the splinter mats. His sobriety put him in a bad temper and he
was dying for a drink. As the last man found his place, the ramp
was raised and secured and LCT 11 became quiet.

'Let go,' Carter said, and the sound of the engines, murmuring
at the stern ever since they'd arrived, grew in volume as slowly
the ungainly-looking vessel backed off into deep water.

Another engine exploded to life among the launches where
more men were filing aboard, carefully watched by Hockold and
Murdoch and Amos and Rabbitt, to make sure no one got on the
wrong vessel. As the naval launches filled up, the HSLs moved
forward, their exhausts rumbling, their decks crammed with extra
petrol tanks and collapsible dinghies. As they, too, disappeared
into the shadows, *Horambeb* and a naval drifter edged alongside
and the press of men moved forward again, nobody noticing in
the dark that Tit Willow, sore knee and all, was among them.

They were all aboard an hour ahead of schedule and, certain that something must have gone wrong somewhere in the orderliness, Hockold began to move round the little fleet with Amos and Babington in an RAF seaplane tender. As they drew alongside ML 112, Lieutenant Dysart was waiting on the bow.

'An hour to go, Dysart,' Babington said. 'You ready?'

Dysart gestured behind him. Vaguely in the shadows they could see seven dim shapes stretched on the deck. On one of them they could see epaulettes and the gold rings of a lieutenant.

'Be glad to leave, sir,' Dysart said. 'This lot's beginning to pong.'

'Nothing likely to go wrong with the charge?'

'No, sir. All checked and rechecked. Our boat's alongside the bow. All we have to do is pay out the wire and touch the ends.'

'Better synchronize watches. It's 2315 exactly. One hour, forty-five minutes to go. The launch here will take you ashore.'

In *Umberto,* beneath decks that were crowded among the packing cases with gangways and ladders, put aboard at the last minute after dark and not yet properly stowed, the men of 97 Commando were still staring with horror at the space they were to occupy.

'What do you do with your gear?' Sugarwhite asked.

A slightly-built sailor who looked like a schoolboy grabbed his pack and stuffed it on top of a locker.

'We're more crowded than this, mate, in corvettes,' he said.

' 'Ow long 'ave *you* beed in corvettes?' Waterhouse asked.

'Three years.'

'You're not old edough.'

'I'm nineteen.'

'No wonder you're not very big. You 'aven't had room to grow.'

Incredibly, when they sorted themselves out, there was even space to sit down. They began to wander about, awed by their surroundings and a little scared by the difference between the sea and the land. To Taffy Jones, his unease nagging like a nail in his boot, the place looked like a steel tomb and, when a thump somewhere outside clanged against the side, a thin sharp flick of fright touched him and he jumped and stared round, expecting the metal wall to fall in on him under a gush of roaring water. 'Torpedo,' he said loudly.

'Naw,' one of the sailors said. 'They're at it all the time. In case of charioteers.'

Bradshaw caught the look on Taffy's face and knew what it meant. 'Cheer up, Taff,' he said. 'Have a fag. It's only the old blood lust working up in you.'

'Yes.' Taffy almost snatched the cigarette. 'That is what it is, see. The old blood lust.'

A few of the luckier men, or the cleverer ones, got invited to 'sippers' and joined in the matelots' rum ration. The unlucky ones, those who felt seasick even in the bath, began to feel ill already. A few were even treated in the crews' quarters to the incredible sight of an elderly three-striper knitting.

'What is it, mate?' Belcher asked. 'Are we going to hear the patter of tiny feet?'

The three-striper looked up at him with cold contempt. 'It's for me grandchild,' he said.

The thought of being a grandfather and having to fight in a war awed Belcher and he went away, silent.

It was 0025 when Hockold climbed aboard *Umberto* and headed for the ugly bridge, made even uglier with steel plates, splinter mats and sandbags that were still being put in place. Lieutenant-Commander Hardness was waiting for them. He handed round cigarettes.

'Duty free,' he said. 'Don't spare yourselves.'

They lit up and waited, none of them saying much, all of them going over and over in their minds what they were supposed to do.

At 0055, Hardness turned to his first lieutenant. 'Gun ready, Number One?' he asked.

'Ready, sir. Loaded with blank.'

'Good.'

'Three minutes to go,' Sugarwhite said below deck as he bent over his watch.

'Two,' Bradshaw corrected him.

'Two and a half,' a voice said behind them and they turned to see Cook-Corporal Rogers, devoid for once of his dirty white apron, and hung about instead with weapons and packs.

'What are you doing here?' Sugarwhite demanded.

Rogers stared back at him indignantly. 'They'll need someone to brew up, won't they?' he said.

They spent the next two minutes glancing surreptitiously at their watches.

'0059,' Hardness said as he stood on the wing bridge by the wheelhouse. 'Stand by.'

'Stand by, sir,'

Hardness was watching the sweep hand of his watch.

'Fire!'

The gun banged and the flash lit up the ship and the tense faces. Almost immediately there was another bang and a flash on the stern of ML 112 fifty yards away.

'Good shot,' Babington said dryly.

ML 112 was already crackling and banging like a jumping cracker, and ammunition was flying in all directions. Lieutenant Dysart was not a particularly energetic young man but he had ideas.

'Start our own fireworks,' Hardness said, and a few thunder-flashes and flares were set off along the side of the bridge. They were dazzled for a while and deafened by the bangs. Then, hanging over the bows by the anchor cable, the first lieutenant called out his report. 'Up and down, sir!'

At that moment, the RAF tender roared alongside *Umberto*, and a pilot ladder clattered down for Dysart's crew to scramble over the low rail amidships, all wearing steel helmets and armed to the teeth.

'Who the hell's that?' Hardness demanded.

'Dysart and his chaps,' Babington said.

'They're not supposed to be here.'

'No,' Babington said dryly. 'But I thought they might be, all the same. Tell 138 to come alongside and pick 'em up. Dysart might as well be where he can be most use and 138's short of an officer. The rest of 'em can be spread around among the other launches.'

Horambeb and LCT 11, as dark as the coaster, were already pushing their blunt noses through the water to take up their positions behind *Umberto,* followed by the launches which were swinging to form up in pairs astern. ML 112 was blazing merrily now, the ammunition still exploding and the flames sparkling on the water. Then there were a couple of heavier crashes and they saw planking fly through the air and splash into the sea. The stern began to sink. They knew the explosions had not gone unnoticed from the shore. Binoculars would be trained on the spot at first light next day.

The last few flames flickered and died and, as they dragged their eyes away, they realized that *Umberto* was on the move.

'Qaba, here we come,' Babington said.

Operation Cut-Price was under way.

4

Means had been taken to delude the German garrison who were worried by the successes of the Eighth Army which were already becoming apparent.

As the sun crept over the rim of the Mediterranean on 30 October 1942, the dark waters of Alexandria harbour were busy. A destroyer moved whooping towards the west. Freighters waited with the harbour clearance vessels behind the boom, ready to move into captured ports along the coast as soon as the army arrived and the demolition experts had finished their job.

The air was full of the drone of aircraft, and small boats dashed like beetles between the waiting ships. White harbour launches began to appear, green Egyptian flags fluttering from their trim sterns. On board were officials in red fezzes with portfolios under their arms, who tapped their legs with leather-covered canes. From somewhere a plaintive Bedou melody floated over the water.

Near where *Umberto* had been anchored, an Arab felucca had stopped, her forty-foot mast reaching to the sun. On her waist deck, still dripping water, was a grey-painted plywood dinghy marked with white digits, '112'. Its stern was splintered and scarred, and alongside it on the deck were two corpses which had been found inside it. Around the felucca, floating in the sea, were planks and cushions and pieces of wreckage. Then a man standing on the bow pointed and the felucca moved up. A boat-hook jabbed and a putty-coloured horror in naval uniform rolled and turned in the warm water, the face ruined and un-recognizable.

A rope was passed round the corpse's chest and it was hauled on board because there was a reward for British bodies found in the sea. As it flopped on the wooden deck, a thin dark hand moved through the pockets. A few coins vanished at once; then a letter and a soaked wallet were dragged out. The Egyptians stared at each other and as they did so, the man on the bow pointed again. There was another body floating further away.

There were seven altogether and as the felucca delivered its grim cargo ashore, the Royal Navy men who had arrived with a lorry took the name of the owner and told him to report for his reward. As the lorry trundled off, one of the younger members of the felucca's crew set off at a jog-trot for the native quarter. Within half an hour his news was being handed over to an Egyptian girl with a flat overlooking the harbour, who passed it on to a friend with a radio, who transmitted it in turn to those who might be interested in Qaba.

Kirstie McRuer was writing a confidential report, sitting in a typist's chair and banging away at a typewriter with two fingers, when Murray appeared in her office at lunchtime.

'It worked,' he said. 'Bryant's contacts think Jerry's swallowed it hook, line and sinker.'

She looked up but didn't stop typing. 'I'm glad,' she said shortly.

'A lot of it's due to you, Kirstie. You put a great deal of work into this.'

'I wanted to. I was glad to do it.'

Murray looked at her over his spectacles, fishing a little. He was a shrewd man and hadn't failed to notice that Hockold had spent less time with him than he had with his planning officer.

'I rather had to throw you on Hockold's tender mercies,' he tried.

She tapped out another sentence. 'Yes, a bit,' she said.

'Rum sort, Hockold.'

She frowned as she replied. 'I never thought so.'

'Oh!' Murray was intrigued. 'Nice chap, though, really.'

She still kept her eyes on the typewriter but he saw her lips tighten. 'George Hockold's a good man,' she said.

'You've seen a lot of him over the last few days. Even over and above the call of duty.'

'Yes.'

Murray lit a cigarette and allowed a long pause. 'Come to mean anything to you, Kirstie?' he asked abruptly.

She lowered her hands from the typewriter and swung the swivel chair until she was facing him. 'Yes,' she said firmly.

Her eyes were blazing and she spoke with such defiance, as though challenging him to dispute her opinion or question her any further, that he drew in smoke unexpectedly and was glad to turn away coughing. When he recovered, she was picking calmly at the typewriter again.

'Well,' he said, trying to make his peace. 'Good luck to him, Kirstie. I think he'll pull it off. At least *Umberto*'s at sea.'

Not half she wasn't.

There was a small lop running, and it gave the ship an uneasy lurching motion that was sheer hell to the seasick men below.

Because the decks were packed with sailors trying to push the landing ladders and gangways into place and lash them alongside ready for dropping ashore, and men were still screwing steel plates to baulks of timber erected round the bridge and stacking sandbags in appropriate places, there was no room on deck for the troops. Forced to remain below, they fought with their queasy stomachs and clung grimly to the few places where fresh air was available. By common consent, those with stronger insides left them to it and kept out of their way.

With its steel bulkheads, the place looked like a prison, the men grouped chiefly near the ladders because there might be a torpedo and it might be necessary to get out in a hurry. Taped to the bulkheads were roneoed maps of Qaba, but not many looked at them because they knew them off by heart now. Five hundred paces, turn left. Three hundred more and there you were. It was as simple as that because Hockold's knowledge and Murdoch's experience had made it so. A few men muttered to themselves, but most of them were bored and simply talked of wives, children and families. A few smoked, wrestled and indulged in horseplay. A few played cards – the officers bridge, the men poker or rummy. A few of the more experienced slept peacefully. Watching them, Hockold decided that he loved the army. In no other civilized unit did men mean so much to each other.

The men on *Umberto* were the lucky ones. Their ship was at least reasonably stable. Despite the calm sea, the smaller vessels were moving up and down like horses on a roundabout and the soldiers were suffering terribly from sea-sickness so that the smell below decks was already appalling. A stink of petrol, vomit and blocked-up lavatories filled the air, and the crews, knowing it would be their lot to clean it all up when the pongos left, could only regard the whole business with disgust.

Yet they were all glad to be on the way, despite what lay ahead. They were emotionally drained, and the prospect of action was welcomed because it meant an end to doubt. If it had to be done, was the feeling, then let it be done and over with as soon as possible.

One or two had prayed quietly to themselves during the night, but the time had passed slowly because most of them had been too excited to sleep. As dawn had broken, a few had directed uneasy glances at the sea for prowling U-boats, and a few had kept their eyes on the sky for the Luftwaffe. But there were no U-boats and only RAF planes in the sky.

Because he needed to be busy, Taffy Jones was showing off his belt with its collection of regimental badges. 'Seaforth Highlanders, Scots Guards, 17th Lancers, Buffs and Diehards,' he was saying in a curious cracked voice. 'I have got them all, look you.'

The tea and the food came round. It was chiefly bully sandwiches and soup. The smaller vessels had taken theirs aboard the night before and the bread was curling a little at the edges, but they ate it without complaint. At midday, the launches went·in turn alongside *Horambeb*, chugging away on the beam, long enough to receive hot boxes and large Thermos flasks which had been prepared in the galley. Only Cook-Corporal Rogers complained at the tepid stew but during the afternoon, with nothing left to grumble about, he occupied himself with a game of poker.

' 'Tes a nice pot you 'ave there, me dear,' Eva said.

Rogers stared at the money in front of him. 'Won't do me much good if I stop one, will it?' he said.

Eva's face was expressionless. 'You could leave 'un to me,' he suggested.

Rogers seemed to be caught by a sense of foreboding. 'Fair enough, Tinner,' he said. 'It'll be in my wallet in my blouse pocket. Just make sure I've had it first, that's all.'

In the wheelhouse of the landing craft, Carter lounged near the compass, idly watching the card. He was happy. He didn't even have to worry about navigation. Not far below him, Corporal Cobbe was cheering up a group of young soldiers who had suddenly got cold feet. 'Why worry?' he asked. 'We'll either get shot at or we won't. If we don't, that's all right. If we get hit, we'll either die or we won't. If we don't, that's all right. If we do, we shan't be in a position to bloody worry, will we?'

On the bridge of *Umberto*, Hockold sucked at a cold pipe, his thoughts on the job ahead. From time to time, they strayed to Kirstie McRuer and he wondered what it would be like to visit her after the war as she'd suggested. Then he remembered that for him there was to be no after the war, just an empty darkness among the wreckage of Qaba, and he frowned and wrenched his mind back to the present. Alongside him, Babington tried to remember the family he hadn't seen for two years and to his horror found it was growing harder to imagine what the two individuals he'd left as children could look like, now that they were in their teens and growing into adulthood. In the officers' wardroom Captain Watson was busy over a sheet of paper, trying not very successfully to let his wife know what he was feeling.

'Last letter home?' Amos asked.

Watson nodded. 'Trying to give the impression that I'm about to become a hero without suggesting a massacre. Since she'll get it after it's all over, she'll be able to make her own mind up anyway.'

He paused, his mind far away. Sometimes his body ached for his wife. But above all he needed to see her, to know that her face was as it was on the photographs she sent, that her hair was as soft as he recalled, that her eyes were as warm. She was only twenty even now and, because they were to be parted so soon, she'd been voracious on their honeymoon. 'I must have something to remember,' she'd kept saying with a desperate ferocity, and in his heart of hearts he hoped he'd collect a Blighty wound and be sent home. He'd tried often enough in the past but he'd come through two years of being chased up and down the desert without a scratch.

Amos was brooding. 'It makes you wonder who'll inherit the earth after this little scrum's over,' he said.

'Not the meek,' Watson said. 'That's for certain.'

'Office wallahs, file-carriers, pen-pushers and other fly blighters, I expect. They're the ones who'll get the knighthoods and the seats on the boards. I wonder sometimes, in fact, if they really know at home what we're up to out here.'

Watson looked up and grinned. 'Oh, I think so. The British have always been confirmed in their belief that everything bad happens abroad.'

Below them, at the bottom of the ladder, Willow was also clutching a piece of paper. He was nervous and the paper gave him a lot of comfort. Sidebottom, who was prowling about, his mad eyes bright, watched him for a while, seeing him yawn prodigiously and then snap his jaws together, looking faintly sick. 'You all right, son?' he asked.

By this time Willow had decided that he must have been barmy to fight his way into an operation like this when the sore on his knee had offered him a legitimate excuse to stay out. 'I don't feel very brave, Sarge,' he said.

'You never do, son,' Sidebottom said mildly. 'Tired or worried or hungry or alakeefik. But never brave, son, never brave.'

'When was *your* first time, Sarge? 1940?'

'Bit before that, son. North West Frontier, 1930. Up at Razmak. Guarding a conner-dump in the cud.'

'Was it bad, Sarge?'

'Mostly just uncomfortable. It got worse later when the Fakir of Ipi arrived.'

'Were *you* scared the first time?'

'Couldn't stop me knees knocking.' Sidebottom nodded at the piece of paper Willow was clutching. 'What you got there, son?' he asked.

'It's a charm against death, Sarge,' Willow said, faintly shame-faced. 'This old Egyptian sold it me when I first arrived. He was a nice chap. Even his galabiyah was clean.'

'Let's have a look, son. I can read Arabic.' Sidebottom took the proffered paper, glanced at it, and handed it back. 'Inta-quois,' he said. 'Pukka gen. Ought to protect you a lot, lad.'

Willow smiled nervously and tucked the paper in his blouse pocket. 'To protect the heart, Sarge,' he said.

Sidebottom nodded. The paper was an old laundry bill, but, though Sidebottom might have been mad, touched by the sun, tapped by a deolali stick, whatever you liked to call it, he wasn't so bloody silly as to take away Willow's feeling of security.

On LCT 11, Murdoch stood in silence, not bothering even to smoke. He didn't seem to need conversation. He had his two pistols and sniper's rifle with him, but his face was still that of a professor when you couldn't see the deadly glow in his yellow eyes. On ML 138, second in the file on the starboard side of *Umberto*, Swann was still badgering his men. 'Soon be there, chaps,' he said.

'That makes four hundred and seventy-nine times he's said that,' Jacka announced. 'I've counted 'em.'

On HSL 117, second in line on the port side, Sotheby was equally edgy. His stutter always grew worse when he was excited and he was terrified that when the time came to give orders he wouldn't be coherent. He was also frightened, not of being hit, of being wounded, of dying, but of getting in Collier's way, of dropping his Sten gun just when he needed it, of his bootlace breaking, of tripping when they jumped ashore and going flat on his face, of everything in fact *but* getting hurt. In his white-faced tenseness, he looked a born victim.

The Raid

'I wish to Christ he'd go to sleep,' Sergeant Berringer muttered
in disgust.

The battle had now been going on for six days and nights,
and the desert air hummed with an impenetrable jargon of
English, German, Italian, French, Greek, Urdu and Afrikaans.
The flash of the guns was still lighting the horizon, and in
Qaba Hochstätter had decided to make certain that what little
he had to defend the place with was in good working order.
Accompanied by Nietzsche and von Steen he drove round the
town, insisting that everybody redouble their efforts and ordering that a battery of Schlabrendorff's flak guns be turned to the
east in case of an attack from that direction.

They had no sooner got them in position than a colonel from
Flakartillerie HQ arrived to claim them for the desert, together
with Schlabrendorff himself. Hochstätter complained that his
defences were being taken away, but the artillery colonel had
seen the panzers being shattered in the desert and his guns
smashed one by one. To him the issue was simple. If the Tommies
got past his positions, nothing they'd got at Qaba would stop
them. So before Hochstätter and Nietzsche really knew what
was happening, most of the gun positions Wutka had so pains-
takingly built no longer had weapons in them.

'Thank God they left our two 75s,' Hochstätter commented
bitterly.

Stories came in of hundreds of burned-out vehicles scattered
across the desert and of groups of Englishmen holding out
against even the fiercest of the counter-attacks, hanging on like
grim death and doing more damage to the panzers than they
could afford to take. Hochstätter's office was bedlam, with
Hrabak furiously demanding lorries because some officer with
authority from panzer headquarters had snatched more of his
own away from him.

'My men can't carry shells away one under each arm,' he was
storming. 'I've got to have transport!'

Hochstätter was still trying to work out a new scheme, with

half of his men occupied in unloading and the other half in the desert with the commandeered guns, when a *Sanitätskorps* colonel arrived to demand tents.

'We've got no spare tents,' Hochstätter said. 'They've all been taken!'

'I've been told to expect two thousand wounded. Where am I supposed to put them?'

'There's the Mantazeh Palace,' Dr Carell, the medical officer, suggested.

'It's almost a ruin.'

'If the wounded have been in the desert,' Carell said, 'they won't complain.'

Then Captain Veledetti, in charge of the POW compound, asked when they were going to get his prisoners away. They were growing restless, he said, and he suspected they were making wire-cutters.

Through all the panic, the roaring of the guns continued beyond Qaba and the news from the desert became increasingly grim. It seemed the Tommies had broken through near the coast and that though the panzers had been strengthened by new and repaired vehicles, there were still only half the number there had been when the battle had started, while the artillery was being shattered, crazed and exhausted by the sustained pressure from tanks, guns and aircraft.

Yet by the afternoon of the 30th, as Babington's little fleet began to draw near, things in Qaba were actually beginning to look up. Though the pioneer officer had been whipped away to take over a staff job at Fuka, what was left of his pioneers remained and a signal arrived from army headquarters ordering that under no circumstances were the two 75s that Schoeler had acquired to be removed and that the defences were not – repeat not – to be reduced any further.

The tension was further eased by the news that Rommel had decided to pull back towards Fuka. This was brought in by the pioneer officer who reappeared to pick up his kit as he passed through Qaba en route for Bardia where he was hoping to rustle up fresh vehicles for the panzers.

'He's concentrating everything in the north,' he said. 'At Sidi Abd el Rahman so that he can either resist or withdraw.'

It was while they were still feeling a little more confident that Tarnow received a report passed on from Fuka that *Umberto Uno* had escaped from Alexandria.

'Shot her way out of the harbour last night,' he announced. 'Overpowered the guards and turned her gun on the guard-ship. They've been picking up bodies all day.'

'Where is she now?' Hochstätter asked.

'The Luftwaffe's not reported her but they're a bit busy, aren't they? For all I know, she's heading for Sicily.'

'Or here!' Veledetti said excitedly.

As they stared at each other, the elderly commodore who had brought in the four supply ships joined them. 'She's got guns aboard,' he said. 'New 88s, some 76.2s they captured in Russia and some Italian 47s. I saw them loaded.'

Nietzsche smiled. 'We'll hang on to a few of those,' he said. 'It looks as though we're going to be all right, after all.'

By this time, *Andolfo* was almost unloaded and von Steen was trying to organize the means to haul her out so that they could get at *Guglielmotti* and *Cassandra*. He had already spent what seemed like hours on the telephone demanding that the tug which had been taken from Qaba for Bardia three weeks before should be returned immediately, but all he could get in reply was a promise that it would probably leave the following morning.

As it grew dark, sensing that it might be their last chance for a while, Hochstätter sent round a little note inviting them all for drinks at his headquarters.

The party went on longer than anyone had expected, and feeling pleasantly drunk, Wutka moved on to the verandah overlooking the harbour. There were a few dim lights about and men were still moving drums down the mole, so that he could hear the occasional rumble of wheels as handcarts crossed his wooden bridge to the waiting lorries. Above him the moon hung like a squashed yellow orange over the desert and the hill behind the Shariah Jedid was touched with gold. He felt more homesick

than he'd felt for weeks and his soul seemed to reach up to the
motionless stars.

As he held his breath, afraid to break the fragile spell of the
evening, he caught scraps of native chatter from near the mosque – all *Insh' Allah* and *Ou Allah* – and the toneless wailing
of flutes, aggressive but somehow lacking in result; then a sailor
in the barracks opposite playing '*Muss i' denn*', the naval song
of farewell, on a mouth organ. As though it had stirred up a
heart-sick desperation for home, an Italian near the Mantazeh
Palace began to sing. The notes came up to where Wutka stood,
sharp in the still air, clear and sad against the distant rumble of
artillery.

> '*Tutte le sere, sotto quel fanal'*
> *Presso la caserna . . .*'

The words lifted in the sort of crystal clarity only Italian tenors
could manage and other voices began to join in, in German. If
they could have been heard in the desert, they would have been
taken up in English, Afrikaans, French, Polish, Greek, Urdu and
half a dozen other languages, because they were known to every
man in North Africa.

> '*. . . con te, Lili Marlene*
> *Con te, Lili Marlene.*'

There was something in the air. It was something nobody
could define – a sense of unease – and long after Hochstätter's
little get-together finished they hung around headquarters talking. Then the voices in the streets died away and, apart from the
men still working under the shaded lights by the harbour, Qaba
became silent.

At headquarters, the feeling of anxiety returned and Wutka
went out on to the verandah again to stare into the darkness.
The thudding of guns was still coming from the east and he
could see the sky shifting in a fitful flickering of light.

Hrabak appeared alongside him and stared at the sky with
him.

'Thinking of home?' Wutka asked.

'I have no home,' Hrabak said.

Wutka turned to look at him but the supply officer's face was blank.

'Haven't you heard anything?'

'I shan't now.'

They could hear the other voices beyond the black-out curtains, Hochstätter's everlastingly diplomatic; von Steen's high pitched, an old navy voice; Tarnow's harsh and imperious, a Nazi voice; Dr Carell's quiet, persuasive and scholarly; Veledetti's milky with Italian consonants. Then Wutka cocked his head, listening to the sounds from the desert.

'They must be closer,' he said. 'You can hear the tanks.'

For a while they strained their ears and Hrabak frowned. 'That's coming from the sea,' he pointed out.

Wutka turned, his eyes on the stars again, looking for dark shapes. 'Aeroplanes,' he agreed.

They hurried back inside the room to give the warning, and everyone came out on to the verandah. Ibrahimiya airfield was only five miles away but it remained dark and silent and, as they watched, the lights round the harbour went out one by one.

Slowly, without hurry, they went to their positions – von Steen to his office in the naval barracks; Schoeler to his command post in a hut near the 75 on the Ibrahimiya side of the town; Dr Carell to the bunker under the harbour wall where mattresses, running water, disinfectants and bandages were waiting, and his surgical instruments, syringes and morphine were already being laid out. The others remained in Hochstätter's office where they could be called upon at once and could issue orders.

The aeroplane engines seemed louder now and they all found their eyes turning upwards to the ceiling. Tarnow, whose cold face never showed much emotion and who never seemed moved by the possibility of death, swallowed the last of his drink.

'It doesn't seem a very big raid,' he said.

And neither did it. But Private Bontempelli, standing outside his dug-out among his friends, stared unhappily at the sky. He'd been asleep when the alarm had been given, dreaming of Sundays in the fields outside Naples, of girls, bowls, wrestling matches and hunting hares – and of Maddalena Corri's warm lips and soft body in Taranto. Near him the breeze raised the dust from the roadway. That day, knowing that the British weren't far away, the priest had managed to hold a mass, preparing an altar on a slab of marble resting on sandbags and covered with a linen cloth. But it didn't seem to have helped much; the British were still coming.

Baldissera arrived and they saw him moving round the defences with Sergente Barbella.

'More sandbags,' someone observed. 'More digging.'

'We've already dug up the whole of Libya,' Bontempelli said. 'Now we're digging up Egypt.'

In the silence over the town, it was possible from Hochstätter's verandah to hear the voices of the men moving to their positions. For a while Hochstätter stared at the plan of the town attached to the wall of his quarters. It seemed extraordinary that after ten days of hard work, all that was left to him of the weapons he'd been sent were the two French 75s. Still, he thought, with the addition of his original three 47s and a percentage of well-placed light and heavy machine-guns, they were heavy enough to stop any normal landing from the sea.

He glanced at the list prepared for him by Nietzsche and von Steen. With the pioneers and von Steen's sailors and the men he could call on from Wutka and Hrabak, he had 523 men to defend the town. It was surely enough for so small a place.

Had he only known it, by a strange coincidence, and with the assistance of Cook-Corporal Rogers, it was exactly the same number of men as Hockold was proposing to throw ashore.

The ships had long since passed Fuka, well beyond the Eighth Army's farthest forward outposts, and everybody aboard them began to look at his weapons again. The gunners checked their ammunition, and down below the engineers glanced anxiously at the concrete and steel plates erected round the engine rooms to protect them.

There wasn't long to go now. They all knew it and you could have cut the tension with a knife. Cook-Corporal Rogers was still playing cards. Willow was still occasionally fingering the paper in his pocket. Sergeant Berringer was still muttering savagely about Sotheby's nervousness, and Lieutenant Swann was still badgering his men to the point of fury. The one thing nobody was doing was voicing his fears, or wondering aloud what it was like to get the chop, and what death was like, apart from being dark and cold and lonely.

Sidebottom and Jacka were talking quietly in a corner.

'The wogs was all round us,' Sidebottom was saying, 'and they're not bad with their bundooks at three hundred yards. Quiet as mice they was, and all you could see was rocks. Then this shot comes and the officer – pukka chap, called Gavin – he just says "Oh!" Just like that. Nothing else. Just "Oh!" And falls plonk off his horse.'

'Where was that, Sidi?' Jacka asked.

'Loe. Up near the Malakand. In 'Thirty-four. Or was it 'Thirty-three? Buggered if I remember.'

At about that moment someone on LCT 11 noticed that the breeze which had been blowing on their cheeks all day was now blowing into their faces, and they realized they'd changed direction.

'We're going in,' Cobbe said and a few hands started to reach for equipment.

'Leave it alone!' Murdoch was there. Nobody had seen him arrive but he had appeared, as though through the floor like the demon king in a pantomime. 'There's plenty o' time. No need to exhaust yourselves carting heavy equipment about yet. You'll be told when to put it on.'

His voice was oddly soft for a change, all the harshness gone, and he stopped occasionally, as they'd never seen him stop before, to exchange a word here and there, usually with the youngest men, or to offer a cigarette or a match.

Above him, they could hear a faint tuneless song coming from the bridge that sounded a little like the hymn, 'Holy, Holy, Holy'. It was Lieutenant Carter. He was riotously happy. He was doing the thing he was trained for. He had a ship under his feet and he was going into battle. He was also a little drunk because he hadn't been able to resist having a tot to celebrate and then another and another. But he was still capable of doing his work, if only instinctively, and the rum insulated him from fear. He was singing the "Minesweepers' Song" –

'Sweeping, sweeping, sweeping,
Always bloody well sweeping'

The first lieutenant, a boy of twenty, stared at him, worried and wondering if he ought to take over. But he liked Carter, for all his faults, and he knew better than to try anyway.

The talking became desultory and on every ship men merely sat and stood and leaned, smoking, waiting, busy with their own thoughts again. Grisly last-minute preparations for death were made on *Umberto*, and the ship's surgeon in his 'butcher's overall', stethoscope in his pocket and gauze mask dangling under his chin, was laying out an array of instruments and bottles. First-aid dressings were handed round and bundles of them stacked in odd corners about the ship. Carbide lamps were placed alongside electric bulbs, hoses drenched woodwork and splinter matting and the stacks of ammunition by the guns. Over all was the sound and feel of men preparing themselves for action – the creak of webbing and the clink of weapons, the sudden nervous cough hastily suppressed, and the thunderous silences emphasized by the bitter swearing of those fortunate enough to be busy.

A lot of them were introspective now and spoke of all sorts of private things that they wouldn't have dreamed of disclosing to anybody at a different time – talking with unusual candour, drawing closer to one another in the harsh bowels of the ship, confiding in men they'd never spoken to before, about home and the past and what they hoped would be a future.

By the ladder, Bradshaw smoked a cigarette and read, his face dark under his helmet. Docwra was playing softly on a mouth organ as he'd done so often before in the loneliness of the Cumberland fells.

Sugarwhite's thoughts were on his home. 'Think of all those folk back in England worrying about us,' he said.

Waterhouse, who was engaged in a heavy discussion on the delights of the Alexandria waterfront, turned sarcastically, his ginger hair as wild as if it had had an electric current passed through it. 'And thingk of all the bastards who dod't give a sod,' he said.

A few men were swopping smutty jokes and a few more telling of the times they'd had with women. Taffy Jones, desperate to keep his mind off what lay ahead, had just finished explaining how he'd halted the invasion of England in 1940 by joining up, and was now laying it on ad nauseam about a girl he'd had in Cardiff.

'Poor old Arienwen,' he was saying. 'Duw, she was a pretty girl, man. She could play the piano lovely. Used to help at the glee club. But there's a state she was in that night, behind Geary the Emporium's. Begging me for it she was. The moon was out and I could see it shining on her – all white – '

'Ghost-like?'

'No. Not ghost-like. Soft. You know what I was thinking then?'

Tit Willow, bored to tears, lifted his head. 'That you fancied sixpennyworth of fish and chips,' he said.

Sergeant Bunch, who had just appeared, heard him and swung round. 'You was supposed to be in hospital,' he said heavily.

'I didn't want to miss it, Sarge.'

Bunch glared, rigid as a poker. 'You was ordered to hospital, you dozy idle man,' he barked. 'An order's an order and you're supposed to obey it. You're on the fizzer.' Then the hard leathery face, marked by barrack-room brawls and years of acne as a youth, softened alarmingly. 'How's it go, son?' he asked. 'Hurt?'

'A bit, Sarge.'

'Like the parrot said, when it laid square eggs.' Legs stiff, back straight, Bunch stalked off and Willow stared after him, startled, aware that it was Bunch's way of trying to put him at his ease.

Someone started singing, the same song for the hundredth time – 'I don't want to be a soldier. I don't want to go to war . . .' and slowly everybody began to join in softly. Then the Welsh element changed it to a hymn. They seemed to have been singing hymns on and off every bit of the way, Taffy Jones in the lead parts whenever he could check the squirming in his stomach.

'I wish they'd try something more cheerful,' Sugarwhite said. 'Or even just have a fight.'

It was Waterhouse – dogged, irrepressible, profane and riotous – who stopped it.

'Ringg the bell, verger,' he sang in a high pitched nasal falsetto you could have threaded a needle with, 'Ringg the bell, ringg! Till the fuckin' coggregation condescedd to singg . . . !'

Even the Welsh couldn't defeat Waterhouse and in the end they took the hint. But the interruption smacked of blasphemy to Sugarwhite, and now didn't seem to be the time or the place for offending God. 'Think we've got a chance?' he asked.

'I don't give a monkey's either way,' Waterhouse yelled and Sugarwhite looked quickly at him, trying to make out whether he really was unconcerned or only putting on a brave face. Bradshaw was still reading, holding a tiny book in his hand, and Waterhouse removed his helmet and ran a hand through his ginger thatch so that it stood up like an old yard-brush.

'I wish I was like 'im,' he said. 'Standig there as 'appy as a budgie on a kitchen table. What is it you're readig, Bulstrode?'

Bradshaw looked up. 'Omar Khayyam.'

'What's that? A dirt book?'

'It's not an "it". It's a "he". A Persian poet.'

'Cad you read Persian?'

'It's a translation.'

'Why are you readig it?'

'Because it's the smallest book I've got and it goes in my blouse pocket.'

'Is that the only reason?' Sugarwhite asked.

'It's as good as any I can think of.'

'Aren't you worried?'

Bradshaw lifted his head. 'Of course I'm worried, you bloody oaf !'

Sugarwhite was puzzled. 'You don't show it.'

'Well, I *could* smear my emotions all over the bulkheads, but I don't think anybody'd enjoy it, do you?'

Sugarwhite frowned. 'I wonder why we don't?' he said. 'I'm shit-scared really.'

Bradshaw's smile widened. 'That's pride, old son. You're concerned with what your friends might say, and they feel the same because of what *you* might say. That's what makes the army tick. It's what makes all armies tick.'

They were still staring in bewilderment at Bradshaw when Bunch appeared. 'Right-oh, darlings,' he said. 'Time to put your party dresses on.'

As they entered the swept channel in the minefield the talk on the bridge died.

'This is what they call the moment of truth, isn't it?' Hardness said.

Though there was no announcement, the news soon travelled below. A few eyes swept round the ill-lit hold but no one made any comment. Hearts began to beat so hard they hurt the chest and, noticing that his fingers were trembling, Taffy Jones hid them between his thighs as he sat near the ladder. Sweat trickled at his armpits, and the thin slash of fright he'd felt earlier came again, icy against his flesh so that he felt sick. He stared round at the other men, his throat dry, wondering if they could tell he was afraid. They showed no sign of it and he knew that even if they could they'd never judge him.

They were all tense despite their chatter. Only the card players, absorbed in their game, seemed not to have noticed.

'Five bob,' Rogers grunted.

'I'm in,' Eva said.

'Me, too.'

'Your five an' up three.'

'Raise five.'

'I think you'm bluffin', me dear.'

On the RAF launches on the port side of *Umberto*, the collapsible rubber dinghies were being inflated, making even less room for the overcrowded men, while the extra petrol tanks fitted on deck were being emptied to reduce the risk of fire. Someone started handing out burnt cork and tins of dark make-up. It smelled of olive oil and cocoa, with a bit of something extra that seemed like carbon and was probably lamp-black.

'Faces and hands,' Rabbitt said. 'Make sure you're well covered. It might save your life.'

Waterhouse dropped on one knee. 'Mammy!' he began to sing at the top of his voice. It sounded like 'Babby.'

When they were all looking like nigger minstrels, they once more checked their weapons and braced themselves again as they'd braced themselves the night before and on the night of the postponement. Speculation and fear galloped through their minds and they felt cumbrous under their kit.

Faintly they heard telegraphs jangle and felt the shudder of the engines become different so that they knew their speed had changed. Then the tannoy crackled. 'All hands muster at disembarkation stations.'

Bradshaw sighed and put away his book. Near the stern of ML 138 Lieutenant Swann moved his shoulders under his webbing. 'You ready, chaps?'

Nobody answered because they all knew there was no hurry, and it was only Swann getting up his own wick.

'No panic when we get ashore,' Swann continued. 'Just keep together and keep your eyes on me.'

'Any minute now,' Belcher whispered, '''e's goin' to start whizzin' round in ever-decreasin' circles and finally disappear up his own fundamental orifice.'

There was an explosive cackle of laughter and Swann whirled. 'Who's that? Who's that laughing?'

Nobody answered and he calmed down, jerking at his equipment and fingering his moustache.

'Make sure you've got all your equipment,' he nagged again. 'Cigarettes out. No smoking.'

Belcher turned to the dour ex-fisherman, Comrie, as he

stubbed out his fag-end. 'Do you smoke after you've had a bit with your bird?' he asked.

'Ah dinnae ken,' Comrie said with an unexpected flash of wit. 'Ah've never looked.'

There was another cackle of laughter so that Swann looked angrily about him, convinced he'd got a lot of idiots to look after. Nobody seemed to be taking the thing seriously except him.

5

*The first shots were fired at 2347 when the
Germans became aware of our approach.*

There had been several reports of enemy bombers approaching
Qaba, so nobody imagined that the noise they now heard out to
sea had any special significance. Despite the depredations of the
desert force, there was still enough flak at the airfield and on the
outskirts of the town to keep the Tommies high. Fears of a raid
were confirmed, however, when Fighter Control at Ibrahimiya
telephoned them to expect trouble, and the alarm bells began to
ring.

'Achtung! Alarm! Fliegerwarnung!'

The guns began to swing and the soldiers assembled at their
posts, their officers shouting orders. Among them was Private
Bontempelli, holding his rifle by the muzzle, its butt trailing behind him in the dust so that it looked curiously harmless. He was
chiefly concerned that one of the aeroplanes would get off
course and drop one of its bombs not on the airfield where it
belonged but on the spot where he happened to be standing. He
often wished he could be taken prisoner – painlessly, of course.
In fact, he once *had* been a prisoner – in June – but before they
could be put in the bag, the tide had turned again and a whole
crowd of Afrika Korps lorries had swept round the group, taking the British guards prisoners instead and freeing the disgusted
Bontempelli so that he was now back with a gun in his hand and
expected to stand up to a charging Scot or a New Zealander or
an Australian or a Gurkha, or one of the other barbarians the
British employed to fight their wars.

Standing on the roof of the Boujaffar Hotel, Colonel Hochstätter stared at the waning moon. With him were von Steen, Nietzsche, Wutka and Hrabak. Below them were Tarnow and a sergeant, with two telephone orderlies who were waiting by their instruments. Round the harbour area they could see men running, and caught occasional faint flickers as lorries passed with shaded headlamps.

Hochstätter stared at the sky, and wondered again how his wife and two young daughters were faring in far-off Düsseldorf. He hadn't heard from them for months now and it seemed years since he'd seen them. Von Steen's thoughts were on his career. A man with a stiff leg hadn't much future at sea, and in any case, German naval activity at that moment seemed to be dwindling rapidly.

Wutka was watching the stars again and deciding that when the war was over he'd probably take up astronomy. It was a subject he knew nothing about but here in Qaba and in the dusty North African desert the stars had always fascinated him – perhaps because they seemed the only dust-free things he could see. Hrabak's thoughts were much simpler. His old wounds were hurting and all he wanted was to sit down.

The sound of the aircraft became louder and Hochstätter's head turned nervously as the telephone rang on the floor below.

The sergeant put his head through the hatchway to the roof. '*Sie kommen, Herr Oberst!* The Luftwaffe say it looks like a big raid. Radar's picking up hefty signals from the north-east.'

'Warn the gunners,' Nietzsche snapped and the sergeant nodded and disappeared.

There were shouts among the buildings below them and Hochstätter stared at the flickering horizon to the east.

'I'm glad it's the airfield,' he observed.

Von Steen frowned. He had an inexplicable feeling that it *wasn't* the airfield.

The drone of the aircraft grew louder and Hochstätter's head went back.

'Almost overhead,' he said. 'Coming in from the sea.'

The guns were still silent and the searchlights had not yet

opened up, and it wasn't until the first missile came whistling down to explode fifty yards from a parked Junkers 52 that Ibrahimiya finally came to life. As the men started to run, the first of the flares filled the sky with a white eerie light. The guns began to bark and the searchlights snapped on, probing with their silver beams. An aeroplane was caught in the over-spill of light like a small fish and flickering pin-pricks began to sparkle round it. At once it began to take violent avoiding action, the anti-aircraft shells following it as it went into a dive.

Despite the warnings of a heavy raid, the Tommies seemed to be approaching only in ones and twos and small groups from widely dispersed directions. Then a nervous *Flakartillerie* corporal and his men, manning an isolated gun position on the eastern perimeter of the airfield, saw parachutes. They appeared briefly in the glow of the searchlights, then disappeared; then another two or three were seen, then more and more. Hurriedly counting, and adding a few for good measure in his panic, the corporal reached for the telephone.

'*Fallschirmjäger!*' he yelled into the mouthpiece. 'Paratroops!'

The telephone in Hochstätter's office shrilled again, and the sergeant called up to him.

'Sir!'

Hochstätter almost fell down the stairs, and in a moment Nietzsche heard his voice.

'Paratroops? Where?'

'We have them on the airfield,' the Luftwaffe colonel at Ibrahimiya yelled. 'We need every man you can spare!'

Hochstätter also began to shout. 'I have no men to spare! I have instructions from headquarters to maintain a strong hold on this place!'

'Look –' the Luftwaffe colonel's voice was harsh ' – if they land men here, you might as well go out of business!'

Hochstätter put the telephone down and signed wearily to Nietzsche.

'Send them the Italians.'

The Raid

As the few lorries they could muster rolled to a stop near the Roman arch, Private Bontempelli decided that fighting parachutists was something that just didn't appeal to him. He didn't enjoy the thought of being hurt and he hated loud noises. He'd once been in a gun position at Bardia when the gun had fired, and it was as if someone had crammed his head inside an oil drum and tossed in a hand grenade.

He could hear Sottotenente Baldissera and Sergente Barbella shouting now, and on an impulse he turned abruptly into the shadows and headed for the latrines.

From the ships they all heard the drone of aircraft.

'Thank God the RAF's on the dot,' Hockold said, realizing for the first time that since the operation had started he had hardly thought about death. Preoccupation with Cut-Price had driven it from his mind and he forced himself to concentrate on what he had to do so that it would stay that way.

Below him in the hold, Taffy Jones was also trying desperately not to think too much about death and had succeeded in starting a heavy argument, involving everybody near him, on whether you could dodge the army by failing the medical through drinking too much alcohol, eating too little food and having too little sleep.

'When I took my medical,' Bradshaw said blandly, 'the chap next to me couldn't do the necessary when they told us to fill the test tubes. I offered him some of mine. He was pleased to accept.' Bradshaw smiled. 'I considered it a very comradely action.'

As usual it stopped the argument dead, and Taffy was just searching his mind for something else to get them all going again when the first of the RAF's bombs went off on the airfield. As the searchlights snapped on, against their pale glow the men on the bridge could see low-flying cliffs and even the shape of buildings. They could pick out the Mantazeh Palace on the headland and the square outline of what they knew from the mock-up to be German headquarters.

A shaded light winked from *Umberto,* and *Horambeb* closed

up on her port side. On the starboard side, LCT 11 also closed in until she was swinging in the wash from *Umberto*'s bows and the helmsman was having difficulty steering her. On HSL 116, Lieutenant Collier caught the signal too, and signed to the officer in command.

'Time to turn off,' he said, and the HSL began to swing to port, leading the other two RAF launches in a slow curve towards the low cliffs below the prisoner of war compound. ML 146 had led the Fairmiles after the landing craft, the gunners working the breeches of the three-pounders to make sure they were loaded and ready. 'For what we are about to receive,' Lieutenant Dysart said.

The word went round to stand by. Cigarettes were put out and there was a last minute rush to use the latrine buckets. On the bridge of the landing craft, Lieutenant Carter decided that, having got this far without mishap, he might be entitled to another quick snifter and dragged out his hip flask again. On the flimsy launches, lacking armour and heavy weapons, everyone held their breath, all isolated in their own enclosed oases of loneliness, throats dry, stomachs twisted with the gagging feeling of fear. Only Lieutenant Swann was trying to persuade himself that he was looking forward to action.

This was the most highly charged moment of the operation – the fragment of time between the setting in motion of the attack and when the guns began. They sat on their kit, their eyes moving constantly and giving the impression that they were listening intently. Every one of them was gripping something, a bamboo assault ladder, a rifle, a pack, their hands unrelaxed and knotted into heavy fists. They didn't look at their watches because they knew the time only too well and were counting every second.

The tannoy clicked on and eyes lifted to it immediately as though the speaker were there inside the little box where they could hear him breathing.

'This is the naval padre,' the disembodied voice came. 'We are now running in to the coast, and that seems a good reason why we should have a prayer. It's one that Sir Jacob Astley offered

before the Battle of Edgehill and it seems very apt. "Oh, Lord,
Thou knowest how busy I must be this day. If I forget Thee,
do not Thou forget me." Good luck to every one of you.'

That was all and they were grateful that it was no more.

'Are you religious. Oxshott?' Sugarwhite asked.

Bradshaw's head turned. 'Not really. In any case, I'm not all
that sure I'd enjoy Heaven if I went there. It sounds to me a bit
like a non-conformist social evening with no beer and the girls
determined to hang on to what they've got.'

Sugarwhite was silent for a while. 'I wish I was married,' he
said unexpectedly.

Bradshaw turned and stared at him. 'In the name of God,
why?' he asked.

'Oh –' it was hard for Sugarwhite to put his thoughts into
words without feeling embarrassed ' – you know. All that
stuff about Abdul and so on – I've never been with a woman in
my life.'

Bradshaw nodded. 'It's a thing that bothers a lot of men at a
time like this,' he agreed.

As the tannoy had switched off, the main lights had gone out,
leaving only the dim secondary bulbs glowing, and Taffy Jones
was staring up at them with haggard eyes.

'Black-out,' he announced loudly, driven by his mounting
terror to say something. 'Got your carrots?'

On board ML 138, Swann hitched at his straps yet again and
felt his buckles for the thousandth time. 'Stand by, you chaps,'
he said once more. 'And remember, if you give it everything
you've got, it'll be a piece of cake.'

Nobody answered, chiefly because, unlike Lieutenant Swann,
they weren't kidding themselves. Someone in the shadows began
to murmur the Lord's Prayer. When he finished there were one
or two murmurs of 'Amen.'

On the bridge of *Umberto*, Hockold stared ahead with Babington. His face was haggard in the dim light.

'Any minute now,' Babington said.

There was still no sign from the shore.

'Must be watching the fireworks on the airfield,' Babington

commented. 'Let's hope de Berry can keep it up, because those bastards ashore must have spotted us by now.'

They had. Just.

'Herr Oberst! Radar reports ships approaching.'

Hochstätter, Nietzsche and the others tumbled down the steps from the roof to the darkened radar room. The sergeant in charge pointed to the dial and the sweeping arm.

'What have you got?' von Steen asked the operator.

'One medium-sized ship, two smaller ones and several others that are probably motor boats.'

Hochstätter swung round. 'We must have the Italians back,' he said. 'Get hold of Ibrahimiya.'

By this time, Nietzsche's orders were going out to Schoeler in his command post above the POW compound and Wutka's shouts were stopping all the work on the mole. Men reached for equipment and, bawled at by Unteroffizier Upholz, others were running through the streets, strapping on webbing and humping weapons into position. In the compounds, the last rolls of wire were dropped into place.

Hochstätter was yelling down the telephone to the Luftwaffe colonel at Ibrahimiya. 'Send my Italians back! They're coming at us from the sea!'

There was a moment's silence and a little muttering, then the Luftwaffe colonel's voice came again above the din of bursting bombs. 'I gather they haven't arrived yet,' he said.

Hochstätter frowned. The Italians hadn't hurried and they were now in limbo, of use neither to the Luftwaffe nor to him. 'I must have them back as soon as they appear,' he snapped, and slammed down the telephone before turning to Nietzsche. 'Warn all the look-outs,' he said.

'It's done.'

'And advise Veledetti to make sure his prisoners are safe. We don't want any attempts at a break-out.'

Standing in the little concrete bunker near the 47 mm on the end of the mole, Private Alois Jumpke, aged only nineteen and formerly of the Stiffelmayer Battle Group but now attached to the garrison of Qaba as he recovered from a bad dose of dysentery picked up in the desert, stared at the bursting bombs five miles behind the town. As he watched the flickering lights along the horizon, the telephone alongside him made him start with its shrilling.

'Mole,' he reported automatically. '*Alles gut!*'

'We have ships on radar,' the voice in his ear said. 'Keep a sharp look-out.'

Jumpke replaced the telephone. As he swung his glasses across the horizon, he picked up the dark mass of the Abba Sid peninsular, towards Fuka; then he swept across the sea, bored, uncertain and caught by a gnawing unease. But there was nothing on the dark water except the wreck of the German freighter, *Lotte*, which had been hit by bombs three months before and been beached on a sand bank in the bay.

He was about to move the glasses on when he realized that *Lotte* seemed to be growing in size. Then he realized that behind the shadowy shape of the wrecked freighter another ship was coming into view. It looked like a small coaster and he knew it shouldn't be there.

Colonel Hochstätter and the other officers had taken up positions on the verandah overlooking the harbour when Jumpke's message arrived. To their right the 75 near the POW compound and the 47s by the Mantazeh Palace and on the mole began to swing to the east.

They trained their glasses out to sea.

'I have it,' von Steen said. 'It's a coaster by the look of her.'

'Well, they don't set up raids in coasters.'

'It could be *Umberto*,' Hrabak said quickly. 'Coming in, in the dark.'

They turned and stared at him, smiling and relieved, and von Steen turned to the yeoman of signals alongside him.

'Make the challenge.'

On the bridge of *Umberto*, Babington turned to Lieutenant-Commander Hardness.

'Where's that Italian-speaking chap, Fusco?'

'Here, sir.'

'Right, Fusco. Give him "*Umberto*." That's all. Nothing else. And slowly. Badly. As if we're in trouble.'

'Aye aye, sir. "*Umberto*." Badly.'

The lamp clicked. After spelling out the first three letters the signalman sent the erase signal and began again. The word went out once more, slowly, hesitantly.

The lamp in the square building ashore flickered.

'It's the challenge again, sir.'

'Perhaps they're not satisfied.'

'Right,' Babington said, 'let's give 'em a bit of Italian, Fusco. Keep it simple. Remember we're in trouble. Tell them, "Captain and mate dead. Wounded on board. Request permission to enter." And keep it hesitant. Can you do that?'

'Aye aye, sir.'

The lamp flickered again. There was a long pause and the shore remained dark. With every second the ship crept nearer to the land.

'Perhaps they can't read,' Hardness said.

'Or perhaps they're Germans and they've sent for one of the Eyeties to help 'em.'

In fact, that was exactly what they had done.

Tarnow had swung round to the telephone and yelled into it. 'Send Tenente Rizzioni up here. At the double.'

Tenente Rizzioni, one of the few German-speaking Italians on the staff in Qaba, had been outside watching the air raid when the telephone went and it was several minutes before he arrived in Hochstätter's office.

Hochstätter waved his hand. 'We want you to read signals,' he explained. 'There's a ship out here. What's this mean?'

He handed Rizzioni the form with the message the yeoman's mate had written down to the yeoman's call.

Rizzioni stared at it. 'It says, "Captain and first mate dead. Wounded on board. Request permission to enter." '

'Not possible!' Von Steen turned to the yeoman. 'Tell him to anchor outside the harbour.'

'Why not open the boom?' Hochstätter said. 'There's room alongside *Giuseppe Bianchi.* Just.'

'No!' Von Steen turned. 'We shall only have to haul her out again when the tug arrives tomorrow. Let her anchor outside. She'll be safer, anyway, if bombs fall in the harbour.'

'Suppose the raiders come?'

'How do we know *these* aren't raiders?'

'*Umberto?*' Hochstätter smiled, but von Steen wasn't in the mood for humour.

'How do we know it's *Umberto?*' he demanded. 'Make "Who are other ships?" Put it into Italian, Rizzioni.'

They had moved another quarter of a mile by the time von Steen's signal came.

Leading Seaman Fusco turned. 'He wants to know who the other ships are, sir.'

'Tell him, "Escort from Fuka".'

The lamp clattered once more and there was another long pause while they all held their breath. Then the lamp ashore flickered again. Fusco turned to Babington.

'It's the "Proceed", sir. Anchor outside.'

The tension on *Umberto* could be felt now almost as if it were a material thing.

'A few more knots, I think,' Babington said, and Hardness increased *Umberto*'s speed a little, but carefully so that it would not be immediately obvious to the watchers on shore.

'Three-quarters of a mile to go,' Babington said. 'Warn *Horambeb* to stand by.'

The water boat began to creep closer in to *Umberto*, so that it was almost nuzzling her and the water between them was boiling like a mill pond.

Everybody was keeping their fingers crossed now, or more exactly, were clenching their fists and praying. LCT 11 was well in to *Umberto*'s starboard beam so that it was impossible to spot her in the darkness and the Fairmiles were clinging close to the landing craft.

'Soon be there,' Babington said. 'Oh, God, our help in ages past, our hope for years to come, just a little bit further, please!'

The ship was only half a mile from the end of the mole when von Steen came to life.

'Why the devil would they escort *Umberto* from Fuka?' he snapped. 'I'd have thought they'd got enough to do there at the moment with watching their own back door.'

'The army's pulling back to Fuka,' Hrabak pointed out. 'As far as the Rahman track. Perhaps they're clearing the place.'

Von Steen said nothing, still unconvinced, and stared again through his glasses. To his surprise the profile of *Umberto* had altered and it dawned on him her bow was swinging to starboard.

'He's turning,' he said. 'He's heading west of the entrance.' He stared through the glasses again and this time he picked up the shape of the smaller *Horambeb* in front of *Umberto*. Her low profile had kept her hidden in the darkness up to that point.

'What the hell's that?' he snapped. 'It looks like a water boat. It's coming past on the port side.' He lowered his binoculars and spoke over his shoulder. 'I'm not so damned sure that *is* Umberto.'

'Half a mile,' Babington said. 'Keep it up, Hardness. And a few more revs, please.'

Once more the speed increased imperceptibly.

'Right.' Babington turned. 'Yeoman, flash the landing craft to break off.'

The lamp flickered towards the sea and they saw the nose of LCT 11 begin to swing and could pick out the white foam under her blunt bows. The Fairmiles began to close in alongside to take her place.

Down below nobody seemed to be breathing, then Jacka's

voice came through the hatch. 'On deck, gangway party. In your places. Stand by, mole party.'

' 'Ere we go,' Cook-Corporal Rogers said. 'Eyes down for the count. Never mind your 'at. 'Old your ears on.'

' 'Ow long, Sarge?' Waterhouse asked Jacka.

'Five minutes. Why? You scared?'

'Not 'alf, Sarge.'

Jacka grinned. 'Nemmind. Barring shooting the sergeant-major or raping his wife, if we pull this off you'll be out in about ten years.'

They were scrambling up the ladders now in the order they'd been instructed, Brandison's party first, to crouch on deck with their gangways. The man behind the forward gun gave it a tentative swing, made sure it was cocked, and applied his eye to the sight. Inside the dummy crates on deck, the Oerlikon parties put their faces to the holes drilled in the wood and waited for the command to drop the sides.

'Oi told the sergeant Oi didn't want to go on church parade,' a nervous Birmingham voice was saying in the darkness at the bottom of the ladders. 'He said, "Whoy?" An' Oi told 'im Oi didn't believe in God. You know what he said?'

Nobody answered.

'Charlie, you know what he said?'

'Go on.' The long-suffering Charlie sounded bored. 'What?'

'He said, "If you don't believe in God, 'oo the 'ell do you think makes the fuckin' flowers grow?" '

The invisible Charlie made no comment and the speaker became silent.

'Nerves,' Sugarwhite whispered nervously to Bradshaw.

On the bridge they were still staring towards the shore.

'Quarter of a mile,' Babington said. 'I think they're going to let us go right in, by God!'

They weren't, though. Not quite.

Von Steen was still staring suspiciously through his glasses as *Horambeb* moved towards the mole. 'It's not *Umberto*,' he snapped. 'They're going to lay her alongside the wall!'

'They can't!' Hochstätter said. 'It's not possible.'

'It is with that damned water boat!' As he stared again, von Steen saw the shape of *Umberto* growing perceptibly longer. Then he saw what appeared to be two bow waves, and realized there was another vessel beyond her, hidden up to now. He saw blunt bows and swung round.

'That's a landing craft!' he snapped. 'It's not *Umberto*!' He snatched at the telephone. 'Searchlights!' he yelled.

'For God's sake,' Hochstätter said. '*Umberto*'s full of ammunition and the RAF's still overhead!'

'I'll take responsibility,' von Steen said. 'If we don't hit her now, we certainly shan't be able to if she gets alongside!'

As the searchlight near the Mantazeh Palace picked them up, they all instinctively ducked.

Babington lowered his glasses. 'Here we go,' he said.

'Dead slow ahead,' Hardness ordered. 'Port five, cox'n.'

'Port five, sir.'

'Hoist the battle ensign, Number One. Stand by all guns.'

As the great white jack fluttered from the masthead the crates on *Umberto*'s deck flattened and the sides were tossed overboard.

'Hit that searchlight, Guns.'

The time was 2347.

6

Tanks were put ashore and the mole and adjoining buildings quickly occupied.

Umberto's first shot hit the end of the mole near where Private Jumpke was standing, and the ear-splitting crash and sear of flame nearly made him leap out of his skin. Yelling with fright, he was knocked sideways against the wall and dropped to the bottom of his post while the chunks of concrete flew through the air. A second shell sailed over his head to land in the town where it wrecked a house, and killed three people, a donkey and two camels. The third hit the Mantazeh Palace searchlight. As it went out, a boot with a foot in it and a helmet with a head in it sailed out in a long slow curve and plopped into the sea, as though they had been hurled at the attackers by someone who had put his hand on the first thing that came within reach.

Those three shells were to have quite a considerable effect on Private Bontempelli's behaviour during the rest of the night.

Just before the attack had started, he had managed to slip away from the company latrines and between the gun crews' huts at Mas el Bub, and had sidled in the darkness along the sea front towards the seaward side of the Borgo Nero, where he had waited until the coast was clear enough for him to dive into the narrow alleys behind the mosque.

The Borgo Nero was very familiar to Bontempelli. It was a squalid area full of ravenous flies and the inane sound of Arab music, where once a week a patrol entered with great deliberation to buy *eggis,* the midget-sized products of Arab hens, for the officers' mess. Most of the garrison thought it necessary to learn to walk backwards before you entered the Borgo Nero because it was well known that the Arabs hated them all, but with Bontempelli it was different. Uneducated, unskilled, and to a certain extent unemployable, he had the gift of communication, and could move confidently among the shuffling men and veiled women. Indifferent to standing orders which placed the area out of bounds, he had never made the slightest concession to racialism but could still get the Egyptians whom he met in there hooting with laughter at his imitations of Sottotenente Baldissera and Unteroffizier Upholz.

Now that the lorries had set off for Ibrahimiya with all his friends, he was having second thoughts about his impulsive ducking out of sight. Coming to the conclusion that he might as well be hanged for a sheep as for a lamb, he had called at the house of the Arab who usually supplied him with beer and had just moved on to the home of Zulfica Ifzi when *Umberto*'s first shell exploded against the mole. The bang seemed to lift him through the door and Zulfica Ifzi, who was just preparing for bed, swung round, stark naked, her eyes wide with fear.

'It's the British,' Bontempelli yelled. 'It's an air raid!'

He reached for her, intending to rush her into the caves that had been dug in the cliff face below Mas el Bub, but at that moment the second shell exploded among the native houses and, as the flying tiles rattled on the roofs and walls, she flung herself at him, shrieking with fright. At the third explosion, she clung even tighter, wrapping herself round him in her petrified terror, so that he found himself fighting against her, hampered by her arms and legs, his rifle, and the bottles of beer he had bought.

'Holy Mother of God,' he was panting. 'Let go!'

Now that he could hear the guns of the port defences firing, he realized his first assumption that this was an air raid must be wrong. He could hear whistles blowing and could already imagine himself cowering in a dugout with the rotten sandbags bursting, the candle guttering in the blast, and the dust and pebbles dropping from the quivering roof. Since he had always had a horror of being buried alive, he decided he'd be wiser to stay where he was.

Then his ingrained sense of survival began to tell him that in the Borgo Nero, in Zulfica Ifzi's room, he was as safe as he would be anywhere. It was surrounded by dozens of mud-brick houses and protected from blast by half a hundred walls and the bulk of the Ibn al As Mosque. Only a direct hit could harm him, and the British, Italians and Germans – all eager to keep on good terms with the native population – had always insisted that the Arab town should never be harmed. As his fear slipped away, he became more conscious of the naked girl clinging to him. His thoughts began to turn from safety to other things. He pushed her away, laid down his rifle and the bottles of beer, and dragged off his jacket.

If he were caught now, he would probably be shot; but with a British force apparently about to descend on Qaba from the sea and the Eighth Army heading through the desert from the east, he had a strong suspicion that he wasn't going to be free to enjoy the fruits of life much longer anyway. He had no intention of dying if he could help it, but if the war dragged on he could well be a prisoner for a long time. He decided to make the best of what he had.

'Holy Mother of God protect and keep us,' he said and, crossing himself quickly, began to push Zulfica Ifzi towards the bed.

Private Jumpke, at the end of the mole, couldn't believe his eyes as the ships swept past him. The crew of the nearby 47 had come alive too, but they were almost too late.

Their shots whistled past the stern of *Umberto* just as her guns cracked again. With all hope of disguise and deception gone, the Oerlikons on *Umberto*'s deck were bursting into flame along with every gun on the launches which could be brought to bear. Streams of tracer were spattering the stonework round Jumpke's post and he again flung himself to the bottom of his little concrete box, his hands over his head.

Then he realized that though he could hear the bullets whanging off the concrete, they were doing him no harm, and he reached up for the telephone and cranked the handle. It was connected to the bunker below the Kriegsmarine barracks, and as soon as he heard the answering click he screamed 'Raid!' at the top of his voice. It wasn't the proper way to give a report but Jumpke was more keen to keep his head down than be a good soldier.

The youthful naval ensign at the other end of the line had been waiting for a quarter of an hour now for the air raid, which still seemed to be taking place in leisurely fashion out at the airfield, to switch to the town. Already somewhat alarmed and in a state of nervous excitement, he naturally assumed that Jumpke said 'Air raid'.

He knew exactly what to do because it had been drummed into duty officers half a dozen times since the four supply ships had come in. Swinging round, he checked that the black-out switch was up, sent a man to crank the air raid siren, and pressed the button that set off the line of smoke floats circling the harbour. Immediately, smoke began to pour out, pungent, greasy and yellow. But the shell from *Umberto* which had knocked out the searchlight near the Mantazeh Palace had also severed the electrical circuit to the smoke pots on the landward side of the harbour and only those on the mole worked. With the wind blowing from the south-east, the smoke was carried out to sea, leaving the harbour area clear.

As they plunged into the smoke, the men on *Umberto*'s bridge couldn't believe their incredible luck. Though the greasy folds made it more difficult to see where they were going, it also blunted the beams of the searchlights at Mas el Bub and the Bab al Gawla.

'Bridge! Are you all right?' As they edged closer Hockold could hear the first lieutenant, calling from the conning position above the hand steering aft, and the unemotional reply from the yeoman that they were.

Their speed and course appeared to be exactly right and it was time to join his party on the deck. But as he made his way from the bridge, the heavy machine guns ashore found the ship.

His heart began to hammer against the cage of his ribs as luminous yellow slots sped past like beads on a string, and he heard screams as they furrowed and ploughed up the deck. As he pushed through the crowded cursing men struggling to make their way to the ship's side, instinctively waiting for the shot that would kill him, above him the bridge protection was already being torn to shreds, while splinters flew from gangways and ladders.

The ship's guns were making a tremendous clamour now and there was an incessant crackle of small arms fire. To the men on the deck near Hockold the moment was one of flame and anger; to the men still below it meant waiting with ice in their bowels, unable to tell whether the crashes they heard came from their own gun or from shells exploding aboard.

In Hochstätter's headquarters, Nietzsche turned furiously to von Steen.

'Jesus Christ,' he said. 'We don't want smoke! We can't see to hit the bastards now! For God's sake, shut it off!'

As he spoke, a heavy machine-gun started probing across the front of the hotel and they all dropped to the floor. Oerlikon shells spanged and cracked against the walls, chopping out great chunks of stone and mud-brick. Then, as they stopped, a lighter weapon took over.

'Stop that damned air raid siren!' Nietzsche shouted, and Wutka scrambled on all fours to grab the telephone and bawl into it. A moment later the wail died in a drone of anguish.

'Get the harbour lights on so we can see what the hell we're doing!' Von Steen was in contact now with naval headquarters. 'The damned place's full of Tommies!'

As the message was passed on, the loading clusters strung round the harbour came on and they could see the smoke drifting grey-yellow and ghostly across the water. Then a freak wind momentarily cleared it and at last they got a glimpse of the upper works of the ship beyond the mole.

'That *is Umberto*,' Hochstätter shouted.

'Well, she hasn't got *Umberto*'s crew aboard,' Nietzsche yelled back.

As he reached for the telephone to issue orders, the heavy machine-guns on *Umberto* began again. The shutters leapt and clattered as they dissolved into splinters, the black-out curtain was ripped to tatters, and the light went out as glass began to tinkle and plaster fell in chunks from the ceiling. Hochstätter and the other officers flung themselves to the floor again.

On his knees, Nietzsche clawed for the telephone and contacted Schoeler. 'Guns!' he roared. 'We need your guns!'

As the searchlight by the palace had gone out, the whole of Qaba had become aware that the danger lay not out at the airfield as they'd believed but here in the town.

The remaining two searchlights tried to bring their beams round; the smoke was confusing, however, and as *Umberto* was now passing the tip of the mole they couldn't properly be brought to bear on her. *Horambeb* was already in the shadow of the great arc of stone but the smoke floats were situated on top of the guard wall so that though the thick grey-yellow clouds poured through the rigging at the top of her mast, they left her uncovered as she turned to port and wide open to the view of the 75 at Mas el Bub.

Crouching with his party among the splintered ladders on the deck of *Umberto*, Hockold's head jerked up at the flash of acid white against the loom of the cliff as the heavy gun fired.

'That's not a 47!' Amos turned as another brilliant flash came from the cliff at the opposite side of the town and a spout of grey water lifted beyond the RAF launches, the spray sparkling in the glow of the searchlight. 'There's another there, too!'

Hockold's heart seemed to stop. It was always one of the chances of war that an enemy could change his dispositions after dark or bring up unexpected weapons in secret. The entire Eighth Army attack was based on just such an assumption, and Hockold realized that the whole plan for Cut-Price was now in jeopardy and the battle would have to be fought by rule of thumb, its success depending not on pre-arranged tactics so much as on individual courage and initiative.

Amos was shouting again – 'They've got *Horambeb*' – and

Hockold turned to see tracer skidding past and shells flashing against the bow and bridge of the water boat.

The unexpected weight of artillery fire hadn't gone unnoticed on *Umberto*'s bridge and Hardness was endeavouring to adjust to it.

'That gun there,' he shouted to the officer on the foredeck. 'Get it, Guns!'

But before *Umberto*'s little popgun could fire, the 75, having hit *Horambeb* twice already, switched targets. Its first shot was a lucky one. There was a tremendous crash and the little popgun disappeared over the side in a tangle of torn metal and flying splinters that killed the gunnery officer and three men and wounded seven others in a fraction of a second. More splinters knocked the glass out of the wheelhouse windows and Hockold heard them thump into the woodwork above his head.

The heavy machine-guns at Mas el Bub and near the mosque were also hammering away, by now, and the smoke had cut visibility to a few feet. There was blood on the decks and frantic sailors were heaving the dead aside. As they dragged the wounded below to the surgeon, more flying splinters found targets. The Germans were firing haphazardly, however, and, though almost every shot hit something, they were not hitting *Umberto*'s vitals. The upperworks were in ribbons but the steel-covered bridge was still functioning and the engines were still turning.

On *Horambeb,* now curving away to port from Umberto's side, the engineers were keeping up an enormous head of steam in the boilers, but then a shell from the 47 above the slipway hit her wheelhouse and her captain was flung aside dead with the helmsman, while the first lieutenant crawled away stupefied. A second 47 millimetre shell hit her from only a few hundred yards as she headed in but the determination of her captain had already done its work. Steered by an elderly petty officer with a face like a set of nutcrackers, who kept his head just above the sill of the wheelhouse, she continued to move away from *Umberto,* her bridge a wreck, her mast trailing over her stern. Trembling under the thrust of engines held at a gland-shattering pressure of steam, she bore ahead. Then another shell from the 47 tore through her side, to explode in the grimy cavern of her engine room. A high shaft of red-orange flame, ancient soot and roaring steam shot up from her funnel and she immediately began to lose way, her rudder and engines useless.

From *Umberto* they watched her with agonized faces, then a shell hit *Umberto* herself with an aching shuddering crash and they felt the ship roll against the explosion.

'Another two hundred yards,' Babington prayed, 'and we've made it!'

As he spoke, the bright glare of the searchlight in the centre of the town disappeared and they realized they were in the shelter of the great stone mole. Hardness had just ordered the wheel to be put to port and rung down to stop engines when another shell from the 75 at Mas el Bub hit the roof of the wheelhouse. It killed Hardness and Babington outright and wounded the helmsman, the yeoman and the Italian-speaking signaller. At the most crucial moment of the approach, *Umberto* was no longer under control.

Von Steen saw the explosion through the smoke. The shell had passed dangerously near to where *Giuseppe Bianchi* was lying astern of the other three ships.

'Stop those guns,' he screamed, and as Nietzsche crawled to the telephone the firing slackened. Despite the bullets still chipping plaster from the ceiling, Nietzsche lifted his head to look out. He could just see the topmast and upperworks of *Umberto*, caught by the overspill of the searchlight, sticking out of the smoke as they glided past *Giuseppe Bianchi*. He stared at them helplessly.

'For God's sake,' he said. 'What do we kill them with?'

Von Steen swung round. 'Not with guns,' he shouted. 'Get your men down to the mole!'

As Nietzsche scrambled to his feet and headed for the stairs, *Horambeb*'s port bow thumped against the mole. As the steel scraped the stone, groaning and flinging out sparks in protest, the petty officer at the helm, coughing at the smoke in his lungs, put the wheel hard-a-starboard. The old water boat swung outwards and slithered along the wall, tearing off her rails against a projecting stone. As they lifted, screeching in protest and snaking through the air, they skewered a sailor crouching for shelter near the bridge. His screams as the rusty iron stabbed into his stomach went unheard as *Horambeb*'s bow dug into the mud-bank ahead to fling everybody off their feet. Then her boilers blew and the engine became a tangled mass of steel and she slid to a steaming, spluttering, crackling halt with her nose on the mud, her stern sticking out at an angle of thirty degrees from the wall.

Lieutenant Carter was still singing to himself as he drove LCT 11 towards the beach. Smoke enveloped his ship and nobody seemed to have spotted her yet so that he thought he might even get her ashore without being touched. They might actually give him a gong for it, and then he could go out and get happily drunk. Or even, he decided gaily, go home and strangle his wife.

He heard the tanks start their engines and caught the smell of exhaust fumes, and saw turret lids clang shut. There were only a hundred yards to go now and the well-deck was full of blue smoke. It was going to be a piece of cake. His song grew louder.

'Pin a rose in your permanent wave,
The navy's at the door.
There's cider down the eiderdown –'

But at that moment LCT 11 burst from the smoke and the crew of the 75 at Mas el Bub saw her. The gun barrel swung and, even as Carter saw the muzzle flash, the shell hit the side of the bridge. The wheelhouse, together with Lieutenant Carter's plans and his song, seemed to disintegrate in a blood-red blur as the place fell in on him. The signaller standing alongside him, together with the helmsman and the twenty-year-old first lieutenant fell in a heap. As Carter dragged himself to his knees, he saw that the wheelhouse was on fire and the signaller's clothes were already burning. The first lieutenant's head, the steel helmet still in place, was at the opposite side of the wheelhouse, staring at the body it belonged to with an expression of startled bewilderment, and the helmsman was so peppered with splinters he looked like a colander oozing blood through every hole.

The wheel was spinning and the landing craft's head was beginning to fall off, so that she was aimed now towards the cliffs instead of the slipway. Carter could hear shouts from the well deck in front of him where the soldiers were staring anxiously back towards the bridge. Grimly he struggled to his feet and grasped the wheel to bring the head round again. Then he realized that something was soaking the front of his uniform, and with his free hand he pawed clumsily at his body. Curiously, he didn't feel any great pain, but as he stared at the palm of his hand, glistening and red with his own blood, he knew he was badly wounded somewhere.

Automatically, he started to sing again, in the same tuneless monotone he always used.

> 'When I get out of the navy
> What a wonderful wife I'll make –'

Staring ahead, he started a mad conversation with the dead men around him. 'Proper cock we made of that one, Number One,' he said, uncertain whether to address the first lieutenant's head or his body. 'And what a bloody helmsman! Lying down on the job!'

Another shell burst near the bridge and the blast knocked him to his knees. Down below in the well the soldiers were crouching with their heads down.

'Officers don't worry me – not much,' Carter sang as he dragged himself to his feet again. 'The bastards'll pay for this, Number One. If I don't get a medal for this night's work I'll shit in the admiral's hat, you see!'

They were almost on the beach now, and the crew of the 75, unable to depress the barrel of the gun any further, had switched back to *Umberto*. The 47 by the slipway picked them up instead. Its first shell screamed over them but the second hit the bow and the air became full of singing splinters, and steel peeled back as if it were the rind of an orange. Someone started screaming in the well deck and, unable to see properly for the blood that streamed into his eyes from a wound on his head, Carter made out the rusty loom of a wrecked freighter on the beach. As he felt the bow of the landing craft scrape the sand, he knew he'd arrived. A petty officer started to lower the ramp but the shell on the bows had cut the chains and it fell with a crash into the shallow water.

'Made it,' Carter said aloud, and reeled back to sit down heavily on the body of the helmsman. Slowly, feebly, he fumbled in his pocket for his flask. Lamps seemed to be going out, and little doors were shutting one after the other in his mind, each one cutting off one more cord in his brain, so that he could remember his song only in fragments. Then, for the first time in his life, he found he couldn't recall the words at all, couldn't even lift the flask to his mouth. He stared round him at the shambles in the wheelhouse and felt a terrible lassitude, as if he'd done what he ususally did and had one drink too many.

New song, he decided. New song. Sober him up.

'Rolling home,' he mumbled. 'By the light of the silvery moon...'

Then his own light finally went out and, as they dragged him from the wheelhouse, he was silent at last.

As *Umberto* thumped out of control against *Horambeb*, her riddled main mast came down and another piece flew off her funnel. A man jumped over the side, glad to be out of the flying splinters, and secured a rope round one of the water-boat's bitts, but with no one to correct her and only her high bows touching, *Umberto* began to swing and it was impossible to get ashore.

ML 146, having discharged her men across *Horambeb*'s bow, reeled away with her fuel tanks on fire, her crew jumping into the water. ML 138, just behind and outside her, had to back away from *Umberto*'s swinging stern or be borne under. At that moment, a burst of machine-gun fire shattered her bridge and killed her captain and her coxswain. Half-blinded by cuts on the face, Lieutenant Dysart saw the danger and punched frantically at the vast body of Leading Seaman Gaukrodger, hunched alongside him.

'Get on that bloody wheel, Gaukrodger,' he screamed. 'Shove 'em in!'

Umberto's first lieutenant had now got the secondary controls working and had swung the wheel over. Then the *Fairmile*'s bow thumped against her stern, springing the launch's planks and lifting the winch. As the third ML joined Dysart and they pushed together, *Umberto* at last began to swing alongside. Her weight shoved the lighter *Horambeb* towards the wall, the trapped water between the two vessels surging and thrashing as it leapt and boiled, to rock the ships like cradles.

By now, *Umberto*'s upperworks, were like a sieve. In the din, another shell crashed into her funnel and reduced an Oerlikon position to a tangled nest of smoking ruin and blackened bodies, but she was still swinging in, bearing *Horambeb* with her. As a second rope went down to the ruined deck of the water-boat, Hockold rose to his feet. There seemed to be no point in trying to dodge the bullet that was going to kill him, and his indifference as he stood upright put heart into the men about him.

'Mole parties!' he yelled and Lieutenant Brandison's men rushed forward, slamming their gangways across to *Horambeb* and racing over them. A ladder lifted from *Horambeb*'s port side against the wall and a man scrambled up into the smoke at the top. But the German gunners were flaying the air above the mole with their weapons and a blast of machine-gun fire flung him back on to Belcher who fell to the deck half-stunned.

Brandison was behind them, however, and, crouching low, dived across the mole with the ropes to secure the top of the ladder. Immediately, more men swarmed up, to fling themselves flat behind oil drums, crates and piles of rope, and direct their fire towards Wutka's wooden bridge and the 47 at the end of the mole.

'Bridge party!' Brandison and his men jumped up and went clattering away long the mole, with the smoke floats hissing and poppling from the wall on their right. The rest of *Umberto*'s complement began to swarm across *Horambeb* after them.

Then a burst of firing caught the bridge party and Brandison went down on his face with a crash, sliding along the concrete with the speed of his run until he came to a stop against a wrecked hand-cart. As the rest reached the bridged gap, Sergeant Jacka saw Germans hurrying up the mole from the landward end where there were huts and stone-built sheds and the crew of a 47 working at their gun. He flung himself down, his Tommy gun up, and as the Germans approached, the dazed Belcher flattened out alongside him.

'Laid out like dog's dinner,' Jacka said and, as the two guns chattered, the Germans dropped to the ground. All but one, who went on running, leaning over at an angle as if he were trying to dodge the bullets, his head lolling, his mouth wide open. Then his legs crumpled and he crashed down, his helmet bouncing away, to roll over on to his back, his arms spread-eagled.

Jacka couldn't tell which of the others was alive and which was dead, but they'd captured the wooden bridge. When another group of Germans made a rush forward, one of them with a grenade in his hand, Jacka's burst caught them before they'd gone a yard and the grenade went straight up in the air to fall back against the man who had flung it. The explosion tossed his body over the edge of the mole into the harbour.

'That'll stop him coughing in church,' Jacka said.

They scrambled to their feet and pounded across the wooden bridge to fling themselves flat again at the far side. Almost immediately behind them, Hockold crashed across the planking and began to run along the mole.

On the beach, clear of the smoke, Meinertz had got his Honey out of the landing craft and was heading towards the slip. The tank didn't move very fast, but he reached the bottom of the slope hard under the cliff where he couldn't be hit either by the 75 above or the 47 on the mole, and stopped to wait for Sergeant Gleeson.

He could hear both guns firing just above him and the clatter of machine-guns, and, pushing his head out of the hatch, he saw that Gleeson's tank had stuck on a patch of soft sand and was sinking deeper with every turn of the tracks. A shell from the 47 hit it low on the port side and a cloud of sand, water and grit shot upwards. Thick smoke came from the turret and he saw the glow of an explosion inside. There was rubber in the burning smell, and hot oil mingled with something else that was nauseating, and he heard someone howling like a sick dog. He stared, helplessness quickening the horror as the ball of flame that seemed to surround the tank grew, fattened and bloated. After what seemed an age, the turret opened and he saw Gleeson's head appear, his hair ablaze. But then the flames shot up round him like a gas jet and Meinertz had to shut his ears to the screams.

By this time, men were running through the streets of Qaba carrying weapons. Unteroffizier Upholz, magnificently indifferent to flying shards of metal, was standing at the bottom of the Shariah Jedid, waving a carbide torch to direct them into the buildings at the end of the mole. The whole town was alert now, but the Germans were so preoccupied with watching the harbour and keeping their guns on the mole that at first no one noticed the three RAF launches rushing in alone on a separate course to the eastern beaches. Then one of the guards in the watch tower of the POW compound spotted them and pressed the alarm while his mate snatched at his Schmeisser MP 38 and started firing. The MP 38 didn't do much harm but it brought the crew of a heavy machine-gun below to life and as it started directing a stream of bullets out to sea, it was followed immediately by the 47 near the palace.

In HSL 117, Second-Lieutenant Sotheby, standing dry-mouthed with Sergeant Berringer, saw the launch in front stagger in the water, then there was a tremendous thump as the explosives on board went up. In a moment the whole boat was enveloped in fire and Sotheby could see men with their clothes ablaze jumping frantically into the sea and trying to swim away from the spreading area of burning petrol.

'That's cuck-cuck-Collier's lot,' he said nervously. 'It looks as if it's up to us.'

They passed the burning wreckage and screaming men in the water without stopping. The 47 seemed to have missed HSL 117 and was now firing at the last launch in the line, hitting her repeatedly. Sotheby turned to the officer in command, a boy no older than himself.

'We'll never be able to gug-get ashore with the dinghies,' he said. 'The bastards'll knock us out.'

'I can put her bow on the rocks there,' the RAF man said. 'Will that do?'

'It'll bub-bloody have to,' Sotheby said.

They moved in until the bow of the launch butted against the rocks that lined the low cliffs and, keeping the engine going ahead, the RAF man held her there.

'Cuck-come on, Berringer,' Sotheby said as he leapt ashore. 'I think we'd bub-better get cracking.'

Hockold had been the first man of the main party across Wutka's wooden bridge but the machine-gun near the 47 at the end of the mole was dropping his men as they ran. They could see a barrier of wire in front of them dancing and pinging as the bullets struck the strands, and hear the whine as they lifted and whirred into the air over their heads. As they flung themselves down behind drums, crates, and piles of rope and chain, the rush along the mole came to a stop. Hockold joined them unwillingly, his mind seething as he saw the whole plan for Cut-Price falling apart.

'Mr Rabbitt,' he said. 'See if you can get over the wall and on to the rocks, and settle the 47 before it stops the tanks. We're going to need them!'

'Right, sir!' Rabbitt signed to the men alongside him, and with a rush they scrambled over the shelter wall. Two were hit but the others hung down by their hands above the rocks and dropped into the darkness. Two more men had to be left among the rocks with twisted ankles, but the rest began to work their way towards the slip. Then, spotted by machine-gunners near the 75 at Mas el Bub, they had to dive for cover again.

'For God's sake,' Rabbitt snarled. 'Where are those bloody tanks?'

Hockold and his party were still struggling to reach the shelter of the stone store-sheds at the end of the mole from where they might run for the buildings near the mosque. From there they could work their way to the Roman arch at the Bab al Gawla. They could actually see the arch now, dark against the whitewashed stone of the Boujaffar Hotel. There was a searchlight near the harbour wall and Hockold gestured towards it.

A Bren stuttered and, as the searchlight went out, the firing slackened momentarily so that they were able to make their dash to the sheds, threading through them in ones and twos until they could see the buildings at the end of the mole. But the crew of the 75 at Mas el Bub, using spades, sandbags and wedges, had managed to bring their gun to bear. As it began to blow chunks off the stonework about them, they had to edge back the way they'd come to put the debris between them and the sheds they could safely occupy.

The 75 above the POW compound was firing at short range towards *Umberto* now, tearing her upperworks to ribbons, and the 47 by the palace was firing across the harbour past the bow of *Cassandra* to add to the damage being done by the 75.

'For God's sake,' Amos yelled above the barked orders and the stammer of weapons to add his plea to Sergeant-Major Rabbitt's. 'Where are the tanks?'

Gleeson's tank was a blazing wreck and Meinertz, who had been violently sick, was still wiping his mouth and trying to make up his mind what to do as Murdoch, Cobbe and Captain Cadish roared up the beach in the old Humber brake and skidded to a stop alongside him in the shelter of the cliffs.

'We'll get round the back!' Murdoch shouted up. 'We'll pin 'em down so you can get up the slip!'

'No, hang on!' Meinertz's brains were temporarily addled by shock and nausea, and he was fighting to clear the fog.

A group of men were behind the blazing landing craft and another behind the beached freighter, crouched half in the water waiting for the machine-gunners on the landward end of the mole to be silenced, while the rest had dashed for the cliffs where they couldn't be touched.

Meinertz stared round him. The gun up above him was something they hadn't bargained for, its shells pinning down the men on *Horambeb* and *Umberto*.

It seemed to be up to him.

'Let's go,' he said.

They were still in darkness, though the harbour and the slip were a blaze of light from the loading clusters. There was no longer any point in regarding the black-out, and Hochstätter had switched on everything he could find.

As they reached the bottom of the slipway, Meinertz saw that it was narrower than he'd expected; only just wide enough for the Honey to get up it. Here was a job that seemed to call for care and precision, but at the top a 47 was waiting for them, and on the cliffs above the bigger weapon which it was also clearly his job to knock out.

'Up the slip, driver,' he said. 'And go like the clappers!'

The gears crashed and the driver, knowing well what would happen if he missed his aim and the outside track crumbled the edge to topple them upside down to the sand, stared with wide eyes as the slip drew nearer. The tracks were throwing up the sand behind them in showers now and the men round the brake watched with grim fascination.

There was a violent clang as the tank lurched on to the stones; then it was clattering up the uneven slope, swinging and rolling on the heavy boulders that made up the surface. Its bogeys rattling, its springs creaking, as it reached the level ground at the top it seemed to leap into the air, its tracks spinning wildly; then its nose banged down and it disappeared from sight.

The driver had kept his eyes on the edge of the slip every inch of the way, but there wasn't time to think much before they arrived with a crash by the harbourside, sending a native felucca, parked there for repairs, reeling away, its mast whipping like a riding crop as the tank barged against it. As it rolled over, its planks splintered, and crashed to the beach, Meinertz realized that the 47 he'd been expecting was just beyond where it had stood and was waiting for them to appear, its barrel trained towards the top of the slip.

'Keep going!' he shouted. 'Keep going!'

There was a tremendous bang and a screech of metal as the gun fired, tearing off the Honey's starboard track and slewing it completely round so that it was almost facing the other way. But the gun was a wreck too, beneath them, and its crew were dead underneath it.

As the tank came to a stop, Meinertz, his nose bleeding where he'd banged it on the butt of the machine-gun, became aware that the whole inside of the tank – radio, ammunition racks, every nut and bolt and rivet – was now sharp and clear in an icy white light. They'd been picked up by the searchlight on the cliff near the other gun.

Dazzled, he tried to pull himself together and swing his own searchlight, but it was a puny affair compared with the one on the cliff and he knew that beyond the glare the crew of the gun would be struggling to bring the barrel to bear on him.

'Get that bloody light,' he yelled. 'Driver, bring her round!'

The screech of the gears told him they were stuck.

'Gunner.' He screamed. 'Traverse right! Get that light, for Christ's sake!'

Caught by the overspill of the light, he saw the end of a gun barrel, dropping lower as the crew fought to depress it further. The flash and the crash against the outside of the tank came together. Fragments of metal flew through the air and for a moment Meinertz thought he was dead. But, as he realized that the shell had actually missed them and exploded on the concrete alongside, he began to yell again.

'Get that light!'

'For Christ's sake, sir, the turret's given up!'

As the gunner, his eye to the hot rubber of the sight, fought with the traverse handle, shouting despairingly, 'It won't bear! It won't bear,' Meinertz yelled again.

'Driver! You've still got one good track! Use it!'

As the outside track jerked, the old Honey lurched another

foot to the right and the gunner's voice cracked with his excitement. 'Got her, sir !'

The gun roared, deafening them, and Meinertz saw the flash as the shell hit the emplacement below the big grey barrel. Living up to expectations, Meinertz's gunner had missed the searchlight completely but, with a shot as lucky as that which had destroyed *Umberto*'s popgun, he had placed his shell right in front of the 75.

'Give 'em another while their heads are ringing!' Meinertz screamed.

The crew of the gun were as stupefied by the explosion as the crew of the Honey had been, but they were slower to react so that Meinertz's gunner got his next shell in first and they saw the gun barrel lift and swing in a dipping half-circle as if it were free of its moorings.

'Got the bastard,' Meinertz said with satisfaction. 'Now the searchlight, gunner!'

The gun banged again and this time Meinertz's gunner hit what he was aiming at. The shell struck even as the crew were hurriedly switching off for safety, and the dying red glow was lost in the glare of the explosion.

For a brief moment there was a silence that seemed to smother even the sounds of battle from the harbour behind them, Then, as Meinertz and his crew dropped to the ground beside the wrecked Honey, Murdoch came roaring up the slip in Hockold's old brake to shoot past them, unnoticed by the Germans in the houses at the bottom of the Shariah Jedid, and disappear among the trees by the mosque, followed by the rest of the group from the landing craft, running as fast as they could go.

7

The POW compound and a lorry park were attacked.

Sergeant-Major Rabbitt's party had watched Meinertz's little battle from the rocks just below the slip.

'Jesus,' one of the Stooges said. 'These cavalry boys certainly do things in style.'

With the destruction of the guns, the machine-gunners at the end of the mole where isolated and, as Rabbitt's party dashed to the slip and tossed a couple of Mills bombs over the top, the survivors threw down their weapons and raised their hands.

As they did so, Hockold lifted his head. To his surprise he was still alive, and it seemed a good idea to utilize what little time he had left in securing the centre of the town and organizing a defence. Though a lot of the loading clusters and harbour lights had been shot out, the searchlights at Ibrahimiya probing the sky for de Berry's isolated groups of aeroplanes were destroying any pretence at darkness.

There was wire beyond the sheds, stretching from Meinertz's wrecked Honey to the mud at the other side. A soldier flung himself down across it, and Hockold used his body as a stepping stone and dived for the shelter of the buildings at the end of the mole. As he vanished, a machine-gun near the Shariah Jedid came to life and the man following him was caught by a slicing burst which spun him round and flung him into the wire. Its barbs snatched at his uniform and held him half-upright, one arm outstretched, the hand dangling crazily every time the wire moved.

With Hockold already using his Sten, the fire from the troublesome machine-gun slackened and more men crossed. Watching from among the sheds where he crouched, Taffy Jones found he couldn't make himself follow. He desperately wanted to display the sort of courage the others were showing and had made the first rush down the mole in a blind panic, forced onward by the still greater fear of what his friends would think if he stopped. But now, since the first terrifying crashes of shells had started around them and the shuddering stutter of machine-guns had knocked men over alongside him, nothing he could do would produce any further response from a body frozen by terror. This wasn't at all what he'd expected. From the day he'd volunteered for the commandos, he'd been living in mute and unspoken fear of what battle would be like. But, though he had all along imagined something terrible, he had never foreseen anything as terrible as this.

Sergeant Freelove noticed the expression on his face and, used to the momentary panic of soldiers in the first shock of a fight, he gave him a shove. 'Get on, man!' he shouted.

But Taffy was even stricken dumb in the paralysis of fear, and Freelove literally dragged him to his feet so that, exposed to the firing, he had no option but to run, panting, his equipment clanking, to leap the wire and fling himself, breathless, his tongue stuck dry and tacky to the roof of his mouth, down again among the others.

A lorry was moving nearby, heading away from the buildings. Someone threw a grenade at it and the petrol tank exploded and it went up in flames. A man jumped out and started to run, and Taffy saw that he, too, was burning brightly.

The obscurity of the smoke gave them a moment's grace, and the men around him jumped up again and began to run across the road and through the trees by the mosque to gather round a group of small mud-brick buildings nearer the arch. Trying to keep up with them, Sugarwhite saw a few fleeting figures in the dark and was just going to shoot when in the nick of time he recognized them as Arabs. A couple of lurching shapes appeared – camels which, sleeping among the trees by the mosque, had stumbled to their feet in alarm at the din and were bolting with hobbled legs. As he ran, one of them blundered into him and he went over, stunned, while the camel appeared to trample all over him before a stray bullet caught it and it collapsed, blowing blood through its nostrils, its bound feet threshing the dust.

Perspiration streaming down his heavy handsome face, Taffy watched Sugarwhite go down. Then Sergeant Freelove gave him another kick so that he leapt up in alarm and went after the others, running with clattering equipment for the mud buildings at the side of the mosque. The raking stutter of a Bren was answered by a rippling crackle which, even through his panic, he knew came from a Spandau, and he flung himself down again. Wriggling under a hand-cart containing half a dozen drums of petrol and a water-skin used by Arab labourers, he hunched tensely against the wheel, frantic unintelligible words coming between his lips in the anguished whine of a bullied child.

The men around him glanced at him but made no comment. Knowing they hadn't finished by a long way yet, they sat with their backs to the mud walls, panting, to rest their heavy packs. Willow dragged the water-skin off the cart and they passed it round. Then, surrounded by Eva and the snipers who were holding down the fire of the Germans trying to hit him, Hockold tried to peer through the smoke. As he lifted his head, Docwra gestured at a palm tree further along the road. 'Keep your 'ead doon, sir,' he said. 'There's a felly wi' a gun up yonder.'

'Where be the mucky toad?' Eva asked. 'Among they trees?'

'Fourth one on the right. Tak' a dekko, Tinner!'

'Mun' be bloody thin,' Eva commented. 'Just 'ang on a tick.'

He found a place alongside the cart where Taffy Jones cowered, and crouched down. Though aware of the terrified man alongside him, it never occurred to him to question his fear and, cradling his rifle against his cheek, he wriggled himself to comfort.

'I see 'un.' The rifle cracked and he lifted his head. 'That's served 'urr wi' 'is chips,' he said.

Docwra shook his head, peering with narrow eyes through the smoke. 'Na,' he said. 'You missed, hinny!'

Eva smiled. 'Just 'ee wait.'

As they watched, a body wavered behind the tree and fell forward into the road, still grasping a rifle in one clenched fist.

Docwra grinned. 'I'm bloody glad ye're on oor side,' he said.

There was still a lot of firing coming from the buildings by the Roman arch and the direction of the Boujaffar. Hockold knew exactly where he wanted to be. Just ahead was a second-floor office with an outside iron stair, from which he could cover the hotel and the buildings nearby. But there was a brick-built hut that looked like a storehouse in the way, and in the darkness beyond its wide-open doorway a machine-gun had been set up and was firing spasmodically towards them.

'Get that building, Sergeant,' he said to Sidebottom who went off at once between the trees with half a dozen men. As the machine-gun stopped for a moment, two of them tried a dash across the road, but it opened up again and they staggered away, one shot in the face, the other in the ankle.

Crouching among the trees, Sidebottom studied the doorway for a moment or two. 'Stanna shwaya,' he said and ran back to where Hockold crouched. Indifferently, he kicked Taffy Jones from under his feet, snatched the water-skin from the hands of Eva who was drinking from it, and emptied its contents into the dust.

'For Christ's sake, Sarge, 'tes water, that!'

'Mallesh!' Sidebottom's crazy eyes gleamed in his blackened face. ' 'T'ain't the pawny I want, it's a buckshee skin.'

As the last drops of water splashed into the dust, Sidebottom turned to the hand-cart and drove a hole in the top of one of the drums.

'Yon's bloody petrol, Sarge!' Docwra shouted in alarm.

'Taro!' Sidebottom was holding the open mouth of the water-skin under the spouting liquid. 'It'll soon drain down!'

Filling the skin, he ran back to where his party were bent over the two wounded men.

'Sidi's gone spare,' Docwra said.

There was nothing spare about Sidebottom, however. Watching from the mud huts, they saw him pat his two wounded men on their backs as though comforting them. Then he jumped up and made a dash across the road, the water-skin spraying the earth round his boots with petrol, to fling himself down alongside the storehouse. Crawling to the door, he rose and stood with his back against the wall, then he swung the goatskin and tossed it with all his strength inside. As it landed, splashing wildly, he wrenched the pin from a grenade and rolled it in after it. There was a scream from the darkness as it exploded, a belching flare of flame, and the whole interior began to burn like a torch. Plunging inside, Sidebottom saw the gleam of an iron cross and yelled the only German he knew. '*Achtung, Schpitfeuer!*' he roared as he pulled the trigger of his Sten.

With the machine-gun silenced, the firing had slackened a lot and Rabbitt came pounding up to crouch alongside Hockold. 'Mr Murdoch's away, sir,' he reported. 'I saw his party go.'

'Right!' Hockold gestured at the iron stairway and, carrying Brens and captured German Schmeissers, they pounded towards it past the burning storehouse. Cook-Corporal Rogers found a crowbar and began to knock a hole in the wall so that Rabbitt could set up the Spandau he had dragged with him from the end of the mole. Alongside him, Sergeant Curtiss opened contact with *Umberto* on his radio.

'In position,' he said. 'In position.'

Amos grinned. 'I think we've made it,' he said.

It seemed so, too, to the men in Hochstätter's office. They had seen the first two searchlights go out and the clusters of hanging lamps round the harbour shot away one by one, but they could still see the grey-yellow smoke drifting from the harbour wall, obscuring everything beyond from the very men who needed to know. On the beach below Mas el Bub the landing craft was burning fiercely, lighting the ceiling with its flames, the smoke rolling out to sea picking up the glare on its billows so that they looked like clouds at sunset. It was clear that the British had reached the end of the mole and the beach. A few had probably even got into the town, but they had no idea where the rest of them were. Then the 75 above the Borgo Nero had fallen silent together with the 47 at the landward end of the mole, and Nietzsche crawled on hands and knees beneath the bullets that were tearing Hochstätter's office to shreds, to summon what was left of the pioneers from the POW compound where he'd placed them as a reserve.

'I want them down here at once!' he screamed into the telephone.

A heavy machine-gun on *Umberto* was still hammering steadily at the windows. The shutters were already in splinters and the bullets were gouging great holes in the plaster at the opposite side of the room. Hochstätter was a fastidious man and one of the jobs of his orderlies had been to keep the place presentable. Even a few vases of flowers had found their way in, and the machine-gun was chopping the heads off the blooms and demolishing the vases, along with the books, the glasses, the bottles, the files, the dancing tattered map on the wall, the very wall itself.

It was while they were all crouched under the window, ducking and wincing at the crashes and covered with white plaster and fragments of stone, that the telephone rang.

Wutka snatched at it. It was a call from the airfield.

'It's all right,' the man at the other end said cheerfully. 'It's a false alarm. They weren't parachutists. They were dummies.'

'You're lucky,' Wutka roared. '*Ours* aren't. They're coming straight up the street with Tommy guns!'

As Rabbitt got the Spandau going, the two men he had detailed to run the captured German machine-gunners down the mole towards the ships found themselves face to face with the rest of the shore parties. With the disappearance of the guns and the searchlight at Mas el Bub, it was now possible for the men crouching below the wall on *Horambeb*, to get on to the mole and they were already beginning to move towards the town.

'Come on, chaps!' Swann was standing among the drifting swirls of smoke, magnificently exposed to the flying bullets as he gathered his men around him.

'Get going, you silly bugger!' It was the job of the survivors of Brandison's party to join Swann as he passed and, as he stared back at the officer nagging his men into a group in the smoke, it seemed to Sergeant Jacka that it would have been much wiser to go like the clappers for a bit of shelter and let the rest follow as they could. For Christ's sake, he thought, they weren't on bloody parade!

But Swann was doing it his own way. He'd been told 'No panic' and he intended there should be none. 'Let's go,' he said at last, and began to pound down the mole and across the bridge Jacka had captured.

'Come *on*, Sergeant,' he encouraged cheerfully.

Jacka muttered his opinion of Swann as he and his men scrambled to their feet and tagged on behind. As they burst from the drifting smoke, they saw Meinertz's wrecked Honey and Hockold with his men now established among the buildings at the Bab el Gawla.

As they flopped into shelter by the trees outside the mosque, a machine-gun in one of the houses near the Boujaffar opened up on them and Swann's RAF demolition expert grunted and folded up. Jacka snatched up the bag of plastic explosive and, slinging it over his shoulder, ran after Swann and crouched down alongside him among the trees, waiting for an opportunity to get up the main street. After Murdoch's dash, however, the Germans had recovered and were pinning them down firmly again. As the bullets whined over their heads, chipping splinters from the trees, Swann's determination not to get worked up grew a little frayed and he became excited to the point of exultation.

A Spandau opened up, its intimidating rate of fire making it easily distinguishable, and a group of Germans started to run towards them. Jacka fired and they all fell to the ground, except one man who dashed for shelter. Jacka shot him within ten yards of safety.

Swann nodded, sternly approving. 'We have to get up that street there,' he said.

'I should wait a bit, sir,' Jacka advised. 'We've plenty of time.'

Swann frowned. 'I think we'd better go now,' he insisted, but as he stood up a bullet whanged in a glancing blow against the curve of his steel helmet and spun him round to sit down heavily alongside Jacka, his head ringing, his brain addled, his eyes rolling in his head like marbles in a cup.

Far beyond Swann, and already well clear of the smoky centre of the town, the fuel dump party were running as hard as they could go. Murdoch was way ahead of them and waiting by the lorry compound, with the brake parked among a group of trees. With him were Corporal Cobbe, Captain Cadish, one of the RAF demolition experts, and Hank Broecker who, being an American, had decided riding was always better than running and had snatched open the rear doors and piled inside with the others.

The German guards were standing in shallow trenches by the gate of the compound, staring towards the town, wondering what was happening, and the first man to appear was Honorary Aircraftman Uri Rouat, Devenish's Palestinian. He was leading the rest of the party by yards and, as he came up, running like a stag, he ignored all the warnings he'd been given and went pounding on at full speed. One of the German gunners spotted him as he emerged from the darkness and immediately started to swing his gun. He was too late by seconds and the Palestinian jumped clean over the barrel to land with both his size eleven boots in the German's chest. As the German went down, Rouat swung his Sten by the barrel to knock the gunner's mate's teeth down his throat and, before the loader could collect his senses, he found himself being strangled by a pair of great brown fists.

The sheer speed of the attack threw the Germans into a confusion from which they had not recovered when Murdoch's party, led by Cobbe, arrived. As a German head appeared, Cobbe jammed his Sten straight at it and pulled the trigger so that it seemed to burst apart like a ripe melon, then, flinging himself down, he sent a blast of fire to clear the running figures in the compound.

Rouat dropped the dead German and looked round. 'We are winning, sir?' he asked.

'Cadish!' Murdoch appeared with a swing of his kilt and indicated the bungalows near the lorry park where the German maintenance staff, drivers and guards lived. 'Use your chaps to kill the park, but save a dozen lorries in case we need 'em to take us into the desert. And we'll have yon buildings winkled out and fortified in case we have to make a stand for Hockold to come out. Grab any weapons, food and water you can find! Corporal Cobbe'll help. He kens a fair bit about this sort of thing.'

As Murdoch signalled Cadish forward, the drivers inside the compound were trying to get the lorries away. The leading one was already heading for the road when a burst from Hank Broecker shattered the windscreen, blinded the driver, and sent it swinging off at an angle. It ran into the rear of another lorry, puncturing the petrol tank and pushing it into a third. Broecker immediately saw the possibilities and tossed a grenade towards them as men started to jump down with their weapons at the ready.

They went down like ninepins as Broecker fired, then the grenade went off and all three lorries went up in flames.

'Not bad!' The British habit of understatement appealed to Cadish. 'Not bad, Broecker!'

Murdoch nodded approvingly. 'We'll be away,' he said. 'Yon bastards at the petrol dump will be wide awake by this time.'

The Americans watched the brake head further out of town, trailing a cloud of dust and with the rest of the party trotting after it, bowed down under their heavy packs. Then Cadish swung round to his own group. 'Right, you guys,' he said. 'Fingers out! Get stuck into these goddamned lorries!'

At the other end of the town, also out of the smoke, Second-Lieutenant Sotheby was finding things a little more difficult than he'd expected. Out of what was to have been a party of sixty men, there were only nineteen left; and he was the only officer, with Berringer as his only sergeant. A lot seemed to depend on him.

He had climbed the low cliffs and crossed the road and was now crouching on the slope below the POW compound where Captain Veledetti was watching nervously from the window of his command post, wondering if it were best to surrender or put up a token resistance to satisfy honour. A gun was firing over the compound and it worried Sotheby because it hadn't been shown on the plan of the town he'd seen. What was more, it seemed to be a damned sight bigger than the 47s he'd been expecting. It occurred to him that perhaps he ought to do something about it but, lacking Collier's experience, he wasn't sure what. The firing was only sporadic, however, because now that *Umberto* and *Horambeb* were behind the mole and sheltered by the supply ships there was nowhere the gun could shoot with safety. Sotheby decided thankfully that it could wait for the time being.

Firing started round the Roman arch in the centre of the town and he assumed Hockold and his party had managed to establish themselves there. The 47 behind the Mantazeh Palace seemed to be unsighted because it wasn't worrying them, though he could hear the clatter of machine-guns from that direction. Then the gun on the cliff above him fired again and he saw the shell burst among the Arab boats in the harbour. As feluccas disintegrated in a cloud of flying splinters and whirring planks it dawned on him that the gun-crew had managed to bring it to bear towards Hockold's party and that before long it could be smashing to ruins the houses where they sheltered.

He became aware of Berringer watching him, and then that all the eyes in the other blackened features round him were on his face. He was horrified by the responsibility that had been thrown on him and his adam's apple jerked as he swallowed with difficulty. Conscious of his nervousness and lack of skill as a soldier, he bent to check the magazine on his Sten but managed instead to wrench it free. Blushing under his blacking, he sighed and shoved it back into place. He looked like a hesitant sixth-former.

'Actually, Sergeant,' he said, 'I think it's tut-time we were off.'

As he straightened up, he was astonished to see three lorries and a motor-cycle escort come round the shoulder of the hill, heading down the dusty road from the POW compound. The pioneers Hochstätter had demanded appeared so unexpectedly, the sound of their engines drowned by the clatter of firing, that they were almost past before Sotheby's party fully realized they were even coming. The first lorry roared on down the slope, but as the second one came alongside Sotheby woke up to the situation with a start and pulled the trigger of his Sten gun. Nothing happened and he realized he had the safety catch on. As he freed it, the third lorry drew level and he emptied the whole magazine into the driver's cabin. As he did so, his men woke up, too, and Sotheby had the satisfaction of seeing the lorry swerve and roll off the road, turning over and over down the slope before bursting into flames, while one of the following motor-cyclists, either dead or in a catalepsy of fright, shot over the low cliffs, still sitting bolt upright, still grasping the handle-bars, and dropped with a splash into the sea alongside the startled crew of HSL 117.

Surprised and pleased with the results of his work, Sotheby turned a grinning face towards Berringer. It appeared he could do things after all if he tried, and he waved his arm and started up the slope towards the POW camp.

Alongside him were Keely and the terrified Fidge. A product of the Gorbals, fighting was nothing new to Keely; war was only a difference of conditions and weapons. He loathed everything about the army because it imposed rules on him, but now that he was away from camp he was enjoying himself and itching to do something about killing Germans. Fidge was frankly horrified at what he'd let himself in for. When this lot was over, he kept telling himself, he'd muster out of commando training as fast as he'd mustered in.

As they scrambled over the top of the slope on to the flat ground beyond, they saw the compound in front of them.

Sotheby had expected it to be full of huts, but there were only two or three by the entrance where Veledetti and his staff worked. All the compound itself contained was a large number of ragged men, now lying flat on their faces for safety.

With one half of his men keeping down the fire of the few Germans and knocking chips off the huts where the Italians were crouching, Sotheby ran forward. Alongside him were Keely and Fidge. There were five Italians standing by the gate and Keely flattened the lot with one burst. But then an explosion of sustained firing came from a parked lorry in the shadows beyond and, just as he dived for the ground, Sotheby saw Keely stagger. It occurred to him that the POW compound wasn't going to be quite as easy as they'd expected because he'd noticed peaked Afrika Korps caps near the lorry and realized that the men who wore them were the last of the group they'd ambushed on the hill, who for some reason or other had been delayed.

Keely was still on his feet, with Fidge close behind him for shelter, and as he pulled the trigger again, the firing from the lorry died away. When Sotheby looked up, Keely was lying on his face and Fidge was standing terror-stricken, wondering what to do next. It seemed to be Fidge who'd done the damage.

The firing from the lorry had stopped only momentarily. Its crew had dived for safety and, flinging themselves flat, they opened up again so that Sotheby had to scramble up and leap forward to knock the petrified Fidge flying.

'Wu-well done,' he said as he sprawled on top of him.

They could hear yelling now from the compound as heads lifted and British cheering started. But Veledetti had finally decided to make a stand in the guard-house, and as he and his men began to fire across the compound the prisoners' heads went down again and the cheering stopped abruptly as the bullets flew, twanging on the wire and whining off into the darkness.

Sotheby lifted his head. Fidge was moaning. A bullet had nicked his ear and he was bleeding like a stuck pig. Without thinking, Sotheby half-dragged, half-carried him out of the firing, and almost hurled him into Berringer's arms.

'You all right?' he asked.

'Oi think Oi'm doying!'

As Berringer pushed Fidge away, Sotheby waved his arm. 'Get those bub-bastards with the lorry, Sergeant,' he said. 'The rest of you, come with me.'

Diving across the road to the shelter of the bank beyond, he climbed up to the huts. There were a few Italians among them but they were shot down as soon as they appeared. Then Sotheby tossed a grenade through the window of the guard-house and the shooting stopped abruptly. A moment later two Germans burst out of the hut, firing from the hip.

Sotheby yelped and fell flat on his back, but someone killed one of the Germans with a single shot and, as the other began to run across the compound, a sailor stood up among the sprawled prisoners with a stone as big as a football in his hand. He was a huge man and he flung the stone with all his strength. It struck the German at the back of the head just where his peaked cap finished, and felled him as if he'd been pole-axed.

In the sudden silence, Sotheby sat up. Inside the guard-house there were a few moans of '*Mamma*' and '*Aiuto!*' as Sotheby got to his feet, blood staining his sleeve and dripping off his finger tips.

'Lor',' he said.

'Where'd it get you, mate?' the sailor asked through the wire.

'Fore-arm.' Sotheby pulled up his sleeve and stared at the wound, surprised to see how slight it was. 'Don't think it's much.'

The firing by the lorry seemed to have stopped and they could see Berringer moving back to them at a crouch. The men with the wire-cutters ran up, and as the gate was torn to pieces they were surrounded by shouting, excited men. A few of them ran into the guard-house and, picking up dropped weapons, pushed out the surviving Italians, their hands in the air. An infantryman in tattered shorts kicked Veledetti just for spite and Sotheby turned on him.

'Stop that!' he said.

'The bastard's an Italian.'

'I said sus-sus-sus-stop it!'

A few more of the prisoners had picked up weapons and crowded round Sotheby.

'What happens next, sir?'

'You gug-gug-gug – ' Sotheby's jaw worked wildly and he began to blink rapidly ' – you go down into the tut-tut-tut – ' His excitement at his success was so intense he found he couldn't speak, and he turned in disgust to Berringer. 'Tut-tell 'em, Sergeant,' he managed.

Berringer explained. There was a yell of delight and the horde of men streamed off. Sotheby watched them go.

'Where's the signaller?' he asked.

'Here, sir.'

'Warn *Umberto* that the pup-prisoners are on their way.'

As he spoke, there was an ear-splitting crack and another icy-white flash from the cliff above, and they flung themselves to the ground. The explosion seemed to suck the breath from their bodies and, even as they whiffed the cordite fumes, they saw the shell explode near the Roman arch.

Sotheby lifted his head, frowning. 'I think we ought to dud-do something about that bastard, Sergeant,' he said.

8

Strongpoints were set up and warehouses full of Luftwaffe, panzer and transport spares were set on fire.

To Major Nietzsche, surveying what he could of the battle from the windows of a house near the Bab al Gawla, it was obvious that the struggle for Qaba had now reached a critical phase. The din was still tremendous but the British, established in the buildings round the Roman arch, weren't moving forward and they weren't showing their heads. From the naval barracks opposite the German headquarters, von Steen's sailors were keeping up a heavy fire towards them, and Nietzsche was just wondering what else he could do to dislodge them when the pioneers arrived from the POW camp.

Instead of the hundred he had expected, there were only fifty because two of the lorries seemed to have gone astray somewhere; but they were all toughened soldiers and he began to spread them out among the houses and shops of the business quarter. As he worked he heard a fresh outbreak of firing from the direction of the POW compound and he swung round to Wutka who had appeared alongside him. 'Better take a dozen men and see what's happening,' he said. 'We can't raise Veledetti. *Macht's gut. Hals und Beinbruch!*'

Wutka signed to the men around him and moved off at a run between the houses, while Nietzsche turned his attention again to the British. He had sent snipers to occupy strategic positions and they were already diving down alleys and pounding up stairs, to kick doors open and stamp past startled civilian occupants to occupy bedrooms and windows.

The fire coming from the area of the Roman arch and from what sounded like a captured Spandau set up in one of the buildings at the end of the harbour was heavy, and it was hard to do much in return. The 75 on the cliff above the POW compound was firing but it was still unsighted and its shells were only hitting the fringe of the British positions, so it was necessary to get the 47 near the Mantazeh Palace to bring its fire to bear. There was also a telephone line in Hochstätter's office to the 47 at the end of the mole, which could be swung round with a bit of initiative for a clear shot at the buildings round the arch. So far, for lack of orders, it seemed to have done remarkably little.

A motor-cycle was standing near one of the lorries that had brought the pioneers down from the POW compound. It belonged to one of the outriders who had accompanied them and Wutka decided he'd better use it to go and get the gun into action.

Reaching Hochstätter's headquarters wasn't too difficult but the Boujaffar was a wreck now and as he dived into its shelter he saw the body of the elderly commodore who had brought in the convoy lying with one of the Italian captains under a pile of chairs and tables. Somewhere in the darkness he could hear a voice moaning, 'I wish to die for the Führer. I wish to die for the Führer.'

Hochstätter's office was a shambles and Hochstätter had joined von Steen in an attempt to set up a new headquarters in the naval barracks across the road, but the telephone still worked and Wutka grabbed it and rang the crew of the 47 across the harbour.

'Get that damned gun firing!' he screamed. 'The Tommies are in the houses round the Roman arch!'

He slammed the instrument down and ran outside again to head for the 47 by the palace before going on to find Veledetti. As he crouched in the doorway of the wrecked hotel, he glanced upwards. Aeroplanes were still heading over the town towards the airfield, but they were coming in penny numbers that puzzled him as he stared at the sky, trying to pick them out. The flare of flames and the flash of guns seemed to have drawn the brightness out of the stars so that instead of hanging like great shining lanterns in the African sky they seemed dim and small and insignificant in a way that troubled Wutka.

Near him the wounded soldier in the wreckage had changed his tune – '*Mutter! Hilfe! Wo bist du, Georg? Wann kommt der Arzt?*' – and he moved into the shadows looking for him. He turned out to be little more than a boy, and his uniform was saturated with blood. Near him lay the bodies of his comrades. As Wutka stooped over him, the boy's cry changed. 'My name is Otto Knaben. I live at Mariatheresienstrasse Drei. My name is Otto Knaben –'

As he saw Wutka, his moans stopped. '*Wann kommt der Arzt?*' he asked feebly.

'*Bald,*' Wutka said. 'Soon.'

'*Immer bald,*' the boy moaned. 'They always tell me that.'

Wutka turned away, knowing he could do nothing. 'Christ damn the war,' he said bitterly, and glanced up at the stars again, as though they were the only stable things in the world.

It was at that moment that Sugarwhite, after lying stunned for a good ten minutes following his collision with the camel, picked himself up. His mouth seemed to be caked with salt, he had twisted his ankle and had a cut on his nose, while the two smallest fingers of his left hand appeared to have been damaged. He still felt dizzy and his chest was bruised where he'd fallen on his Sten. Why he hadn't blown a hole in himself he couldn't understand, because his legs and arms felt as though the camel had danced a fandango on him. It still sprawled a few yards away, like a heap of old coconut matting, all long legs and neck, snorting its life blood out through its nostrils in a red froth into the dark dust that jumped and quivered in the fire from the naval barracks and the business quarter towards the Roman arch.

Staring at the leaping dust, it seemed to Sugarwhite that it would be a good idea to find somewhere safer, but as he scrambled to his feet, his body rolled to the vacuum of a passing shot. The crack that followed was as if the shell had exploded right alongside him, and he heard the whine of flying fragments of steel and the clatter of them falling to earth with the scraps of stone they'd gouged out of the nearby buildings. Swathes of smoke were drifting past, choking him, as if he were in hell, and he could hear the harsh chatter of machine-guns.

As he got a grip on himself his fear dried in his throat. 'Steady, the Buffs,' he said aloud and he began to sort himself out slowly, still dazed but surprised to find he wasn't afraid. Anger was growing in him. So far he hadn't shot anybody, hadn't committed mayhem of any kind and, bruised as he was, he was very anxious to do someone some harm.

Looking round, he saw that Hockold had edged forward with a group of men under Amos and Rabbitt into the buildings on the water's edge directly opposite the Shariah Jedid. But the German gun by the Mantazeh Palace suddenly opened up on them and Sugarwhite, still trying to get his breath, saw heads go down like a lot of coconuts in a coconut shy. The shell struck the base of the Roman arch and stones were gouged out of it. Almost immediately another shell struck it and, as more stones crumbled from almost the same spot, it occurred to Sugarwhite that the arch was beginning to look a little top-heavy and that it wouldn't take much more to bring it down.

There was a wooden jetty, surrounded by native boats, extending into the harbour in front of the gun, and the gun crew was having difficulty in bringing their weapon to bear. It had never been intended to fire the gun into the town and the wooden masts and rigging of the feluccas were in the way so that the shells were missing the low buildings where Hockold's party were established. Even as Sugarwhite considered the situation, a third shell hit the base of the Roman arch. His eyes widened as he saw it teeter, moving almost like a tree in a high wind. Then it toppled and crashed, bas reliefs of Roman legionaries and all, thundering down in a heap of ancient stones and a cloud of lifting dust. To Sugarwhite there seemed something terribly sad in an edifice which had defied nature for two thousand years being knocked to pieces by some bloody rotten little Nazi gunner; it helped to poison his attitude a little bit more.

The bullets were still stirring the dust nearby. He had no idea where anybody else was and was terrified of being shot by his own side.

'War Weapons Week, Weymouth,' he yelled into the whirling dust.

'Over here, you soft sod,' a voice called back from a group of mud-brick houses alongside the mosque and, taking advantage of the confusion that the fallen arch had caused, he set off for them in a crouching run. As he did so, a burst of firing from the houses across the Shariah Jedid made him dive rather more hurriedly for shelter than he'd intended and he knocked his knee badly and jarred his injured fingers.

As he sat up he saw Sergeant Freelove staring down at him. 'Where've you been?' he demanded angrily.

Sugarwhite looked up indignantly. 'I've been getting shot at,' he said. 'That's where! I think I've broken my ribs!'

Freelove seemed unimpressed and gestured towards the remains of the Roman arch and the settling dust. 'Well, you're needed up there,' he said sourly. 'Up by them houses. Get stuck in!'

Sugarwhite had expected at least a 'How are you?' or a mug of tea and a word of sympathy, but all he'd got was 'Get stuck in' as if he'd been shirking. But then, as he crouched down by the mud dwellings, he realized what was causing Freelove's impatience. Hickey, the American doctor, was using the shelter of the buildings as a dressing station and the area around him was like a scene from a nightmare. Small groups of men were huddled there, clutching injured limbs, their faces pale and desperate in the glare of the flames which made their bloodstains look black. They had lost all interest in the battle and were concerned now only with getting to safety. Around them, stones and rubble were scattered across the road under the drifting dust and smoke. Not far away two or three dead Germans sprawled like half-empty sacks of flour. Behind him, a stone-built hut was burning fiercely, someone still screaming inside. Alongside it there was a dead mule and a bullet-chipped cart, and in its shelter Hickey was crouching over a man who still clutched his rifle with pain-filled desperation.

Another man was lying on his side, his trousers slit to the thigh, a bandage round a shattered knee, and near him an RAF corporal lay propped against a pack, snoring with a wound in the head. Mitchell, one of the Stooges, was by the side of the road, quite still, his hips and legs twisted unnaturally. A fourth man was trapped under a collapsed wall, moaning, his hair white with dust. 'Oh, Christ,' he was muttering. 'Oh, Christ, my back!' Two or three other men were trying to drag him out, tossing bricks and rubble aside with a ferocious, desperate speed. As Sugarwhite stared, sudden tears in his eyes, he saw Hickey, his hands red with blood, crawl over to him and, breaking the seal of the morphia capsule of a hypodermic, calmly begin to screw on the needle.

Someone was mewing with terror nearby and Sugarwhite saw it was Taffy Jones, cowering under a hand-cart containing drums of petrol, his head down, his face chalk-white, a string of saliva hanging from his open mouth. Remembering his old ebullience, Sugarwhite gaped at him aghast. Yet somehow he couldn't condemn as a coward a man who could so publicly display his funk when all the rest, just as afraid as he was, felt obliged to hide theirs in case their friends should sneer. Sugarwhite gulped, hating every German in the world for the suffering they had caused, even for the humiliation they were bringing on the wretched Taffy.

There was another explosion and the air buffeted him, knocking his helmet over his ear with a hard jolt; somewhere nearby a machine-gun shuddered in a long run and a geyser of smoke which had lifted into the air began to drift past him. The whole bloody place was full of gusts and cracks and flashes of light, and as he lifted his head he heard Gardner who was firing around a corner of one of the huts give a little gasp and saw him start to sway. His head began to roll, his face turning blindly as if trying to make out where he'd been hit, and he slid down the wall of the hut; one arm still moving feebly as he gradually sank to his knees, his head bowing forward, a hand clutching his chest, so that he looked like an Arab making his obeisances to Mecca.

One of the American orderlies ran to him but the machine-gun started again and, just as Sugarwhite joined him at Gardner's side, he fell across the wounded man, a gaping hole in his neck. Sugarwhite stared in horror, wondering in a panic which of the two men he should attend to first. There seemed to be little sign of injury on Gardner but the American was losing blood with great speed.

Trying to remember what he'd learned about first-aid, Sugarwhite dragged out his field dressing and tried to bandage him, but the blood spurted over his hands, drenching his sleeves and splashing his face. The American groaned and twisted as Sugarwhite tore at his shirt to staunch the flow. Then, with unexpected suddenness, he became quiet, his face grey, and Sugarwhite laid him down, choking with a sense of futility. Gardner was also silent by this time and Sugarwhite looked round, desperate for someone to tell him what to do, seeking encouragement, even a faint sign of success somewhere among the slaughter.

But Sergeant Freelove was now busy with Mitchell while Taffy Jones still crouched with his head down, indifferent to everything. He had reached the end of terror now, the extreme of emotional degradation. Half delirious, he was grasping at the dusty earth, hunched, panting, not looking up, one hand combing through his greasy hair, his eyes dilated, his cheeks blanched with horror.

'Let's get out of here,' someone said, infected by his fear, and Freelove turned from where he was bent over Mitchell.

'Shut up,' he snapped. He lashed out with his boot at Taffy. 'Pull your bloody self together, man! You!' He glared at Sugarwhite. 'Get up forward!'

Sugarwhite nodded speechlessly, thankful for even the smallest indication of leadership. He glanced at Gardner still kneeling head-down alongside the wall and, concerned for him, remembering that he'd been the first man at Gott el Scouab to show any sign of friendliness towards him, he pawed at him unhappily, wondering if he could do something to help. But the Yorkshireman didn't move and Sugarwhite saw that he'd gone as grey as the American.

'Go on!' He realized Freelove was staring at him. 'What are you waiting for?'

Sugarwhite nodded again and, grasping his rifle and scrambling to his feet, scuttled through the drifting dust from the fallen arch towards the buildings opposite the mosque. As he flung himself down, he saw Hockold crouching behind a wall with Amos who had a bandage round one of his hands. With them were Waterhouse, Belcher, Tinner Eva, and Docwra who had blood on his face and looked as though he'd like to be sick. As Sugarwhite stared around him, trying to make out who was alive and who was dead, a shell from the 75 above the POW compound whistled past the front of the German headquarters and exploded on the harbour wall. The blast knocked Sugarwhite's helmet over his ear again and sent him staggering. As he picked himself up, he saw on the wall a canary in one of the little wooden cages the Italians seemed to like. It was terrified by the racket, fluttering inside its prison and beating its wings frantically against the bars. Sugarwhite gazed at it for a moment, thinking angrily what a bloody silly lot the Italians were to bring a singing bird into a place like Qaba to be frightened to death.

As he took the cage down, a sniper's bullet spanged against the stonework a foot from his head. He collapsed in a heap, his eyes full of gritty dust and shocked by his narrow escape. He was burning with hatred against the Germans. It seemed they were venting their spite on him alone. His ribs hurt, and his futile rage was laced through with an agonizing misery at the death of his friends. Placing the cage in a corner, he watched the canary's panic die away to sporadic flutterings. Then he patted the cage as if to say, 'It'll be all right now,' and gripped his rifle, looking round for something on which he could work off his loathing of the Nazis.

It was at that moment that Wutka burst out from among the buildings by the Boujaffar on the motor-bike. Firing was coming from the houses opposite and most of the men with Hockold were occupied with keeping it down, so that only Hockold and Sugar-white, facing directly towards Ibrahimiya, spotted him. Sugarwhite froze, the skin tight across his jaw. Wutka was clearly an officer and, to the infuriated Sugarwhite, the sort of brutal SS Nazi who had caused so much wretchedness in the world. It was a long shot but the bullet hit Wutka in the small of the back to sever his spine as if it had been chopped with an axe.

As Wutka let go of the handlebars and toppled backwards, the motor-bike went careering onwards to crash into the corner of the naval barracks and fall over with spinning wheels, leaving him spreadeagled in the middle of the road, staring at the stars, aware with his last shreds of consciousness that before long there would be no stars, no sky, nothing but darkness.

'Good shot, Abdul,' Hockold said, and Sugarwhite turned, startled and more pleased that Hockold knew his nickname than by the fact that he'd killed the German. It was almost as good as if he'd shot Hitler.

As Wutka died, Nietzsche was turning his attention to the men infiltrating the buildings by the ruined arch. His snipers were in position and every time anyone in the centre of the town raised his head a rifle cracked. But the British were not giving ground, and he turned to the sergeant alongside him.

'I think we might get them with mortars,' he said. 'Bring them up.'

As the sergeant hurried off, bent double, Nietzsche crept to the window to look at the position below. A sniper was crouching there, his face pressed against the brickwork, only the edge of his cheek and his eye showing. As Nietzsche reached him, he gestured to him to keep down.

Then the sniper pulled the trigger and Nietzsche lifted his head again for a quick look. The firing below had died a little and the British seemed to have gone to ground again.

In fact, they had just discovered Dr Carell's bunker below the harbour wall.

'Sir –' Sergeant Freelove came running bent double to where Hockold was crouching ' – there's a German dressing station just behind us. There's a doctor there.'

'Right.' Hockold turned and scrambled back with him to Dr Hickey by the mud huts. 'Sergeant Freelove's found somewhere for you to set up an aid post,' he said. 'You'd better get going. We'll cover you.'

As the firing broke out again, the American and his orderlies ran for the harbour wall, bent double, carrying and dragging the wounded with them. Hockold went after them and Dr Carell, wearing a white apron, turned to meet them as they appeared. He had three wounded Germans and an Italian with him.

'*Sprechen Sie Englisch?*' Hockold asked.

Carell nodded.

'I'm taking this place over. Are you a doctor?'

Again Carell's head inclined.

'Well, you can consider yourself my prisoner or you can help with the wounded. Whichever you like. You need fear nothing from my people if you help.'

Carell's head came up. 'You have no need to threaten me, Herr Oberst,' he said. 'I'm a doctor and there are no nationalities among injured men.'

When Hockold got back, Amos was bending over Sergeant Freelove who'd just been hit in the neck.

'Sniper,' Amos said. 'He's up there among the houses somewhere.'

Eva, crouching among the bricks near Sergeant Sidebottom, turned. 'Would 'ee like me to get 'un, sir?'

'Know where he is?' Hockold asked.

'In yon window wi' the red blind, sir! 'E keeps shovin' his head up for a look.'

'Think you can?'

'I can take a mouse's eye out, sir.'

As Hockold called for stretcher-bearers for Freelove, Eva rested his rifle on his pack and squinted along it.

There was still a lot of firing, and Hockold turned to glance at

Swann and Jacka crouching down beside him. It was time they
were moving off towards the warehouse but there was no point
in their getting themselves killed for a matter of a minute or so of
waiting.

He directed the machine-gunners towards the windows where
the firing was coming from and it died a little. Then Eva's rifle
cracked, and he looked round to see a figure rise in the window
with the red blind and flop back out of sight.

'Got the mucky toad,' Eva said happily. 'That's two!'

The sniper stared round at Nietzsche laying flat on his back
alongside him, one eye a bloody hollow, his face mildly surprised,
then he turned to shout to Unteroffizier Upholz in the next room.

'They've got the major! He's dead.'

Upholz gestured and a corporal ran to the sniper's room. But
he was foolish enough not to keep his head far enough down,
and the joyful Eva put a bullet straight through his temple to
slam him against the far wall.

'Three,' he yelled. 'They don't know the first thing about it!'

The sniper squirmed on his stomach to the next room where
Unteroffizier Upholz and half a dozen men were firing
industriously towards the remains of the Roman arch.

'They got the corporal as well,' he said flatly. 'This place's
getting too dangerous.'

As the firing from the house opposite died, Swann stood up.
He was annoyed at the narrow escape he'd had but by no means
scared. Crouching among the trees with the bullets whistling
over his head, his exultation burst out in a great shout of excitement.

'Come on,' he roared, leaping unexpectedly to his feet. 'Come
on!'

None of his men was ready and they were slow to move. Bullets whacked into the trees about them and one of them went
down with a crash. It only served to excite Swann still more
and he stood erect, yelling and waving his arm.

Hockold saw him from the ruined arch. 'Get down, man!' he

yelled, but Swann was oblivious to everything now and had set off running. He rounded the corner by the mosque into the Shariah Jedid in fine style, yards ahead of the heavily-laden Jacka and the rest of his party.

'For God's sake,' Jacka muttered in disgust.

Swann was charging happily up the hill now, elated by the fact that he was out of the German fire and by the knowledge that this time he was going to show everyone what he could do. Turn right, he'd been told. An opening appeared alongside him. It was nothing but an alley and was clearly the one he'd been told to avoid. Just ahead of him was another opening wider than the first.

'Not that one!' Jacka yelled, but Swann didn't hear him in his excitement and swung round the corner, so blind with elation he hardly knew what he was doing.

Jacka saw him go. 'Oh, Christ,' he said. 'The silly bugger didn't have to do that!'

On the corner of the alley down which Swann had disappeared, Jacka stopped dead. Almost immediately it narrowed and turned again, and there was no sign of Swann. Jacka knew it was dangerous to go in there, and he signed to the men to follow him up the Shariah Jedid instead. Twenty yards further on he saw the opening he wanted.

'Here we go,' he said.

Immediately in front of him there was a warehouse surrounded by a wire fence with a notice bearing a skull and crossbones and the words, *Achtung! Lebensgefahr!*

There was a little guard-house by the entrance, from which a burst of firing came as they approached. They flattened themselves against the wall; then Jacka pulled out a grenade and tossed it at the guard-house. It bounced off the door and burst with a shattering crash in the narrow street.

It didn't seem to have done any damage but the door of the guard-house opened and two Germans stumbled out with their hands in the air. In the excitement one of Jacka's men shot them.

'You silly sod,' Jacka said furiously. 'They'd packed it in!'

He blew the lock off the gate with his Tommy gun and, as he did so, he became aware of another man lifting his head from behind a crate just beyond. He fired quickly. Splinters leapt from the crate and the head disappeared. In the silence he could hear moaning.

As they pushed through the wrecked gate, they found themselves in a small compound, with the doors of the warehouse at the end of it. Again they shot the lock to pieces. Dragging the doors back, they found themselves staring at crates, piles of shavings and stacks of tyres.

'That lot'll burn nicely,' Jacka said with satisfaction. 'I wonder what that silly bugger Swann's doing?'

Swann was staring down at the bodies of two people he'd just shot. As he'd hurtled out of the Shariah Jedid and down the winding alley he'd found himself face to face, not with a warehouse as he'd expected, but with a group of small flat-roofed native houses that gave off a smell of urine. They'd looked wrong and he was just wondering where he'd made his mistake when he saw two figures moving in the shadows by a doorway and fired automatically.

They fell into the street and, as he edged forward warily, he saw that both were Arabs. One was a mere boy with a fez on his head who was sprawled against the wall, stone dead, his nose punched in by Swann's bullet, his crossed eyes staring blankly at his bare feet. The other, who looked like a bundle of dirty washing, appeared to be an old man, his eyes opaque with trachoma; he was moaning quietly and Swann could see blood oozing from underneath his rags.

Realizing in horror that the man was blind and that the boy had been leading him to safety, he looked round for Sergeant Jacka for advice. To his surprise, there was no one with him and he moved back a little down the winding lane. But there was no one there either and he swung once more towards the two bodies, worried about the old man. He was still standing there when Private Bontempelli, shoving his head out of Zulfica Ifzi's room to see if it were safe to leave, stumbled into him.

He was as startled as Swann and quite prepared to put his hands up in surrender. But Swann was troubled, lost and shocked at having shot two harmless people who weren't even in the battle, and he was slow to respond.

Bontempelli recovered first and lifted his rifle. '*Mani in alto!*' he said. His voice was almost falsetto with fear.

Swann stared. 'Pardon?'

Bontempelli coughed and swallowed. '*Hände hoch,*' he tried. 'Hands – oop!' He drew a deep breath and lifted the rifle. '*Per favore, Signore,*' he added politely.

9

Attention was then turned to fuel supplies, gun positions and supply ships.

The smoke which had aided all the other parties had served only to hinder Captain Watson. It was blowing back from the smoke floats at the end of the mole and, caught by the blast from the guns, was drifting over the supply ships in whirling swathes, thick, choking and obscure.

Watson had been the first man on board. The draped folds of the heavy camouflage nets, threaded with broad strips of coloured canvas, made the decks gloomy, but there were areas of speckled light where the glare from the flames shone through and as he had leapt aboard *Andolfo*, the inner ship of the trot of three, he saw a startled officer pop up from a hatchway.

'*Wer da?*' the officer said, wondering what was happening, and Watson, still running, kicked him in the face like a footballer taking a ball on the run. The officer's head snicked back, his neck broken, and he slid out of sight. Followed by Devenish and a group of soldiers, Watson continued without a pause across the connecting gangplank to *Guglielmotti*, the next ship. A soldier carrying a gun appeared round a winch. Automatically, the man alongside Watson lunged forward with his bayonet and the soldier fell back with a scream. On *Cassandra*, the last ship, the guards, who'd been inside the galley making coffee, had more time to collect themselves. But when they appeared and found themselves faced with the horde of black-faced men bristling with weapons, they weren't sure what to do. They knew all too well what was beneath their feet and had already decided among themselves when they'd first heard of the likelihood of a raid that it was probably unwise even to fire a rifle. An Italian merchant seaman who appeared confirmed their fears. '*No*!' he screamed, diving behind an open hatch. '*Non tirare!*'

The British, better organized and better briefed, didn't have to worry and the three guards went down under a swarm of dark figures with flashing knives and bayonets.

Led by the naval guides, Watson's party scoured the officers' and crews' quarters of the three ships. It didn't take long and as they began to come up on deck, their hands in the air, Devenish started to climb into the hold of *Andolfo* with his plastic explosive.

As he disappeared, an unexpected burst of firing from the end of the mole stopped the other party dead in their tracks as they headed for *Giuseppe Bianchi*, further along. Watson was standing under the drooping netting at the end of *Andolfo*'s gangplank where he could keep an eye on all four ships at once, at the same time shepherding the captured crews over to *Umberto*. He was quite safe from the machine-gunners on the end of the mole, but a chance burst from the houses across the harbour swept across the decks, ripping through the netting and making the strips of canvas leap and dance. As Watson's head jerked up, the next burst ripped into his face, neck and shoulders, and sent him staggering sideways across the mole to crash into the wooden shelter Upholz and Wutka had used as they checked the cargoes.

For a moment, he clung to the shelter, his fingers clawing the wood, startled by the lash of pain and his inability to do anything about it. Then, slowly, as his knees gave way, he slid down, his face scraping the rough timber to leave a dark smear across its gritty surface, and fell into a sitting position before rolling gently sideways. Shocked by the suddenness of his dying, as he felt the cold stone of the mole against his cheek, he knew without the slightest doubt that he would never see his wife again and would go groping through eternity to find her, his last conscious thought the question, Why? Why? Why?

As Devenish emerged from the hold of *Andolfo* and pushed aside the camouflage netting, Sergeant Bunch appeared from the *Giuseppe Bianchi* party. He carried a haversack and looked worried. 'Sir,' he announced, 'our party copped it and the navy chap's stopped one. These are his charges but we've nobody to place 'em.'

'Oh, dear,' Devenish said. 'Well, just hang on a minute, Sergeant, please. I'll be along when I've finished here.'

Bunch stiffened to his plaster mould salute and went back to where his men were crouching behind bollards and piles of rope, a little startled at the good manners of RAF officers. As the wounded were dragged away, he indicated the stone warehouses further along the mole. 'I think we ought to do something about that,' he said. 'There's a crowd of nasty old Jerries down there.'

Almost as he spoke, the 47 at the end of the mole fired across the harbour. Like the gun near the Mantazeh Palace it had never been intended to fire into the town, and only Wutka's telephone call had stirred its bewildered crew to life. It was hard to see what was happening round the Roman arch for the dust and smoke, but as they dragged the gun round, they saw HSL 117, a sitting target as it waited for Sotheby below the POW compound. At the crash, the camouflage netting on *Giuseppe Bianchi* leapt and the HSL, the last one afloat, went up in flames. As it began to settle, the crew of the 47 got to work again to manhandle their weapon further round towards the town. They were occupied with drawing a bead on what looked like a group of men round a machine-gun when the smoke cleared unexpectedly, and Bunch's party were seen edging forward along the mole.

As the machine-gunners opened up and Bunch and his men flopped down behind the drums and crates and timbers once more, they were spotted by the 47 by the Mantazeh Palace. Its crew worked the barrel round and let off a round across the harbour, which knocked a rusty ventilator from the sunken freighter in front of the warehouse and whanged into the wall of the mole near where Bunch was lying.

'Bit nasty round here,' Bunch observed mildly as chunks of concrete and metal flew through the air. 'I think we'd better nip back and bring up a few reinforcements.'

The Raid

Still wondering what had happened to Swann, Sergeant Jacka had prepared a splendid bonfire. He had even found a second warehouse attached to the first, which was full of clothing and other stores. Manhandling drums of petrol from the little compound by the gate, he and his party forced them open and poured their contents among the crates, shavings, tyres and bales of clothing. Then he opened skylights and doors to make a good draught and, withdrawing his men, placed two charges with five-minute time pencils and retreated to the gate. Just to make sure, he withdrew the pin from a Mills bomb, tossed it into the store, and ran.

It didn't need the plastic explosive.

He had just reached the corner when the grenade exploded, and the blast of the petrol going off sent him skidding on his chest into the arms of his men. In a matter of minutes both warehouses were ablaze.

The glare lit their sweating, dusty, blackened faces and Jacka watched for a while to make sure everything was well alight. Then he gestured. 'Right,' he said. 'We can think about getting back now.' He looked round. 'I wonder if that silly sod Swann's found his way out of Wogtown yet.'

As a matter of fact, Lieutenant Swann, seething with fury, was sitting on a none-too-sweetly-smelling bed in Zulfica Ifzi's room not very far from Jacka's blaze. His revolver and Sten gun reposed on the floor by the door and a perspiring Private Bontempelli sat facing him on a chair, pointing a rifle at his chest. Zulfica Ifzi stood alongside the Italian, chewing gum and occasionally taking a drink from a bottle of beer.

'Look,' Swann tried. 'This is silly.'

Bontempelli frowned. '*Signore?*'

'I mean, you've lost the war.' Swann tried to gesture while keeping his hands in the air. 'It's obvious. You might as well give yourself up.'

Bontempelli could understand quite a lot of what Swann was saying but he preferred to feign ignorance. '*Signore?*'

'I mean, give yourself up to me now and I'll see you get jolly good treatment.'

For a moment Swann wondered – as he'd wondered on and off for some time now – whether he could take a dive at Bontempelli and wrestle the gun from him. But Bontempelli's finger was on the trigger and he looked nervous.

In fact, Bontempelli was *very* nervous because he'd just remembered that his rifle wasn't loaded. There were bullets in the pouches on the belt resting across his knee but he'd forgotten to thrust a clip into the magazine and he had a suspicion that if he tried to now, Swann would take the opportunity to pounce on him. Despite their well-known sense of fair play, he had a feeling that the British didn't stick to the rules when they were in trouble.

It occurred to him he might use Swann's Sten, but he had no idea how a Sten worked and he felt that if he took his eyes off Swann long enough to find out, it would be just *too* long. There was also the revolver, of course, but British service revolvers were reputed to have a kick like a mule so that you couldn't hit the side of a house with them even at ten yards. No, he decided, it was safer to keep the muzzle of his empty rifle pointed at Swann's chest and hope for the best, conscious that nobody but he knew how his life hung entirely on the Englishman's ignorance.

Zulfica Ifzi was watching him, her eyes bright. It was obvious she thought him a hero and he knew that the next time he arrived on her doorstep the fun and games would be twice as erotic as hitherto. She was an accomplished performer when she gave her mind to it and, by the look on her face, in future she'd be a mass of concentration.

The more he thought about it, in fact, the luckier he realized he was. When it was all over, somebody would be bound to ask questions about him failing to appear at Ibrahimiya with the other Italians, but if the British were driven away it was going to be possible to emerge with a prisoner. If the British *weren't* driven away he could graciously hand over the rifle to the Englishman and surrender instead. He seemed to be covered both ways, and it seemed very much by now as if the raiders were just about everywhere it was possible to be except in Zulfica Ifzi's room.

Bontempelli was dead right. They were.

Out at the lorry park, Captain Cadish had already extracted fifteen Lancia trucks – more than enough, he reckoned, to carry a hundred and fifty men – and dispersed them around the group of bungalows which he had fortified and stocked with petrol, tinned food and water. Then the rest of the lorries had been driven together, their tanks punctured, and destroyed with a grenade tossed in the middle.

'Piece of cake,' Cadish said.

So far it had been a piece of cake for Murdoch too. Expecting the most difficult job of all, he had fallen, in fact, for the easiest, though he had made it easier by the speed and certainty with which he'd moved.

When Murdoch arrived among them, the handful of guards and stores staff at the fuel depot had still been watching the glare of flames from the town and the lorry park and the occasional flash of a bomb to the south on the airfield, and trying to make up their minds which ought to occupy their attention first. They were all either dead, wounded or prisoners within a matter of minutes.

While the survivors were being shepherded into the road, Cobbe, Auchmuty and a few others went round the hundreds of drums which by Wutka's diligence had already been stacked there, piercing them with ice-picks while By's great fists hurled them to the ground to spill their contents in the dust. Then the RAF explosives expert and Honorary Aircraftman Rouat placed five-minute time charges and ran.

There was a drainage ditch alongside the road to carry sudden winter downpours to the sea and they all took shelter in it. While they were waiting for the bang, Baldissera's lorries arrived on the scene. The Italians had wasted a good twenty minutes arguing with the Luftwaffe at Ibrahimiya before it had dawned on them that their presence was no longer required there. The air raid seemed to be over and the alarm about parachutists seemed to be a false one; but, no more keen to face black-faced commandos than they were to face black-faced parachutists, they had turned their vehicles about unwillingly and headed slowly back. They were just approaching the petrol dump when the first charge went off and the stacks of drums went up, less with a bang than a whoof. A whole series of explosions followed, as if a giant were blowing huge breathy belches across the face of the desert.

Without waiting for orders, the Italians dived from their lorries and pressed themselves to the earth while fragments of scrap iron and wood and brick bounced with little puffs into the dust around them. When they lifted their heads again the whole hundred-yard-square expanse of the compound was roaring, sending huge black clouds of smoke into the sky. The heat was so tremendous it created its own draught and they could feel the air being sucked past them to feed the flames. Dust and uprooted shrubs began to roll with it and disappeared as cinders into the heavens with the smoke.

'Holy Mother of God,' Baldissera said. 'What happened?'

One of the men behind him started to pray. '*Siccome Voi, o gran Dio –*'

'Shut up!' Sergente Barbella gave him a kick, and they began to move forward towards the flames to see what was happening. Eventually they were standing in groups, illuminated by the glare not fifty yards from where Murdoch's party crouched in the ditch.

'God damn it,' Cadish whispered, shocked. 'We'll be shooting 'em from the back!'

Murdoch shrugged. 'Gey sight safer than shooting 'em from the front,' he said.

It was possible to see the glare of the burning petrol dump from the centre of the town, and Hockold knew that Murdoch had done his job well. The mortars that Nietzsche had brought into action before he was killed were now dropping their bombs among the buildings by the remains of the Roman arch. Docwra had been killed, while Cook-Corporal Rogers, a little startled to find the war rather more bloody than he'd expected, was lying on his back among the scattered stonework. Eva bent over him. There was blood on Rogers' face and he was dazed and shocked. 'They got me, Tinner,' he said. 'Better take me money.'

Eva did as he was told. Then he took another look at Rogers in the light of the flames. 'Tedden that bad, Rodge,' he said. 'Tedden only a scratch.'

Rogers' head lifted. 'You sure?'

' 'Course I'm sure.'

Rogers heaved. 'Then give us back me wallet,' he said.

As he struggled to sit up, however, another of the mortar bombs dropped nearby with a nerve-shattering crash and he forgot his money, even the wound that had knocked him over, and dived for shelter with a yell of fright.

The explosion left another man sprawled grotesquely over a captured Spandau and a second badly wounded. Sugarwhite and Willow struggled to lift him out of the rubble, Sugarwhite – his hurt ribs making him catch his breath – wondering as he strained under the weight, if it was as difficult for a dead man to be hoisted into heaven. Carrying the injured man into the bunker, smeared with his blood and with his arms flopping round them in a parody of affection, they were shocked by the pain they faced. There was a stink of death in the place and they were glad to get away.

'God,' Willow said, his mouth trembling. 'There's more stiffs than living in that place!'

They wormed their way back to their shelter among the rubble and, as they gripped their rifles, a German ran from the buildings across the Shariah Jedid towards the mosque in an attempt to outflank their party. Sugarwhite shot him before he reached shelter and he rolled over in a whirl of arms and legs. Almost immediately a sergeant appeared in an alley between the buildings, waving and shouting other men into a rush, and Sugarwhite shot him, too. But as the rush died away in a spatter of fire from the ruins of the Roman arch, the mortar began to fire again. An abrupt crash lifted him from the ground and slammed him down again with a force that jarred his teeth and knocked the breath from his body. His helmet seemed to be crushed on his head and his lungs became filled with a rush of sand and grit that scraped at his injured ribs.

He gave Willow a stiff wooden grimace that was meant to be a smile. 'They've got us taped,' he panted.

A shell from the 75 above the POW compound whacked into the rubble, and while the stones and dirt were still falling on them the Germans tried another rush. Sugarwhite brought one of them down and Eva shot another, and the rest dived back into shelter. Then the mortar started again, the crashes seeming to shake the flesh loose over their nerves.

'I reckon we ought to move over a bit,' Sugarwhite said.

He had just heaved himself painfully to his knees, looking for a better shelter, when another shell from the 75 exploded alongside them and the shock wave snatched him up like a rag doll in the shrivelling heat of a molten flash and flung him head-first into the wreckage of the Roman arch.

Willow lifted his head and stared with haggard eyes at the pair of legs sticking stiffly up in the air. 'Poor old Abdul,' he muttered.

The main party was under heavy pressure from three sides. Unafraid of death because it seemed inevitable, it had always been Hockold's intention to draw as much fire as he could so that the demolition parties could work unhindered. But, whatever his own fatalism, he felt he owed life to the rest of his party, and with the mortars, the two 47s and the 75 above the compound firing at them, he could see their numbers dwindling away to nothing.

Another mortar bomb landed with a deafening crash, and bricks and stones bounced among them.

'I think it's behind the hotel,' Amos said. 'Let me have a go at getting it. I can get into the Shariah Jedid and to-and-fro a bit round the back door.'

'How many men will you need?'

'Ten should be enough with Sergeant Sidebottom.'

Collecting his men, Amos snatched at a haversack containing

ammunition and, waiting for a lull in the firing, dived for the trees across the road. They made one of the houses opposite without difficulty and, as Sidebottom shot the lock off the door, they burst inside. The house was furnished luxuriously and there was even a piano. Waterhouse crossed towards it and, caparisoned as he was for war, his concave cheeks black, his ginger hair over his eyes, he began to pick out the National Anthem.

'Nice tone,' he observed in his flat catarrhal voice.

As the rest of the party arrived they gathered round Amos. 'We're going further up the street and through that door there,' he said. 'Ready?'

'Right,' Sidebottom said.

As they dashed out again, they were spotted and a machine gun on top of the naval barracks opened up. They flung themselves into the doorway, and a flying splinter of stone whipped over Sidebottom's shoulder to lay Amos's forehead open from his eye to the hairline.

Pausing to blink away the blood and the shock, he shook his head in an attempt to get his senses back. With an effort, he succeeded and looked round at Sidebottom who was watching him.

'I'm all right,' he said. 'Come on. Inside.'

They had reached the entrance to what had clearly once been the home of some wealthy Egyptian. As they smashed the door open they heard a scream and, whirling, Amos saw a plump, terrified girl in a yellow dress crouching behind it, holding an enamel jug to her chest. They were in a small tiled courtyard, with a fountain surrounded by plants. The roof was open to the sky; bullets had smashed the leaded window and shattered the figure of a dolphin in the centre of the fountain so that the jet was spraying wildly across the floor. The wet tiles were covered with plaster, glass, and fragments of pottery, stone and wood, and the girl's cheek had been cut by a splinter. She was obviously quite certain she was going to be raped.

'Tell her to shut up, Sergeant,' Amos said, his forehead dripping blood on to his blouse. Sidebottom crossed to the girl and began to address her in his quaint mixture of English, Egyptian and Indian Army pidgin.

She stopped screaming and said something, but her wide, shocked eyes never left their faces.

'She says her old man's the caretaker, sir,' Sidebottom reported. 'He had to go home because he was ill. They were comty feloose so she took over for the night. She'd locked herself in.'

'Tell her she's all right.'

Sidebottom spoke to the girl again, bending over her so that she cringed back, her wet skirt up over her fat thighs, her feet pulled under her, her hands still clutching the jug, her eyes staring at them in terrified black orbs.

Amos had been watching through the back window and had located the mortar established on a small patch of green behind the Boujaffar, its bombs sailing over the low out-buildings into the Bab al Gawla.

'I've found it,' he said. 'Let's go.'

Leaving Sidebottom and two men to cover him, he led the rest of the men through the back door. But they were seen by a group of riflemen on top of the Boujaffar and the first man out was flung back against the wall, his Sten hitting Waterhouse in the face, so that he went down with a crash, stunned and bleeding from a split lip. Amos was also hit, this time in the cheek, and it sent him spinning back against the wall while the girl behind the door screamed again as the bullets came through, bringing down ugly enamelled pottery and plates ranged on shelves along the opposite wall in a shower of flying fragments, and making the plaster jump into the air in a cloud of dust and grit.

Amos shook his head, spattering the girl's dress with blood from his torn cheeks as he spat out broken teeth. His mouth was a livid gash and he could hardly see for the pain, but he grasped his Sten and waved soundlessly towards the door. Sidebottom threw a grenade and the mortar disappeared in a cloud of smoke. Two or three German heads popped up from a shallow trench just behind, and as Amos, half-blinded and desperate, shot at them they disappeared again at once.

Gagging on his words, he gestured ahead and the party pounded across the patch of grass to the trench. Among the Germans was an elderly sergeant who was crouched with his head pressed against the earth, waiting for death. Dazed by his third wound, Amos couldn't bring himself to drive a bullet between the thin shoulders and instead he jabbed the German with the muzzle of his gun and indicated that he should shove his hands in the air.

As they grabbed the mortar and headed back to the houses, with the two surviving Germans, the men on the top of the Boujaffar started firing once more and, even as they stumbled back into shelter, Amos was hit in the face yet again. He spun round, his jaw broken, his tongue shredded, and fell with a crash into the room where the girl was crouching.

As he sprawled on his back on the wet floor, Sidebottom bent over him and dragged out his field dressing. Amos feebly waved it away but he couldn't speak and as Sidebottom stared down at him, he saw the girl crawl to the broken fountain with the enamel jug and begin to fill it. Pulling open the field dressing he silently handed it to her and, dipping it into the jug, she knelt on the swimming tiles alongside Amos and began to bathe the blood from his face.

The silencing of the mortar brought some relief for Hockold's party, but the 47 across the harbour had got their range perfectly now and the buildings were literally falling apart about their ears.

A group of German sailors led by a young ensign burst out of the barracks further along the waterfront and rushed at them, yelling. Hockold shot the officer and his slender body bowed backwards while his feet were still moving forward. But they were moving more slowly now, almost as though they were feeling their way in the dark, and as they came to a stop, the youngster half-turned and went down with a crash on his side, to roll over, one hand groping at the air. The yells of his men became reedy and shrill as the rush died away.

But Willow had been wounded now, and as Stooge Smith

returned from carrying him to the first-aid station in the bunker a shell from the 47 sent him flying into the debris.

Crouching, watching his party dwindle, sweating with anxiety, the whole of his body cold in spite of it, Hockold glanced at his watch, wondering how Devenish was getting on.

Devenish was beginning to grow worried. He had set his charges on *Andolfo*, *Guglielmotti* and *Cassandra* and the acid in the time pencils was already working away. He had only twenty minutes left but it had become impossible by this time to get to *Giuseppe Bianchi*. She was further away from the other three ships than he'd expected and it was by no means certain that she would go up with them.

To make matters worse, a machine-gun below the Boujaffar was now firing through the thinning smoke across the harbour into the space between the first three ships and *Giuseppe Bianchi*. Some of the bullets were hitting the mole, and Devenish had been half-blinded by flying chips of stone. As he lay on his face blinking away the grit, he was hit in the backside by a ricochet which gouged a large piece of flesh from his right buttock.

'Sergeant,' he called to Bunch. 'Could we shut that machine-gun up across the harbour?'

'Yessir!' Bunch said. 'Shut the machine-gun up.' He paused. 'Unfortunately, sir, there's them other nasty bastards at the end of the mole, and every time we try to move they poop off at us. We got to knock *them* out first.'

The fight by the ships could be seen clearly from the POW compound and, while Sotheby was trying to make up his mind how to tackle the gun above him, it switched its aim from the Bab al Gawla and began to fire at the mole just beyond the stern of the *Giuseppe Bianchi*.

'It's about time we got cuck-cracking with that bub-bub-bub-bloody thing, Sergeant,' he said to Berringer. 'The bub-bastard's only up there.'

Berringer grinned. During training he had come to regard

Sotheby with the affectionate regard of an elder brother for a willing but rather stupid junior, an attitude which had changed during the voyage to Qaba to one of irritation at his nervous fidgeting. Now he was beginning to feel a warm glow of genuine comradeship for him because Sotheby had discovered he could do things if he tried; his nervousness was slipping away from him as if it had been a cloak, so that he became concise, clear-thinking and fearless.

'We lost Keely and three men wounded at the compound, sir,' he said. 'But we've picked up nineteen prisoners with German and Italian weapons who seem keen to have a go.'

'Ought to be bub-bags,' Sotheby said. 'Come on.'

By this time the released prisoners of war were streaming round the back of the town. As they slipped through the vineyards and orchards and turned into the Shariah Jedid they saw the whole street was lit up by Jacka's burning warehouses.

It was possible to get by, however, and in groups they began to edge down on the other side of the road and between the trees. But the Germans were still firing at Hockold's party from the naval barracks and the ruins of the Boujaffar and, as the prisoners burst from behind the mosque, several of them were hit. The rest immediately bolted for shelter to await an opportunity to reach the mole.

As they flung themselves down near the mud huts, Taffy Jones under the hand cart lifted his head. He was holding his steel helmet on with both hands as though afraid the top of his skull would fly off, his rifle had disappeared and the haversack of ammunition he'd been carrying had long since been snatched up and used elsewhere. Half-delirious, he clawed at the earth, ignored by the men around him who tried not to look at him in the humiliation of his fear.

The firing was still intense and the mole was being flayed by bullets, but one after another the prisoners crossed the road and began to drop over the sea wall and down the slip, past Gleeson's still-burning tank and Carter's ruined LCT. Taffy watched them go with agonized eyes, his mouth hanging open, his knuckles white with tension as he gripped his helmet. His mind drove him to follow them but his limbs were like water.

By now the prisoners were picking their way over the rocks and mud to where *Horambeb* lay. It meant a chest-deep wade at the end but most of them didn't object to that and the first of them were already beginning to scramble aboard *Umberto*, where petty officers crammed them below.

The ship's funnel was a wreck by this time but the mast had been chopped away and dragged free. The first lieutenant had also cleared the dead and wounded from the shambles of the bridge and got it functioning again; but men were propped everywhere along the decks and in the passageways, packing the mess and holds while the stretcher-bearers pushed past them. Alongside, ML 146 was still drifting away in flames, but Lieutenant Dysart had got MLs 138 and 147, both looking like colanders now, their planks holed and splintered, attached by their bows to *Umberto*'s stern, ready to haul her off into deep water the moment the signal came to cast off.

When Sotheby and his party reached the huts near the 75, they could see men busy about it behind the barbed wire. As they watched, the gun cracked again and they saw a shell burst on the corner of the stone warehouse on the mole. There was also a machine-gun firing from just in front of it, keeping up a stream of bullets across the harbour to pin down Devenish's party.

'Ready?' Sotheby whispered.

There were nods.

'Right, get the bub-buggers.'

They were through the wire before the gun crew knew what was happening. Men appeared, only to be cut down, and Sotheby himself burst through the door of a hut marked *Hauptmann und Batterieführer*, where Captain Schoeler was screaming into the telephone to the naval barracks for help.

The German had his revolver in his hand and he fired automatically as Sotheby appeared so that he spun round, flung aside by a heavy bullet scoring his rib cage, and fell to the floor. But before Schoeler could fire a second shot he was almost cut in two by a burst from Sotheby's Sten that tossed him across a folding table, one end of which collapsed and deposited him on top of Sotheby, while the telephone still squawked in his hand. Struggling up with difficulty, Sotheby snatched up what papers he could find and, stuffing them into his pocket, stumbled outside again. By this time it was all over. The crews of both the 75 and the machine-gun were all dead or dying, at the cost of one dead prisoner of war, three wounded commandos and a nasty gash over Sotheby's ribs.

Berringer stared at him. He was bent double, his blouse was soaked with blood, his face a crimson mask.

'For Christ's sake, sir,' he said in alarm.

'S'all right,' Sotheby said cheerfully. 'Not as bad as it looks. What's the damage?'

Berringer told him, then pushed an undersized German forward, his hands clasped on top of his head.

'Also one prisoner, sir. What do we do with him?'

Sotheby managed a grin. 'Too small to keep,' he said. 'Throw him back.'

His eyes were darting about as they talked. Although the 75 was silent, a machine-gun across the harbour was now firing down the length of the mole and they could see Bunch and Devenish and the rest of the ship's party crouching under a cluster of lights behind a group of oil drums.

'Any gunners here,' Sotheby asked.

One of the ex-prisoners stepped forward. 'Sir! Corporal Jacques, Northumberland Hussars, Anti-Tank Regiment, RA.'

'Could you knock out that bub-bastard on the mole,'

'Couldn't miss, sir, at this range. They've already jacked her up.'

'Right. Get cracking.'

The hussar examined the gun for a few moments. Then, aided by Sotheby's men, he squatted in the gunlayer's position, his eye against the rubber eye-piece of the sight. The barrel shifted.

'Bang on, sir.'

'Right, bub-bung one up the spout.'

Still crouched alongside *Andolfo*, Devenish saw Sotheby's
shell explode on the gun position at the end of the mole. Men
were flung into the water and the gun barrel drooped. The
machine-gunners, numbed by the blast, stopped firing and for
a moment there was silence. Bunch jumped to his feet at once.

'Bayonets, lads,' he roared.

Private Jumpke saw them coming and didn't wait. He flung
down his rifle and leapt into the harbour. Coming to the surface,
he was surprised to see how different everything looked from
down there and how big the ships seemed from water level.
Stray bullets were splashing into the sea alongside him, and he
decided it might be wiser to get the hell out of it. Treading water,
he wrenched at his equipment and let it slide from his shoulders.
Then, hampered by his heavy boots, he began to head slowly
across the harbour towards the beach where he could see HSL
117 still burning, watched by the surviving members of its crew
on the cliffs below the POW compound.

As the firing from the end of the mole stopped, Devenish
picked up the bag of charges and struggled on to *Giuseppe
Bianchi*. A glance at his watch showed that he had just less than
a quarter of an hour before the charge on *Andolfo* exploded.
They were clearly not going to get everybody away because in
ten minutes *Umberto* would start hauling off.

His behind hurt and his leg was stiff and he was already
feeling a little weak and shocked. The Germans had already
started unloading *Giuseppe Bianchi*, so that they didn't have to
knock out the wedges to open the hatch and Bradshaw and a few
others were already wrenching at the canvas covers. As the planks
were flung aside Devenish moved forward, but his leg gave way
and he stumbled and fell to the deck.

Bunch looked at him. 'You going to manage, sir?'

Devenish winced and Bradshaw stepped forward. 'How about me helping, sir?' he asked.

'Can you?'

'They keep telling me I'm intelligent.'

'Right. We'll make it a three-quarters-of-an-hour charge. Then, if she doesn't go up with the others, she might take a few Jerries with her.'

Supporting Devenish, Bradshaw climbed into the hold and began to heave boxes aside to find a spot where the charge wouldn't easily be discovered.

'In here, sir,' he said. 'There's a pipe.'

With Bradshaw's help, Devenish strapped a nine-pound plastic charge behind the pipe and a second to a valve. It took longer than they'd expected and Bradshaw began to glance at his watch.

'Shan't be long,' Devenish said as he pushed the detonators into the plastic and attached the time pencils.

Sotheby, his face a mask of drying blood, seemed to have the bit between his teeth now. 'Actually, Sergeant,' he said, 'we're doing so bub-bloody well, it seems a pity to stop. There's another gun down there beyond the Mantazeh Palace. It's playing hell with that party round the Roman arch. See any reason why we shouldn't knock that bastard out, too?'

Berringer grinned. By this time he would have followed Sotheby anywhere. 'Let's go, sir.'

'How long have we got left?'

'Six minutes, sir.'

'Shouldn't take us more than fuff-four.' Sotheby turned to the RAF corporal humping his bag of charges behind him. 'Can you sort this bub-bugger out, Corporal?' he asked.

'Easy, sir.'

'Okay. Get cracking.'

As the anti-tank gunner opened the breech of the 75 and the RAF man began to set his charge inside, Sotheby led his men down the slope of the escarpment below the gun position. From the wide expanse of dusty ground to the west of the POW compound, they could see the 47 by the palace knocking pieces off the buildings on the seaward side of where the Roman arch had fallen, while machine-gunners in the naval barracks and in the shops and buildings round the German headquarters prevented any further forward movement. A few stray bullets from Hockold's group were thumping into the trees, but they were having to keep their heads down and their firing was sporadic.

'Up alongside the bub-barracks,' Sotheby said. 'Then behind the palace. Get the bastards in the rear. Don't stop for anything.'

'Right, sir.'

'Okay! Go!'

The twenty-odd men still with Sotheby scrambled to their feet and started running. Almost immediately, they were spotted by a machine-gunner on top of the naval barracks and two of them went down at once. But those still on their feet had reached safety alongside the wall and crouched out of sight. Unsighted, the German sailors dragged their gun along the roof to the eastern end of the barracks and, as Sotheby's men made their second dash, three more of them fell. But there was no stopping the rest of the party who hurtled round the side of the palace and across the stretch of concrete to crash into the 47 from the rear. Three Mills bombs were tossed ahead of them, and, as the flash and roar subsided, they went in with bayonets. The last gun worrying Hockold stopped firing.

There were nineteen of them still on their feet but as Berringer looked round, panting, he realized Sotheby wasn't among them.

They found him by the corner of the palace. Slowed down by his wound, he'd been caught by the machine-gun just as they'd dived out of sight and he was huddled on his face, muttering to himself with pain. He knew he'd been more seriously hit this time but he was glad he'd gone to Qaba. He had a feeling that he'd achieved something for once and probably done enough to have avenged his father. Without realizing it, he had begun to cry with the emotions welling up through his hurt and had put his face against the earth so that no one should see his tears.

Berringer moved him gently and, as Sotheby lifted his head,

he saw his wet cheeks. Squeezing his shoulder, Berringer bent
over him.

'Where did it get you, sir?' he asked.

'I dunno.' Sotheby pressed his face against the concrete
again in his misery. 'All over the shop, I think.'

As they turned him over, Berringer noticed his right leg was
twisted at an unusual angle. 'Shin, sir,' he said. 'Nasty one there.
There's another on your hip, too. Mebbe chipped a bit off the
bone.'

Sotheby's eyes rolled up wretchedly. 'Will I die, Sergeant?'

Berringer managed a reassuring laugh, and at that moment a
flash of white on the slopes above the compound lit their faces
and they heard the crash of the explosion.

'That was the gun going up, sir,' he said.

'Five,' Sotheby murmured. 'We've gone nap.'

Berringer grinned. 'You were bloody terrific, sir.'

Sotheby managed a twisted smile and tried to explain that it
was the thought that *somebody* had to do it that had driven him
on. 'Somebub –' he stuttered. 'Somebub –' But he was so embarrassed by Berringer's praise, the tears came again and his
stammer became so unmanageable he had to give up.

Berringer rose and jerked a hand at the men huddled in a
group by the wall of the palace. 'You lot,' he snapped. 'Get a
door off its hinges. Quick-sharp.'

'We taking him with us, Sarge?' one of them asked.

'Yes.'

'I thought they said we wasn't to take no wounded.'

Berringer glared. 'Did they? Well, we're taking *him*.'

There were three minutes left when Bradshaw climbed to the
deck of *Giuseppe Bianchi* behind Devenish.

'Right, sir. Better get going.'

With Bunch half-carrying, half-dragging the RAF man down
the gangway, Bradshaw began to replace the planks on the
hatch. It was heavy work, but he got them into position and
was heaving the tarpaulin back when Bunch shouted to him.

'For Christ's sake, Bradway, you dozy idle man,' he yelled,

stiff as a poker among the smoke and flying bullets. '*Umberto*'s off!'

'You go, Sarge,' Bradshaw said. 'I'll just fix this so they'll not look inside.'

Bunch lowered Devenish down to *Horambeb* and willing hands hoisted him to the deck of *Umberto*. Staring anxiously down the mole, the first lieutenant turned to the yeoman of signals alongside him. 'Anything from them yet about with-drawing?' he asked.

'No, sir.'

The first lieutenant stared down the mole again. 'There are a hell of a lot missing,' he said.

There were. As soon as Sotheby had silenced the 47 behind the palace, the firing from the houses round German head-quarters increased with the desperation of defeat. It was obvious that if they didn't clear them, nobody would get down the mole.

'Mr Rabbitt,' Hockold said. 'Wait here. Direct everybody you see to the ships, then go after them yourself. The rest of you, come with me.'

They went in ones and twos across the road, heading into the houses round the German headquarters, kicking down doors and tossing Mills bombs inside. Almost immediately, they found Amos. He was obviously dying and the Egyptian girl was kneel-ing on the floor with his head in her lap.

Hockold stared at him wretchedly. There was a saying in the North of England, when something happened that you'd already seen in the imagination, that it broke your dream. Amos's dying had done exactly that for Hockold and he felt now that he wouldn't die after all. Staring down with empty eyes at the man lying in the puddle of water on the rubble-strewn floor, sur-rounded by broken tiles and scattered plaster, it was as if he was staring at the picture he'd seen so often of himself, his head bloodied, his body twisted in pain, his hands groping blindly at his hurts.

'I'm sorry, Frank,' he said, bending down.

Amos didn't move but his eyes lifted and he gestured weakly
with his hand.

'Four times, sir,' Sidebottom said. 'Three in the face.'

'Any others?'

'Three, sir. They're next door. Two prisoners.'

Amos was signing to Sidebottom to find his pencil and notebook and, while the Egyptian girl supported him, he began to
write. Sidebottom handed the notebook to Hockold.

'He says we've to leave the wounded where they can still fire
their bundooks,' he said in a flat voice. 'So the rest of us can
clear out.'

Inside the naval barracks, Hochstätter was standing by the
telephone when Hrabak appeared. He was covered with dust
and dirt and his uniform was torn. 'Wutka's dead,' he said.
'Nietzsche, too, I think. They're heading this way now and they're
damned close. We're doing no good here. It's time we cleared
out.'

'Very well,' Hochstätter said. 'You go. I'll follow.'

As Hrabak and the naval signallers disappeared, Hochstätter stood by the window, hidden by the wall, staring down
on the scene of destruction below him. He had imagined that
the British had come to destroy the ships across the harbour, but
their objective now appeared to have been only the petrol dump
and the stores. Schoeler and his artillery had gone with them,
however, together with a great many of his men.

He saw Tarnow watching from across the room, half-crouched
by the door because chips of plaster were falling from the ceiling,
a bandage round his head, his face streaked with dried blood.

'Better come now,' he said.

Hochstätter sighed and nodded. Then, refusing to crouch, he
walked upright to the door.

Murdoch had sent every man who could be spared down into
the town, and they arrived just as the firing began to slacken.
Rabbitt was waiting for them among the trees by the rubble of
the Roman arch.

'Get going,' he shouted. 'Look slippy.'

As he waved them on he was moving through the sprawled shapes among the rubbish, turning them over, examining them. Taffy Jones was still crouching under the hand-cart, still holding his steel helmet over his eyes.

'Where are you hurt, son?' Rabbitt demanded gently.

Taffy lifted his head, unable to speak.

'*Are* you hurt?' Rabbitt's voice was harsher now. Then he stood up and gave Taffy a push with his boot.

'Get going,' he said. 'Down the mole! Go on, hook it!'

Taffy stared at him for a second then, like a cornered wild thing grasping at a chance of safety, he scrambled to his feet. Rabbitt gave him a shove and he joined the hurrying figures, running into the smoke drifting about the mole, his face soft and white and puffy, his chin wobbling, his eyes blinking at every bang, thankful to be out of it alive.

He was only just in time. Aboard *Umberto*, the first lieutenant was looking anxiously at his watch. 'For God's sake,' he said. 'Where are they all? Where's Hockold?'

He glanced again at his watch. 'We've got to go,' he continued. 'Those are the orders.'

He leaned over the side of the splintered wing bridge. 'Stand by, motor-launch! Let go aft!'

It was just as *Umberto*'s stern was hauling off, with Dysart's Fairmiles straining their engines, that Taffy Jones and the last group of men appeared in a crouching run. Rabbitt followed, upright and walking.

'Avast heaving!' The first lieutenant leaned over the wing bridge and bawled down to Dysart. 'Shove us in again, for God's sake, Dysart!'

As Dysart reversed engines and the ML's bows whacked against *Umberto*'s steel side, the running men scrambled across *Horambeb* and were hauled aboard *Umberto*.

Panting, still terrified, but recovering quickly now that he was not being shot at, Taffy found himself alongside Auchmuty.

The Scotsman's eyes met his, pale and wild-looking in his blackened face. As usual he had no comment to make, but he smiled and Taffy realized that he knew nothing of what had happened by the mosque.

He glanced round. Rabbitt was out of sight. He smiled back, shifting his big shoulders, feeling better, almost the Man of Harlech himself again already.

'Them Jerries will remember us for a bit after this, look you,' he said.

Then they were shoved below and, as the last man was hauled aboard, a voice bawled over the wing bridge. 'O.K. Dysart! Let her rip!'

As the launches' engines went astern once more, *Umberto* swung out, leaving the smoking wreckage of *Horambeb* still stuck on the mud.

'Let go forrard,' the first lieutenant yelled. 'Dysart, stay close till the bang goes off. You might be glad of big brother's protection.'

Dysart grinned and waved, and with the two remaining launches lying close alongside her, *Umberto* began to head slowly north-west out to sea. The first lieutenant was staring back at the mole.

'For God's sake,' he said. 'Aren't the bloody things going to go off, after all?'

At that very minute the whole sky over the harbour turned red.

10

Though there were some casualties, Qaba's value as a supply base was seriously impaired...

The crash as *Andolfo* went up flattened Bradshaw against the stone warehouse. He had been heading there for shelter as the ship exploded, and the blast lifted and carried him about twenty yards before it slammed him against the wall.

There was a roar like sustained thunder going on around him, as if some titanic stonk had dropped nearby. His lungs emptied with a rush and a cry of protest burst from his lips. There was another enormous flash and he was rolled into a corner as if he were a ball of fluff before a breeze. He tried to shout for help but his mouth was like dry wood and all he could get out was a gasp. Things seemed to be dropping all round him and he was surrounded by a kind of inky cotton wool which was rolling up into the air. In one catastrophic moment of time as the shock wave swept back to him, the world seemed to have been jolted off its axis and he felt like a man travelling through space.

Why he was still alive he couldn't understand, but somehow he scrabbled for safety through an open door and crouched down with his head between his hands, wincing with a pain that had started in his ears. Almost immediately, it seemed, *Guglielmotti* went up as well.

From the building at the other side of the harbour Hockold saw the first sheet of flame climb skywards as though it had livid red hands clawing at the heavens to drag itself up. The

camouflage netting on the other ships lifted and billowed as if
in a high wind, and then burning fragments from *Andolfo*
came whirring down like glittering bats to set it on fire. Doors
slammed open, the native boats moored in the harbour swung
wildly on their moorings, and a native cart parked just under
the trees by the mosque slid sideways into the roadway.

Just recovering his senses after being sent head-first into the
wreckage near the Roman arch by the shell from the 75,
Sugarwhite had just scrambled unsteadily to his feet, bent like an
old man with the pain in his ribs. The canary he'd rescued was
silent now, a flattened dusty little body at the bottom of its
crushed cage, trodden on in the confusion. Nearby, Gardner
still knelt against the wall, his head down, mutely at prayer, and
Sugarwhite stared at him stupidly, bothered that a life could be
blotted out so completely – that a decent, kind man could be
there one minute and gone the next to whatever darkness death
consisted of.

He drew a deep painful breath. He knew Brandison was dead
as well, together with one of the Stooges and Docwra. And
doubtless Bill Brewer, Jan Stewer and Old Uncle Tom Cobley
and all.

'Oh, Jesus,' he said in a welter of despair.

He wiped the back of his hand across his face and his mouth
opened and shut slowly, as if the hinges of his jaw were clogged
with dirt; his head seemed numb but full of rushes of pain.
Realizing he was the only man left alive in the rubble by the
strongpoint, he began to weep with rage, fright and self-sym-
pathy. His mouth sour from the taste of bile, he brushed a hand
across his eyes to free them from the paste of sweat and grime.
As he blinked, he saw Hockold's party moving among the
houses opposite, their water bottles flapping as they ran. He
scrambled to his feet, wincing with pain, and shot across the
Shariah Jedid after them, in a panic that he'd be left behind.
He was just pounding up a flight of stairs where he'd seen them
disappear, when the blast from *Andolfo* caught him and dumped
him neatly at the bottom again. Somebody, he decided, had it in
for him that day.

Determined not to be left behind, he grimly pulled himself up again, his mood changing as he realized that in spite of everything that had happened to him, he was still miraculously alive. Suddenly he felt he was going to survive and the thought sufficed to encourage him. Mad enough to bite somebody, he determined once more to do someone some damage. He had already shot several Germans but this latest insult decided him to shoot more. As he got to his feet, a portion of the ceiling collapsed on to his steel helmet with a clang that almost broke his neck and he felt certain he'd been hit on the head with an anvil. *Guglielmotti* had joined *Andolfo,* and more blazing fragments of netting were swept upwards to join the others that were descending on the town like crimson snowflakes. The roof above Sugarwhite, already weakened by the exploding *Andolfo,* lifted then sagged towards him in a shower of tiles, bricks, timbers and dust.

The two ships had been torn open by the blast and now sank hissing into the water, their decks a mass of white-hot flame. But *Cassandra,* the outside ship on the trot, was still afloat. Her ropes severed, her bridge flattened, her masts and funnel gone, and licked by flame from *Guglielmotti,* she drifted into the middle of the harbour. Then she went, too, and a final shower of bricks, timbers, tiles and other debris, all that was left of the roof, fell on Sugarwhite and buried him.

To Bradshaw, crouching inside the warehouse, it seemed as if the end of the world had come. He was aware of flashing lights and timbers falling on him as the roof collapsed, of the ground coming up to hit him, and sheets of corrugated iron sliding down out of the sky to clank to the concrete around him. He prayed that none of them would fall on him because, if they did, they would probably cut him in half.

Moving out towards the POW compound on the higher ground, which they were hoping to defend, Hochstätter, Tarnow and Hrabak stopped and turned.

'*Gott im Himmel!*' Hrabak gasped. 'They got the ships after all!'

The machine-gunners on top of the naval barracks had been lifted neatly over the edge of the roof with their weapons and deposited in the roadway, and were now trying to crawl to safety, bruised and breathless, several of them with broken limbs. By the Mantazeh Palace, crouching down out of the blast, Sergeant Berringer bent over Sotheby to protect him from the debris falling in showers from the ornate turrets.

'Got the bub-buggers,' he heard Sotheby whisper.

The blast seemed to send *Umberto* rolling over, so that her torn upperworks heeled against the sky and her mizzen topmast crashed to the deck in a tangle of ropes and blocks and a shower of old rust.

As she straightened herself up and the crew began to hack at the debris, Devenish, propped up alongside the bridge, grinned at the men around him, their faces lit up by the flare of flame.

'That'll make the bloody Afrika Korps think!' he said.

Lifting his head as the pieces of metal and wood and fragments of burning camouflage net stopped splashing into the water of the harbour and spattering into the roadway, Hockold could see *Umberto* in the glare, standing off to the west. Above him, the drone of the last of de Berry's aeroplanes was fading. The searchlights were going out one by one now and the bark of the anti-aircraft guns had stopped.

Mentally counting numbers, Hockold knew his group had been cut to pieces and he looked around, trying to identify the men who were still with him. Under the grime the blackened faces were almost unrecognizable but he was able to pick out Sergeant Curtiss, struggling with his set to pluck strangled signals out of the interference.

'Are we still in touch?' he asked.

Curtiss's head turned. 'Yes, sir. Just.'

Hockold looked faintly embarrassed. 'Tell *Umberto*: "Having *wonderful time. Wish you were here.*" The navy likes funny signals.'

The dressing station in Dr Carell's bunker was full of wounded now, sitting about in untidy heaps, their clothes cut away to show stained bandages. The place reeked of blood, ordure, sweat and the scent of death.

As Hockold entered, he saw pleading, unsteady eyes and faces close to hysteria. At one end were nine bodies, lying on their backs staring at the concrete roof. Near them a sailor was dying with fifteen bullets in his chest, and an RAF corporal shot through the back of the head was snoring as if asleep. His skin was already grey. Another man's stomach wound had been plugged, and an orderly was now filling the hole with sulpha. Most were suffering from shock but Hickey was keeping them well doped with morphia while a medical corporal was writing with copying pencil on their foreheads the dose they'd been given. There were a few groans and cries and a low voice muttering in delirium; but for the most part, as they hugged their hurts to them in the modesty of pain, emotion was frozen on each face, so that it possessed its own permanent look of dumb bewilderment and eternal questioning, so sharp that Hockold found himself glancing at his own face in a small mirror hanging on the wall to see if it were the same.

Hickey had straightened up, his white apron stained.

'We're leaving,' Hockold said quietly. 'Are you ready?'

The American smiled. 'I guess I'll stay,' he said.

'It was the understanding that the wounded were to be left behind.'

'I guess I'll still stay, Colonel.'

'Very well. And thank you. I hope it won't be for long.' Hockold nodded at Carell, waiting, stiffly precise, to one side. 'Keep him here, if you can. We don't want him to let his friends know we're pulling out.'

'Okay, sir. I can handle that, I guess.'

When Hockold returned to the buildings by the Shariah Jedid, a wounded man had taken Curtiss's place on the radio. 'I can keep on sending, sir,' he said. 'Make 'em think you're still here.'

Hockold nodded. 'It won't be long,' he said. 'Eighth Army

can't be far away and they'll come faster than ever now.'

Withdrawing the last of his men, he joined Sergeant Side-bottom. Jacka's party had just appeared.

' 'Lo, Sidi,' Jacka said flatly.

'Sham, Jacka. Greetings!'

Belcher was staring at Waterhouse's swollen mouth. 'Fink somebody's done for you, mate,' he said flatly.

Waterhouse's grin was lopsided and bloody. 'Right id the soddig bouth,' he agreed.

They moved the wounded to the windows and gave them their weapons, trying to comfort them with grim jokes and rough tenderness. Then Hockold bent over Amos. 'So long, Frank,' he said.

Amos nodded feebly, his eyes full of blank uncomprehending pain.

'We're going now,' Hockold said, and Amos nodded again; his eyes watched them all the way to the door.

Withdrawing the last men from the surrounding houses, Hockold set off up the Shariah Jedid towards the back of the town. After a while, they reached the vineyards and then the road. As they emerged, they were recognized by Murdoch waiting by the bungalows near the fuel dump.

Blackened faces split in broad grins as the two groups greeted each other and thumped each other's backs. Hockold quietly shook hands with Murdoch.

'We seem to have done what we came for,' he said.

'Did they all go up?'

'All except the ammunition. But ammunition's no good if there's no petrol to carry it to where it's wanted.' Hockold glanced towards the south where the racket at the airfield seemed now to have stopped. Over in the east they could still hear the thunder of guns and see the flashes in the night sky.

'Eighth Army seems a bit nearer,' he said. 'I think we'd better head south.'

They were still bent over the injured when Sotheby's party arrived. As they appeared, Hockold stepped forward.

'Who's that?' he asked.

'Mr Sotheby, sir,' Berringer said.

'Is he bad?'

'I don't think so, sir.'

'I'm glad you cleared the compound. We saw them coming through the town.'

'We did more than that, sir,' Berringer said. 'We captured the 75 and used it to knock out the 47 on the mole. Then we sorted out the 47 behind the palace.'

'So that's why they stopped,' Hockold said. 'Well done, Sergeant.'

'Not me, sir,' Berringer said, nodding at Sotheby. 'Him.'

After a while, it dawned on the Germans and Italians in Qaba that there were no British remaining in the place except for the dead and the badly wounded who'd been left behind. Warily, they began to emerge.

As the noise died down, it left the town so silent it seemed to be panting, trying to get its breath back. Wild-eyed, shocked men, their clothes torn and stained, their faces covered with dust, came into the streets in groups. A few of the natives started moving among the trees towards the mosque to send up a prayer while it was still possible, to stare at the damage, or inspect their wrecked boats in the harbour.

There were a few prisoners, most of them wounded but also one or two who were unhurt. Among them was Swann, prodded forward by Bontempelli who had taken the opportunity as Swann stumbled ahead of him, his hands in the air, to jam a hurried clip of ammunition into the rifle at last. By sheer coincidence, he bumped into Sottotenente Baldissera leading in the remains of his mixed engineer company. There were considerably less than had set out for the airfield and they didn't have a single lorry left.

'For the love of God!' Baldissera was blackened, filthy and exhausted, his clothes scorched. 'Look who's here – Double Ration!'

There was also the indestructible Sugarwhite who rose out of

the debris of the shattered roof, still twisted from the pain in his
ribs, bloody, blackened and covered with dirt, just as Unteroffizier Upholz stopped the *Kübelwagen* he was driving by the
harbour.

They stood and stared at each other. Sugarwhite and the German sergeant-major. One of them tough, middle-aged and experienced, the other young, frightened and bewildered, his face
streaked where the tears had run. Sugarwhite's hair was white
with plaster dust, his clothes were torn, he'd lost his Sten gun
under the broken roof, and he felt his brain had been shredded
by the explosions. But he was the card of the outfit, wasn't he,
and he still had to behave like a card. He managed a grin at
Upholz standing by the jeep.

'Taxi?' he said, and even Upholz, who knew no English,
caught the insult.

And finally Bradshaw. They found him in agony from
shattered eardrums, his face blackened so that his eyes looked
spectral, just struggling from the debris of the stone warehouse,
and pushed him, stumbling, along the mole to where the German
officers were standing in a group.

Tarnow, the least shocked by the battle despite his wound,
started to question him.

'How many of you were there?' he asked.

Bradshaw's face was blank. 'I am Lance-Corporal David Evan
Oxshott, Number 2089675.'

'You'd better tell us,' Tarnow snapped.

Bradshaw couldn't hear him properly. 'I am Lance-Corporal
David Evan Bulstrode, Number 2089675.'

'You said "Oxshott".'

Bradshaw gestured wearily, guessing at the words that
Tarnow's moving lips framed. 'Oxshott-Bulstrode,' he said.
'Hyphenated.'

Tarnow indicated the debris in the harbour and the still surviving *Giuseppe Bianchi*. 'Why didn't you blow them *all* up?'
he demanded.

Bradshaw knew what was worrying him and he glanced at his
watch. It was still going and the minutes were ticking by. 'We

did,' he said. 'Or we shall. There's a delayed action charge on that one.'

Tarnow's face went white. 'When?'

Bradshaw grinned. 'Any minute now.'

The Germans glanced at each other. Then Bradshaw was bundled into a house, and Hrabak and Tarnow began bawling at the sergeants. A few men who'd wandered down the mole to stare at the wreckage began to run back into the town; others were sent to clear the harbour area. Within three minutes there wasn't a living soul in sight. No Germans, no Italians, no Arabs.

Five minutes later *Giuseppe Bianchi* went up. Devenish had done his work well, and they all heard the charge go and ducked their heads. A fraction of a second later, the ship split wide open. The funnel went clean over the wall into the sea. The masts shot into the air as if they were javelins hurled by a giant hand. A huge ventilator lifted across the harbour and dropped with a clang in front of headquarters. For about two minutes pieces of metal and wood and iron showered on the town, shattering tiles, removing roofs and doors, flattening the dome on top of the mosque as if it were brown paper instead of copper, and completing the ruin of the Mantazeh Palace. Palm trees were stripped of their leaves and reduced to bare poles. Most of the surviving Arab boats in the harbour became matchwood, and those that didn't were washed up on to the roadway by an enormous wave.

What was left of the Boujaffar collapsed like a pack of cards, burying a sergeant and six men who were dragging out the bodies of the commodore and the ship's captain who had died there. So did half a dozen houses along the front and the warehouse where Bradshaw had sheltered. Wutka's wooden bridge dissolved into splinters and a long stretch of the mole was reluced to scorched and torn concrete as stark and empty as the moon.

11

. . . with resultant assistance to the army advancing from El Alamein. Qaba was occupied for the Eighth Army on 10 November.

By the time Operation Cut-Price slipped back into Alex on 1 November, it was already becoming clear that the Axis had been dealt its first real body-blow of the war.

Every unit of the Eighth Army was on the move now, passing swiftly through the destruction they had wrought, even staff cars, ambulances, water carts, signalling vans, rear workshops and casualty clearing stations racing to get ahead, nobody knowing where their headquarters were and nobody giving a damn. Nose to tail they were pouring past all the old familiar places, tanks and guns without end, their tyres and tracks making marks like zip fasteners in the sand.

The news of the victory had been flashed from a destroyer which had met the remains of Babington's little fleet, and everybody aboard *Umberto* became conscious of a wonderful feeling of elation. They'd fought their share of the battle, and though for them it had taken only around half an hour – in some cases a mere matter of minutes – it had been fierce throughout and they'd done exactly what they'd set out to do. A few hadn't survived, a few had been hurt, a few were missing, and for most of those who'd returned, it was enough fighting for the rest of the war, enough even for a lifetime. Indeed, a lot of them would scrounge free drinks off it for years to come, and would certainly bore their relations with it for the rest of their natural lives.

The signal, 'Smash-hit', had reached Alexandria within

minutes of *Giuseppe Bianchi* going up, and had been relayed to
Murray by telephone. During the whole of 31 October, he and
Kirstie McRuer had held on to their patience and their nerves
as they'd waited, still not quite able to absorb the full implica-
tion of the news that was coming in from the desert.

A great wedge had been driven into the German line and their
counter-attacks had achieved nothing but the destruction of
their own tanks. Rommel, the great myth, the ever-successful
general, had been out-thought for once and attempts by Stukas
to halt the advance had come to a dead stop in an inferno of
anti-aircraft fire. The Littorio, Trento and Trieste Divisions were
known to have vanished in the maelstrom and the 21st Panzers
very nearly so, and the whole landscape was a mass of derelict
vehicles sending up their spirals of smoke to the empty blue sky.

Then, in the afternoon, with the belief already growing in
every heart that the tide, which had run so strongly against
Britain for so long, had turned at last, news came in that the
navy had picked up Babington's ships. There were smiles at once,
but faces fell again when it was learned how few there were.
When the little fleet sailed into the harbour, half of Alexandria
turned out to watch them arrive. *Umberto*'s funnel looked as
though it had been peppered again and again by a gigantic shot-
gun, her main mast was gone with the top of her mizzen, and
her wheelhouse was a mass of blood-stained splintered planking
and punctured steel.

The cheers that greeted her died as she came alongside and
the ambulances drew up and the wounded were helped ashore.
The unwounded survivors followed, a little overbold now – even
Taffy Jones, quite recovered and as noisy as ever. Then the tele-
phones began to ring. In Bryant's office. In de Berry's. In
Murray's.

Kirstie McRuer, waiting with the door ajar, heard Murray
speaking, heard him asking about the dead, the wounded and
the missing, and the thunderous silence as he listened intently
while names were given. As she heard the click of the telephone,
she rose and went to the door. Despite the heat, she felt as cold as
ice.

The Raid

In the corridor people were still discussing the battle in the desert. Montgomery had been right all along. The feeling they'd had that this time it was all going to be different had been correct. The Afrika Korps was as good as beaten – completely, finally and for all time. Rommel's rear areas were already in a state of panic. The information sent back by Intelligence was that the panzers were running down like an unwound clock for lack of petrol; the whole desert was alive with British vehicles, every man in them aware of the exultation of victory.

The excitement made the return of Cut-Price all the more poignant and Kirstie waited silently by the door for Murray to speak. He was sitting with his hands on the desk, his fingers entwined, staring at the telephone, and as he became aware of her at last, his expression changed with an effort.

'Complete success, Kirstie,' he said. 'All four ships, spares, petrol and lorries. Also, as far as we can make out, several guns and God knows how many Germans and Italians.'

He was talking quickly, deliberately, spinning it out, she knew. 'What about the men?' she interrupted. 'Who's dead?'

The words were brutal enough to make Murray look up sharply. 'Babington,' he said, frowning. 'Hardness. Two of the HSL skippers and one ML skipper. The captain of *Horambeb*, Watson and Brandison. Those are known. Carter, the captain of the LCT, is alive but he'll be a long time in hospital.'

'What about the shore parties?'

Murray paused, staring at the telephone again, troubled by the evenness of her voice. 'Murdoch's not among them. Nor are the Americans. Devenish is wounded. Amos is missing –'

'What about George Hockold?'

Murray's head lifted as though it weighed a ton, then his eyes moved to her. He drew a deep breath that seemed to hurt him.

'He's not with them.'

Kirstie stared at him for a moment, suddenly sensing what had been troubling Hockold through his silences. When she spoke her voice seemed dry. 'Thanks,' she said.

She turned away and, closing the door behind her, aware of Murray trying to explain – 'They may be in the desert, of

279

course!' – she leaned against it. 'Oh, damn,' she whispered. 'Damn! Damn! Damn!'

Then she drew a deep breath, blew her nose and, going to the desk, drew a sheet of paper from the typewriter she'd been using and began to look for mistakes. It was difficult because she couldn't see very well.

'The British raid on Qaba,' Rome radio announced on 2 November, 'was a complete fiasco. A small amount of fuel was destroyed and one or two lorries were wrecked, but it is worthy of note that even the night clubs in the town are still flourishing.'

No one in Qaba took the slightest notice. The only night clubs Qaba had ever possessed were brothels, and it was already growing clear that the results of Cut-Price were causing tremendous damage far beyond the town itself. Reports were coming in of guns left by the roadside because there was no transport to haul them away; of tanks and tank workshops surrendered intact because they'd run out of fuel; of aircraft destroyed by their own crews for lack of spare parts; and trucks abandoned with their petrol gauges empty. The old routine was ended. They all knew it. North Africa would never be the same again and the feeling that it would all go on and keep on going on for ever had vanished.

Over the town there was a hush, sorrowing and austere. The streets were those of a dead place and everybody seemed to be white with dust. There were still a few flattened bodies lying about and a few wounded groaning among the shattered houses. What was left of *Andolfo*, *Guglielmotti* and *Cassandra* were mere scorched hulks. Of *Giuseppe Bianchi* there was no sign except an upturned stern and a few steel plates sticking out of the water. The ruins made the place look like the end of the world.

The dead, some of them out of sight among the wreckage, were beginning to smell now, and all over the town they were being buried where they were found. Many of them were smoke-blackened, mutilated and slippery; peeled and contorted human shapes atrociously defiled. Here a face was split almost in two so that the eyes were not human and only the rough hands showed the owner to have been a man; there dead fingers still tried to thrust a grey tangle of intestines back into a torn body. Down on the beach Sergeant Gleeson, half out of his tank, his arms over the edge of the turret, was still struggling to escape, his blue face staring at the men approaching gingerly with ropes to get him out of sight before they all had nightmares.

Where *Umberto*'s shell had wrecked the searchlight behind the palace, the earth had caved in, the ground was churned up, and the barbed wire fence had been ripped to pieces. There was a dead German lying there, his face black, a coagulated trickle of dark blood oozing from his mouth, and an Italian minus everything but his head, his face fixed in horror; flesh, hair and uniform matted together in a purple mass crawling with flies. They used the hole the shell had made for the grave, lifting the bodies in silently, and hurriedly shovelled the dust on to the upturned faces and staring eyes.

All over the town, little groups of men stared at the opened earth, and here and there mouth organs filled the air with the notes of '*Ich hatt einen Kameraden*'. Near the flattened area round the harbour Jumpke was still expounding on his escape when he ought to have been dead like the other men at the end of the mole. 'I didn't even know I could swim,' he kept saying. More groups were trying to clear the debris at the fuelling post, the lorry park and the petrol dump, and men from the airfield were digging a grave for those of Baldissera's Italians who hadn't survived the return to Qaba.

A few Arabs, some of them with looted cigarettes, a few with abandoned British weapons with which they intended to pay off old scores in the Borgo Nero, wailed round their own dead and the wreckage where stray shells had brought down their homes. Their leaders shouted angrily at the destruction of the Mantazeh Palace and the roof of the mosque, or gestured wildly over the splintered planks of their boats. Though Hockold had stressed that native property was not to be touched, the sweep of the arm of war was always a wild one. Even the camel drivers stared at the splintered poles of the palms and realized they would have to find shade elsewhere from now on.

Smoke still hung over the town, and everybody knew that defeat was at hand. They'd heard that British tanks and infantry had reached the Rahman Track, the last defence behind the lines, where they had destroyed the Ariete Division and were now smashing the German units there, cutting off whole groups of bewildered men from the rear. Then news came in that von Thoma, the commander of the Afrika Korps, had been captured, that Fuka and the forward supply base at Daba had gone, and that the British were pushing into Libya in the direction of Sollum, and going like a pack of hounds for Tobruk itself.

The first shattered Italians who passed through Qaba improved on the story. 'There was no petrol,' they said, 'and no armour, and when they came with bayonets we legged it.'

Then a major in a staff car appeared from Rommel himself to find out if it was true there was no petrol. He didn't have to ask twice, and Hrabak demanded to know more.

'There's been an order,' the major said. 'We've got to return.'

'Return where?' Hrabak said.

'To the front. It's Hitler's order.'

'Then Hitler should come out of those damned headquarters of his,' Hrabak said bitterly, 'and take a look at Qaba. Or better still, get hold of a gun and help.'

Tarnow was watching him but Hrabak didn't care because he had a feeling now that Tarnow didn't care either.

The sun was hot and some of the Italians tramping through the town had thrown away clothing and weapons and bandaged their feet with rags. One group started a fire by the roadside. They had found a can of petrol and, because they'd thought it was water, had smashed it in fury and set it alight. More cans were added to the blaze, and then anything they could think of – jackets, sandbags, straps, bandoliers, puttees, webbing belts, jerseys, packets of letters, postcards, even money – everything, but what they stood up in. They gave it the Fascist salute, shouting sarcastic *Evvivas* for Mussolini, and finally someone found a large portrait of Hitler and held it up in an attitude of mock obeisance so that everyone could see it before, with a shout of '*Sieg Heil*', tossing that into the fire, too.

282

Hochstätter watched them. His body frail and shrunken underneath his uniform, he looked an old man, his face lined and haggard, his grieving eyes dark in his head.

'I think, Hrabak,' he said, 'that it's about time we left.'

Even Tarnow didn't argue, and they found a car and filled it with the last can of petrol in Qaba, then drove up the Shariah Jedid, past the ruined Roman arch, and the burned-out warehouses, towards the wrecked lorry park and the blasted area of the petrol dump. As they reached the top of the hill, Hochstätter stopped the car and, standing up, looked back.

'I think we shall lose this war,' he said.

He was still looking back, when, coming over the brow of the hill, out of sight and soundless until the last moment, the Hurricanes found him.

The remains of the car were there when the dusty vehicles came in out of the desert, heading back past what was left of the fuel dump and the lorry park with its blackened skeletons.

Narrowed eyes stared at the grave alongside. 'Oberst Eitel-Friedrich Hochstätter,' the name on the cross proclaimed, '*Geboren 6.6.92, gefallen 5.11.42*'.

Nobody said anything. They were too tired, their eyes dark slits peering out of grey masks, unshaven, stinking of sweat, dirt, grease and gun oil, and so tattered they'd been shot at by trigger-happy Australians who'd thought they were Italians. They had very nearly reached the limit of their endeavour.

They had buried the wounded who had died well to the south near the Rahman Track on the 6th, placing them in the earth by a solitary wooden cross they found bearing the words, *Ein unbekannter englischer Soldat* – a faded reminder of some long-dead fight – and as they'd thrown the last spadeful of dusty earth over them, heavy grey storm-clouds had rolled up and great hailstones had come down to fill the arid wadis with water. Already the westward-moving convoys were slowing to a crawl and, as the mud started, the roads became jammed and they had remained motionless for hours among the thousands of halted vehicles, able to do nothing as the Germans streamed away; nothing but take off the gluey coverings that went by the name of socks and wait.

The desert looked rinsed and cool as the rain died away. As they had moved on again in fresh implacable sunshine on the 9th, it soon became clear that nobody was bothering about Qaba out on its little peninsula to the north, and the idea of returning to it as somewhere to recuperate grew stronger in their minds. When they reached Ibrahimiya, they saw the burned-out trucks of Baldissera's command still containing what they had always flippantly called *soldati fritti*; empty flapping tents; and blackened, wind-ripped aircraft, with bent propellers, broken backs and shattered wings, for once all bearing the hated swastika. Along the southern perimeter, past a knocked-out 88, its endless barrel like a fallen pine, a vast column of prisoners was trudging into captivity with doped rhythmic steps and weary stony faces. The dust from the drying desert rose in a great cloud from their feet as they plodded along four abreast, an endless crocodile stretching away to both horizons, only an armoured car and a few British privates shouting in mixed English, Arabic and Italian alongside.

Among them was Private Bontempelli. His guess had been a good one. Baldissera and his few remaining men had been ordered south to stop the British advance – and this time Bontempelli had gone with them. No one had argued when Baldissera, his knees showing through his torn trousers, had stepped forward to surrender to the first tanks that appeared. '*Sono prigioneri*,' he had said unhappily. '*Ci arrendiamo. Tedeschi non bono. Viva l'Inghilterra*.'

The morning was bleak and the wind whipped at the yellow grass. The marching men were unkempt and dirty, their steel helmets down over their eyes to break the force of the wind, their hands blotched with desert sores. Staring at them, the survivors of Cut-Price were surprised to find they felt no sense of triumph, even though they knew the war in North Africa was nearing its end. All they could feel was the tragedy of hunger, wounds and defeat, and a deep concern for their own safety because they, too, were fatigued and tacky-socked; men of dirt and tatters, their beards dusty, their red-rimmed eyes glaring into the sun, feeling they could sleep for a hundred years.

From the top of the hill, Qaba seemed a place of utter desolation, the empty Italian camps containing abandoned boxes of half-packed clothes and tables bearing half-eaten food. A few Italian tanks stood where they'd run out of petrol, and in breaches in sandbagged walls men lay crumpled or grotesquely spread-eagled. A few mules and an occasional dog nosed mournfully among the debris in search of food or water and, half-hidden by the blown sand that covered corpses, carcasses of dead animals and broken machinery, there were millions of cartridge clips, belts of ammunition, rifles, machine-guns, hand grenades, rolls of wire, pieces of clothing and equipment, lifted mines, batteries and blackened piles of ruined metal. The chirping crickets and the rustling of letters blowing among the thorn bushes provided the only sound.

The town was a maze of broken tottering buildings, its white walls stained with scorch marks so that they frowned with embarrassment at the terrible destruction they had wrought. Nobody stopped the lorries as they moved in. A few Arabs demanded cigarettes and a few Italians appeared holding white flags. The grimy men divested them of their watches and wallets and marched them in groups to the POW compound they had built for the British. There they found Swann, still seeking excuses; Bradshaw, who had come to realize he would probably be deaf for the rest of his life; and Sugarwhite, bent double now but grinning and shouting, 'It took you long enough' – a determined card to the bitter end. Hickey and Carell were still in the bunker, surrounded by millions of flies attracted by the smell of blood. The Egyptian girl was with them now, but Amos had disappeared.

Opposite naval headquarters, von Steen, Hrabak and Tarnow, determined to do the thing with dignity, had lined up what remained of the garrison outside the ruins of the Boujaffar. A huge ventilator, which had peered myopically at the world from the deck of *Giuseppe Bianchi*, lay by the remains of the front door, along with a dead mule and a car which had been blown on to its side.

As the lorries stopped, von Steen saluted, not a Nazi salute but a naval salute. Hockold's men stared back at him not without sympathy because there was something they all possessed but could not communicate to each other. The war correspondents in London and Berlin were describing them to their readers as 'Our boys', shining heroes bursting with enthusiasm, when in fact most of them hated the war, and would much have preferred to have been drunk or full of food or in bed with a girl. Exhausted and dried-out, their bodies bruised by battle, their brains addled by the sun, their skins abrasive under the dust and mud, they had no high notions of glory. All they wanted was to win the war and go home to the wife and kids and English beer.

Hockold accepted von Steen's pistol without comment. Then, as the Germans were marched away to join the other men in the POW compound, Murdoch raised his eyebrows in a question.

Hockold nodded and turned to Curtiss.

'Contact Eighth Army,' he ordered. 'Tell them we're in possession of Qaba.'